The Well of Loneliness

This book is a work of fiction. Names and characters are products of the author's imagination or are used fictitiously. Any resemblance to persons, living or dead, is entirely coincidental. Some sites and places are historical and are portrayed and/or described as closely as possible within the telling of this fictional story for realism as well as educational purposes.

ISBN-13: 978-0-9822189-6-9
ISBN-10: 0-9822189-6-6

Cover design by ThomasMax (Lee Clevenger & R. Preston Ward).
Edited by Lee Clevenger

Published by: Divacity Press, a ThomasMax Company

ThomasMax Publishing
P.O. Box 250054
Atlanta, GA 30325
404-794-6588
www.thomasmax.com

The Well Of Loneliness

By Michael Tanner

Divacity Press

Also by Michael Tanner:

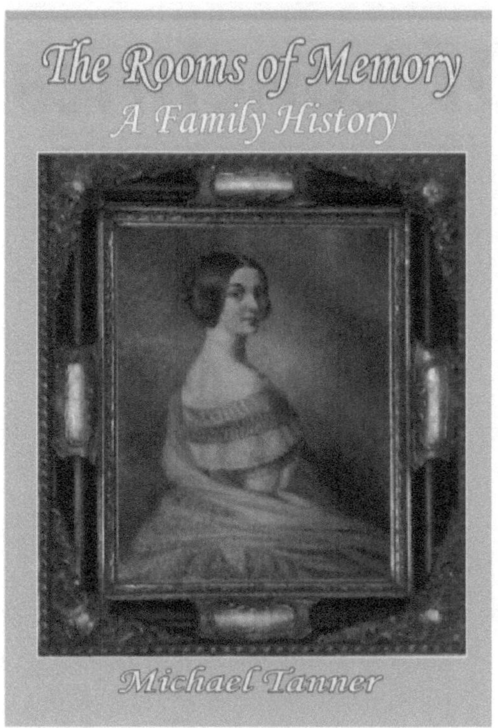

The Rooms of Memory
$ 15

This non-fiction accounting traces the genealogy of the author on both the maternal and paternal sides, including a king of England and President William Henry Harrison. Includes narratives about the family names, family photographs and documents and genealogy charts. Available wherever books are sold and through internet sellers such as Amazon.com. Published by ThomasMax Publishing.

For Dr. Maya Frieman Hoover --- Prima Donna Assoluta

Io ti sequii come iride di pace
Lungo le vie del cielo:
Io ti sequii come un'amica face
De la notte nel velo.

E ti sentii ne la luce, ne l'aria,
Nel profumo dei fiori;
E fu piena la stanza solitaria
Di te, dei tuoi splendori

In te rapito, al suon de la tua voce,
Lungamente sognai;
E de la terra ogni affanno, ogni croce
In quel sogno scordai.

Torna, caro ideal, torna un istante
A sorridermi ancora,
E a me risplendera, nel tuo sembiante,
Una novella aurora.
Torna, caro ideal, torna... torna.....

(Paolo Tosti: Ideale)

(English translation follows on next page)

I followed you like a rainbow of peace
Along the paths of heaven;
I followed you like a friendly torch
In the veil of darkness.

And I sensed you in the light, in the air,
In the perfume of flowers,
And the solitary room was full
Of you and of your radiance.

Absorbed by you, I dreamed a long time
Of the sound of your voice
And earth's every anxiety, every torment
I forgot in that dream.

Come back, dear ideal, for an instant
To smile at me again, and in your face
Will shine for me a new dawn.
Come back, dear ideal, come back...come back...

Part One:
David

One
November, 1953

On a blustery November morning eight-year-old David Atkins rode with his mother in her 1950 black Chevrolet coupe along a recently paved stretch of Union Street in Selma, Alabama. Little did he know that this short drive was to mark a change in his life that no one could have foretold.

Though he did not understand it all, he knew his parents' marriage was ending in divorce. His brothers told him their father, Daniel, had run off with a Yankee woman from Pennsylvania. Their mother had managed to find a job with the U.S. government as a clerk in the finance department at the nearby air force base. Daniel had deeded to her the house on Evans road, where she and her three sons lived. The eldest boy had been born just before the Great War with Germany and Japan. David, the youngest, had been born after the war's end.

David smiled as his mother reached over to smooth a wayward lock of dark-auburn hair that had fallen across his forehead, not quite reaching his lustrous, dark-brown eyes . . . eyes which stood out in contrast to his pale skin. He wondered silently to himself where they were going and why she had insisted on taking music to a church hymn with them when they left the house, but he sat in silence, looking out the window. She was the one person in his world that he unconditionally trusted, and he relished times like this when he had her all to himself.

He had found a secret place within himself where the hurt from his father's absence could not reach. Although his mother seemed increasingly concerned with him, he figured it was because he wasn't doing that well in school. He had never excelled in subjects that did not interest him. His mother abruptly turned into a long drive, bordered with rows of tall oak trees, and stopped in front of a large old house. He didn't know that a friend of his mother's had suggested this visit to the new Conservatory of Music and the voice teacher who had opened it after coming to this country with her marine colonel husband, a man she had met in the ruins of her native Italy at the war's end.

"Well, David, come on. I have a surprise for you."

The frail child looked apprehensively back at her, then slid over to her side of the seat, lingering for a moment at the warmth left behind as she got out of the car. He ran his hands across the warmth of where she had been sitting, feeling the same security he felt in the bed that he shared with her since his father's exit. He recalled the smell of her favorite perfume,

Evening in Paris — it lingered on her pillows. The remembrance comforted him.

"David! Get out of the car *now!* The music. Don't forget it."

He roused himself from his thoughts and dutifully followed her up the steps of the house.

Two

Imogene paused part-way up the long stairway. *What kind of dream world does this boy live in? Is he ever going to learn the difference between reality and the make-believe world he lives in? If this keeps up, I'm going to have to take him to that doctor in Montgomery that I read about. There has to be something that can be done for this poor child.* David continued ahead of her for a couple of steps, then she caught up with him, took his hand, and continued up the seemingly unending expanse of steps to the huge porch.

As they reached the top, she looked around the wide veranda, her eyes resting with pleasure on two old-time green wicker rockers. She smiled approvingly at the six fern stands from which cascaded beautiful Kimberly ferns, their graceful fronds drooping nearly six feet. *What a beautiful warm setting on such a chilly day. Soon they'll have to take the ferns to a safe place to keep them living through the winter.* She was pleased too, with how the high windows gleamed. *And I had heard this place was falling to ruin. Why it looks the way it must have when The Colonel's mama was still alive!*

A great door of deeply stained hard oak beautifully framed the entrance to the Queen Anne-style home built in the early 1900's. The house emitted a feeling of unassuming old southern elegance of a sort she rarely encountered. It was surrounded by tall pecan trees and bordered by foundation plants, mainly ancient hollies with thick hedges of mountain laurel. The pecan trees were bare now in late November, but here and there Imogene spotted clusters of vine-like mistletoe high up in the branches like parasites. She also admired the double row of great oaks that lined each side of the long driveway. The branches of the trees at the top had reached each other, forming an arch. *How beautiful this must be in the spring when the leaves come out and form the canopy!*

She looked for the doorbell and found none. A heavy brass lion's head in the center of the door had a ring through its mouth. As she reached out to grasp the ring and strike the plate beneath it, the door suddenly creaked open from within.

A deep voice said "*Avanti! Avanti*, please come in!" The lady who stood in the door was The Colonel's wife and the resident voice teacher. Gossip, both good and bad, had been circulating for the five years this Italian woman had lived in this small south Alabama town.

"Good afternoon," the younger woman stammered as she prepared to introduce herself. Always emphasizing the southern pronunciation of the letter I, *like eye*, she began, "I'm Imogene Atkins, and this is my son David. Did I speak to you on the phone?"

"Yes, Mrs. Atkins, I recall having spoken with you. So is this the child?"

"Why, yes. This is my son, David Alan Atkins, my youngest child."

The teacher heaved a great sigh and answered in a strange clipped way, "David . . . that's a good strong name. Come in, both of you, to the music room."

Imogene, struggling to understand the teacher's heavily accented English, and David followed her breathlessly to the room to the right of the door. A wide hall dominated the entrance with rooms opening to the right and left. A staircase rose toward the rear of the very high walls. Imogene glanced furtively toward the staircase; light became increasingly dim as she looked up the stairs. Beautiful portraits and mirrors graced the imposing vestibule. She snapped back to attention as the teacher, who stood in the middle of the music room called out to them.

"Well?" The teacher's tone was laced with irritation, her hands on her hips, "Come in, I haven't all day. I am waiting." She turned toward them and approached a Steinway grand piano which gleamed in ebony blackness near the huge front window. She thought to herself, *Mio Dio! Does it never end?* She made a sweeping gesture towards an over stuffed sofa near the center of the room. "Now let us talk! I am Carlotta Antonia Vasselli, teacher of *singing*."

Imogene and David trembled as she spoke. Before them stood a tall, slender, blond- haired woman of undetermined age with deep blue eyes and a highly theatrical manner. She carried herself in a very erect and imperial style of beauty and poise; her clothes fashionably accentuated her still-striking figure. She raised her hand in an elegant gesture, wet her lips and smiled at them patronizingly.

"I teach the method of Garcia, the greatest teacher who has ever lived. He was the son of the tenor Manuel Garcia who created the role of *Il Conte De Almaviva* in Rossini's *Il Barbiere*! His sisters were Maria Felicita Garcia-Malibran and Pauline Viardot-Garcia, the most famous singers of the nineteenth century. Their method was first taught to me in my youth by Madame Blanche Marchesi, the daughter of Salvatore

Marchesi and the incredible teacher, Mathilde Marchesi. Alas, old Madame Marchesi was dead before my time, but in London her child Blanche taught for many years. I was blessed as a child to have had from her the good fortune of learning the *only* correct method of singing."

Madame Vasselli stood, studying the faces that merely looked blankly back at her, not comprehending a word she had said. She stood, thoughtfully looking at them for a moment as her hand touched the piano keys. As she turned, she looked directly at Imogene's chalk-white face.

"You may go, Mrs. Atkins. You, child, remain."

Imogene hesitated, then said, "Well, Madame Vasselli, my son is a child and this is all new to him, so I believe I should stay while you talk to him."

"Mrs. Atkins, that is absurd. You told me you wanted to see if the child could possibly have a voice. Now you are looking to me to draw him out. How am I to gain the child's confidence while his mother, like some hideous bird of prey, stands guard over him, intimidating him by her presence? He hasn't so much as spoken a single word, nor lifted his eyes from this carpet. Now, I repeat, *be gone*! Leave me with the child."

David raised his head, watching this power play between the two women, his face blank. Timidly he said, "Madame, what does *Mio Dio* mean*?"*

"He talks! It means, 'my God.' Get used to it, because I use it a lot. As well as *che fai,* which means 'what are you doing,' also p*arlami,* which means 'speak to me.'"

Imogene rose from her seat, admonished David to do as he was told, then turned to leave the room. "He won't give you any problem. He knows what's waiting for him if he does. I'll be back in an hour."

"By all means go, but do not believe I limit my lessons to an hour as so many do, and then stop a student in mid-lesson as though the cash register had suddenly slammed shut. I teach as I will, and it is I who will call to summon you back here when I am ready. Now . . . go. I will take it from here."

David's eyes glistened with tears as he watched his mother back silently out of the room. He had never seen her dismissed in such a way by anyone. He gazed at her till the door closed silently behind her. He heard a slight movement near his right shoulder. Carlotta's hand touched him on the head. As he looked up, two tears stole down his thin cheeks as he contemplated this new person who spoke in a strange way and talked about times long ago, mentioning names he had never heard. His left eye began twitching .

Madame, as he ever-afterwards called her, smiled benevolently and said, "Now, my child, it's our time, let's talk. Shall we hear the hymn your mother said you would sing for me? We will then see where it goes."

He clutched the wrinkled pages of music. *What shall I do now? They look horrible.*

Carlotta seated herself at the piano, beckoning for the boy to approach. "Is that the song that you are going to sing for me? Well, hand it here. What is the title? Ah, never mind, it doesn't matter. Give it to me, child, and come closer." She frowned as she saw the title at the top of the first page. Raising her eyes heavenward, she let out a great sigh at the name, *Let the Lower lights be Burning*.

"Lower lights indeed? Well then, let us sing." The contempt in her voice for the simple nature of the hymn was clearly evident.

David was visibly shaking as he stood to her left. She played an opening flourish, complete with a sweeping cadenza on the keyboard that extended at least three octaves and back. He sang, "Brightly gleams our father's mercy, from his lighthouse evermore, but to us he gives the keeping of the lights along the shore." He had opened his mouth to sing the chorus when Carlotta suddenly threw up her hand, signaling him to stop.

"Ah, *Mio Dio*. What is this trite nonsense? It will never do. Now, be still. We will see what the compass of your voice is. Just follow me, singing the vowels I say as we go through them. Do not tremble, boy, just do as I say." She played scales, arpeggios, and octaves.

He followed — hesitantly at first, then with ease as his confidence rose. They went through the scales on the vowels A, E, I, O, and U. Higher and higher rang out the bright soprano voice as he followed every flourish, continuing uninterrupted as she played them faster and faster.

She stopped, staring blankly for a long moment. She looked at him and said, "Do you realize that you have just vocalized over more than two and a half octaves, from the Low E to the high E above the staff? *Incredible*. Of course the sound is weak. You are just a skinny child with a natural high-set soprano. You will begin, of course, with vocalizes and exercises that I had from Madame Blanche. This will take at least two years of practice on your part and application of the breathing techniques that I shall teach you. Then we can see what direction we will take from there. Naturally when your voice begins to change, we will have to restudy for the masculine voice that you will have. How do feel and what do you have to say for yourself?"

In a flood of nervous terror the boy's words came quickly. "Oh, Madame, I know nothing. I have only sung with the children at church. I know nothing about what you are talking about, but I like it here. I don't feel afraid with you as I thought I would when I walked in here. You are a very pretty lady, and swell too. Nothing like the things my mother's friends have said."

Suddenly he went white with fear and came closer, speaking urgently, "Please, Madame, don't tell my mother what I just said, she would whip my ass for saying this."

He looked at her beseechingly and something about the terror in his eyes left her for a moment speechless. Then she threw her head back and great peals of laughter rang forth. Just as quickly the smile faded and she again looked at him in deadly seriousness. "I know you are but a child, yet there is something different about you, something your own, detached from this town where you live. I have seen this before, but not often. In fact, hardly ever in my experience have I seen this. God knows, not in this miserable town. Among the few pupils I have, you are by far the youngest. It is like a blank canvas that one can use to create the most beautiful picture in the world. Come closer, child; let me look deep into your eyes and perhaps your heart as well. Alas, you know nothing of the world, nothing beyond the narrow compass you live in with your family. But enough of that, you will learn to trust me. It will be difficult, but you will come to understand as time passes that what I say and do is true." She looked earnestly at him, then taking his face in her hands she quietly said, "Believe in all you are capable of, apply yourself to the exclusion of every distraction and I will make something extraordinary of you."

David looked more like a miniature adult as he said in all seriousness, "Madame, my mother says I am to obey you as if it came from her. I will do as you say."

She stood and told him quietly, "I think this is enough for today, go along down the hall to the kitchen and tell Viola I said to give you a dish of charlotte while I call your mother."

He backed out of the room like a courtier before a royal personage, never once taking his eyes off her until he was in the middle of the hall, out of her view. He looked cautiously toward the light at the end of the long hall, hearing someone singing *The Old Rugged Cross*. He lingered, not wanting to leave the nearness of Madame, and he overheard her talking to herself. He very quietly listened, unobserved.

Carlotta looked at the signed photos on the piano. Black and white autographed and dedicated pictures gazed back at her . . . the *crème de la crème* of the opera world in France, Italy and Germany of the 30's and 40's. She had seen and appeared with many of them in the greatest theaters

— *La Scala* of Milan, the *La Fenice* of Venice, the *San Carlo* of Naples, the *Teatro Massimo* of Palermo, The Rome Opera, Covent Garden of London . . . the list went on and on. She sat, as in reverie, and looked at the portrait of Madame Blanche over the fireplace, and whispered out loud, "Yes, my friends and foes, the past is mine, and I remember everything."

David hid himself behind a marble column as she walked out into the hall and picked up the phone in the alcove. "55895," she told the operator. "Hello, Mrs. Atkins? You may come now for David; however, when you arrive, don't touch the door knocker, I will be waiting for you. We need to talk. How is he? He is fine. No, of course there is no problem. He is quite safe, eating a dessert in the kitchen that my old maid Viola has prepared. I will see you in a few minutes." She hung up, then walked slowly to the other side of the hall into the library where she could better see Imogene's car approaching the house. She moved the vase of flowers to one side and drew back the white eyelet curtains and stood waiting in silence.

David slowly looked around the corner into the kitchen where he saw a thin, old colored woman standing in a corner beneath massive glass-faced cabinets. A huge rectangular table of painted white pine stood in the center of the room. The stove, refrigerator and other fixtures were of 1930's vintage. A large old Sunbeam mixer stood at one end of the two long counters. The ceilings seemed lower here than in the front part of the house as if the kitchen had been added on after the original house was built . . . a fact confirmed as he saw from a window at the rear a small brick building with two chimneys. Viola would later explain to him that was where the kitchen stood when the house had originally been built.

"Come on in, honey, Viola ain't gonna bother you none. She too old and decrepit to cause anyone any trouble. Don't be bashful now, child. Ain't you ever spoken to a colored woman before? I heard you singing in there with Miss Carlotta. It sounded nice, though I ain't ever understood that mess she carries on in there with them young ladies who come in and holler back and forth with her. Just don't take no hankering to that kind of music I reckon."

"Madame Vasselli told me to come back here and tell her servant to give me something to eat while I wait on my mother."

"Well, I'se a servant, stuck up white boy, but not a slave in the tone you are taking with me, young man. You white folks just don't understand colored folks. Lordy! Even Miss Carlotta, for all her high-class ways, don't even know the first thing about cooking. Still can't figure out how a woman like that could have snagged The Colonel over yonder in that place she came from. He found her starving there in some bombed-out opera house. All her folks had been shipped off to some camp by the Germans.

Think she ain't got anyone no more. She don't ever hear from no one except some of them singers she writes back and forth to. Guess she must have been a great lady once upon a time, and then the war came and it all changed. She's lucky The Colonel found her. Damn sho is, cause she's mean as hell. For some reason that I don't even think he understands, he fell crazy in love with her, married her, and brought her back to this old place where he grew up, where his momma and daddy and baby sister Georgiana all died."

She sighed, and her eyes grew cloudy at the memory now lost in the mists of time "Why, honey, that gal don't know the first thing 'bout taking care of a man." She stood, her eyes raised towards heaven. "I tried to learn her fried chicken and macaroni and cheese, but she didn't have a clue. Finally threw up her hands and told me to just fix the stuff The Colonel likes. Ha! No problem, I been doing that all his life. But how I just go on. Child, have a seat, and I'll bring you something."

He sat alone at the table, watching her in silence, trying to remember what all that jabbering was about and what all Madame had been saying to him and to what he heard her say in the music room.

Viola, who said she was ninety-six years old, wiped her face on her long apron, washed her hands in the sink and then wiped them across her ample bosoms. She shuffled to the refrigerator, opened the door and drew out a couple of small crystal bowls. She put the bowls on the table, pulled up a chair, and put out two spoons and napkins. She plopped down in her chair and looked across at him. "Eat up, boy; this here is your charlotte!"

"Charlotte? I don't see a girl in here, just you and I and you are so old."

She looked at him through narrowing eyes and spat snuff juice into her spit jar that she usually hid behind the cookbooks on the counter. "Lawdy, darling, ain't you ever had charlotte before? It's that dessert sitting in front of you. Its good, now dig in and enjoy!"

He looked down at what appeared to be a vanilla pudding with some pink liquid floating on top. He took a tentative bite and immediately made a face. He had never tasted anything like it before.

"Now, baby, I knows it's new to you, but its boiled custard, chilled with a dash of sherry over the top. Lots better than them candy bars you young folks favor so much. The Colonel's momma was from Texas. She brought the secret with her when she came here as a bride back in 1893. Everyone who was anyone said she had class, and she sho nuff did. What a lady. Anyhow, eat it up but savor it, you'll like it."

David took another taste.

"That's it. Does I see a smile curling up on them lips? I told you it was good and I never lie. Colonel's momma always made it. He loves it. She wouldn't even let me fix it, though, till her eyesight started to go, then she broke down and taught me before she died so she'd know he'd always have someone to fix it for him. Lawdy, this Miss Carlotta ain't never gonna learn it. Old Viola feels sorry for The Colonel. I gonna die soon and then the secret goes, it's gone."

"Well, why don't you just write it down and someone can fix it for him and then he won't even miss you when you're gone!" He laughed in spite of himself. *Funny, I can talk to this old woman, she's southern folk, but Madame is so different than other folks here in Selma.*

"Why I never! You hateful young'un oughta have mo' respect for old folks. Nothing ever changes with you young kids. I done raised a bunch myself, but do they have time for me? Oh no, wouldn't be fittin' to come visit an old nigger woman. But I've outlived all of them 'cept my youngest, Mattie. Oh, child, and grandchillen? I must have a hundred. But none of 'em ever come around 'ceptin when they wanna try to take my pocket money for drink, or women, or worse."

David looked across at Viola running off at the mouth and just smiled. He'd never sat at a table with a colored person before.

His old grandmother had always said, "Things were so much simpler when they belonged to us. They knew their place back then. Never gave white folks no trouble, and then them damn Yankees came down here and ruined everything."

They sat in silence until she got up and fetched him another bowl of charlotte and said, "Well, child, you just sit right there till you're called. Viola has to tend to picking up some pecans. Colonel just loves my pecan pies. I gotta make him a couple. God knows *she* ain't never gonna do it. If you is gone when I get back, maybe I'll see you or hear you in there screaming back and forth in the music room." She smiled and ambled out the back door with a large basket. "Oh, Jesus! These steps are gonna be the death of me, fallin' down rotted just like me."

David listened as she sang a verse of *The Old Rugged Cross* until her voice faded away.

Three

Carlotta saw Imogene turn into the drive, walked briskly out to the front porch to meet her and suddenly felt her hands shaking as Imogene started up the steps. She took a breath, steeled her nerves and said, "Hello again, Mrs. Atkins. Please come over here to the chairs and we can talk like two old friends!"

Who is she calling old? mused Imogene as she looked at the smiling Italian who had been, she thought, insufferably rude earlier. *What's she up to?* She sat in one of the wicker rockers. An afternoon wind had arisen. *Why in heaven's name does she not ask me inside?*

Carlotta considered carefully what she was going to say. Convinced that the boy had a genius for singing, she was determined not to lose this opportunity. She cleared her throat. *God, give me the words to convince this woman of my sincerity — she can make or break this thing.* "Well now, Mrs. Atkins. I have worked some with the boy and I feel he has a gift if you will be so good as to let him come over here, say three or four times a week as his school work permits, or even all day Saturday, so he can listen to my teaching of other students to reinforce things I cover individually with him. What to you think? Does that sound reasonable?" *Am I coming on too strong? Too enthusiastic?*

Imogene jumped to her feet, "Reasonable? Three or four times a week? And maybe all day Saturday? Are you out of your mind? Do you think I'm made of money? My husband barely gives me $100 a month for my three sons; with what I earn at the air force base, and keeping our bodies and souls together, that doesn't leave much for any voice lessons. Now I let my friend Margaret, who also makes no bones about your strange ways, talk me into bringing David by here. He is such a shy child, so hurt and inside himself, but what you're talking about, I could never afford that. We'd be out on the street and in the poorhouse, or begging our bread at the church door!" She paced back and forth, wringing her hands, with her eyes fixed on this strange woman.

"Mrs. Atkins, please calm yourself." She too, rose and glared. "Perhaps my ways are different than what all of you here are used to. I know I dress differently, talk differently, have old world ways, but please remember that until a few years ago I had no idea where Alabama was, and certainly in my wildest nightmares had ever heard of Selma." Then, forcing a smile, she said through clenched teeth, "Let us talk frankly. Your child has a gift, something I sense inside of him to aspire to a life of singing, of knowing a kind of life he might never know had you not brought him here today. This isn't about you . . . or money. It is about the latent talent I see in him. His voice is naturally placed, a high soprano now, but when it breaks one day he will have had the training to cover those awkward months till it deepens to what it will ever be." She looked patronizingly at Imogene.

"Oh please, Madame, you talk about things that shoot right over my poor head. I have no idea what you are talking about. I do love the child, or, believe me, I wouldn't be here, wouldn't have put up for a moment with the indignity you offered me this morning when you practically threw me out of this house. Your words are like a bee dripping honey. I remember hearing people talk like that when I was a girl. I was just a country thing. We didn't have much, but we were decent God-fearing folks, and we slept well at night after working hard all day. You seem as nice now as you were rude to me earlier. And all this because an eight-year-old boy you say has a gift?"

Her eyes blazed with inner fury. "I can't afford more than a few dollars a week — do you see this dress?" She came close and pointed, "The elbows are threadbare. Of course the children don't know this, they don't see it, nor do I want them to know that after working all day and coming home and fixing their dinner, making sure they get their lessons, getting them to bed, that all I want to do is fall in bed too.

"But no," she arrogantly spat out, "you wouldn't know any of this, living out here in this fine house, being married to one of our leading citizens and doing nothing but giving music lessons and probably going down to that Catholic church." Her voice rose as she took a step toward Carlotta. "What would *you* know of struggle, of having to fix their lunches for the next day, washing, ironing, cleaning, and then I finally drag myself half-dead to bed? What would some woman like you know of what our lives are like?" She was beside herself, shaking violently.

Carlotta listened while Imogene worked herself into her frenzy, red streaks coming into her neck and face. Watching her jump up and go to and fro in her tirade, she waited until the passionate outburst was over and said, "Now then, Mrs. Atkins, sit down. You are going to listen to me. Don't you dare move because now it's *my* turn." She brought her face to within an inch of Imogene's and said in a tone of repressed rage, "First of all I am not a Catholic, I am Jewish. Yes, some of us Italians are, you know, and I was born to an affluent family. But we were foolish. We didn't see the darkness taking over Europe during the war. We thought it would never come to Italy and we stayed till one day it was too late. My parents, my brothers and sisters, almost my whole family were taken away to the camps in Germany and Poland. I never saw them again." Her face grew redder with each new word. *Oh, God, the pain of not knowing what became of my parents, my Grandparents, brothers and sisters, probably consigned to the gas chambers with no one there to comfort them in their final moments, pain, unending agony knowing they died and I still lived.*

"Our property was confiscated, everything taken away. I survived because I happened to be in a touring company in South America singing in Buenos Aires. When I made my way back to Milan they were all gone. I never had a chance to say goodbye, and I had to go into hiding with people who protected Jews. The allies came and the cities were bombed, my magnificent *La Scala* opera house lay in ruins. I was forced into the streets to beg to survive. It was there The Colonel came and found me, and in his compassion he loved me, took me away from my own country — and married me even though I wasn't a Christian. So you, woman, don't believe I have not suffered, something I hope you will never have to face in your life." She had cast off her icy reserve and stood waiting, waves of heat coming from her face in spite of the cold wind that whistled over the porch. At length, she stood, composed, the regal bearing of a *Prima Donna Assoluta* reasserting itself.

Imogene took a step backward. "Ah, my God, I had no idea. Somehow I hope you can forgive me, I'm so very sorry, Madame, please excuse my words and forget them if you can."

"Mrs. Atkins, it is all right. I will take David as a full scholarship student. There will be no charge. I do this because I believe in talent. It is a rare gift. He has it in spades! I have seen the greatest, and this child could eclipse them all. Give him to me all the time you can spare, and I promise you, he will have a life that people in this close-minded place could never imagine."

Imogene hung her head. "I put him in your hands. I was wrong about you. Everyone has been. I let the prejudice around me color my thoughts and actions and I am ashamed. Thank you for caring so much that you offer free lessons for him. My gratitude will be yours so long as I live."

"No need for an apology, Mrs. Atkins. So we understand each other then? It is the child who needs a chance at a different life now. So, let us go in and fetch him so he can leave with you." *Thank God she agreed to allow him the chance to have the future I can give him.*

"Oh my, yes, it's getting late now. We need to be going, I need to fix the boy's dinner."

Together the two women, so different in many ways but now united in a common good, walked back into the house.

"David? Come on, honey, we have to leave. Where are you?"

David peeked around the door of the kitchen and saw his mother standing in the doorway with Madame. He came down to them and seemed surprised when his mother knelt down and hugged him in a strange new way. She knew when she saw his face that something had happened that day. He had a glow about him. "Goodbye then, Madame," he said as he hurried past them, ran down the steps, and got into the shiny black Chevrolet.

"Goodbye, David, I'll be seeing you again very soon," said Carlotta.

Imogene turned and walked out the door with Carlotta. As she started down the steps, she turned around and said, "I'm not sure what David might have learned today about singing, it's only the beginning, but I learned something today about assuming things without knowledge, about the things people have in common, no matter where they are in their lives, or where they might have come from. Thank you for that. I'll have him back here first thing next Saturday. We are going up to see relatives in north Alabama for Thanksgiving, but we'll be back by then and he'll be here bright and early."

Carlotta reached out her hand and Imogene grasped it gratefully. Then she and David drove slowly away, turned onto the wide newly paved avenue and were gone.

How long Carlotta stood on the porch after they had gone she would not recall. Time seemed to have stood still. Something stirred within her as she recalled the way the boy's voice sounded as she took him through the scales. She said aloud, "What a pleasure it will be to work with such material through his young years, to mold it to perfection." She turned and walked back into the house closing the great, heavy door behind her.

Four

The next day Imogene and her sons arrived at her mother's country home in Albertville, Alabama. Her older sister, Barbara, dashed out to meet them and enveloped the boys in huge hugs. Barbara was the oldest of Imogene's siblings, an old maid designated by her parents' wishes to be nursemaid to all the subsequent children. She grew used to her position as sister matriarch and seemed happy in the role fate had ordained for her. Imogene loved her as a second mother and ran with joy to greet her sister's embrace.

"I thought we'd never get here, Barbara, but seeing your face makes it all worthwhile. My goodness, it's windy today, I'm glad to see you remembered to put on your sweater before coming out here."

"How was y'all's trip? Were there any problems on the way? I've been cooking, making all the boys' favorites." She kissed Imogene. "Come on in, Mama's been all excited and fussing with impatience for y'all to get here!"

The old lady, Alexandra, sat in an overstuffed chair beside her bed. Partially paralyzed on her left side, she had not taken a step again since her stroke four years ago. An old crank lift moved her in and out of bed. She had once been tall, six feet, and lanky, but now she had grown heavy from inactivity. She wore her hair in two long braids fastened to her head with old tortoise-shell combs she had in abundance, souvenirs left to her by her own mama. She grabbed each boy in turn, lingered over David, always her favorite, and then gave her youngest daughter a kiss. The boys always thought it strange that she was so old when their mother seemed young. Alexandra had been 49 years old when Imogene, the last of her ten children, had been born.

"You boys go on out to the kitchen. Barbara has made you a blackberry cobbler and has some homemade ice cream too. Imogene, get my snuff tray and spit can and bring it over here and sit and talk with me a while about that low-down trashy husband of yours who's done run off on you with some Yankee gal. Make haste now, girl, and get me that snuff. Barbara, turn off that radio, I can't stand that station. Those folks don't know anything about singing the Lord's music. Come on now, girl. That's right, where's my wood spoon? I can't dip the snuff without it. Be still now, or I'll get up from here and wear you out if you don't mind me. There now, let's talk."

The bedroom at the rear of the old farmhouse was bright and airy, with a small fireplace in the middle back wall. A coal fire burned brightly in the grate beside an ancient coal bucket. To the right stood an old hall tree, on which still rested one of her daddy's old hats and his favorite wooden cane.

Imogene wondered why they kept his things around; he had been dead for more than eight years. He had been a carpenter and had built this house for his wife and daughter, dying shortly before they moved in the spring of 1945. His death from colon cancer had been a slow, painful and humiliating death. At the end, in the days before mind- and pain-numbing drugs, he had cried out in agony in his delirium, calling for God to release him from the living hell of his life. He was buried in the old Bethlehem Cemetery on a hill overlooking the tiny primitive Baptist church. His parents and Alexandra's all rested there as well. At the church during the funeral, several of his sisters had gone down to the open casket, covering his cold face with their tears and kisses. Imogene's children hadn't been there. The two oldest were too young; David would not be born until November that year.

At the graveside one of her daddy's sisters, Aunt Della, had been so overcome with grief that folks thought she had gone crazy. As they lowered his pine box into the red Alabama clay, she had let loose with a scream of woe so terrifying that even the staid old Alexandra looked up in surprise. Before anyone could stop her, Aunt Della let out another yell and hurled herself into the grave. It took three men to extricate her. She later had to be taken to the state hospital in Montgomery for shock treatment but was never the same again and grieved herself to death within a year.

Imogene picked up a picture of the graveside service from the mantle. *Funny how there always seemed to be some charlatan photographer around asking to take a picture for the family's memory book at funerals.*

"Tarnation, Imogene. Stop looking at that old picture. Put it down and do as I told you and sit down here beside me. Now ain't that better? I ain't seen you and the boys for so long, but do any of you care? Why of course you don't. Y'all are just waiting for me to die since I'm so old and useless now. No, gal, don't you open yo' mouth to deny it either. You just be still and listen to me. This is my house and what I say goes, now, just like it always was before. I'm going to stick around a while yet, I reckon, because not a one of you girls, or the boys either, ever had a lick of sense. Well, at least you of all of them finished school and went down to Birmingham to that business school and worked till you met that city boy you just had to marry. Well there you have it. What you got to show now, girl, for your haste? Three young'uns and a husband you weren't woman enough to keep from going after them painted northern women. Now he's up and left, and here you sit. Well, you are my child, but you got to live with your mistakes and make the most of it."

"Oh, Mama" Imogene murmured. *I am, after all, divorced.* "How deep you twist the knife in me. All I ever wanted was a better life than all of us had here. So I tried to make something of myself. I went down to Birmingham to learn office work. Why, you and Barbara were the only ones who came when I got my diploma. Daddy was off possum hunting with the colored men like he always did. You'd have thought he would have thought enough of me to put if off for one night, but no . . . and now he's dead. None of y'all called me till he was stone dead, and I had them babies and my husband was off in the war. God only knows what I went through in those dark days, never knowing from one day to the next if he wasn't going to be killed. Do you think he ever worried about his family? Every time his ship pulled into a port he'd be off after them painted up hussies and never thinking about what foul disease he might get and bring home to me. No, it was always what was in it for him. But I stayed. I mean what else could I do? I had them two babies and y'all preaching to me about staying with a man no matter what he did short of killing me. I know how all of you feel about divorce, but what could I do, Mama? One person can't make a marriage."

"Now, girl, you hush. You hear me, Imogene? Fluff up them pillows behind my head; pull that quilt up on my lap. None of you will ever know what suffering is. I had all of you one by one in this old iron stead bed. Never could keep that man from exercising his marriage rights. Now here I sit in this chair or that bed there waiting my life out, praying the Lord would lay it on your heart to come up here and let me see them boys. Brad and Tony ain't got no use for me no more. All they're concerned with is the dollar I'll give 'em when they go. But David? He's still mine, he *loves* me. Who else would I let take down these thick braids and brush out this long hair? No one but that little angel gift of God. Now get up, go on in the kitchen and see if you can help Barbara and then send David back in here. I want to be alone with him."

"All right, Mama, I'm going." She reached down to hug her mother, but the old lady shrugged her off.

"Get on with you now, girl, ain't got no time for that nonsense. Now, git."

After Imogene left, Alexandra lay back, resting her head against the feather pillows and gazing upon a black, oval-framed picture of her son, Sherman, who had died of whooping cough at age three, just before Imogene was born. In the picture he lay dead in the undertaker's arms in his little white suit. She had grieved all her life for him and another son earlier who had been stillborn. Both were buried on the hill overlooking the church. One day she knew she would join them there. She wasn't afraid of death's bright angel folding her in his icy arms. But she just wasn't ready to go just yet. "Barbara! Imogene! Send David on in here! Get him in here now before I wear the lot of you out!"

David was laughing as he ran into the room, "Hi, Granny, what are you doing? Aunt Barbara's blackberry cobbler was so good."

"What am I doing? Child, what does it look like I'm doing? I'm right here beside this iron bed, one day just like the other. So you liked the cobbler? That's good. Wish I could eat me some, but that stuff don't sit well with my stomach now, it'll cause them to have to crank me up in the air and put those newspapers and that rubber sheet under me. But never mind that, come closer David, let me hold you and look at you." *How like my Sherman he is!*

"Oh, Granny, you know I don't like it when you've been dipping that snuff. It just dribbles down your chin when you spit in the can, and sometimes gets on your gowns. It's horrible, just like them places on your face." He spoke of spots of skin cancer for which treatment had not yet been developed.

Alexandra uneasily shifted and fixed steely blue eyes on the little boy. "So, you are being ugly towards me today? That snuff there is about the only pleasure this old woman has in life anymore. You'd deny me that? You know I'd rinse out my mouth before I kissed you, don't you? What's wrong with you, boy? Cat got your tongue? Well, I knows you want to go outside, but I want you to come back later and see me, okay? Play your cards right and if I feel like it I'll let you brush out my hair. Come on, honey, don't hold back now. Gimme a kiss. Oh, all right, go on then, I ain't going to beg for it!"

* * *

David rushed out of the room and went outside. He looked around at his Aunt Barbara's old shrubs and pots of begonias of all colors. He loved the shrubs. They were large and had little leaves and thousands of tiny white flowers. They attracted honey bees and the beautiful large swallow-tailed butterflies that fluttered around, hungry for nectar. He walked to the back and saw several of the wild cats that came and went. Aunt Barbara would occasionally throw grits, biscuits, and green beans to them and always kept a big bowl of cool water for them. They fled at David's approach, running under a part of the house supported by stacks of bricks carefully arranged to support the weight above them. The house was all white. No shutters back here, but around front he knew they adorned every window, dark black against the stark white clapboards.

Immediately behind the house was a smokehouse where meat was hung — hams wrapped in salt drenched white cloths hung from the ceiling — and rows upon rows of preserves, soups, canned blackberries to see the old folks through the winter. Behind that, before the old cow pasture, stood the outhouse. Years later Aunt Barbara would have an indoor bathroom added onto the back of the house beside her bedroom. He was both horrified and intrigued by the little three-seat building. Dark purple grapes grew nearby in the rich soil, but he was reluctant to eat them because of the outhouse's proximity to the vines.

He looked for his brothers. Probably they had gone a few houses down, playing games in the woods with the local boys. They never wanted him tagging along, but he didn't care. He didn't like them anyway. They liked all the things he hated, stuff like little league baseball games, playing football and talking about girls. He didn't like girls either. Something about their long hair and dresses and the way they giggled and acted silly. He just wanted no part of it and he had grown used to being alone. It gave him time to think about serious things. He had never been allowed to be a child. He had to do his chores . . . and his brothers' also because they intimidated him. He had always been expected to act and think like an adult. He could never remember having a toy or playing as other children did.

He sat on an old tree trunk that had fallen long ago beside barns that now lay dusty and empty, the animals long gone save for a few chickens that ran here and there, pecking at corn thrown out to them. He knew he was his mother's favorite and he tried hard not to think about the father who was so frequently gone, but he thought of him now . . . of the rough stubble of his beard and how it felt like sandpaper against his cheeks. His parents loved him; at least he felt they did. But the hugs he craved rarely came. Often he longed to be held, to be rocked in their arms. His father, Daniel, would hug him, but only for a tiny moment. Then he'd feel himself being gently pushed away, as though somehow touching his male children sparked some unspoken taboo that forbade it.

He looked toward the woods in the back and thought he heard far-off voices of boys, then realized it was just the cackle of the crows in the crowns of the trees. Crows, and sometimes even the larger ravens, were always around here, always watching, always hungry. He shivered against the wind but did not move.

He thought of the meeting with Madame back in Selma. What was it about his singing she liked so much and what was it that she spoke about? Yes, about Garcia, whoever he was, and his method. He remembered her house and the beautiful piano and the strange look on her face as she played and they sang all those notes without words. What did it all mean? He didn't know or understand, but he trusted Madame's words, just as he trusted most adults.

He had been taught to be mannerly and didn't mind doing as he was told. Good behavior often produced some ice cream and cake for him, or maybe some slices of ice-cold watermelon from the tin ice-filled tubs in summer. He thought, too, about Viola and her leathered, wrinkled dark skin, her musky smell and the gray, wooly braids all over her head. His brothers would laugh and holler names at the colored children when they rode or passed close to Harlem. Sometimes he'd hear them use that word, *nigger*; Mother said they must never say that word. He just knew colored people were different. But Viola was nice and she gave him charlotte. He thought back to that kitchen with the immense white-pine table and the strange sensation of the sweet custard in his mouth with the taste of sherry on top.

He was unaware of time as he sat beside the grove of trees, listening and thinking. Then he saw fireflies start to light up as they flew to and fro. He listened to the chirping sound the crickets made as they crawled in the fresh red pine straw. He knew they'd be gone soon. Winter was coming. Then there would be no more life outdoors, only silence and cold. And death.

* * *

"David? Where are you, honey?" called Imogene from the back porch. "Come on back to the house now, we have to eat our supper, wash up, and get ready for bed. Come on, David, its getting dark out here!"

She shivered. She didn't like the dark, had always been afraid of it since she'd heard stories as a child of things that came for you if you ventured too far from the house, especially in the woods. Her mother had told her of witches disguised as kindly old ladies. She looked out into the gathering darkness and saw the leafless trees, their branches going in all directions against the fading light in the sky. Wind whistled through the trees which stood like dark sentinels. She shuddered, looking and remembering other times so long ago.

Suddenly she saw David coming up the path in his tattered jeans and flannel shirt. She stood motionless watching him, his dark auburn hair fluttering in the wind. Her jaw hardened as he approached. "Well it's about time! Didn't you hear me calling? Now get inside and let's eat. Don't forget to wash your hands in the basin now." She slapped him on the backside as he bounded up on the porch. She stopped him for a moment and looked searchingly into his face. She touched his shoulders with her hands and felt the bones move underneath. She took his hand and they walked inside. She looked back for a moment and thought she saw something moving in the darkness that had now overtaken all daylight. She closed and locked the door behind them as they walked to the brightly lit kitchen.

Five

December's first day found Imogene and her sons back in Selma. It was Friday evening when they drove past the Selma city-limits sign, just after the old Bradford Drive-in Theater. They were all tired and quickly unpacked the car, each taking care of his own belongings. The small three-bedroom house allowed Imogene and Brad, the oldest son, their own rooms. Tony and David shared a room with twin beds, although David usually slept with his mother.

They had a supper of sandwiches and iced tea. Imogene had gone out and picked several ripe tomatoes from their vines, sliced them and put the dish on the table as the meal's token vegetable. Brad, Tony, and David all loved her iced tea, true to the southern tradition of "sweet tea," with at least two cups of sugar per gallon pitcher. Like most of the families in Selma who could not afford the luxury of television, the only entertainment was the radio, around which they would all gather and listen in the evenings. Imogene went to the kitchen to try to prepare a grocery list.

Brad was studying, memorizing poetry assignments to recite at school. His grades were good thanks to a great memory. Schoolwork, regardless of the subject, came easily to him. As the first boy grandchild, he had been petted and pampered since birth. He sat with his feet on the table, clad only in ragged denim shorts. Nearly fourteen, puberty had struck, and a little cluster of darkening hair showed just above his shorts. An athlete who played football, baseball and tennis, he sported "six-pack" abs; with a handsome face to go with his physique, it was no surprise that girls — even some a couple of years older than he — gave him admiring looks. He was popular with other boys, too, and even the rich kids' parents loved him.

Tony, eleven months younger than Brad, sat bare-chested, looking at an old magazine. A story in contrast to Brad, they were in the same grade, their birthdays falling on different sides of the cutoff date to start school. Tony always was in his older brother's shadow. He found school difficult, never making the honor roll, and seemed to run with the "rough" crowd. Tony had the promise of being a handsome young man too. He was taller than Brad, with a long, slim torso, slender but not "skinny." His body had begun to change also. He had been introduced to cigarettes and beer filched from his friends' parents, and the girls that eyed him were those drawn to the "bad boys." Manipulative, he could always get his mother to buy him nice clothes when she could afford it.

As he looked at Brad, he silently swore that someday he was going to be a guy that people would take seriously. He shifted his eyes to David, who sat quietly looking at the book of voice exercises his voice teacher had given him. He resented his younger brother; Mother seemed to coddle him so much. He knew he should love him, but there was something different about David. The other boys he knew used to look at and laugh about him.

Some of Tony's friends talked about a couple of men who lived together, men who always seemed to have boys around doing work for them, giving them money for it. When watching the boys wrestle outside, they would laugh and throw fluffy white towels to them, encouraging them to come over and swim whenever they liked. Tony had been once to their house. He remembered feeling uncomfortable with how the men always seemed to be touching him on his shoulder, his arm or his stomach. His friends laughed, told him he was crazy to turn down beer, cigarettes and even the stag movies that some of the boys had seen. Tony thought, *Well maybe they're okay, but I just didn't like the way it felt the day they each had put their hands on my side , just below my shorts. It made me feel strange, I had to get away.* Those memories hit him as he looked at David. *How tiny he is, small like a girl, but almost pretty with his big eyes and that long hair and a fawn-like softness of his body.* When he saw David naked the thought arose: *If it weren't for that little dick he has, no one would know he was a boy.* He shuddered inwardly as he felt his own start to rise. He got up and shook his head as he left the room. *He is a boy, not a girl, and he's my brother. How I hate him!*

* * *

David was blissfully unaware of Tony's feelings. He loved both his brothers, and tagged along when he was allowed. Usually that led to them screaming at him to get lost, sending him running home in floods of tears to lose himself in his picture books of handsome knights and beautiful ladies with wonderful clothes, where everyone seemed happy. He had heard many snide remarks at school that he was different, someone to be avoided. Pretty and girlish, some of the older boys, with the curiosity of those passing into puberty, eyed him with lust. He even secretly liked the boys who would bully him; at least he was being noticed.

Such undercurrents of thought from Tony and some of the others boys had never figured in David's imagination; at eight, he was totally naïve about sex as were most children of that era. He had noticed that his brothers' bodies were changing, and the changes puzzled him. He always thought a penis was for peeing. But lately, when they had been to Grandmother's house and were getting ready for bed, he saw a marked change in Tony's behavior. They shared an old feather bed upstairs, and Tony started sleeping naked. Late one night in bed, he felt a pressure against his back. He moved away, frightened and puzzled. Why was it that Tony did something in the night to himself and made noises?

A few minutes ago when Tony got up from the table something had bulged in the front of his athletic shorts. He smiled and thought, *Tony is so weird, but he's my brother and I love him. How I wish he would love me too and keep the mean boys away.*

He went back to the voice exercise book and hollered out to Imogene,

"When are you going to buy me a piano, Mother? I have to learn the names of these notes and what they mean. Maybe Madame will let me practice there on one of her other pianos, like the one in the parlor."

He yawned, it was bed time and tomorrow he'd see Madame Vasselli once more.

Six

It was Saturday, and Carlotta was more excited than usual. It was the day she'd have David to herself. Of course her other pupils would come and go during the day. There were six others, all girls who had pleasant voices; she wouldn't have taken on students she didn't feel had promise, but these girls, aged twelve through fifteen, were easily distracted. They were uniformly pretty, popular daughters of the more prominent families of Selma. Still, Carlotta felt that they could go places if they became as intense about their vocalizing as they did about school activities and boys. *Always the boys with these girls.*

She turned in bed toward the morning sun. The cold December morning's bright light peeked through the gauze-like curtains that swept the floor with swags and cascades, all white and stiffly starched in the manner of the old south. She frowned. Although she liked the old house, she had never entirely gotten used to it. The furniture was old, passed down from several generations who had lived there. Heavy sideboards, magnificent chandeliers, marble statues from Italy, tapestries of many styles, portraits of ancestors . . . it remained a magnificent showplace. She lay in the huge four-poster bed with its high back carved with rosettes and winding vines, all in dark oak. To her right lay her husband, known to everyone, including her, simply as The Colonel. A descendant of a proud family with inherited wealth, he remained unaffected by it, favoring instead to dispense with the dances and festive occasions his parents had so loved during their lifetimes. He was a quiet, private man. He loved nothing better than to spoil his wife, to take any worry off her shoulders, and she loved him for it. He would disappear to his private hobbies when the students would come. Carlotta watched him sleep. *What a pity we didn't meet earlier; it was too late for children.* She filed that thought in some secret mental alcove and slipped out of bed. She would need to see to her toilette, dress carefully to receive the students.

She was careful to tiptoe so as not to wake him. As she approached the bathroom door, she heard a rustle in the bed and looked back to see him smiling at her, his salt-and-pepper hair askew. She rushed back for a hug. Oh, my own dearest," she said, "how much I love you."

"I love you more though," he said. "I feel so blessed. Now you get going, my treasure. I'm going to play some golf and take advantage of this sunny day."

"Well, take care to keep your throat and head covered, I don't want you catching cold. You remember last winter how bad it was, you must be careful."

He smiled. "Just like a singer, always worrying about the throat. I'll be careful. Now run along, dear, I have to get going myself." He headed for his own bathroom, pausing just a moment for a quick kiss. "I'll see you tonight; enjoy your work with the children."

* * *

David arrived at nine wearing the scarf around his neck that she had told his mother he needed for his throat, and a hat, which he hated because it messed up his hair. He had walked the five blocks unaccompanied, and Viola answered the door and directed him to the music room where Madame was waiting. He stopped before going in; she was singing. He admired the size and volume of her voice. *What language is that anyway?* She finished on a very high note.

"Come in, child. We need to begin our work in earnest this morning, after which you will stay the remainder of the day to observe and learn as I teach the girls. Have you been looking over the exercises I gave you? Of course we already went over most of them that first day your mother brought you by, but no matter. You may remove your hat and scarf now, there are no drafts in this room!"

After some vocalizing to limber up his voice, they started going over the twenty-four exercises one at a time, repeating them as she thought appropriate. He enjoyed the discipline more than he thought he would, happy to focus on something other than the mean boys at school. Here was a person who liked him and who wanted to spend time with him; for the first time in a long while he felt happy about doing something worthwhile. After what seemed a long time, but actually was less than an hour, Carlotta stopped and said, "Let us sit and talk now, David. I am rather pleased that you are one of those rare people whose voice is naturally placed and that you do things instinctively that others spend years in learning. I understand you have no piano at home, so you may come over here every day after school and practice in the parlor. There is an adequate piano there which stays reasonably in tune and will serve the purpose. *This* piano, on the other hand, is for performing! You do read music, don't you?"

"No Madame, I've never had piano lessons before. I can't read music. I've only sung the things at church that the children's choir does. I just memorized those things, they seem so easy."

"Ah, *mio Dio!* Of course you wouldn't know. I myself will teach you for now. I have here diagrams of the notes on the scale and you will practice them in *there*. I know it won't take you long; you have such a quick mind. But, my dear, you must learn to recognize them when you see them on a sheet of music. When you do this, all things will open for you and you can take wings. There's plenty of volume in your voice, it just needs to be developed by ardent study. The notes are all there. Now, before the next student arrives, let's do something for fun. Listen while I sing this melody and then I'll play it for you and you imitate what you heard. Now the words are in Italian, but when you repeat it just sing 'la' or 'oh.'"

She began to sing an aria from *Lucrezia Borgia* by Donizetti, which began, "*Si voli il primo colierge, d'un bacio, d'un santo amore!*" He noticed that she seemed to stop at moments but he could clearly hear the melody. When his turn came, she played the melody and he followed, having memorized it instantly on first hearing.

She stopped, her mouth open in astonishment. "David, you must have heard this music before. There's no way you could have sung that line without mistakes. Your phrasing, your intonation, is as if from someone who has worked for years. Tell me, how did you do that?"

"Oh, Madame, I have never heard of opera until now. We don't have records like that in our house. My father's father, my grandfather, once told me of hearing Caruso and Melba, whoever they are. I think he has some 78's by them, but no, I have never heard that melody until you played it just now. I have always felt easy in imitating what I've heard; it's just something I've always understood how to do." He smiled, amused that such a noble and elegant lady would find him astonishing.

"That's all well and good, my child, but without knowing the words in their original language, true understanding and interpretation are impossible to attain. I shall teach you the words myself, what they mean, then magic, beauty . . . unimaginable things will be revealed to and through you."

She took him several times through the exercises of Madame Marchesi, always watching him and listening closely. He sang them without fault, over and over. Each time she would sing something, he would follow like an automaton. *I swear, oh God,* she thought, *as by your grace I was saved from the horror of war, that I will never cease working with this child, your gift, until the day he stands on the stage demonstrating the glory of the Garcias to a public who has forgotten all that is beautiful in the world.*

His lesson over, he sat as Madame had commanded in the huge old armchair at the back of the room. He listened as first a soprano, then a mezzo-soprano came for lessons. He listened for what he felt sounded right and filed it away in his mind. What sounded wrong he dismissed as he saw Madame's reactions to each one. With one girl, her face would light up as she saw the girl had mastered something especially difficult, then he would smile as he would hear her curse and scream at another who was lazy and hadn't studied her scales.

The day passed quickly with just a break for lunch with Viola in the kitchen. Carlotta fussed about the lack of freshness of the watercress, the slightly stale rye bread, and the pickles that weren't cold enough. Viola in indignation cried, "Have mercy, Miss Carlotta. I'se done the best I could with what they had at that fancy store you sent me to. T'aint my fault they ain't got your fancy tastes or all those crazy cheeses you keep yelling for. Lawdy, you gonna be the death of this old woman."

"Be silent, you vile old hag, before I beat you for the ungrateful wretch that you are. You may have pulled something over on The Colonel, but I swear to God, I will see you in chains before I'll let you take advantage of him. You had better have his dinner ready when he gets back here before you drag your decrepit carcass out, or I'll have you outside picking cotton again like your betters did before you. Another thing you'd better remember is that I am *Madame* to the likes of you. You are never again to address me as Miss Carlotta. Do you hear me, old woman?" Carlotta whirled this way then that as she worked herself into a fury. Fists-to-hips, she screamed "I am she who must and will be obeyed. Now be gone to your corner and dream of how easy you had it before I saved The Colonel from a slave like you. Come along now, David, back to our music."

They walked to the music room hand in hand, Carlotta with her head up, an erect figure looking this way and that, checking for dust old Viola missed. *God*, she thought, *I will be that woman's death or she mine before I am finished with her.* Then, brushing aside all agitation she gleefully and radiantly greeted the next pupil, a brilliant coloratura soprano. Again, David sat in the overstuffed armchair, listening, learning. In between she would give him an Italian-English book, commanding, "Learn this!" She also gave him books on how to read music. Time passed swiftly and it was soon time for him to leave.

"Return tomorrow when you get out of that miserable hovel they call a school and come straight here to practice. You will see, knowledge will come and you will take wings." She gave him a huge hug.

His mind raced. *How nice she always smells. Mother told me she could afford the best.* He walked . . . or floated . . . into the cool December sunshine, home to reality.

Seven

David's world increasingly became intertwined with Carlotta's instructions in voice training. He learned to read music. She taught him to play the piano well enough to know the notes on the page. Perhaps most importantly, she taught him Italian, the language of opera.

She would teach him about the lives of the composers, interpretation of drama in plays where dialog was song, where the voice becomes the instrument which brings music to life to lift the audience's knowledge and enjoyment of this most difficult art form. They had their work cut out for them. Very few people in Selma had ever seen an opera; Montgomery was the closest place where one might hear anything above a primitive level. Carlotta frequently took students there to perform before a more discriminating audience. Even with just piano to accompany them, she would encourage them to color their voices to bring melodies alive. She herself played for them, cursing the mostly wretched available instruments.

She took them, whenever possible, to churches in Selma for afternoon concerts, where they performed opera songs, including solo arias. Carlotta insisted on strict adherence to the method of Manuel Garcia. She would not tolerate laziness, goading them on to difficult feats of bravura, leaving the old dowagers and ancient grand dames gasping in amazement. Carlotta would gush and carry on with these old women, some of whom dragged along their grumbling, reluctant husbands. She would later tell all the students, "My dears, you must be firm but kind with ignorant, inferior people whose sole virtue is the fact that they have money. Did you notice that old Mrs. Benson? That hat was obscene . . . straw, a very low quality at that, covered with a menagerie of flowers, birds, and fruit. Of course we must remember she is married to the President of the C&S Bank of Montgomery, and as such could be a valuable asset to cultivate. People with money are so often fools, coming to musical events and imposing themselves on artists just simply because they know nothing. They think genius is something that rubs off. It does not, I assure you. However, remember such people can be useful. You can get them to sponsor a recital for no more than saying in the program that the flowers are courtesy of Mrs. Benson and so forth. She gets to feel important seeing her name in print and will be there forever with open checkbook just to be associated with art and culture."

David and the girls would laugh when remembering poor Mrs. Benson, but when it came time to perform their concert selections, they became very serious. Carlotta would not allow any foolishness when performing. She often said, "Opera is something that has been dead quite a while ago. If it isn't presented with great seriousness and persuasion, it isn't taken in with pleasure. Keep focused, my sweet children, on the goal. Slacking off from concentration for an instant could be fatal for a career. Now, smile. We will go to the reception and at least get fed for our efforts. Maybe if you're all sweet to the old witches, there might be a donation or two to our divine conservatory in Selma."

David sang soprano arias with the best of the female students at concerts. Along with the staggering demands from Madame to learn new music, daily practice and lessons in deportment, Italian and piano took up all his free time. Schoolwork and socializing with friends his own age took a back seat to music. His mother, obviously content to take bows when her son's singing drew praise, did not interfere. Carlotta helped keep Imogene at bay, patronizing her with such things as compliments on her taste in clothing. Imogene didn't have much money but always had a few very nice things that she saved diligently to buy. If warning clouds were on the horizon, Imogene was oblivious to them.

David's world became so attached to Carlotta's that not a single day passed without them seeing each other. At times he would meet The Colonel too. *Now this is a man,* he mused one afternoon as he saw him climbing the wide front steps. He watched from the music room window as Carlotta raced out to greet her husband, literally jumping into his arms. They clasped their arms around each other. *How happy they are. She is so beautiful and he is so strong and tall.*

"Come on, David, enough music. Say hello to my husband. Don't be shy now. I know you like him. I've seen how your eyes light up when he is near."

The child thought, *If only he could have been my father!*

The room rang with The Colonel's laughter. "David, Carlotta tells me how special you have become to her, and whatever makes her happy makes me happy as well. Come here, boy, let's have a bear hug."

David put his arms around The Colonel, and the man held him close to his body. *How unlike my father, he doesn't push me away. He lets me hold on to him.* His head rested just above the man's waist and he held tighter, wrapping his arms around and feeling The Colonel's back while his head rested against the tight muscles of his stomach. *Only this thin shirt keeps me from touching his skin.* All this took only a moment, but to David it seemed an eternity. Still The Colonel didn't let go of him, sliding down to his knees to hug the boy tighter. The Colonel's eyes glistened with tears. David was transfixed with love for the man.

"Well, you two have quite forgotten me," Carlotta exclaimed as she gently separated them. She put her hand gently on David's neck, "After all, isn't he *my* husband?"

The Colonel frowned; husband and wife exchanged a glance at each other over the boy's head as he put his arms around their waists.

"All right, you two," she said. "Let's go out to the porch and have some hot chocolate. Viola? Oh where can that old crone be? You two go on out and wait for me, I'll make the hot chocolate myself. I can do that in spite of what that witch thinks." She fluttered her hands.

The Colonel took David by the hand, and they walked to the porch. David headed for his favorite rocking chair. "No, David, come here and sit by me." He stretched himself out on the chaise lounge with its thick cushions. The boy climbed into the lounge beside him. The Colonel threw a thin blanket over them and David put his arms around him again, arching his back so the boy could slide his right arm around his body. David rested his head again on the man's chest, almost drifting off. With his left hand he felt the muscles of The Colonel's stomach again under his shirt.

The Colonel shifted his body a little and David's hand slid under the shirt and against the skin. He moved his hand higher across his chest, brushing the nipples without knowing why.

The man groaned, took the child's wrist, moving his hand down to where it rested in his lap. The Colonel unzipped his trousers with one hand, never taking his eyes off the boy. He took the small hand and put it inside his trousers. "How does that feel?" he asked smiling.

The boy didn't answer. *It feels big, I wonder if it's big like my father's that time I saw him naked.* The Colonel smiled into his face, a deep look of loneliness and longing. No adult had ever before looked at him that way.

The Colonel kissed his neck and cheek, brushed his fingers through the dark auburn hair, sighed a sigh, deep and long, from some secret place deep inside his heart. He drew the boy's hand from his trousers as he heard the clanking of the tray. "Now sit up, go to your chair, Carlotta's coming." They looked across at each other wordlessly, as the moment hung in the air.

Eight

Over the next two years, David absorbed the Garcia method until he made it his own.

Madame said that once perfected, one could sing anything and could expect a career that could last thirty years or more. The method stressed breath control and correct focus . . . clear notes with a seamless scale with no perceptible breaks in the three registers from bottom to top . . . and coloring the voice and acting with it to expertly bring to life the character portrayed. Madame stressed reality. Less was best. "Never move your hand unless you follow it with your heart and your mind. The mind must work, but not too much. When someone sings their lines to you, your reactions must be as if you'd never heard those words before. As for your gestures, just look to the music. The composer has already seen to that. In the music you will find everything you need to bring to life a character that people can see, hear and enjoy. Master this, my child, with complete control of languages and the world and all it has to offer in realization of artistic perfection will be yours."

Carlotta taught David great soprano arias and diligently sought venues to present her prodigy to people who mattered. They made trips with one or two of the best of the other students to Georgia, North and South Carolina, Florida, Mississippi and Louisiana. The word was getting around that her studio was one of which to take notice.

People were astonished when David sang, a glorious coloratura soprano. The sight of a small ten-year-old boy singing the Mad Scene from *Lucia di Lammermoor, Bel Raggio* from *Semiramide,* or *Ah forse lui, Sempre Libera* from *La Traviata,* brought gasps of amazement. Newspaper accounts of their concerts glowed with superlatives. Basking in the attention, Carlotta engaged a superlative pianist so that she could sing at the concerts with them.

At New Orleans one night she and David sang the two great duets from *Semiramide*, *Serbarmi ognor* and *Giorno D'Orrore,* evoking thunderous ovations from all parts of the theater. They were called back several times. David wore a black suit and Carlotta a green gown sparkling with shimmering bugle beads and a necklace and earrings of huge emeralds and diamonds. As an encore they sang the great duet from *Norma, Mira O Norma, si fino a l'ori.* The overcome audience rose to their feet, screaming in delight as the two singers embraced. But such times of glory were infrequent as David had to be home in time for school on Mondays.

He had matured to a point of self assurance that no one could have imagined before he first came to his beloved Madame. Yet at school, he was still teased mercilessly, called a sissy by bullies who tormented him relentlessly. He was indifferent to academics, excelling only in subjects that interested him like history. He knew many students looked at him jealously; the reputation of his phenomenal voice and the stories of the concerts in other cities and states became known to all in the school.

Brad and Tony, now entering high school, drew jeers from friends because of the little brother who sang like a *girl.* Both took pains to avoid being seen with him. David loved them all the same. With Brad he enjoyed a protector. One look from Brad sent bullies running, and while Brad laughed at him too, it was good-natured. Even those who teased him about David did it without malice, knowing Brad's temper could flare up in a second. And no one wanted to get Brad angry.

* * *

Tony was another story. He hated hearing the boys call his younger brother a *queer* and spat hateful words at David, always telling him to shut up when he sang. They slept in the same room, now furnished with twin beds. Tony ran with a rough crowd, wore tight jeans and had his hair styled like James Dean, the current Hollywood bad-boy teen idol. At night Tony would look across at David with increasing anger and smoldering resentment. David was Mother's pet; adults raved over his singing, and David had turned into a snob. *The little shit needs to be taught a lesson, making my buddies laugh at me over his sissy ways.*

Tony had reached sexual maturity. He and his friends visited ugly whores, trying to outdo each other with sexual prowess, comparing penis sizes, and planning what girls they were going to mess with as soon as they could be persuaded

* * *

Tony's behavior was enough to cause his mother concern, but she seemed to shrug off any warning signs, staying out of the boy's private lives and pursuits. She had her church activities, played bridge several times a week, stayed engrossed in her job at the air force base and quietly went about her days. Daniel had increased her child support after their divorce was finalized. With alimony payments, they lived comfortably though never extravagantly. They ate together every night through the week, though David would tear out of the house as quickly as he could to his music practice.

They were regarded as a "regular Selma family" except of course for Imogene, *poor thing*, who had no husband. Still a very attractive woman, well-meaning friends often introduced her to eligible men. But because of her children — regarded as extra baggage to most would-be suitors — her dates were few.

An old-fashioned girl determined to maintain her unsullied reputation, Imogene disdained affairs. And when word got out that she wouldn't put out, the calls from men stopped. It mattered not to Imogene, content with the way things were, always putting her children ahead of her own desires.

Nine
January, 1956

A bitterly cold winter hit Selma, several heavy frosts reaching southward into the bowels of Alabama by late January. Outside, the leafless trees shuddered against a brisk cold wind. One Friday evening David found himself alone after school. Imogene had been gone for several days, reluctantly leaving the boys alone in response to calls to visit her ailing mother in Albertville. After she left, Brad and Tony immediately set into misbehavior, Brad staying out late while Tony often stayed out all night.

Brad came home from school, had a quick shower, and was getting ready to go out. Tony still hadn't come home from the night before. Brad showed a moment's concern for David. "It's going to be dark soon. Are you going to your teacher's for a lesson tonight?"

"Yes, but not for a lesson. Madame said I could practice and maybe have a cold supper with her and The Colonel. I'm supposed to go over there around seven thirty, I think she said. It's only a few blocks away."

"Well, I'm going. You be careful and take your key with you. Are you listening to me, boy? Just lock the door when you leave, okay? I don't know what time I'll be back. I have a date. When you get back, just go to bed if you aren't too geared up from all that screaming you do over there." He laughed. "Why don't you take a shower before you go and wash your hair? I don't know what you've been up to today, but your hair smells." He smiled at David and was gone.

David gathered his sheet music, set it on the dining room table with his house key, and headed for the kitchen. He came back through the dining room with two cookies and a small glass of milk. He carefully treaded his way around the throw rugs, letting his feet slide a little on the highly polished hardwood floors, careful not to spill any milk. He wasn't supposed to take food out of the kitchen or dining room, but tonight was different. Tonight he was alone. He sat the milk and cookies down in the bathroom and began to undress for his shower. He tossed his clothes into the corner and climbed into the tub, pulling the shower curtain across behind him and enjoying the feel of warm water cascading over him. He lathered up his hair with his mother's shampoo. *This always smells so good. Madame likes the scent; The Colonel too.* He soaped up his body with the washcloth. He had grown taller yet his body was still like a wand. He scrubbed everywhere, especially his face. Madame said one needed to very clean, and that a freshly washed face was beautiful to behold. He smiled, knowing she would be pleased. He stepped out of the tub and dried off quickly, taking pains to towel dry his long dark hair. He looked at himself in the mirror, brushed back his hair till it gleamed the way Madame liked. *Maybe he'll like it too. He is always so kind, telling me what a good boy I am and what a handsome man I'll be someday. I really love him. He's so different than my father. I wish he were my father and then I could be close to him always.*

He stepped out into the hall, naked, and started toward his room to dress. Suddenly he heard laughter as the front door opened. *Brad must have forgotten something.*

But it wasn't Brad.

He stepped around the corner into the living room, where Tony and five of his friends — all boys of fifteen or sixteen who David recognized — lounged on the sofa and chairs. David stood, frozen in shock, as Tony got up and started towards him, his eyes blazing with fury at the sight of his naked brother standing in the doorway in front of his friends. David turned to leave, but it was too late. Tony reached out and grabbed him by his hair, dragging him into the room and throwing him to the floor.

"You Goddamned faggot. You aren't going anywhere!" he screamed, kicking David in the head, causing blood to trickle from his lip. All the boys stank of alcohol and cigarette smoke.

"Please, Tony, let me up. I'm *so* sorry that I walked in here in front of your friends like this. I'll go to my room now." His face was white with fear. He had endured their teasing and taunts for months now whenever he was out and would run into them.

All of them were laughing now, watching him try to get up. Tony railed down on him again, snatching his head up by the hair and then slamming it to the floor. David tried to grab a throw rug to cover himself, but one of the boys, tall and blond, tore it from his hands.

"No, David, you aren't going anywhere, you little dick tease," said one of the boys. "You go around town like you are some kind of fucking

struck him again in the face as hard as he could. Blood trickled from a fast-swelling eye as David stopped struggling. Tony knelt now between his legs as the others watched, fascinated by the sight of Tony having intercourse with his brother. He came quickly and laughed at the blood all around his stomach. He reached over and whispered savagely, "It's okay that I fucked you too. It's okay because we're brothers."

At length the boys grew tired of their game, though they were too drunk and too full of the thrill of desecrating the *sissy boy* to care. They all dressed.

Tony got a towel and wiped up the blood from the shining hardwood floor. "If you say a word about this to anyone . . . anyone . . . then next time we will fuck you till you're dead. Do you hear me?" He laughed, completely drunk, and said, "Come on, guys, lets get the fuck out of here." They were gone without a backward glance at the broken and bleeding boy curled up in a ball on the floor.

How long he lay there David couldn't calculate. For the first time in his life he felt pain that he didn't know could exist. He raised his head and realized that blood was coagulating in his hair, nose, mouth and ears. As he shifted upwards on his elbow and then on one knee, there came a stab of pain from his ass that made him groan in agony. Semen and sweat mixed with streaks of blood left slimy trails down his thighs. He tried to rise, but his head swam so violently he stayed on his knees. The room was in chaos, Overturned chairs and lamps littered the floor. He saw the wet towel Tony had used to try to wipe up the floor. *God! My mother is going to kill me if this place is left this way!*

He crawled through the hall, into the bathroom. He turned on the cold-water tap in the bathtub and splashed water into his face. His head slowly cleared. He washed his mouth out and looked about the room. *Where are Mother's old towels that she uses for rags?* He remembered that she kept them on the floor of the linen closet. He got several of them, dampened a couple and wiped up the floor, crawling back out through the hall, looking for and wiping up anything that had come off his body.

As he reached the door to the living room, he felt a wave of nausea envelop him, and his whole body shook violently. He remembered his mother's words, "You boys are going to be in big trouble if I get back and this place is a mess."

Slowly and methodically, he began to get the room back to the way it had been. He managed, after several tries, to right the fallen chairs, set lamps back on the tables. He wiped away every trace of what lay on the floor. He pulled back the scatter-rugs to the place Imogene had left them.

Several times he had to rest, to catch his breath and stop the violent shaking spasms that kept him from standing. He put the towels beside the door. *I have to take them out of here, she can't see them.* Suddenly his mind filled with terror. *What if they come back?*

He headed for the bedroom he shared with Tony, his mind reeling in fear of this brother he loved. He pulled on his jeans and a hooded sweatshirt. He couldn't fasten the jeans; his fingers hurt too badly. But he did get on his loafers. His gaze fell on the small, framed picture of his mother on his bedside table, and without knowing why he reached out for it and slipped it into one of his jeans pockets. He made his way back to the living room, his face burning with shame. He pulled himself up to his feet by the door handle. Slowly he opened the door, half expecting the boys to have come back for more, but all was quiet and dark outside. The cool air rushed into the room, and his head at least partially cleared.

He remembered Brad's words: "Don't forget to take your key with you and lock the door behind you." He had left the key on the dining room table with his music. He went to get it, turning sideways so as not to look in the large mirror over the sideboard. He stepped out, being careful to take the soiled towels with him. His left eye was almost swollen shut; the blood in the lashes stuck his eyelids together. *I have to get out, have to get away from here.*

Ten

He made his way carefully through back alleys, nearly jumping out of his skin at every night noise. At last he game up to the alley that ran behind Madame's house. *What will they think, seeing me like this? But I can't go home, and I know they love me.* He made his way around the side of the house, finally reaching the front steps. The porch light burned. They had, after all, been expecting him. He managed the steps one at a time, holding tightly to the banister, stopping four times to rest. At last he reached the porch. He fell again as he tried to pull himself together. He reached out for the brass knocker in the mouth of the lion. It clanged down loudly. He heard footsteps coming from inside, down the stairs. He leaned heavily against the frame of the door.

The door swung open, flooding the porch with light. David turned away.

"David! Well it's about *time!* Where have you been? The Colonel said we couldn't eat till you got here. David . . . David . . . ." He had turned away, advancing towards his favorite wicker rocker. His mind was in turmoil; he only knew he must rest. "David? Why are you going that way?" She stepped closer, reached out and grasped his shoulder.

He let out a blood curdling scream of agony and fell into the rocking chair. *Oh please Madame, forgive me, I had no place to go.*

Carlotta came closer. "David, *carino, parlami*!" But he couldn't answer, just sat with his face averted. She walked around to look at him. He raised his head toward her. *"Mio Dio! Che fai?"* (What has happened?) She was struck speechless for a moment, then, raising one hand to her face, she screamed, "Colonel, Colonel! Come quickly, it's David! Oh my poor child, my baby, tell me, tell me my darling, who has done this?" The Colonel came running onto the porch.

"Come, David, into the light. What has happened? Tell us."

Oh please, not into the light ever again, let darkness cover me.

"David, it's me, your Colonel. Don't be afraid, come to me, my child. Come now."

David slowly got up from the chair and advanced with little steps towards the man. As the porch light fell on his face, Carlotta let out a scream of horror so great that she fell back against the windows. David had his head down as he came forward. "Come, my child, come to me my darling David. It's me, your Colonel. You're safe here with me. Come, you are safe. Just another step." He held out his arms.

"Oh, Colonel," he whispered, coming nearer. "I am so sorry to do this to you and Madame; I hope you can forgive me for being so late." He sobbed uncontrollably as he came closer; he looked up into the Colonel's face. "Please forgive me for looking like this."

"Oh, my beloved child, come, come to me. Oh, my child, oh, my own dearest boy, come now."

David fell into his arms and fainted. The Colonel swept him up carrying him swiftly into the house, his heart breaking. The Colonel raced up the staircase, taking the steps two at a time, turning at the top toward the black-and-white tiled bathroom. Carlotta, shrieking in full Italian, followed closely behind. The large white door was flung back, creaking on its hinges as it hit the towel racks directly behind it. The mirrors with their circular globes gleamed in mute witness as The Colonel gently laid the senseless child on the fluffy white bath rug in front of the old huge claw-foot bathtub.

"Carlotta! Get me some towels, turn on the hot water."

She ran past him to the huge Victorian armoire and grabbed four or five thick white towels, pausing at the pedestal double sink to turn on the hot water. "Darling, what shall I do now? Should I call the police? The doctor?"

"Carlotta, just be calm for a moment. We need to see how badly hurt he is before we do anything else." He stuck one of the towels in the sink, wrung it out and flew back to the child. "Put one of the towels under his head and come here and help me look." With one of the towels he gently began to dab at David's face. The caked on blood loosened, and he wiped carefully at his mouth and eyes. "Get me a wet wash cloth now and fill the wash basin with water!"

She followed the orders as though in a trance, staggering back and forth at the scene before her.

Slowly The Colonel washed away the snot and dried blood from David's nose and mouth. A large knot had arisen on his forehead. His left eye was swollen and black. *What kind of perverted animal could have done this? Oh God! What has happened?* He stifled a scream in his own throat as he looked at the child's thick hair, now all matted together.

"Colonel? What is it? Why have you stopped? Why are you staring at his hair?" Her cry died in her throat as the couple exchanged a glance over the child's small form. They saw to their horror that something beyond blood and sweat clogged his hair . . . Semen . . . white globs of it in his ears and running down his neck.

The Colonel quickly undressed the boy down to his underwear, throwing the garments into the corner by the sink. "Carlotta, snap together for a moment." He reached out and shook her hard. "You're going to have to help me now. Look at me."

She nodded that she understood but was unable to utter a word. Her mouth moved, but no sound came forth.

"Turn on the water in the bath tub. Do it now!" He watched her closely, glancing at David's still face. "Not too hot, just warm. Put the plug in, I have to wash him. Get me peroxide."

She obeyed mechanically, going to the medicine chest, bringing all the things he requested. "Colonel, I think I really should call someone. He is in bad shape. I don't think we can handle this by ourselves." She got up.

"Stop! Come back here. We can't call anyone just yet. Do you want to stay here? I'm going to have to take his underwear off and put him in the tub."

"I'll go and get some wine; he likes that mixed the way I do with just a little mineral water. God knows, I need it myself." She glanced anxiously behind her. "Colonel, is it going to be okay? I need you to tell me that." He nodded and she was gone.

He lifted David up now onto his shoulder, and slowly, with his free hand, took off the boy's underwear. They were stuck to his skin, and he had to peel them off. The hair on the back of his neck stood up as he looked at the boy's bottom. Bruises were everywhere. He stared in mute horror at David's thighs, streaked with dried slime. The boy moaned in his arms. He gently lifted him up and slowly lowered him into the half-filled tub. The Colonel bent over into the tub with the wash cloth, gently washing the thin white limbs. David began to whimper.

"Colonel? Oh, please. I feel so bad." He coughed and shook from a sneeze, his nose full.

"David, tell me who did this to you? I know you are hurting, I'm hurting too. Show me where you were hurt. What are these bruises on your butt? Oh, baby, you are so beat up. You have to tell me what happened."

David remained silent, shook his head and looked away.

The man stood him up in the tub and began washing his back, followed by the legs and between his butt cheeks. David cried out when his rectum was touched. He fell against the man's shoulder, flung his arms around his neck and sobbed.

"David, tell me, did someone do something to you there?" He froze as he said these words, his mind reeling back to that afternoon on the porch two years before and what happened on the chaise lounge when he had placed the boy's hand inside his trousers. *God, what might have happened had Carlotta not been coming with the hot chocolate?* The thought froze before it could even come to his lips. Here he was on this dark night, in the bathroom with this beloved child who had been violated. "Sit back down, David; I need to wash your hair. Carlotta uses this shampoo, it smells so good." He washed away the evidence; the beautiful, thick auburn hair gleamed in the bright light surrounding them.

Carlotta returned with the wine and glasses. When David saw her, he buried his face against The Colonel's chest, not wanting her to see him. "Come, David, just take a sip, it will help you. Let's all have one." The Colonel lifted him out of the tub, pulling the plug out as he did so. He shuddered at the dark soapy water going down the drain. He wrapped a new fresh white towel around the child's shaking shoulders. Husband and wife sat beside him in front of the tub, all three lost in their own thoughts. Carlotta filled the glasses several times. No water in the wine tonight.

"Well, you aren't going home tonight; you're staying here with us. I know your mother is out of town for at least another week. We just need to go to bed now. We will sort this out in the morning. Carlotta, give me a moment with David, I need to wash some places on his body with the peroxide. Go and get one of my night shirts, he can wear that." She gathered up the glasses and tray, walking quietly out of the room.

"Okay, David, it's just us guys now. Stand up and take off the towel." The boy did as he was told, holding tightly to the tub. The Colonel took the peroxide and washed the swollen eye, the bruises, and finally the ripped rectum. It foamed as he poured it over the broken skin. "It won't hurt, David; no one is going to hurt you again if I can help it." He took down a tube from the shelf beside the sink. "Bend over now, I have to apply this to your rectum. It won't hurt, it will heal." He took a bead of it and touched it gently to the broken skin. "Now stand up. Carlotta, where's the night shirt?" No reply came. He stepped out into the hall and saw it hanging from the door knob. He turned back and looked at the boy standing naked by the tub. He shuddered as he realized his hands were shaking. He put the garment over the boy's head and pulled it down over his body. *What whiteness. How small he seems. This thing just swallows him completely.* "Okay, sport, let's go to bed."

"Colonel? I love you." He rushed into the man's arms and began to cry softly once more.

The Colonel swept him up in his arms and carried him out of the room into the dark hall. The glistening dark auburn hair shone and he buried his face in it. The Colonel thought, *God, if I die in this moment so be it. I love him so much.*

The bedroom was dim, lit only by a small lamp at bedside. Carlotta had already gotten into a night gown and into bed. "Why, he is fast asleep! Where are we going to lay him down?"

"He is going to sleep between us tonight, here where he has a refuge, here where he is loved." He put the boy in the middle of the bed between them, gently. "He needs to rest now, no dreams, just safety."

She smiled at the tenderness in The Colonel's words.

The Colonel slipped into his side of the bed and reached for the light, then paused. "Carlotta, we will talk this out in the morning and figure out what to do. It'll be okay." He reached across David and kissed her. She looked intently toward him and lay down. He turned back, turned off the light, and lay down looking at the little figure between them. The wind outside whistled through the leafless branches of the pecan trees. The stillness settled around them. The adults each remained lost in their own thoughts. A bright moonbeam shone suddenly into the dark room. At length, they slept.

Eleven

David stirred in the big four-poster bed. He opened his one uninjured eye and looked across to the wide bank of tall windows. Through the white starched panels, bright morning sunlight flooded the room. He raised his head, confused. A dull throb spread across his forehead, and he settled back into the warm sheets and thick down pillows. He looked up at the ceiling with the chandelier and intricately carved medallion. The wide crown molding ran around the room where the walls joined the ceiling. He wanted to stay there, to drift back to sleep, but the need to urinate became too strong to resist. He shifted toward the edge of the mattress and saw his mother's small picture on the nightstand. His stifled back tears as he smelled a familiar perfume lingering in the sheets.

Madame! Now I remember. Last night, the porch, the bathroom, my Colonel. He slid his legs over the side and sat up. It seemed he ached all over. He reached out, wrapped his arms around one the thick bed posts and slid down to the floor. He took a few tentative steps toward the open bathroom door. He smelled the night shirt that trailed behind him. *The Colonel's? Yes. He took care of me.* Slowly, painfully, he made his way to the bathroom, sat on the commode and released the built up urine from his bladder. As he sat there, a sudden stab of pain came from his rectum. *Oh no, don't let anything come out from there.* He reached up to the sink and rinsed his hands. He looked around the white room with its black tiles. He stepped back, then saw in a corner wadded up towels stained with dark streaks. He remembered. His clothes lay forlornly in a pile beside the towels. He turned away. He would not think about that. Not now. Behind him he heard footsteps.

"Morning, sport," said The Colonel from the doorway. "Have you brushed your teeth and washed your face yet?"

"No, sir, my toothbrush is at home. I did wash my face though and then folded the washcloth and put it here by the sink."

"David, we keep extra ones for guests over there in the armoire. Go on over and get one and brush your teeth then we'll go down for breakfast. Carlotta's down there now. She's had to make do since Viola died last year, you know. How she could cook . . . fresh hot biscuits and red-eye gravy or sweet molasses every morning of my life. . . " He sighed at the memory. "Carlotta does try and we've had to search high and low for anyone she can trust just to do the housework Are you finished? Well, come on, let's go."

"But, Colonel, my clothes! I don't have anything to put on, only this big white shirt."

"Its okay, baby, we'll worry about that later. Right now let's go get some food in our stomachs." He reached out and smoothed the boy's hair.

He put his arm around his shoulders and they walked out into the hall and down the staircase. As they neared the kitchen, Carlotta could be heard singing an old Italian song that David knew well. It was by Bellini and he loved to hear her sing *Malinconia, ninfa gentile.*

She turned and smiled. "Carino, come here and sit down. The Colonel and I need to talk with you about last night." She looked up at her husband and he nodded in agreement..

"We will, but let's eat a little something first, okay? David, we have some pancakes and sausages. Does that sound good?"

"Yes, sir, and maybe some coffee?" He timidly looked from Madame to The Colonel. "I mean if it's okay? My mother gives me some. I've always liked it."

"All right, David, what do you take in it?" Carlotta asked.

"Oh, black please, Madame."

She poured him a steaming cup, then put a plate of pancakes and sausages on the table. She and The Colonel took their seats on each side of the boy.

David had forgotten he hadn't eaten since the day before and dug in with gusto. Carlotta handed him the syrup and butter for the pancakes. The couple sat back and watched. He struggled with a sausage link. His upper lip had been split open, but the swelling was abating. They studied him intently, occasionally exchanging glances with each other. The swelling around his eye had gone down and the eye was open, though very red. The boy suddenly shivered. Carlotta sprang to her feet, fetched a shawl and draped it around him, watching intently as he drew his bare feet up under him to rest on the chair cushion. The moments crept by, the couple each struggling with how to get into last night's events with him.

The Colonel finally led off. "When is your mother due back David, the first of next week?"

"I'm not sure, she said maybe late next week. She said to be sure to get Brad to take me to school each morning and to be sure I had something to eat for my lunch and dinner. She said to mind him and if I came over here to do whatever you and Madame told me to do. I told her I'd be over here to practice, but she said for me to be home each night by dark. But gee, it gets dark so early now. I don't know what she's going to say if she finds out I spent the night over here and Brad doesn't know I'm here."

Carlotta forced a smile, saying, "Well never mind that, I plan on having a talk with her when she gets home. We have been meaning to talk with her for some time anyway, and this incident has pushed the matter to the forefront. I'm not going to put it off again."

"You've been intending to talk to my mother about what?" His eyes grew wide with fear. "Have I done anything wrong? Please tell me, I'll be a good boy. I'm studying really hard with learning the piano scales and keeping up my singing the way you say I should."

"Oh, David," smiled The Colonel, "You haven't done anything wrong. We are both so pleased with your progress. Carlotta says you already sing better than most adults she knew in the old days. Your voice is beautiful. Everyone knows that. You just need to gain more confidence and not be distracted by anything, you know, that's stressful or upsetting. You know we love you and we'd like to have you here with us, so we could see you every day." He wrung his hands, obviously searching his mind for the right words. "Aren't you happy? Don't you feel safe when you're here with us?"

Carlotta took the next step. "David we need you to tell us exactly what happened last night. Who beat you up and abused you? Then we have to decide what we are going to do about it."

"Oh God, Madame, oh please, don't make me talk about that." He stood and began pacing, eyes wide with panic. His hands, bruised and sore, railed wildly in the air. He tried to speak and choked on his words. He couldn't articulate his thoughts. He tried to sit back down and flinched in pain from his sore backside.

"Now, David, come here." The Colonel rose from his seat and grabbed the boy by his wrist and then his shoulders. "You are going to tell us, but quietly, calmly. No one here is going to hurt you." He drew the boy closer, took the cushion from his seat and put it in his lap. He scooped up the child and sat him on his own lap, his arms wrapped around him protectively. "Carlotta, pour us another cup of coffee, and have one yourself, you look pale as death."

Slowly, grudgingly, the ugly sordid story unfolded. David sometimes couldn't even find the words but would just sob against The Colonel's chest. Carlotta drew her own chair right up to his and hugged him too. The couple sat there in shocked silence. They had no idea such things could happen in this little town where everyone knew everyone else.

"Well," she said firmly, "this can't go unchallenged. I'm going to tell all those boy's parents. Let the chips fall where they may. *Bastards!* They aren't going to get away with this!" She rose and went to the counter, looking for the phone book and then reached for the telephone.

Snatching the phone from her hands, The Colonel spoke to her severely," Carlotta, what the hell are you doing? What are you thinking? Are you going to blow our plans right out of the damn water?" He stood, sitting David back in his chair. The couple retreated to the far end of the room, whispering quietly to each other. They returned to the table with resolution written on their faces.

"David, do you think your brothers will be at home now? It's nearly nine o' clock."

"Oh, Colonel, I guess they are, it's early, and they love to sleep late. Not like me, I have to practice!" He looked at Carlotta and she smiled. "I need to go home, but my clothes? I guess I can put the ones on that I wore last night? If Brad is there and doesn't find me in bed when he wakes up there is going to be the devil to pay."

"No, David, you are never going to wear those clothes again! Do you hear me? *Never!*" He could not mask angry eyes. "I'm going over there to get you some clothes and talk to them. If they know what's good for them, they better not give me any problem."

"Oh, no! Oh, please don't do that. Tony will kill me for telling you about this. Brad will be pissed off too; he won't believe it and will say I'm lying to get attention. Tony's friends might come back. One of them said he would kill me if I said anything."

"David, be calm. Trust me, I will take care of this." He grabbed his jacket. "Stay here with Carlotta. The two of you go back to bed and rest. I'll be back soon."

"Colonel, remember they're hardly more than children themselves. Don't lose your temper, you know what the doctor said about that. Talk to them firmly, calmly, without getting upset."

"I will be as kind with them as they have been with their little brother. And for your information, my dear, no child could do what Tony and his buddies have done to David. No child could do that kind of damage. Now both of you, back to bed, its cold in this old house. No singing now. Just rest." He turned, going out the back door, swiftly walking through the dry pecan leaves to his truck.

"Come, my child, let's do what he said and go back to bed. I'll sing to you and we'll rest together." She took his hand, and the child, his innocence shattered, nodded. The two of them climbed the great staircase. Portraits of famous singers gazed down from gilt frames. "Do you see that, David? *La Malibran* is watching you. The Garcias live again through you and me." They reached the top and he went into the bathroom. Carlotta, still dressed in her night clothes, threw her robe across the divan near the bed. She drew down the heavy drapes over the gauze like white starched sheers, closing out the bright sunshine.

David came into the darkened room. "Madame, is everything going to be all right? I'm worried about what Brad is going to say."

"Come along now. You know The Colonel will take care of us." She slipped into the great four-poster bed and patted the place beside her. "Come, let's sleep."

* * *

She tried to draw him close, jealous in spite of herself, as she thought about how easily and warmly he embraced The Colonel. *The boy loves me too, it's just something different. It's fine. He will be a star. We just have to protect him till he's grown and then his wings will fly away from these memories.* David was asleep as soon as his head hit the pillow. She drew the coverlet over his shoulders and ran her fingers through his beautiful hair. *Poor child, if only I could sleep in such peace. Come, let us make one of our two sorrows. You will rise from this more beautiful than before. Your voice will banish this agony to the dark depths of the hell from which it sprang.* She smiled. The house was very quiet now. She sang softly, *"Per la crudel Isotta, il bel Tristano ardea."* She stopped abruptly, realizing he was asleep, and lay lost in thoughts of the future. Both of them slept and dreamed; him of a love eternal, she of redemption and glory.

Twelve

Every moment of the short drive increased The Colonel's fury. His face flushed with indignation at the things David had told him. The memory of last night made him shake with growing rage. He reached the porch of the tiny white-shingled house surrounded by old pecan trees and slammed his fist against the door. "Brad! Tony!! Get up and open this door, now!"

The door swung open. Brad stood in pajamas, rubbing his eyes and shaking himself awake. "Colonel, what do you want? Why are you banging on the door and screaming? I was out late and I'm trying to sleep."

Pushing his way into the house, The Colonel glared at Brad. "Screaming? You haven't heard anything yet. Do you know where your brother is?"

"Tony? David? Why I guess they're asleep in their room. The door was shut when I got in at two a.m.. Like I said it was late and I just fell in bed myself. Our mother is out of town and left me in charge. What's this about anyway?"

"What's this about?" The Colonel's voice grew louder with every word. "It's about your total failure to do what she told you to do. Your concern with your own selfishness has created a horror." He turned away for a moment, brushing away angry tears.

Brad's face grew white with fear. He had never seen an adult act this way, or speak to him in this manner. He struggled to keep his composure. Now this ex-marine, at least a head taller than he, stood in the living room. *Why this anger? What the fuck is going on?*

The Colonel indignantly shoved him first on one shoulder, then the other till he stumbled back against the fireplace. "Get your ass in there and bring Tony out right now."

"Tony? What do you want with him? Do you want to see David too?" Brad's hair was standing on end.

"Oh, I've seen David. That's why I'm here."

"David? When could you have seen him? I know he was supposed to come to your house last night for dinner. Has he done something wrong? Is he in some kind of trouble?"

The Colonel laughed, and as he did so, he felt a white hot lump growing in his throat. He advanced on Brad, grabbing him by the throat. "Now, you little shit, get in there and bring your fucking brother in here, now!"

"Tony!" yelled Brad. "Get your ass in here right now!" Hearing no response, he turned toward the bedroom, when a grip of steel came down on his shoulder. He yelled in pain. The Colonel rushed by him and kicked open the closed door.

Tony looked up from his bed. He never saw the blow coming as The Colonel back-handed him across the face, knocking him out of bed to the floor. He screamed. The Colonel picked him up by his tee shirt and dragged him to the living room, throwing him into the nearest chair.

"Tony, tell me where is your little brother? Where is David? Tell me before you get double what I just gave you."

Tony frowned. "How the hell should I know where that little fuck is? He's probably out daydreaming somewhere, acting like the idiot he is. Who do you think you are barging in here and man handling me this way? You're going to pay for this."

"Oh, buddy boy, someone is going to pay, but it's not me. Now, you shut your filthy mouth and you listen to me. You are *never* going to hurt David again. He is where he is safe from scum like you and your little group of buddies. I'm going to see to it that you are sent to a reform school where what you did last night to him will be revisited on you every night."

Brad still stood by the fireplace in shock. The blood drained from his face. "Tony? What the fuck is he talking about? David was fine when I left here last night. What have you done?" He fell silent. Tony stared at the floor, and Brad came closer. "Oh, God, what have you done?"

"What has he done? Oh, I'm going to tell you. The most monstrous thing I have ever seen in my life!" He drew from his jacket a bag containing one of the towels that David had brought with him to his house and flung it in Brad's face. "Let this tell you."

Brad looked at the towel in mute horror. The crusted blood, the dried semen almost made him visibly shudder. He lifted the towel to his face and smelling it, he staggered and dropped it to the floor. "Oh, sweet Jesus! Whose blood is this? Is that cum on this towel?" He stared at Tony and the full horror hit him. "Oh, God, what happened? Where is my brother? What have you done to him?"

The words had hardly escaped his lips when The Colonel slapped him so hard that he fell to the floor, banging his head into the fireplace. "You are as responsible as Tony and his sick friends for what happened here last night. Your mother left you, the big brother, in control of David, and you, like most stuck-up little fucks your age, thinking of nothing else but yourselves, walked out of this house and abandoned him to this piece of shit and his friends."

Tony sprinted for the door, but The Colonel grabbed him by his hair, knocked him back, slapped him on the left side of his face and then the right as he stumbled backward. The Colonel advanced, his full fury unleashed. Tony fell backwards on the sofa, his mouth bleeding from his split lips. "Stay where you are, animal. If you get up, I'll kill you."

Brad, still on the floor, timidly asked, "Where is my brother? Where is David now?"

"He is where neither of you will ever hurt him again. He is at my house, and as far as I'm concerned he will never spend another night under this roof again. The two of you are to be pitied more than anything else. You have robbed him of innocence . . .thrown his love back in his face. You, Brad, by ignoring your responsibility, you, Tony, by breaking every law of God and man. This is the greatest crime I have ever witnessed. Now where are his clothes?"

Brad pointed toward the bedroom. The Colonel went in and came back with an armload of socks, shirts, sweaters, pants and pajamas. "This is enough for now. We will get him anything else he needs. The two of you need to talk, get your stories straight about what you are going to tell your mother when she gets back. Knowing the two of you, you will think of something to save your worthless skins. We will take him to school next week and take care of him, something the two of you have forfeited your right to for the rest of your lives. Come a step onto my property and I'll have you both arrested. Do you hear me?" He turned; picked up the towel he had brought, and walked out of the house, slamming the door behind him.

Thirteen

Brad and Tony sat in stunned silence and looked at each other suspiciously, each lost in thought. On one hand Brad was shocked beyond comprehension. He had not dreamed that Tony could have possibly done such a thing. *Why would he do this kind of shit when there are tons of girls out there he could have fucked? But his own brother?*

"Are you and your shitty friends really that hard up that you had to fuck your own brother? And why in hell did you choose him? He's just a kid. Are y'all some sort of queer wannabes? Are girls so hard to come by that you have to pick on little boys?"

Tony frowned, got up and went on offense. "Don't talk to me about this shit. We had been drinking and the little shit has been asking for it as long as I can remember. Prancing all over town, swishing here and there like a queer. He was bad enough before, but now that he's been involved with that foreign woman, he thinks he's something so grand. Those people have given him big ideas. I mean who wants to listen to that shit anyway? He makes me feel like an outcast. He looks like a girl, sings like one, has an ass like one. We were just having some fun. I know he wanted it. I've seen how he looks at my friends. Hell, how he looks at me when I'm lying in bed jacking off. So we busted his cherry, what's the fucking big deal?"

"The fucking big deal, you moron, is you think with your dick instead of your head. You think I'm so smart? I'm not smart; I just have a good memory. David has it too. He speaks that woman's language nearly as well as she does. And what difference does it make? Keeps him out of my way, keeps him out of yours. We should be thanking them. Look, all I want to know is why y'all had to beat the shit out of him? I mean he's just a skinny thing, couldn't hurt a fly. It just doesn't make sense!"

"I ain't apologizing for it! I'd fuck him right now if he were here!" Tony laughed, but he was inwardly rattled. *What in hell is going to happen to me if this gets out? Mother is going to beat the living shit out of me and probably send me to reform school. And then she'll love the little fuck more than she does already.*

"Well asshole, this can't get out. What would people at school think? I can't let anyone find out about this, and neither should you. I'm up for class president, beta club, tennis, baseball, not to mention captain of the debating team and football! And what girl would go out with me, no matter how good I am, if what you did got out in this town? Thank God

I'm not going to have to live here much longer, because as soon as I graduate I'm going to Auburn to college and try to forget I ever lived in Selma."

Tony walked over to the window. He stood, arms folded, watching passing cars. *God, I hate this fucking place. Maybe I should just leave as soon as I can too. Brad and I are in the same grade, we can both get out of here, but with my grades, where the fuck would I go? I can't get into college, that's for sure.* He turned back to Brad, who was also staring off into space. "What are we going to do if they call the police or tell Mother about it when she gets home? Brad, I don't think I could stand it if he talks and tells people about what happened. Are you listening to me? What are we going to do?"

Brad turned on him and shouted, "What are *we* going to do? *I* didn't fuck my own brother and beat the shit out of him. God, I despise you. You make me sick. Running around with your bike buddies, starting shit at school, dressing like James Dean with your hair back in duck tails. I can't wait to get away from here, but I'm going to have to help you cover this up if we can, because my ass and reputation are on the line too. When Mother gets back, we'll have some kind of plan to account for him being knocked around, but don't you think for a moment that I give a shit about you. I don't know how bad he looks, but hopefully it'll be gone by the time she gets home. We may also have to deal with The Colonel again before then. Hell, he's the richest man in all of Dallas County. He can ruin us over this, but by God, you aren't dragging me down the drain over this. I didn't do a fucking thing."

"Well, Mr. Big Shot, I'll leave you to figure it out. I've got to go round up the guys and let them know what's happened." He took out his comb, looked in the mirror over the fireplace and slicked back his duck tails. *Damn, I look good. I can get better pussy than Brad ever dreamed about. That little shit better keep his mouth shut.* He paused for a moment, alarmed. *The little fuck already has talked, shit!* Tony returned to his room and dressed quickly. Returning to the living room, he briefly paused to check out his reflection in the mirror over the fireplace. He smiled back at himself, arrogantly, then turned and walked out the door. Glancing back he saw Brad watching him from the window. Brad wasn't smiling.

Fourteen

Brad and Tony were sitting at the dining room table when Imogene returned from Albertville the following Friday. "Hi, boys." She hugged both of them warmly and shot a quick look around; nothing appeared amiss. "Well, what have you three been up to all this time? No answer? Cat got your tongue? Where's David anyway? Oh, right, he'd be over at Madame Vasselli's by now."

Their silence, the way they avoided her eyes, told her something was wrong. "So? What's happening here? Answer me . . . Now."

Tony looked imploringly at Brad, who rose from his chair. "Mother, I think you'd better sit down. Some things have been going on here that we need to talk with you about."

Concealing her rising panic, she pulled out a chair and sat. "Are you boys in any kind of trouble? I swear to God," pointing to Brad, then Tony, "you're 16 and you're 15. Can't I go off for a couple of weeks, trusting the two of you to hold the fort down? I mean, what could be so bad that you both have long faces like this, that you won't look at me? I've been driving for four hours and I'm tired, so whatever it is, tell me right this second."

Brad retreated to the other side of the table. "Well, Mother, it has to do with David."

"David? What about him?" She looked at each boy in turn. Both looked away.

"What has he done now?" Again, they avoided her face.

"Is he in some kind of trouble? Brad, I left you in charge and if you've let something happen to him, I will beat you black and blue."

Brad's hands were shaking. He squeezed the back of the chair.

"Answer me!"

"Mother, I'm not sure, but I think it's you, maybe me and Tony who could be in trouble. Something happened while you were gone, something really bad. I don't know how to explain it, I wasn't here, but David had an accident, fell down, he got himself banged up pretty bad."

Imogene's lip quivered. "Well then, I *demand* that you tell me the truth this instant," she screamed. "I'm the parent here, and you are going to give me this information right now. I don't give a damn how grown up you two think you are, spill it or I swear to God I'll give you a beating that you'll never forget." She glared from one boy to the other, her face growing redder by the second. "What's going on with David? Is he okay? How did he fall? Did you have to call the doctor? An ambulance? The police?"

Tony stood up, shouting, "The police? No, not that. Nothing like that. No need for any police."

"Tony, shut the hell up and sit down. Brad's going to explain this and it had better be good. You say David is okay? He better be. What do you mean the three of us could be in trouble? Is David over at The Colonel's house right now?"

Brad tried to calm his shaking hands once more. He glanced anxiously at Tony, at the floor, the furniture, the ceiling, everywhere but at his mother's face. "Mother, David has been over there for the last week. We haven't seen him, so we have no idea how bad he was hurt, but they've been taking him to school and picking him up so it couldn't have been so bad that he would have been hospitalized. Neither of us has seen him for a week. The Colonel came by here last Saturday morning and just said because of David's fall that they'd be looking after him till you came home."

Imogene breathed a heavy sigh of relief. "Well, there's nothing wrong with that. After all, they are responsible adults. It's okay. So I don't see a problem with that. In fact, if he's been banged up from a fall, it's just as well, since the two of you couldn't be trusted to look after him. But you said he's okay? The Colonel said they'd do whatever was needed? I'll have to go over there and see for myself what he looks like; pick him up and thank them for doing what I trusted the two of you to do."

She looked away as if gathering a new thought. "I still don't understand why you said something about the rest of us possibly being in trouble. What do you mean by that, Brad? I don't understand."

"Well, Mother, you know my friend Marty's dad is a lawyer? I was over there the other night and he asked about you."

"Me? Why would Mr. York be concerned about me? What have we got to do with them?"

"Well, he mentioned that more than one person has noticed your car hasn't been in the driveway now for more than two weeks, and he wanted to know where you were."

"My comings and goings are none of his or anyone else's business. I don't owe any explanations to anyone in this damn town!"

"He said something about parental responsibility. He asked where you were and I had to tell him you had to go up to Albertville because Granny had been sick. He said it just didn't look good and that people were concerned."

"Concerned? Oh, to hell with him and his meddlesome ways. No one is going to tell me how to raise my own children."

"It's more than that. People have seen David at school. His face was banged up pretty bad. Busted lip, black eye, bruises on his face and arms. I mean people are talking. He said someone from children's services might be in touch with you over this!"

"You two don't seem to know the extent of his injuries, but I know The Colonel's reputation, and until I can get the hell over there to see for myself what he looks like, I'll have to leave it to their adult judgment. Now what were you saying? Children's services? What could they want to talk to me about? You two are well able to take care of yourselves and a 10-year old. Or at least I thought so till you proved me wrong. Where's the phone book? I'm going to call Mr. York and give him a piece of my mind."

She sat at the phone alcove in the corner of the room, and looked in the listings for Jerry York, Attorney at Law. Seeing the number, she reached for the phone. Before the operator answered, Brad took the phone out of her hand and put it back on its cradle. She reached up and slapped him hard across the face. "What the hell are you doing?"

"No, Mother, you can't do that. The less you do right now the better. Mr. York told me that what's going on here is suspected child abuse. You could go to jail if this isn't handled right!"

"Did you say *jail*? What the hell does he mean by that? People have family problems; parents have to go out of town now and then. How can that be child abuse?"

"We are minors, Mother. Bottom line is, you left your children without adult supervision for more than two weeks and that is against the law."

Imogene's head throbbed at the thought. It had been a long day. "Well, you two just stay put. I'll go over to The Colonel's and pick David up, and then we'll be home and fix some dinner. Don't look so discouraged, I know you both probably have dates, want to get out and go somewhere, but I just got home and y'all can wait a while before leaving. Promise me you'll both be here when I get back? Okay? David and I will see you shortly." She grabbed her purse and sweater and headed out to her car. As she shut the door she said, "I mean it . . . be here when I get home!"

Tony, who had sat silently during Brad's and Imogene's conversation, stood and walked into the living room, watching her drive off. "Brad, what do you think they are going to say to her? What is he going to tell her?"

"How the hell should I know what they're going to tell her? I'm sure David won't tell what happened. I know him. He'll keep his mouth shut. You know he's afraid of you, but you have to promise that nothing like this is going to happen again. Maybe she'll tell him what Mr. York said. If anyone can pull strings in this town its The Colonel. You know how rich he is. His family has been here for generations. You better hope your sweet ass he will handle this or we'll all be up shit creek without a paddle."

In her haste, Imogene had not called to announce she was coming. As she pulled into the long drive, she simply shrugged at the pang of omission in manners. *They'll understand. It's only natural a mother wants to see her son and what condition he is in when she hasn't seen him in over two weeks.* It was about six o'clock. Night shadows were beginning to gather, casting deepening darkness on the tall windows. Through the windows on either side of the door, she could see the gleaming crystal chandeliers in the library to the left, the music room to the right, and in the center of the entrance hall, the magnificent three-tiered French chandelier which The Colonel's parents had brought over after the First World War. She had never seen the house at night, at least not this closely, and she briefly marveled at its beauty as she ascended the front steps. She drew her sweater closer against the north wind's chill and banged the heavy brass ring in the lion's mouth onto the brass plate below it. She shivered involuntarily as she looked into the gleaming red stones which formed the lion's eyes. She heard approaching footsteps. The great door swung noisily open.

"Ah, Mrs. Atkins," beamed Carlotta. "I thought it might be you. The boys had told The Colonel they thought you'd be home today. Please come in."

Imogene crossed the threshold into the wide hall, looking intently at Carlotta.

"Did you have a pleasant visit with your family?"

"Madame Vasselli, please! I was visiting my sick mother in Albertville. That's all. She is on her way to recovery and from what Brad and Tony have told me, I have been away quite long enough. I have had a tiring drive and I'm quite worn out. I'm here to fetch David home. Is he here? How is he? I was told my baby fell down some stairs?"

"Why of course he is, Mrs. Atkins. He's fine as you'll see yourself. He is much better now. We are having our supper in the dining room. The Colonel and David are there. Shall we go in?"

"I'm sorry to interrupt your supper. I should have called, but I'm anxious to see him as you can imagine, so yes, please lead the way."

As they entered the dining room, Imogene couldn't help but admire the furnishings. Everywhere the chairs, sideboards, the table, gleamed in the light of the candles.

The Colonel rose from his chair and smiled broadly. "Good evening, Mrs. Atkins. How nice to see you again. David, say hello to your mother."

David looked around from behind a high-backed chair. "Hi, Mother, how are you?"

Imogene smiled, ran to David and gave him a big hug. He had returned her smile but made no move to run to meet her. *Well he certainly doesn't seem that excited to see me. I guess he's just tired.*

"Mother, we were just fixing to have our charlotte and coffee now. You remember the dessert I told you old Viola gave me the first time I came to Madame's? Colonel? Madame? Would it be all right for my mother to join us for a dish of it since she's too late to share our supper?"

"Why, of course she may. Carlotta, would you fetch another dish for Mrs. Atkins? Please sit down and join us. Oh, be sure to bring the coffee, I'm sure it must be ready by now."

"Actually, darling, would you join me in the kitchen to help me bring everything in? You know how heavy that coffee service is, and this will give Mrs. Atkins and David a few moments to visit." The Colonel pulled out a chair for Imogene, seating her directly across from David.

Carlotta smiled, "We will be back shortly."

Imogene perched herself on the edge of her chair, smiling at David. *Two weeks and how he seems changed. I can't believe they dress for dinner in evening clothes, sure is a far cry from my old hand-me-down things!.* David gazed back at her, smiling, but quiet . . . unnaturally so. "Well, sweetheart, have you had a nice visit? The boys told me you'd been over here a week. Better be careful not to wear your welcome out. I know how nice they are, and it's been so sweet of them to have you."

She studied him carefully. Deep purple bruises ran down the side of his face, turning black as they reached his neck. Red scabs were visible on his forehead, lips and hands. She could see also that under his left eye a prominent dark bruise stood out. His eyes shone brightly in the candlelight. *How beautiful he looks. How serene and calm. So different than Brad and Tony, like some being of light loaned to me from God. Why they've dressed him up as well.*

"David, where did you get those clothes? They are so pretty. I love the dark green velvet and the gold piping on the collar and lapels. My, they've made a little gentleman of you." She smiled nervously, aware of a distance between them beyond the broad table that separated them. Somehow it frightened her. "Brad told me you had an accident, fell down or something like that?"

"Mother, The Colonel and Madame have been very kind to me. I did have a terrible accident and was pretty banged up there for a few days." He looked away, afraid to return her gaze. "I fell right down our front steps, hitting every one of them, but they took me in and looked after me. I'm feeling quite well now. Madame and I have been doing a great deal of singing the past few days. It has become such a happy place to be with all this room. I'm such a lucky boy to have them care the way they do. It's wonderful being here in this beautiful house with them."

"Well, of course, dear, it's been wonderful of them, so very kind, but we need to go home shortly. Granny and Aunt Barbara send you their best. I've told them what progress you've been making with your music and they'd like you to come up in the spring and sing for them the way you used to do. I'm so tired, honey, and Brad and Tony are waiting for us to get home so they can go out on their dates How did you fall? Oh, never mind, we can talk about it at home." *What's wrong with him? He stiffened when I mentioned his brothers. I saw a flicker of something for a moment in his eyes, but it went as quickly as it came. Could it be fear? This is terribly strange.*

The Colonel and Carlotta returned, pushing the tea cart with the coffee service, four dishes of charlotte, china dessert plates, and a large silver dish with tea cakes. The rich aroma of the coffee filled the room. They smiled at Imogene and served the coffee, charlotte, and tea cakes. As they took their places at the table, she couldn't help but admire the china. *The plates are almost translucent. I have never seen anything like it. Beautiful! But I want to get out of here with my son right now.*

"Colonel, I want to say how much I appreciate you and Madame taking care of my child while I was away. I should have suggested it myself, but didn't feel it would be fitting to overstep in that way. David has bloomed in these years since you've both come into his life. To me he was different from birth from the other boys, and he sings so beautifully now. All the ladies at church are just beside themselves whenever he sings. My, and such music. We had been used to just old hymns, and now we hear really great things. Madame you've managed a miracle here."

"Why thank you, Mrs. Atkins. That's very kind of you to say. David is a phenomenon that comes about so seldom that it's been my pleasure. He is a once in a lifetime treasure to me. Well, of course, to both of us." She smiled at her husband "Isn't that so, my dear?"

The Colonel returned her smile. "Yes, oh, absolutely. So much so that it seems to us that he belongs here," he paused, "where all is harmony, safety, beauty." The couple exchanged a meaningful glance across the table.

Imogene shifted nervously in her seat. "This has all been so nice. The coffee and dessert like nothing I've ever tasted, but David and I should be leaving now. The boys are waiting to go out and I told them we wouldn't be long." She laughed, trying to hold down a rising panic. "David, why don't you gather up your things and we'll be on our way? Right now, dear, okay? We must leave." She rose, went to David, put her hand on his arm. "Come on. What are you waiting for?"

The Colonel and Carlotta rose as well. David looked from one to the other. Carlotta smiled and nodded to her husband.

David nervously said, "Well I'll have to go upstairs for my clothes. They're up in my room."

The Colonel took a step forward. "Come along, David, we'll go up to your room. Mrs. Atkins, Carlotta would like to talk to you. The boys can wait, and if they don't," he looked coldly in her eyes, continuing, "then they don't." He took David by the hand and left the room.

Imogene whirled around, astonished by the insolence in his voice. "What in hell is going on here? Get my son ready right now. We're leaving." She started toward the stairs, but Carlotta seized her arm. "What are you doing, Madame? Do you think you can keep my son here?"

She screamed, "David? David, get down here!" She broke loose of Carlotta's grasp and ran for the stairs. Carlotta, hot on her heels, jerked her backward by the hair; Imogene shrieked in pain and stumbled to the floor. "Why you bitch! Let me go." Carlotta had her in a choke hold of steel. "Let go of me! I'll kill you if you don't."

"Oh, I'm a bitch? You haven't seen anything yet, woman. If you try to go up those stairs again you will first have to throw me to the floor. You wouldn't stand a chance in hell of that. Imogene, I think you'd better come into the music room right now with me and stop acting like some insane she-wolf. There are some things I have to say to you that will bring you back to your senses. Now get in there." She shoved Imogene in convulsed rage. Thoroughly stunned, Imogene walked backward across the hall to the music room.

"Now, you sit down!" screamed Carlotta, pointing imperiously to a low chair near the window.

Breathing heavily, Imogene obeyed.

Carlotta sat regally in the high-backed throne chair from Venice which backed on the entrance to the room, blocking off any possibility of Imogene escaping. It sat slightly higher than the other chairs in the room. She looked at Imogene patronizingly, folding her arms over her waist. "Now, let us talk quietly, and speak reasonably like two adults."

"What do you mean? You can't hold my child hostage here this way. I want to take him out of here right now."

Carlotta smiled icily back at her. "You have seen him. Does he look like he's being held against his will? No, my dear woman, things have changed greatly in your absence. We have engaged counsel in this matter and I must tell you frankly where things stand. You have been gone for two weeks, leaving behind three minors without adult supervision. Perhaps you aren't aware of this, but I believe you have heard of Jerry York? Well, we have had meetings with him and we understand from our conversations that you have placed yourself in jeopardy of having all of your sons taken away from you. It's called abandonment. It's also called child abuse. David did have a terrible fall down some stairs, or so he says. He came over here to us, looking as though he had been beaten. We don't know what really happened, but believe me, pictures were taken, and if they reach the desk of the judge of the superior court it could look bad, very bad for you. We are aware of your struggles. A single woman with three sons, two of whom are teenagers. People talk. You know this, living in this web of gossipy old hags like those who you say gush over David's singing at church. Mr. York is prepared to draw up a petition against you as an unfit mother who left her children to their own devices. We are talking prison here if you're brought to trial."

Imogene rose, wringing her hands, and crossed to the gleaming black Steinway grand piano. She looked at Carlotta in confusion. "Well, yes, I am aware of Jerry York. His son Marty is one of Brad's best friends. Brad said something about it when I got home this afternoon. I find it hard to believe though, that something like this could be taken seriously. I mean, the boys are fine. I'm not about to allow David to stay here with you. It's against nature. I am his mother, he is my son. That should count for something? Surely any judge would understand that?"

Carlotta rose from her throne, went to her French desk at the rear of the room, and drew out an envelope. Watching Imogene closely, she flung the envelope on the shining ebony instrument. "I had hoped it wouldn't be necessary for you to see this, but it appears you must be fitted with the bridle of reason before you will understand the peril you stand in. Now, pick up the envelope and look at those pictures. Do it now. This is how David looked the night of his accident. My husband took these pictures to document what occurred."

Imogene looked inside the envelope at the color pictures of David. She screamed in horror at the battered face, the matted hair, the swollen black eye, the abrasions and bruises. "Oh my *God*! All this from a fall? It's impossible. These must be forgeries. No simple fall could have done all this damage. What is that mess in his hair?" She reeled back and forth, hot tears falling down her cheeks. She sobbed uncontrollably, her shoulders shaking. She sat on the piano bench in utter humiliation.

Carlotta stood back. "I think the less you think about what was in his hair the better for you. Yes, we too, were stunned and horrified that night he came by here. He told us he had a terrible fall. Look at those pictures, Imogene. Do you *really* want them shown in open court in this town? Think well, because if David is called to the stand, and I promise you he would be, he will be asked about those pictures. Who knows what he will say under oath about his, uh, accident? Maybe a different story altogether?" Carlotta drew up to her full height, gazing down on the small broken-hearted mother sitting below her.

Imogene was crushed, her fury, indignation, rage, and protests reduced to soft murmurings.

"Imogene, this can be taken care of quietly, discreetly. The Colonel's father was the head of the law firm where Mr. York works as a junior partner. The Colonel still retains the presidency of that firm. Judge Kelly is also his uncle, and the district attorney is his first cousin. These men are powerful. This matter can go forward as Mr. York wants, or it can quietly fade away and be, in time, forgotten. Mr. York can be persuaded. We are prepared to say, if need be, that we were looking after the boys. That will take the wind out of whatever sails he thought he could unfurl to climb up the ladder. That and his advancement to one of the senior partnerships should do nicely. From there, eventually perhaps he will aspire to political office? All this can be avoided if David remains here, always, with us!"

"But to give up my child like this? How can you ask it of me? I have nothing. I'm just a simple country woman. Brad and Tony will be gone soon. David is all I have. I've avoided remarriage because I know I'd always put my children first. That's not fair to any man. The boys don't realize what sort of man their father is. I've shielded them from that ugliness all their lives. They'll understand one day when they're grown maybe. Perhaps then they'll know what I went through to keep us all together." She leaned over, her arms extended out in misery.

"Come now, poor thing, sit here on the sofa quietly with me. You know I love David. The Colonel does too, more than you may realize. I'm not asking to adopt him. But you've seen the kind of life he can have here with us in this house filled with beauty and peace. He is destined for greatness. His voice, as he grows to manhood, under my teaching, will be something like the world hasn't heard since long years ago. Believe me, Imogene, I have seen the greatest and he will make them seem as though they were amateurs. He will have the world at his feet. He will rise from this place to a triumph without equal on the stages of the greatest opera houses of the entire world. We propose that he remain here with us, to be groomed into a shining star. Of course you can see him whenever you wish. Perhaps you could spend Sundays with him, just the two of you. Doesn't that sound like something that would solve all this threatened ugliness, my dear?"

Imogene nodded in agreement. *God! What is this loneliness eating away at my heart?* "Yes, it is true. You can give him a life I never could. I want him to be happy, and if I can see him often, I'll try to live with it. We can't let this other thing get out. Who knows what might come of it? Your solution makes sense, though I never intended any of this to happen. I can't afford lawyers, and where would I be when they got through with me? I would like to see him before I leave, but perhaps it's best that I don't. I wouldn't like him to see how distraught I am. I'm tired of fighting."

Imogene put on her sweater, gathered her purse and keys, and allowed herself to be led to the front door, Carlotta holding her arm all the way. "Are you sure, Madame? Sure that this is for the best?"

"Yes, sweet girl, it is. You are very noble and brave. You will see as time goes by that this is the only correct thing any of us can do. All this will be taken care of. You will see." She opened the door and Imogene stepped out. She turned around to say goodbye only to see the door close firmly behind her.

* * *

Carlotta walked slowly to the staircase, whispering, "Oh, God, to you be the glory! What a brilliant actress. The child I have longed for is mine at last. Oh, greatness, you will be his. He is safe now. Now I understand what brought me to this moment through all the agony of the past. He is mine. . . mine!"

She turned and saw the lights of Imogene's car as she drove away toward the broad avenue. "Colonel? Colonel?"

He ran down the stairs as she, fainting, slipped quietly to the floor. He knelt and lovingly gathered her up in his arms. He kissed her. She stirred and opened her eyes. "Oh, my darling, we have won. He is ours now."

* * *

Imogene drove along the wind-swept streets, mentally replaying it all. *God, grant that I am doing the right thing. Maybe he can go on to a life away from this place one day where he will know happiness and fulfillment that could never be found in this horrible town. Never have I ever seen him so focused on a goal. And I'll see him anytime, I'm still his mother, I always will have a special place in his heart.* She pulled into the driveway, turned off the motor and sat there a long moment before stepping out and shivering in the bright moonlight. A gust of wind brought a flurry of dry leaves around her feet.

Inside, Brad and Tony were gone. She kicked off her shoes and tossed her purse into the chair beside the door. *What could really have happened here to him? Could there be something I haven't been told? Truth, what is that anymore? There is no truth, only emptiness, only loneliness.*

She walked into David's and Tony's bedroom. She fell on David's bed, buried her face in his pillow, seeking a lingering odor of the boy who no longer would sleep there. But there was none. She wept quietly, clinging to the pillow. The door to his closet was ajar. *His clothes! They're gone. Ah, those people already had this thing planned out; they had no intention of discussing it with me, or giving me any say in the matter. I never did have a choice.* She moved mechanically to David's bureau, opening one drawer, then the others below it. Empty, save for a gleam in a back corner of the first drawer from a small plastic bag. It contained ten shiny silver dollars. *Mama gave him these and he's saved them here. God, oh God, what agony. He is quite removed from this place.* Sighing deeply, she turned to leave the room. She reached over to turn off the lamp and noticed that the small picture of her was gone. *He must have it with him; he'd never have left it.* The thought somehow gave her a sense of comfort. Her eyes brimmed with tears.

Tiredness swept over her, and she moved to her own room and changed into her long nightgown. She lay silently on her bed atop the covers. She turned on her side, closed her eyes and drew her hands up beside her. She cried herself to sleep. Sometime during the night, moonlight flooded the room. Her hands had relaxed in sleep. Ten silver dollars gleamed brightly in the soft moonlight by the pillow where she had laid her head.

Fifteen
September, 1959

David, now three years in the custody of Carlotta and The Colonel, would be fourteen in two months. His singing had reached the point at which Carlotta deemed him ready for a solo concert debut. She engaged a string orchestra for the event and spent a great deal of time organizing the concert, for which she had rented a magnificent hall in Richmond, Virginia. She had advertised heavily in Richmond papers and in musical magazines in neighboring states. She also contacted her extensive network of elite voice teachers in an effort to insure the concert would be well-attended.

She and David arrived several days ahead for rehearsals with the orchestra. Word of their arrival had preceded them, and they received many invitations from socially prominent families in Richmond, anxious to hear and see this prodigy about whom so much had been heard in the tightly knit musical community. Carlotta Vasselli had been a professional singer in her own country before and during the Great War. She had married into the greatest family in Selma, Alabama, and had opened a school of singing which had produced a number of outstanding young artists who were singing in opera houses in cities like New York, San Francisco and Chicago. In the south, word of musical talent spread like wildfire. Old dowagers dragged their reluctant husbands to any recital or orchestral concert to see and be seen. Carlotta's and David's arrival had been anticipated for months.

Carlotta wisely declined the invitations offered by influential citizens, explaining that the work at hand required their full attention, but hinted that a great reception would follow the concert. She had prepared a splendid program of fine music from illustrious composers, fourteen selections in all, some with orchestra, a few with just piano. All were to be sung in English with great emphasis placed on the words. She had been hesitant about that decision because one of the capstones was Schubert's *Der Hirt auf dem Felsen;* a *tour de force* retitled *The Shepherd on the Rock* with piano and clarinet accompaniment. David had received wonderful reviews wherever he had sung this piece, whether in German or English.

Rehearsals went well. Sixteen players and their conductor met with the famous diva and her *protégé* and after a few hours, all was ready. The program was first professionally recorded at a studio Carlotta had rented. She knew that it was important to have David's voice recorded; his voice would soon change as puberty progressed. The two recording sessions went well, stereophonic sound having been recently developed to give listeners a closer approximation of an artist's sound in person.

David was somewhat disconcerted by the microphones. He had never been recorded before, but once he had been placed by the sound engineer, he proceeded to sing directly from his heart as he had been taught. The words were crisp; his intonation and balance with the instruments were in perfect unison. He looked, as ever, to Carlotta for approval, which he joyously received.

On concert night the hall was packed with the *crème de la crème* of society and curious people of all walks of life who had come to hear this prodigy. As the orchestra filed on stage, excitement was at a fever pitch. Imogene had come from Selma the day before and was seated in the front row, receiving due attention as mother of the singer as she was escorted to her seat in the crowded auditorium. Carlotta had spoken frequently in several interviews of this woman from Selma, who had first introduced her to the young man who was to become her prize student. The society grand dames recognized her from the description given in the newspapers and she was aglow with smiles, settling into her seat. The arrangement with Carlotta and The Colonel had settled into a mutually fulfilling mission. She had been able to see David often, and loved him as much as ever; realizing that his future was important to them all.

A hush of anticipation gathered as the orchestra tuned up the instruments. David and Carlotta stood in the wings together. Dressed in a long, black, off-the-shoulder gown of silk damask with a flowing train behind, she was as excited as if she herself were about to sweep out onto the stage. Her blond hair was pulled back into a fashionable French twist; diamonds and pearls glittered from her wrists, ears, and neck. David, standing beside her, had grown taller. He was dressed in a formal black tuxedo, his body still slender, and his face boyish in an appealing way. Carlotta had brushed his dark auburn hair till it gleamed in the backstage light.

The conductor gave his signal. Carlotta beamed, and said. "Go now, my dearest, to your destiny."

He walked out onto the stage to polite applause and took his position to the conductor's left. The orchestra began to play, and the voice responded. He began singing, "If God be for us, who can be against us?" Higher and higher rang the voice in youthful exuberance, his dark eyes blazing with the light of genius. At the conclusion of the first selection, an electric current seemed to run through the audience, many astonished by the sheer beauty of the voice. He was warmly applauded, and the conductor shook his hands. Songs and arias from English operas poured forth. At the end of each set he would walk to and from the wings, warmly acknowledging the applause with beaming smiles, many of which were directed to Imogene, obviously enthralled with happiness. Carlotta seized him in an embrace, then sent him back out for curtain calls. For the final number, David and the clarinet virtuoso came out to perform the celebrated Schubert song, the orchestra gone, a Steinway grand piano rolled out onto the stage. Carlotta insisted on playing the piano. When the audience caught sight of her, applause grew louder; the audience knew she was the reason for this young man's debut. They all bowed. Carlotta made the lowest sweeping bow, then sat at the piano. Palpable silence consumed the audience as Carlotta and the clarinetist tuned up. The long clarinet solo that began the piece was so beautiful that Imogene appeared to be in a trance. At times she turned her head from side to side, beaming.

The piano joined the clarinet and David began to sing *Der Hirt auf dem flesen* in English translation as *The Shepherd on the Rock*. As the audience listened in enchanted wonderment, it progressed to its rapturous *allegro* finale, the voice interplaying with both piano and clarinet in ever-more dazzling cascades of scales. A hurricane of applause descended on the onstage trio gesturing to the chorus of bravos that rang out from all sides of the hall. Four times they were recalled for more bows, each performer putting forth the other for special praise.

At long last, Carlotta threw up her hand to signal for silence. "I'm so proud of this young man. He has worked so hard and has exceeded everything I could have wished for. I would like to acknowledge the participation of Mr. Galvany for his beautiful playing on the clarinet." A wave of bravos and applause followed as the artist took a bow. "And let us not forget Mrs. Imogene Atkins, mother of the singer, who has come from Selma to join in her child's success. Imogene, would you please rise to be acknowledged?"

Imogene stood and turned around to the audience, who warmly applauded her. She was shaking with excitement and blew kisses to both David and Carlotta.

The audience then screamed for an encore and Carlotta signaled with a wave of her hand for the conductor and orchestra players to return. They, too, were warmly welcomed and took their places.

Carlotta said, "David will now sing for you *The Soldier tired of War's Alarms* from *Artraxerxes* by Arne." She and the clarinetist walked offstage and the orchestra began the aria's introduction. Never in living memory had this eighteenth-century piece been heard in Richmond. David's voice rang out in the dazzling *bravura* difficulties of the piece which had been composed especially for the English diva, Elizabeth Billington. David hit perfectly every trill and cascading run up and down the scale, then capped the finale with a magnificent high-D natural. Pandemonium ensued as flowers were thrown onstage; the audience rose in a standing ovation. The players all beat their bows on their music stands in appreciation, and David embraced both the conductor and first violinist. From the wings huge floral tributes poured forth. Carlotta rushed out and embraced David. It never seemed to end.

Finally Carlotta gestured for silence with an upraised hand. "David and I will sing for the final encore a duet from the opera *La Juive* of Halevy. It is our hope that this evening will remain in your hearts always as you will go with us as we go back home." The duet was in French, the one concession to an evening of otherwise all-English selections. Carlotta sang, like a young girl, the part of Rachel; David, that of the Princess Eudoxie. The duet built steadily to a fever pitch until the conclusion, when both voices rang out with thrilling high notes, David's being a penultimate high F.

Screams of joy and wonder descended on them as they bowed again and again. Finally the bravos died away as the curtain fell on the spectacle.

At the reception that followed at the nearby Richmond country club, the artists all stood in a receiving line to greet the three hundred invited guests. Carlotta behaved as Prima Donna Assoluta, acknowledging the flattering compliments with nods in both directions. Imogene also stood with them, dressed in a beautiful gown of dark green chiffon she had borrowed from Carlotta along with her magnificent emeralds, perfectly setting set off Imogene's coloring.

The Colonel and David, along with the clarinetist, stood at the end of the line after the ladies. David's face was covered with lipstick kisses from the ancient dowager ladies who showered him with compliments. He was quite tired, not being used to such late hours. As the guests mingled among the cold trays of sandwiches and sweets, Carlotta took him by the hand and together they stood by a fountain from which flowed fine French wines. David was permitted to drink a glass, and many toasts were offered to his continued success and future. The president of the local chapter of the Daughters of the Confederacy stepped forward and made a speech about how honored they were to be present on such a grand occasion.

One lady, Mrs. Austin, had heavily rouged cheeks and an ample bosom much in evidence as she paraded before them in a beaded gown of blue silk with sapphires blazing from her necklace, earrings, and tiara. Her dyed hair was pulled back in imitation of Helena Rubinstein. Everyone clapped politely at her remarks and even Carlotta smiled, though bored beyond belief.

After two hours of this nonsense, Carlotta signaled that is was time for them to leave. She took David and Imogene by their hands. With The Colonel splendidly dressed in one of his Marine uniforms, they made their farewells and departed for their hotel. At the hotel Carlotta accompanied each of them to their respective rooms, then she and The Colonel turned down the hall to the Imperial Suite which had been reserved for them.

Imogene's room was next to David's, and she soon paid him a visit. "Darling, I want you to know how very proud I am of you. You sang like an angel and I am so pleased that The Colonel and Madame asked me to join all of you here. I know it's been a long journey from that time when I first took you to see Madame, but what a splendid result, don't you agree?"

"Yes, Mother. Madame has been stern with me at times, but it's because a singer must have always a certain discipline to live by." He stood near the balcony. "However, I have learned that no matter how good someone says you are, in the end it is you who must go out on stage and do the work. Not that I'm complaining, but I feel I have had to behave in a very adult and sophisticated manner from a very early age, and it hasn't always been easy. But as Madame says, my destiny is coming and I must be prepared. My voice will be changing soon as I grow into manhood and she and I will have to work very hard to see where it will be placed. It's an entirely different sort of training as I look at music written for and sung by men."

Imogene fidgeted nervously. "Why, sweetheart, aren't you happy? We all have to make choices in our lives and strive for the future which awaits us. You are still so young, not quite fourteen, and I know that being at school hasn't always been a happy experience, but it won't be much longer now. Brad and Tony are away in college, though how I managed to get Tony in is something I still can't figure out. I think The Colonel pulled some strings to get him accepted at North Georgia College. It appears to have curbed his problems a great deal, so I'm grateful for that. Brad, too, is doing well at Auburn. I have my work at the base and of course my bridge playing and church activities." Coming closer and reaching for his hand, she continued, "I still always will have time for you, I hope you believe me?"

David looked at her sadly. "Mother, we all have to live with decisions we make in our lives. I am happy. It is true; school is something I don't care for. The kids just seem to be concerned with having fun, going to parties, dances, and the sort, but I'm apart from that. Madame says that she isn't at all sure if college is something I need to be concerned about. I've become reasonably proficient on the piano and play well enough to learn a good deal of music on my own. She always insisted that I should do that, and I speak her language quite well now. She says I'll need that knowledge when eventually I go to Europe." He sat down beside her.

"Europe? Why, whatever is in her mind? It will be another four years till you're out of high school. There should be plenty of places here you can go to sing. Auditions are held all the time and many Americans are fully trained and able to perform here in our own country."

"You don't understand. I have been schooled in the Garcia method, which basically means the school of beautiful singing of the music of Bellini, Donizetti, Rossini, and early Verdi. Their operas are simply not done in this country due to the lack of singers trained correctly for them.

In Europe, and especially in Italy, a revival is dawning where these operas will be performed once again. That is where my future lies and I must be ready when the chance presents itself." He looked at her patronizingly, realizing that what he said was completely lost on her.

She looked at him earnestly. "But that's still far in the future, there's no reason to think about it right now. I don't want you to leave. I want to spend more time with you. I have hoped now that the boys are gone that you might come back and live with me. Wouldn't you like that?"

David stood, and walking again towards the balcony, he looked out at the shimmering stars in the night sky. Coldly, he said, "No. My place is with Madame. It always will be. That doesn't mean I don't love you, but she and The Colonel give me the sort of life and direction I must have to go forward towards the career which waits in the future. Try to understand, Mother."

"Well darling, I can't say that I comprehend all you've said. It goes quite over my poor head. I suppose in these matters that what Madame has taught you is for the best." She shook her head, looking inanely towards the balcony.

David continued to stare outside. "We really need to go to bed now. It's so late. I'm tired. I want to get out of these clothes and go to sleep."

She walked forward to hug him, which he allowed, albeit with great impatience.

"Okay, dear, you're right, I'm tired too. I'm not used to all this excitement and we have to go back to Selma in the morning. It's such a long drive. Madame just seems to have given you the moon. It's incredible."

He smiled patronizingly at her. "Good night, Mother, I hope you sleep well. We'll talk again in the morning over breakfast. Madame has given me much. It is true. But I don't ask for the moon." Gesturing towards the night sky he said quietly, "After all, she has given me ambition to aspire to be as the stars."

Imogene smiled and turned slowly. David quickly ran in front of her and opened the door for her to leave.

"Good night then, David darling, I'll see you in the morning." She leaned forward to kiss him goodbye, when suddenly he drew back, rejecting both the kiss and the proffered embrace. She looked back at him in astonishment as she stepped across the threshold into the hall. A brief smile flitted across her face as she turned back to him, trying vainly to smile.

"David?"

"Mother, David is gone and will never return! I am now *Ernesto*.

Ernesto Vasselli!"

Imogene blanched white in mute horror and surprise as he closed the door in her face.

Sixteen

One morning in late November, two months after the concert in Richmond, fall had chilled the air. The pecan trees were rapidly losing their leaves, which fell, dried and yellow, to the ground. Wind rattled the tall windows, waking David, who stretched and opened his eyes. He lay in his huge canopy bed in his room, one of the six upstairs bedrooms of the house. Yawning, he drew back the white drapes and slid over the side of the bed to the polished oak floor. He smiled at the small antique drop-leaf table by the fireplace. A steaming pot of strong coffee welcomed him as he sat down in one of the chairs beside the table. Madame, of course, had left it, anticipating his rising at his usual early hour. He poured himself a cup and grimaced for a moment at the bitter taste of the first sip. His stomach growled, and he caught sight of a tray where sweet Italian biscotti overflowed its plate. No one but Carlotta could make it in the old way. The aroma of almond flavoring filled the room as he dipped one of the cookies into the coffee and crunched it hungrily.

A soft knock came at the door. "Dear boy, are you awake?" He rushed to the door and admitted Carlotta. "Good, you're up. Have you had a coffee?"

"Yes, Madame, I was just enjoying it along with the biscotti. Thank you so much for having it here to greet me."

"Ah, child, I am delighted, as always. You have become so like me in your morning routine with coffee and biscotti. How nice that you are out of school for the Thanksgiving holidays. We don't have such a thing in Italy, so that‘s something you'll need to forget once you are there." She glanced around the room. "I wish you had taken one of the bedrooms nearer our suite instead of this one at the far end of the corridor, but I know The Colonel is often up earlier than we, and if you were right beside us, he might be tempted to come in and tickle you awake the way he used to when you first came to live with us."

David turned away to hide the smile that stole across his face. *Yes, The Colonel and his early morning romps, jumping into my bed. I remember the way he would grab me and the feel of his beard and the way he would hug me so tightly like he never would let me go.* He laughed inwardly.

"Hello? Earth to David . . . where do you drift off to, darling?"

"I'm sorry, Madame. Please join me in another cup of our coffee. I would like to talk with you about something."

Carlotta had drifted over to the windows, looking admiringly at the brightening morning. In the distance, the sun had recently risen over the horizon. Golden rays cascaded over the wide front yard, glinting like diamonds over the falling golden leaves that gathered like a blanket "What's that, my dear? Oh, all right, we'll talk for a while, but then we have to get busy with our practicing." She sat in the matching armchair, poured herself a generous cup from the bright-white coffee pitcher. "What was it that you wanted to talk with me about, my sweet?"

He hesitated for a moment, mastering nervousness. "I'd like to ask you about these injections The Colonel has been taking me to the doctor for these last few weeks. They have been making me feel things happening inside that I don't understand. Do you know what they are for? I mean what benefit they're intended to be for? I would ask him, but he would just say they were necessary and not to worry about it."

"Darling, of course it's nothing to worry about. They are male hormone shots. I understand you've completed the ten injections that we arranged with Doctor Von Hilsman. We know that now you have just turned fourteen, and puberty should be advancing quickly. In your case it has been delayed due to factors that frankly we don't understand. It could be because of things that happened to you earlier, you know, several years ago. It could be a chemical imbalance. Perhaps in thoughts that you might not be aware of, you want to remain childlike with your beautiful soprano voice. But, sweet boy, it's time to leave that behind, time for your manhood to take shape. The injections are just designed for your body to catch up with your age."

He sighed heavily. "Well, I've wondered because things are changing with my body when I look in the mirror. I've grown taller lately, and in my body I feel some new things are happening. What does it all mean, Madame?"

She chuckled in spite of herself, keeping her laughter in check. "Is this all, my angel? It just means you are turning into a young man. It's normal; we've just given it a bit of a push. You will start feeling things stirring inside that at first you might not understand. I will have The Colonel talk with you further about these 'men things.' I wouldn't know how to explain it to you. You do trust him, don't you? You must understand our European way of thought . . . there are some things that a man does not discuss with a lady. These changes are things to be discussed only with a trusted male father figure. I will see that The Colonel discusses these, ah, sensitive man things with you."

David turned a deep crimson, feeling the blood coming up over his throat and into his face. "Oh, Madame, I'm not sure I could talk about this with him, with anyone, because I don't understand how my feelings have changed."

"Nonsense!" she exclaimed impatiently, "You know The Colonel adores you as much as I do. In many ways, he thinks of you as his son. You know we met late. I was already over forty and I had never been married, never known before the closeness that he and I came to share. A year before we came here to live, we were to have a child, but it was not to be. I lost the baby and the doctor said there would not be another. We were both so sad, because he is the last of his direct line. The judge, his uncle, has two daughters, but there was no one to carry on the family name. It concerned me so much that I even offered to walk out of his life so he could meet a young woman who could give him children. He refused, saying I was his rose without a thorn that he picked up from the ashes of war. He said I was like an ancient dream from another world sent to fill the loneliness in his heart. He grew up here in this house, but his parents were over forty when he was born, and then his little sister Georgiana faded away to the land of eternal bowers when she was barely five years old. So at the age of ten he saw her tiny casket taken from this house and carried to the family mausoleum at Old Live Oak Cemetery. His parents did not long survive, both of them joining her there before he was barely twenty-five. So, my sweetheart, is it any wonder why he has come to love you as he does?"

David looked searchingly at her, so beautiful with long golden hair falling over her shoulders, her skin so pale, her eyes blue like the cornflowers that grew outside in the flower garden she tended so lovingly. Her dressing gown was full and white against the flame-stitch covering of the armchairs. "I had no idea. He had never spoken to me about any heartache, but I knew at once when I met him that he instantly loved me. I love him, too, so much."

"Dearest, when you are older, you will understand that life can sometimes bring to all of us a bitter cup of loneliness that even a great love can never entirely banish from our hearts, but it's something we live with and try to rise beyond, just as you in your young life have risen from adversity. But let us not speak further of sad things. God has sent you to brighten our lives and that is enough for The Colonel and me, too. Now come along, we need to dress and go downstairs to sing before any of the other students arrive."

"Only one more thing, Madame! I need to ask you how it is that you have said that when I leave here one day that I am to be known as Ernesto Vasselli? Vasselli I can understand, I'm happy to have your name, but Ernesto?"

A shadow, perhaps a long forgotten memory, appeared to pass over her face. "Ernesto? Why he was my older brother. Our parents had groomed him for years to take over our father's position as president of the Vasselli industries they founded in the 1890's. Then in 1943, while I was away in Argentina on tour with artists of the *Teatro Massimo di Palermo*, the Germans came and Ernesto, who could have saved himself, went away with my parents to the camps. He wouldn't — couldn't — have left them to that sad journey north, from which none returned. I only have their memory now. Not even a grave or their ashes to weep over, only what remains here in my heart. I chose his name for you. It will be your professional name always. You already speak Italian, and, more importantly, you think in our language as well. When the day comes for you to go to Italy for your debut, I plan to present you as if you were a native Italian yourself. You have the look for it, and it will be as though you sprang from its earth as naturally as I did. We will speak more about this when the time comes, but you must not reveal your origins as an American from Alabama. You will be to Italy as a true son of hers, and your name is now Ernesto Vasselli. You must be known by that name from this moment forward. Your old name is to be forgotten as though it never existed. I will speak to The Colonel. He and I will address you now only as Ernesto. As soon as it may be arranged we will have it done legally so when you go to Europe it will be only under your new identity. You, too, must use it only and think of yourself only under that name forever. But enough of that for now, we must work. Quickly then, to the bathroom with you, then get dressed and I will be waiting for you in the music room . . . Ernesto." She swept up the coffee pot, cups, and biscotti and whirled out of the room with a loving backward glance.

Ernesto rapidly brushed his teeth, scrubbed his face, and brushed his hair. He looked for a long moment in the mirror. *How I am changing. It's almost like a different person gazes back at me these days. And my body . . . I can hardly believe the things I'm feeling inside and how I seem to be adding inches in places. I'm really becoming a man now. Maybe next time I'll have The Colonel on his back!* He laughed, then methodically dressed in the clothes Carlotta laid out for him. As he descended the staircase, he began to hum the beautiful melody from *I Puritani; Vien diletto en ciel la luna.* Feeling a strange sensation in his throat, he paused on the steps and sang out the words in full voice. The words sounded disjointed, unfocused.

How strange. He rushed down the remaining steps and ran into the music room, where Carlotta waited for him at the piano.

She had heard the attempt when he tried out the phrase in full voice and now anxiously looked at him as he dashed up to her. "Madame!" he cried out in panic. "What is wrong? My voice seemed to have left me."

"No, Ernesto, it has only changed. No more soprano arias for you, my darling. We must now see where the voice lies and strengthen it to the place it will now forever be. Your scales and breathing must now be adjusted. Come stand beside me and we will sing Madame Blanche's vocal exercises in different keys. Your voice is now that of a man. It will always sound an octave lower than the corresponding soprano register that you are used to. Your ear will adjust to it quickly and you will understand its new direction."

He frowned. "Oh, no. No more will I sing the Queen of the Night's arias? No more *Let the Bright Seraphim* from *Samson?* Or the mad scenes from *Lucia di Lammermoor, La Sonnambula, I Puritani, Anna Bolena?* Are those operas now lost to me forever?"

"No, my handsome young man, only the soprano parts, not the other roles. Now come closer, let us begin our exercises." He followed her with caution, almost afraid of his strange new sound, then he relaxed and let the muscles work, adjusted his breathing as she told him. Slowly he accepted his new sound. She played the scales, each time raising a half step in tone. He touched on a high D natural, a new sensation. She stopped abruptly. "Ah, yes, you are now a *tenore leggerio*. Thank God you are not a baritone or bass. This is the voice I had hoped would come when you reached puberty. All sorts of wonders await you. The tenor roles in the operas we have studied will all fall into the range you now have. Your voice is still placed high, only now it will become more powerful. We simply have to make the scale even from bottom to top, but it will come. Have faith in me as you always have, and all will be as it should be. I can hardly wait to begin with you learning the new arias that we will sing. The Colonel will be so pleased to see that you are turning into a man. Let us stop for now. We must not let the voice become too fatigued. That will never do. Besides, the new contralto will be here soon. She began too late. She fancies herself a new Simionato. Can you believe the absurdity of that? You may stay and listen if you like, or go on over to the library and practice a bit on the Clementi sonatas that you've been working on."

The new student arrived, greeted by Madame's bright smile. He smiled inwardly as he left the room after she had introduced him as Ernesto. He loved lingering in the entrance hall and never tired of seeing the portraits of La Malibran and her sister Pauline Viardot-Garcia that smiled down. *Ah, Garcia sisters, your story lives on in your method. I wonder where Madame got these paintings. I know there must be a story there. The Colonel, dear man that he is, could never deny her anything.* He started to the library with its practice piano, then decided he didn't feel like playing anything right now. He was too full of his own inner thoughts to concentrate.

He continued to the large kitchen with its great pine table and gleaming pots and pans, recalling when he first came here and met poor old Viola. As he went out the back door, he saw her ancient old basket, picked it up and made his way out slowly to the pecan trees to pick up the sweet pecans for pies The Colonel adored. *I am like her now, thinking of him and knowing it will please him to be remembered. How wise it was to have learned from her how to cook these pies for him and to sit and watch him devour them and then have him look at me with such pleasure.* The basket soon brimmed over with the paper-shelled pecans. When he heard The Colonel's Buick coming, he ran to the car, proudly showing what he had gathered.

The Colonel smiled broadly. "Well, sport, you've sure been busy this morning. When did you and Carlotta get up anyway?"

"We've been up quite a while now. We've had our coffee and biscotti and then came downstairs to do some singing." He contemplated the man with a quizzical smile. "Madame told me about the injections you've been taking me for and told me their purpose. I didn't know they were responsible for the changes I've been feeling."

"Come over here with me, David, to the gazebo, and let's talk for a while." They sat in the swing suspended from the ceiling of the Victorian building. "Many things will begin to change for you now, my boy. I already see a more mature look about you." He put his arm around his shoulders. "We will need to talk about these new feelings and how you are going to react to becoming a man."

"There has already been a change that I discovered just this morning with my voice. The soprano is gone now and Madame says I'm a high tenor. We went through the exercises and the new sound will take some adjusting to. There's something else though that I'd like to ask you about." He blushed and trembled slightly. "She also told me that from now on I am to be called Ernesto and that she was going to have you call me that also as she would herself from now on. I hope I haven't dropped the ball by telling you this before she could talk to you herself, so please, don't act as if you knew this already. I couldn't stand it if she felt I had superceded her authority. After all, you know Madame must be obeyed."

about these things, too much information too soon. It's just these things are coming in your life, you will know new sensations. You know I wouldn't hurt you. I'd cut off my arm before I'd do that." He turned the boy around and cupped his hand under his trembling chin. "You will learn that when someone touches you with love, with understanding and gentleness, that sex can be a beautiful thing. Now, let's go inside and make some pies with these great pecans you've picked up for me."

Ernesto smiled. The feeling of panic seemed to drain away, replaced with thoughts he didn't understand. The Colonel slapped him on the back and took his hand. Together they walked across the backyard, leaves crunching beneath their feet. Ernesto suddenly turned and wrapped his arms around The Colonel's narrow waist. "I do trust you, I love you. I want you to teach me, to show me about being a man." They climbed the steps to the house together, each lost in his own thoughts.

Seventeen

Months flew by almost imperceptibly. By the time Ernesto turned seventeen, he was in the full bloom of early manhood. He had grown to six feet tall and was shaving almost daily. His chest had broadened, with thick, dark hair spilling across it. He maintained an athletic carriage; The Colonel encouraged swimming, tennis, jogging, and weight lifting. Exercise had become almost as important as singing. He had studied hard. His voice was fully formed, able to effortlessly form a seamless scale without register breaks from the A below middle C to a ringing high D sharp.

Carlotta, meanwhile, cast a wide net with extensive correspondence concerning his career. She resisted entering him in state and regional opera competitions, steadfast in her determination that his first professional appearances in opera must take place in Italy, birthplace of opera. His emergence there as Ernesto Vasselli, native Italian, needed to be carefully planned so that the secret could be maintained indefinitely. So she spent hours at her French writing desk, penning long letters extolling the talents of her protégé to the many musical contacts she still commanded. There were many she could count on when the time was right, but only the most perfect circumstances would do.

* * *

One bright March morning Ernesto lazily remained in his large, old bed as bright sunshine flooded through the gossamer white curtains that blew into the room from the open windows. When he finally stirred he stretched his arms and yawned loudly. *My mouth feels like a roman legion has been in it all night. Gross! I've got to get my ass moving and get downstairs to work on those arias from Rossini's* Semiramide *that Madame has insisted I get perfect. They are difficult, but I've been singing things that are much harder. Why does she insist I work the most on Rossini? No point in questioning. She is always right.* Her exacting method came as naturally now as breathing did. Everything was so ingrained that all he did was open his mouth and technique took control. Even the breathing, so difficult at first when his voice changed, came without visible effort.

He looked in the full length cheval mirror, throwing off the white nightshirt, naked before the mirror with a raging urine-inspired erection. *Down, boy, we'll deal with what you're really meant for later.* He admired his body, toned with rippling abs. Carlotta and The Colonel were fanatics on the subject of hygiene, and he followed their lead and began his ritual by furiously brushing his teeth. He picked up the straight razor and brushed it against the strap that hung from the wall, shaved carefully, then stepped into the shower, using the The Colonel's *Old-Spice* scented special shampoo on his hair. He soaped up and rinsed twice as The Colonel had shown him. He patted his body dry with a huge, fluffy towel (Carlotta would have nothing else). The Colonel had told him to partially towel-dry his hair, then run a fine comb through it, and later putting in a dab of styling gel to give it the darker look. He did as they trained him, adding a handful of *Old Spice* on his face, neck, chest, stomach, crotch . . . and a double pat on his buttocks. *Damn, I feel and look good! What time is it anyway? Nine? Oh crap, boy, get a move on. But wait, Madame isn't here this morning. She's taken three of those stupid girls to Montgomery to sing at the Jewish Temple. She'll know though if I don't practice, she always knows.* He stood naked before one of the tall windows facing the front of the house. The wind blew in. He shivered.

"Don't let that thing shrivel up now. Music can wait; your man needs some loving." The Colonel laughed, threw back the sheets, motioning for him to get in bed, where the older man lay, naked. He pressed David tightly against him. Wordlessly his mouth came down on Ernesto's in a long lingering kiss. Ernesto responded ardently, his hands around The Colonel's back.

The man flung him over on his back. "No more pee hard, son. This is the real thing now." He showered kisses on Ernesto's neck and chest and nibbled hungrily on his hard nipples. Lower his head went till finally he was between the boy's legs and with one gulp nearly swallowed the now-hard penis. Ernesto groaned, arching his back in pleasure. Gone was the horror inflicted on him long ago by Tony and his friends. He was almost at the point of climax when the older man suddenly slid up onto his knees.

He pulled Ernesto's knees over his shoulders, opened a tube of lubricant and applied a generous amount of it to Ernesto's rectum. The boy gasped as The Colonel entered, and reaching down to the man's buttocks, he let him come in deeper. His Colonel had opened the joy of sex in a way that seemed so caring, so natural. The Colonel thrust his hips back and forth and at last emptied a torrent of sperm into the warmth of the young man under him. At the very moment he did so, he took Ernesto's hard penis again into his mouth, making the young man climax.

"Now, how's that for starting your day out right?"

"Oh, Colonel, I love you. My music and your love make me so happy. What have I ever done to deserve what you have given to me all these years? But maybe next time I can put your legs on my shoulders." He smiled broadly.

The older man laughed, and brushed his fingers through Ernesto's hair. "You have made me happy too, son. I know there are those who would be horrified. After all, you are only seventeen; I'm close to sixty. Carlotta has no idea of this side of me. I love her too; it's just that it's always been here, this longing to be with another man. I've waited for you to grow up so I could teach you how beautiful it can be, two men together. But soon your destiny will take you far from here. You must be careful to understand that sex and love are not the same thing. You must try not to get hurt, because there will be many others who will want you, and not always for the right reasons. Emotions, as you will come to know, are things that make us not think clearly. Try to understand what I'm telling you."

"I'm not sure what you mean, Colonel, but I will take care. Now we need to shower again and get moving. Madame is going to expect results when she returns this afternoon, and you know how annoyed she can be when I'm not paying attention."

* * *

Carlotta returned around three o'clock, found Ernesto practicing on the library piano, came up behind him and gave him a huge hug. "How is my handsome young man today? Have you been behaving yourself as I told you to do?"

Oh, if you only knew how our Colonel and I have been behaving! He smiled broadly. "Of course I have, Madame. I worked on the arias of *Idreno* in *Semiramide*. I have worked out the ornaments that you wrote for the cabalettas and they work beautifully." They spoke now together only in Italian; she had insisted on this so that it would come naturally for him.

"Why, Ernesto, you knew they would work. In my day and much earlier, singers were also expected to be composers and often wrote out their own cadenzas and ornaments according to the state they found their voices in at the moment. Always though, when one does this one must be sure they fit the music and are in the style of the composer. Even the great Adelina Patti would sometimes go too far with her embellishments. When she first met Rossini, she sang for him *Una Voce poco fa* from the divine *Barbiere*. He listened in silence. The role had been written for a contralto, but Patti adapted the line to her coloratura soprano, which he had no problem with, as it was the custom for sopranos then as now to sing his music in higher keys than those of the singers for whom the music was originally written. When she finished with a brilliant upward flourish, he merely looked at her and inquired as to who was the composer of the music she had just sung. It had been so altered by the diva's caprices as to be unrecognizable. She was thus properly chastised, and sang again the aria, this time as he had written it."

She gestured for Ernesto to follow her, and they walked across the great hall to the music room. As they entered, she waved her hands impatiently. "You would not have believed those silly girls today. Proper decorum must be observed by women in a Jewish temple, but no, they had to be laughing and behaving outrageously by flirting with the young men. I silenced them with a glance of fury that stopped them dead in their tracks. I told them coming home that how could they expect to aspire to careers in music when they lacked all discipline and thought the most important thing in life was courting the smiles of handsome young men. Thank *God* that you my dearest, are not so bewitched by weaknesses of thoughts in that direction." She glanced up at the portrait of Madame Blanche over the fireplace mantel. "The great diva gave up all for her career and perfecting and passing on the Garcia method. Not even her husband was allowed to distract her from her course of destiny. I would not have obtained the success of my early career had I not followed her instructions to the letter. Love and passion must be subdued in order for perfection to triumph as it must. Remember our diva, Ernesto, in all that you do and you will never falter. Now let us sing the *Semiramide* arias."

She played some scales for him. "Ah, you have warmed up already." She took him through his entire range of the scales. "And now, sing." She played the introduction to the first aria; the opening phrase containing a high C rang true. He continued to the allegro finale with its high D-natural. "Ah, bravo, carino! The ornaments worked perfectly." She flipped to the next act and played the opening of *Idreno's* second aria. It too was brilliantly executed as she had taught him. "Who would have known nine years ago when you first came to me what the future would hold? You have mastered all I have taught you. It will soon be time to spread your wings and take your rightful place in the operatic firmament. You have brought the Garcia's method full circle to the point where they live again through you." She hugged him, tears glistening in her eyes. "Where is my husband? Did he tell you where he was going? I forgot to ask him what his schedule was for today."

Ernesto smiled coyly, remembering his romp with The Colonel that morning. "I believe he was going to play a round of golf. He should be along shortly."

"Well, that's fine, though what he sees in golf is beyond me. Exercise, he says. But he hasn't gotten fat and old like all those slobs I see on the streets when I'm in town shopping. Disgusting! They are digging their own graves with their teeth. You must take care not to ever allow yourself to let go that way. Stay as you are, tall and slim, eat properly, exercise, drink wine only in moderation, and you will sing for thirty years or more without the slightest faltering. I must see about our supper now. You remain and look at the trio in the first act. It's tricky with its interweaving of the voices. It makes a tremendous impression before the entrance of the Queen of Babylon. It can't be glossed over or rushed. I realize there's not much to *Idreno* aside from the two fabulous arias, the trio and some interjections in the scenes with the ghost of Nino, but it's important. The opera can not be performed without his music being included. All parts, whether small or large, my child, must be respected with great seriousness. You may shine in your solo passages, but you must also form part of the ensemble as well. All right, I'll leave you to it."

She embraced him once more and kissed him on both cheeks. "What a handsome young man you've become, my darling.

Ernesto looked at the opening entrance music for his character, *Idreno*, as well as the trio with *Oroe* and *Assur.* The trio had some tricky passages but seemed much less difficult than some of the music he had previously studied. *Madame has something up her sleeve, that's for sure. She's had me learning a lot of high tenor arias. With all the correspondence she's had lately, I can almost hear her mind turning, not to mention the phone calls, where she talks in hushed tones. Oh well, I'll learn soon enough, I suppose.*

The doorbell disrupted his train of thought. He hurried to answer it.

The postman stood in the doorway. "I have a package here for Madame Carlotta Vasselli. Is she home?"

"She's busy at the moment, but I'll sign for it." Ernesto reached for the package, but the carrier quickly drew it back.

"Oh, no, she must sign for it personally. Please call her to the door."

Ernesto turned and was startled to find her standing behind him. Carlotta gushed, "Oh, thank you so much! I've been expecting this for some time now." He noticed as the mailman handed it to her that the return address was the *Teatro La Fenice,* Venice. "Where do I sign? Oh, there?" She handed back the clipboard and shut the door in his face.

"Madame, what's in the package from Italy? More of those wonderful olives you use in our salads? I love them." Ernesto playfully tried to snatch the package from her.

"Child, don't bother yourself with things that don't concern you." She went to her French desk, deposited the parcel in the center drawer and carefully turned the key to lock it. "Now, come with me and help with the final touches for our dinner." Together they walked down the long corridor towards the kitchen.

One hour later they heard The Colonel's Buick. He embraced and kissed both of them. "How are my two sweet treasures? Something sure smells good in here. What's this? My ravioli? Sweetheart, you just outdo yourself all the time. Hell, I'd be happy with some peanut butter and banana sandwiches." He laughed as Carlotta waved him to the sink to wash his hands.

"Heavens, my mother would rise from the grave and slap me across the face if she ever suspected I would not have a proper meal prepared for my husband every evening." Quickly she and Ernesto brought the salad, ravioli, Italian bread and wine to the table. "We have some wonderful Italian ices for our dessert. The ones with the cherries you love so much."

He laughed loudly. "Long time since I had a cherry." He shot a quick glance towards Ernesto, then turned to a frowning Carlotta. "Ah, come on, you two. We need laughter always in this tired old home place."

While they were enjoying their after-dinner ices and strong coffee, Carlotta suddenly rose, walked to the kitchen windows, turned and looked at them. She gestured in the air with her beautiful hands and smoothed back an imaginary strand of hair. "We need to talk, all of us. It is time for the debut of Ernesto Vasselli with orchestra." She threw up her hand. "Before you both start asking questions as you do always, listen to me. I have engaged the players and we will have a tour of several states. From my contacts, the concerts are to be held first in Richmond, then Atlanta, Nashville, Charlotte, Savannah, Miami, Mobile, Charleston, and finally Montgomery. All will be operatic concerts. It's all things we've prepared already, we merely will have to charter the bus, have the programs printed, and we're off. We will have a week of rehearsals in Montgomery. The halls are engaged, and I have seen to all the details as always. All you have to do, my darling, is sing, and you, my handsome husband, to dance with me at the receptions in each city."

"Carlotta, have you lost your mind? We haven't even discussed this and here you go as always, making plans and letting us know after the fact. When is all this madness supposed to happen?" The Colonel colored with frustration as he rose from his chair and glared at her.

"Madame, all opera arias and with orchestra? How can I be out of school like that? I'm a senior now, I have to finish and graduate." He too rose and paced in disbelief.

"Now, as always, you two react emotionally and predictably. When have I ever done anything that was not for the good of both of you? I have sold some of my jewelry to defray the expenses. My emeralds and pearls fetched a great sum. It's all paid for." She gestured impatiently for them to sit, then continued, "Ernesto must have some appearances here before he goes to Italy. The boy soprano is gone, but the tenor is here now and must be heard in this country. Don't fret about your school, my dear. You will graduate on June third, and then it will begin. The dates are to be mid-June through July. We will be away for six weeks." She trembled with excitement and breathlessly waved her arms in the air.

The Colonel broke into laughter as he hugged first Carlotta and then Ernesto. "Well, son, who are we to argue with the diva? There will be no rest for either of us unless we obey. But, Darling, why would you have sold your jewels? I would have covered everything, you know that, don't you?"

"Yes, Madame" Ernesto murmured, "Your jewels . . . I don't deserve this. You have done so much already."

She brushed back tears of happiness. "You are both dearer to me than life itself. How good it is that you realize the folly of questioning me. Aren't I always right, my angels? Ernesto, pour us another coffee while we eat a second round of ices."

He brought back three more desserts from the freezer.

"She's the pied piper. What's the use in wondering if it's good or if it's bad, just trust and obey?" The Colonel and Carlotta exchanged a look, though his right hand under the table grasped Ernesto's tightly.

"Madame!" Ernesto exclaimed, "Won't we have to talk about this with my mother?"

Carlotta advanced menacingly, "You mean, *Imogene?* Please!" She colored indignantly as she rose and leaned over the table and looked into his eyes. "Your mother is looking at you! Your mother is the one who has saved you, who has developed your superb, matchless instrument, who has spared no expense or trouble." She walked around the table. "Since when do *I* ask *Imogene* for anything? Let me tell you, Ernesto, I got her permission long ago. She isn't of any consequence in my plans and never will be. She is merely the vessel by which you came into this world. Your mother and sublime diva knows how things are to be. Now it's high time we went upstairs. Come along, my darlings. Everything will be well."

She laughed her joyous, abandoned laugh, and smiled sweetly at them. "Isn't it always so?"

Eighteen

David Atkins graduated from high school on a sultry June evening in the Selma High School stadium, the venue for such events unless rain forced the participants inside. It was surrounded by a tall brick wall, and dozens of crape myrtles had been planted around its sides. On the main playing field, a huge stage had been erected on which the graduates sat on risers that were kept in storage save for graduation exercises. A huge throng packed the spectator seats, impatient for the spectacle to begin.

The Colonel and Carlotta sat in reserved seats in the front row on thick cushions Carlotta had brought along. Their blank expressions conveyed boredom, although Carlotta had caught a glimpse of Imogene sitting a few rows back. *Poor dear probably wonders why we get places up front*, she thought. *If she only knew where Ernesto will be headed from here.* She stole another glance and saw Imogene applauding with the others as each graduate came forth to receive their diplomas from the school principal, to the tune of the grand march from *Aida.*

Carlotta strummed her fingertips on her knees. "My God! If the divine Verdi could only hear his music played by that wretched upright piano, on and on, endlessly repeated, he would have been as appalled as I am. I would love to see the *Maestro* rise from the grave to slap that silly girl from her bench." She looked around, oblivious to stares from the local women. And why not? She was married to the richest man in town, lived in the grandest mansion ever built in Selma. A smile was frozen on her face as she scanned the crowd and recognized the parents of many of her students. How she despised them. Even their money meant nothing to her. *God, when is Ernesto going to be called, so we can get the hell out of here away from these provincial people?*

Without warning "David Atkins" was called, and a young man stepped from the rows of graduates on the stage. The Colonel grasped Carlotta's hand excitedly. "Darling, there he is. Wow, look at our boy! Isn't he the handsomest man you ever saw?" He applauded and whistled loudly. "Damn, they aren't even doing this in alphabetical order!"

Carlotta frowned and whispered, "My dear, if you are speaking of our Ernesto, yes, I see him there. I do *not* recognize him by any other name. However, may this be the last time we hear him spoken of by any name except Ernesto Vasselli. I know how close you are to him, my darling, but please contain your enthusiasm in quiet dignity." She openly turned a contemptuous gaze at several people who appeared to be craning their necks to hear what she was saying. "We don't want to be seen as stooping to the level of these common people. Ah, well, he has returned to his seat. There are another two hundred names to call, and I am not sitting through all that. Can you believe they had the nerve to ask him to sing? I killed that quickly enough. He is no longer to sing for gratis again. The principal had the temerity to act offended with me when I refused. If only his and Imogene's types had any conception of his worth. Such things are beyond their simple minds. I will see you and our son at home later." She swept up the stairs as other names were called. As she passed Imogene, who smiled, she flung a withering look in her direction.

* * *

The Colonel remained seated. Imogene went down to the front row and timidly approached him. "Good evening, Colonel. If Madame isn't coming back, may I talk with you?"

Startled, he looked up at her, and motioned for her to sit. "What did you wish to discuss with me, Mrs. Atkins, that my wife couldn't hear as well?"

Smiling, yet not reassured by his formal tone, she continued, "Well, it's about David. You know he is the last of my children to graduate from Selma High. It's like an era ending for me. I haven't heard from him lately. I just wanted to know how he's doing, if he's being a good boy and doing as you and Madame have asked him." Without waiting for a reply, she rushed on, "He is strong, and he should be helping you with any chores that may come up at your estate."

Stirring impatiently in his seat, he looked coldly towards her. "Mrs. Atkins, he is doing fine. You know he is preparing for the concert tour. He has little time for small talk with anyone, let alone you. As for any work around my estate, that's what we have servants for. We don't consider David to be required to earn his keep. I know that just like everyone in this closed-minded community that you are curious as to what goes on behind our doors, but it's simply two adults with a young man to watch over."

Barely hiding his resentment of her intrusion he said, "Now if you don't mind, I see one of the student speakers is coming to the platform. I should like very much to hear what she has to say." He turned away from her, directing his attention to the stage.

"I'm so sorry if I bothered you. It won't happen again. Thank you for your time." She returned to her seat with downcast eyes, ignoring the curious stares being directed towards her.

* * *

Carlotta passed the banners on the brick walls advertising the spectacle taking place inside en route to the house, six blocks away. *Strange how in this town you can take long walks, being anywhere in a short while as their narrow lives continue their boring course. At least we are out from the downtown business area. If I have to look at these dress shops one more time I'll scream.*

She thought back to the last time she had walked by the most popular dress shop in town, *Frocks by Frances. My God, what poor taste the women here have. I wouldn't be caught dead in that tacky polka-dot horror they've featured so prominently. People in Italy would laugh these idiots out of town if they could see this crap.* Thinking of her husband, she found herself moved to pity. *My poor darling is trapped by his past in this place. Certain things are expected and looked for by these miserable peasants. It's all right though. I love him, or I wouldn't have agreed to come to this foreign country that's so vast, where everything that means anything musically can only be found in New York, Chicago, or San Francisco. Ah, heavens, how things change, but Ernesto's star will eclipse them all. He, The Colonel and my music . . . there is nothing else. I can put up with the stares I get when I go about in my Valentino dresses. It only widens the difference between these people and the gulf that will forever exist between us. The days are coming when my child will be free of these people and this country. He will be in the land of my fathers, where opera is to us like breathing is to these people. Ernesto will be presented in Italy as a true Italian; nothing else will do. May he forget his origins with the identity of Ernesto he will carry all the rest of his career.*

She came to the back of the house. Somewhere in the darkness she heard far-off barking of dogs. She came up the back stairs and went through the door into the hall of the original house. She stopped for an instant as she thought of Viola and the ghosts of the past, omnipresent always. Absently, she flipped on the lights, showering bright beams from the French chandeliers across the front rooms. She walked along the darkly stained oak floor to the front door and turned on the outside lights.

My men will be along shortly, and then tomorrow we leave to begin the week of rehearsals in Montgomery. My contacts through the old society women have resulted in brisk ticket sales. Nice to know my name carries weight even in this part of the world. God, how I hate the front I have to put up with such people. She looked back at the grand staircase where on the flanking walls the portraits of the Garcia sisters in full stage costumes gazed down from their gilt frames. Ernesto was at the brink of a brilliant career, in full possession of the genius to continue the Garcia method.

She walked into the music room, sat at her Steinway and began to play a haunting Chopin nocturne. Its timeless beauty filled the silent house. She broke off, glanced up at the portrait of Madame Blanche over the fireplace. She smiled and said out loud, "All for art, my diva. You have witnessed the birth of genius in my adored child. Your method is eternal and your memory ever green." She poured a glass of Madeira from the wine cabinet's shimmering crystal decanter, then returned to the piano and picked up the score of Bellini's *Beatrice Di Tenda.* Turning the pages to the final scene, her voice rang out as in days of old. "*Ah, la morte che a me apressa, e trionfo e non e pena!*" She continued to the end, finishing with a ringing high C. She held the vocal score of the opera to her heart. *My Bellini, you comfort me. These words and your music, ah, the death that awaits me is triumph, not pain. Truly the past is mine, and I remember everything. Carlotta, you still have the notes, even if you are fifty-five.* She heard The Colonel's Buick in the driveway and rushed back through the hall and kitchen to greet her two men.

Nineteen

A difficult week of strenuous rehearsals began the following Monday morning in Montgomery. Carlotta introduced Ernesto to the conductor and other members of the orchestra with a speech extolling his talent. "My kinsman from Como in the Italian Alps has been with me for some time, gentlemen. I have arranged this tour in order to introduce him to the public hereabouts to give him the opportunity of being heard by people who matter. He has studied with me these past few months. We need the full cooperation of each of you to guarantee the success of this enterprise." She paused to allow her words to sink in. She smiled coyly at all of them and said, "Of course all of you are being *amply* rewarded for your endeavors. May I suggest, as you Americans are so fond of saying, *let's get with it!*"

She walked to the rear of the hall to listen to the first run-through of the arias she had selected. She very much acted the *Prima Donna Assoluta* that she was with these people, but she had done it so gently that they never realized that they were nothing more than hired help. She looked on them as only a step above the other lesser mortals in her galaxy, to be used for her purposes and then discarded.

"Gentlemen, we will have two daily sessions, beginning today, through this week," said the conductor. As always, Ernesto sang from memory. His voice bounced off the walls easily, seemingly effortlessly. He seemed slightly older than his seventeen years. With his dark brown eyes and dark hair, he looked the part: *Italian.* Over and over the pieces were rehearsed till the little niceties of balance, dynamics, and a thousand other details were meticulously worked out. Only when Carlotta nodded her approval did they proceed to the next aria.

At the break of the morning sessions, Carlotta would mysteriously whisk off her protégé for private consultations. She carefully guarded him from associating with the players, keeping up the distance between the artist and the hired help. As always, they spoke only in Italian. He spoke it as she now, and any trace of his true origins had been banished. In place of his former persona stood her creation, soon to be known to the world. Carlotta's own celebrity assured that he would be received with respect, dignity and awe. But he was no Trilby, and she definitely could not be called a Svengalli, the name of the magician who transformed an ordinary girl into an automaton capable of feats of singing that heretofore would have been deemed impossible.

She had traveled to all the cities on the tour in advance, courting the presidents of the Ladies' association for the preservation of art and culture. Articles appeared about Ernesto in each scheduled city on his tour. The dowagers of nothing, as Carlotta called them, would guarantee sold-out houses with reviews in all the newspapers. The first concert was to take place in Richmond.

Carlotta laughed to herself in pleasure at her subterfuge. Not one of the old ladies mentioned the name of the boy soprano she had presented to them only a few years earlier. People lived in the present, not the past.

The program was to be the same, with slight modifications, mainly in the encores, in each city they visited. The night before the first concert she showed Ernesto the program, bordered in gold coloring with raised letters for each selection to be presented. "Now, my darling, of course you know the order you are to sing, but pay careful attention to the printing of the programs. Be careful to recognize the quality of the paper, the names of the sponsoring organizations, and their lady sponsors. You will need to remember these names to thank them afterwards at the receptions. Be sparing in giving autographs, and never allow questions as to your private life. Let these imbeciles wallow in their own sense of importance, at least until we leave town for the next city." In their suite at the Excelsior Hotel, they relished lavish attention by the staff as they sat together over a light breakfast. Flower arrangements were scattered about on all the tables, and deeply colored crimson velvet curtains hung on the windows.

"Get used to this, Ernesto. You must always travel first class. People expect it, and as artists it is our due. It will be somewhat different in Italy. There, people are a lot more attuned to little details and are sometimes boringly persistent in their efforts to shine in the reflected glory of an opera star. But keep your distance. Only deal with the people who are important, and never grovel, even to impresarios or agents. After all, my child, you are the star. Thus always you will be adored, but most of all, respected." She laughed and sipped her coffee, disdaining the little biscuits and preserves. "We must eat sparingly to keep our figures. One must look good both on stage and off. Never be casual or vulgar."

Ernesto watched her closely, absorbing each *mot* of wisdom and filing it away in his mind as if it were a holy script. "Yes, Madame, it will always be as you wish. I won't let you down. I miss our house though . . . and my Colonel," he said in a loving tone of voice. "I hope he can join us somewhere along the tour."

Carlotta held Ernesto's hand tightly. "That's *our* Colonel, my sweet. After all, he is my husband, and we look on ourselves as both mother and father to you." She elongated a pause to measure his reaction, then continued, "Now here again is the program. Let's look at it together. On the cover, it says, *Ernesto Vasselli: Lyric Tenor.* The date and city follow and the ladies' clubs that are our benefactors. Ah, now to the selections on the next page, they are as listed in the order to be sung after the overtures."

Semiramide: Overture Rossini
Vincenzo Bellini 1801-1835
I Puritani: A te o cara, amor talora
La Sonnambula: Ah Perche non posso odiarti
Gaetano Donizetti 1797-1848
La Favorita: Una vergine, e un angiol di dio
Spirto gentil, ne' sogni miei
L'Elisir d'Amore: Una furtiva lagrima
Don Pasquale: Povero Ernesto! Cerchero lontana terra. E se fia che ad altro ogetto
Intermission
La Gazza Ladra: Overture Rossini

Gioacchino Rossini 1792-1868
Il Barbiere di Siviglia: Ecco ridente in cielo
L'Italiana in Algeri: Lanquir per una bella. Contenta quest'alma
La Donna Del Lago: D'ogni piu sacro impegno
Zelmira: Terra amica, ove respira
Semiramide: La speranza, piu soave

"Now, how impressive is this, my angel?" she beamed. "All of these arias, sung from memory, for all those hog-faced matriarchs. They aren't going to know what hit them. I have gleaned some of these, as you know, from the dust they've sat in for more than a hundred years in the dusty old Ricordi archives in Milan, and the Naples conservatory of music in Naples. One very interesting thing that people will note is that many of these selections have never been heard here in the United States. They are all so beautiful and have only waited to be rescued from obscurity by genius, which we have in spades. Don't you agree?"

Ernesto walked to the windows overlooking the Confederate monuments on the avenue below. "You know, Madame, I owe everything to you. You have rescued and raised me from that horrible place I lived in as a child. You have brought beauty, peace, and music to my life, made me realize the full potential of what can come from dedicated study." He burst into tears and rushed to embrace her, falling down on his knees and grasping her closely. "My debt to you is immeasurable. How can I ever make you understand how grateful I am?"

"Oh, my own dearest," she murmured, "these tears say all to me of what dwells in your heart. It only took me a few moments as we sang through your scales that first time to know that in you I had found the crowning glory of all my own struggles." She looked at him admiringly. "What a student you have been, absorbing everything like a sponge. At times I felt my very soul being drawn out of me by what we have done together. You are to me the reincarnation of Maria Felicita Garcia-Malibran. Her manner of never to be forgotten technique lives again for the entire world to see in you." Touching his face tenderly, she exclaimed, "People will marvel at the resemblance as well, and will note the same piercing dark eyes and heavy eyebrows, the double row of thick eyelashes that made the diva unique and apart with her unforgettable artistry. No thanks are necessary my child, your voice only is my victory."

He laid his head on her lap, lost in thoughts of what the future would bring. She stirred, and running her hand through his thick hair, disengaged herself from his embrace, gently tweaking his chin and kissing his forehead. "All right, enough of emotion. Save it for the stage. Never let it overwhelm your judgment. The temptations will come. You are so young and will be exposed to so much. I won't be there to protect you. You'll have to call on your own reserves to carry you through, but you'll succeed, there is no doubt at all in my mind. Now go along with you and wash your face, get dressed and we'll go for a long walk before it gets too hot." He kissed her, Italian-style, on both cheeks and went to his room. She followed him with a look of studied admiration. *Check it, Carlotta. You will have to let him go soon.*

The next evening found the hall thronged with glittering Richmond society. Carlotta had been dutifully informed by their hostess that the world's next great star was to perform, thus was the interest and curiosity of those who assembled. Chandeliers glittered above the audience, and gold and red accents on the walls gleamed brightly to the delight of the onlookers. The matrons and their circles of friends gossiped in their seats, as every couple's arrival drew comments about beautiful gowns and hairstyles. The ladies, and their reluctant husbands, admired and commented on the beautiful programs with the green-silk page markers. They all pretended, with ill-disguised arrogance, that they knew *exactly* the operas from which the selections had been lifted. Such people amused Carlotta, who had faced innumerable times such ignorance.

With the raising of the chandeliers, and lowering of the lights, the crowd grew quiet and attentive. The massive red curtains parted to reveal the orchestra. The gaunt concertmaster strode onstage from the wings. Lifting his violin, he proceeded to tune the orchestra.

In the wings Carlotta and Ernesto stood, awaiting the signal for him to go on stage. He felt doubly handsome and masculine as he stood in the formal tuxedo that Carlotta had ordered from Italy and had altered in the continental style which outlined his athletic carriage to full advantage. Carlotta was beautiful in a strapless red-sequined gown accentuated by a glittering diamond and ruby brooch at the waist. Sparkling diamonds and rubies, which blazed in the light from the stage, adorned her neck and ears. The Colonel had given them to her after they had come back from rehearsals in Montgomery. He had reclaimed them from her purchaser and insisted she accept them as a token of his love and admiration that she would have made such a sacrifice for their Ernesto. As the concertmaster onstage sat, the conductor signaled Ernesto to follow him onstage. Carlotta embraced him, crying out, *"En Bocca al Lupo!"*

Go into the wolf's mouth, thought Ernesto as he remembered the age-old words spoken by Italians before performances for good luck. He kissed her on both cheeks and followed the conductor out onto the stage to the greeting of thunderous cheers.

The conductor bounded up onto the podium; Ernesto took his place stage left. As the prelude to the first aria sounded, Ernesto gazed out into the audience, smiling. Calmly he began to sing the immortal melody, *A te o cara, Amor Talora* from Bellini's divine opera, *I Puritani.* At its conclusion, the spectators erupted into a hurricane of applause. The old ladies looked back and forth at their cronies, nodding approval. The concert continued, each piece being received in raptures of delight bordering on hero worship. Ernesto sang each aria with limpid tone and strict adherence to every nuance that he and Madame had worked out to perfection. The beauty of his singing held the hearers in the palm of his hand. At the conclusion of the spectacle, he bowed deeply and left the stage to be grabbed and kissed by Carlotta. Five curtain calls followed. At long last, he came back out and stood beside the conductor.

A hush fell as he spoke, in complete mastery of the accented English spoken by Carlotta, "Ladies and gentlemen, it is my great pleasure now to sing for you *Ah Mes amis, quel jour de fete, a mon ame quel destin, Tonio's aria* from *La Fille Du Regiment* by Gaetano Donizetti." He nodded to the conductor, and sang the aria with its nine high C's. The reaction from the audience was electric. Cheers and enthusiastic "bravos" rang out from all corners of the house.

So great was her excitement that the president of the Ladies' society threw a magnificent wreath of white roses at Ernesto's feet, nearly falling into the orchestra pit as she did so. He picked up the flowers and pulled individual roses from the wreath. He presented one rose to the conductor, one to the concertmaster, and saluted the orchestra members who beat their bows on their music stands in admiration. Some of the ladies, who joined their president at the footlights, also flung flowers. Some tore off their corsages and hurled them to the smiling star. He deeply bowed while scooping them up to his heart. Ernesto flashed a wide smile as he threw several of the floral offerings back to the ladies who were now gasping with delight. After several more bows he withdrew to the wings as the orchestra filed off stage.

Backstage, in his dressing room, he wiped his face with a towel and embraced his mentor.

"Darling, your accomplishment this evening was beyond my greatest expectations. Our Gods, the Garcia sisters, stand here with you now saying bravo with me. This night will live in memories of those old hags to the ends of their lives." She danced around the room in delight when a knock on the door called her back to reality.

The theater manager stood at the door as she opened it. "Signora, the audience has gone mad. They refuse to leave until Signor Vasselli returns to the stage. What shall we do?" He stood, wringing his hands in nervous misery, awaiting some response.

Ernesto and Carlotta exchanged a glance and a smile. She picked up a large book of music and looked directly at the poor man before them. "Why, then, Mr. Manager, we must give the public what they demand. We must return to the stage now. Is there a decent piano in tune anywhere in this place?"

"Oh, yes, Signora, we have the Steinway that was used last night. It is still in tune. We keep it always in readiness."

"Well then, my good man, we will go back to the stage. At my indication, be prepared to have it rolled out. Come along dear, let us go."

As Ernesto came back onstage with Carlotta on his arm, the audience stamped their feet in a fever pitch of excitement. The only empty seats were the result of those who crowded down to the front of the auditorium. Proudly, she advanced to the footlights with him; clutching the music. A tremendous roar rose as the crowd caught sight of her. Fresh waves of flowers sailed across the footlights as they both stood, holding hands and nodding their approval to the worshipers. When it seemed as though they would never be allowed to continue, Carlotta raised her hand towards the wings and the grand piano was rolled out. Only then did the mob settle down and return to their seats.

Carlotta strode resolutely to the instrument, opened the book to reveal sheets of music that she placed on the music stand. She again raised her hand, signaling for silence and said, "For his *final* number Signor Vasselli will sing for you *Lo Spazzacamino* by Verdi. It is an old concert aria about a chimney sweeper's passion for his profession. We hope you will enjoy it." She sat down at the piano, beginning the brisk, bouncing introduction.

Ernesto began the song, which consisted of three sections with the melody being repeated with increasingly difficult variations. The audience listened with attention as Ernesto sang out a brilliant, enormous, high D natural in the final flourish. Screams of joy descended on both artists, who bowed deeply and blew kisses and finally were allowed to depart as the curtains closed.

The spectacle continued in the weeks ahead in each of the cities on the tour. Great ovations and receptions followed each performance. With the public enraptured by the glorious voice that rained out in youthful ardor, both men and women looked on him with admiration and interest.

Carlotta, keenly aware of a growing sensuality in her young man, carefully fulfilled her role as mentor, chaperone, and guardian. Her natural reserve prevented her from frankly talking with him about such delicate matters. She knew The Colonel had discussed such things with him, and she was content to leave it there.

The Colonel joined them at Montgomery for the final concert. He and Ernesto went for a long walk early on the morning of his final appearance, each of them lost in his own private thoughts. A beautiful park, shaded by towering trees came upon them and under the great cluster of oaks, The Colonel gestured for him to sit.

"My sweet boy, how has it been with you these last few weeks?" He reached out to the young man with both hands, caressing his face. "I'm sorry I couldn't have joined you earlier, but I thought it best for Carlotta to have her way with things. We will be returning to Selma after the concert tonight and you'll finally be able to sleep in your own bed. It will be so good to have you home again in our own surroundings."

"Colonel, I have grown tired of it. All this traveling, the strange people, the hotels, it's just too much. I love singing. It's not that part that I dislike, but rather the artificial politeness of the people with whom I've had to deal. Madame is so good and shields me from too much involvement." He coyly said, not looking at The Colonel, "It seems though at times that some of the people who want to be close to me seem just waiting to devour me." He paused. "I've seen interesting people, too, some I would have liked to be alone with, but I've held myself aloof. I know I'm only seventeen, but I don't know how to deal with the desires that bubble up from being so sexually aware." He looked back at The Colonel. "It frightens me at times."

He seductively reclined, his back resting against one of the massive oaks.

The Colonel smiled and nonchalantly offered, "I guess you would think what you just said would make me jealous, but I know other men will follow me in your arms. It's only natural." He could tell by the love on Ernesto's face that his lackadaisical attitude struck a chord in him. It was proof that Ernesto was still his, for now. He thoughtfully continued, "I know what it is to be young, believe it or not. In my day in Selma as a young man, things were very different. My parents were elderly. After their deaths, though I was still only twenty-five, I found myself alone and responsible for taking charge of their businesses. I never wanted to be a lawyer like my father and his brother, Judge Kelly, but it was expected. Even though I was a bit older than you are now, I was at least free and responsible for only myself. Going to law school made sense. I graduated from Auburn and passed the bar exam, but my heart wasn't in it. I joined the Marines before the Great War began. For the first time I was away from Alabama. Talk about an education."

He shifted to his side, sliding an arm around Ernesto's waist. Ernesto smiled. The Colonel's free hand touched the young man's chest, his thumb absently tweaking nipples beneath the thin fabric of the shirt. He looked around cautiously. Sighing deeply, he continued. "I knew I was different. Attracted to both men and women, but I knew it was my duty to marry, to produce an heir to continue the unbroken line of male descendants."

"I was in the fourteenth generation of Kellys from the original ancestor who came from England in 1630. I saw things in Europe never dreamed of back in my old home town. Sexual freedom was the norm even in those days. People could care less what you did in private, only that you be discreet. I met Carlotta in the spring of 1945 after V.E. day. It was in Milan; the place had been bombed by the allies. The government there had fallen. Mussolini was on the run. I found Carlotta, sitting in a seat in the great opera house, *La Scala.* Though the walls were intact, the ceiling had caved in. She sat there weeping, covered in dust, with her long blond hair falling on her shoulders. I never understood till that moment what people there had been through. She seemed grateful for even the smallest kindness. We sat there together, talking for hours. She was utterly alone, and though an opera singer, had not been able to practice her craft for some time. No performances were being given. She was so thin and was living only through the kindness of strangers. She spent her days in the ruins of the opera house, rescuing old manuscripts and scores she found there; carefully preserving them till the provisional government took control.

"We fell in love, married soon after. I convinced her to come back here with me. I never regretted it. I loved her then as now. We hoped for children and I was so happy when she became pregnant. It was not to be, however; she miscarried after three months. We were both sad. I gave up on the hoped-for son. She was enough for me. We opened up the house and she took in students. It was wonderful to watch her return to life. Her old self asserted itself quickly once fear was put to rest. The rest is history. And then you came into our world. We loved you; you came to be with us. Watching you grow up has been a joy to me. Seeing your body change into a man's, being able to make love with you, knowing I made you happy has meant everything to me."

Ernesto drew down his head and kissed him long and tenderly. "I love you, Colonel. You have been everything to me too, Madame, our home, our music. You have made me whole again, given me hope and love where before there was only emptiness. Feeling you close beside me has given me the courage to strive for all that is beautiful in life. I hope it will go on forever." He looked over his thick eyelashes into The Colonel's eyes. "I'd like to make love with you right now."

The older man drew up, glancing anxiously around. "Not here. Certainly not now. Time enough for all that at home. I understand Imogene is coming tonight, have you heard?"

"Madame mentioned something about it. It doesn't matter really. My place is with you. I respect my mother, but it's different now. She was never demonstrative like you and Madame. I'm content to let things be as they are."

"Yeah, well that's fine, though you know things are going to change. Carlotta just has so many irons in the fire for you, and to have a career you will have to leave here. You have changed. You are so like her that I could almost imagine you were her child. You think like her. You both live in an artistic, creative frame of mind every minute of the day. You will live long, my dear, but among others soon. Just promise that you won't forget me and what we have shared."

"That would be impossible. No matter what happens, my Colonel, I'll love you, just as I do now, until I die. We have to get back now. I need to rest before tonight and you are very hard to resist in this moment. Let's go."

They walked back toward the clearing hand-in-hand, reluctantly letting go as people came into view. A cool chill came over Ernesto as though he had held The Colonel's hand for the last time.

The evening's concert brought everything full circle. Imogene came, wearing another of Carlotta's cast-off gowns. They saw her briefly after the program at the reception in the hotel. She was only in her early forties, her figure as trim as a young girl's, her hair the same dark shade of auburn as Ernesto's. He smiled and held out his hand to offer her a glass of wine. "How is it with you, Imogene?" he asked.

Her face wrinkled at her son calling her by her name, but she suppressed any further reaction. "Things are well enough, I suppose. I'm still at the air force base. I have my bridge and church activities, so I stay busy. I suppose you and Madame and The Colonel will be driving on home in a little while?"

"Yes, he will be driving us down as soon as we can disengage ourselves from the old dowagers." He looked at her and for a fleeting second wondered how such a cold formality had come between them, then quickly pushed that thought aside. "It's been a long ordeal, but necessary for us to establish myself, which Madame says has been accomplished beautifully. I have no idea of what's to happen from here. I leave it with her."

"Yes, with her." She stiffened as Carlotta approached from across the room. "Well, keep in touch. Your brothers send their love to you."

He looked at her and frowned. "My brothers, what part of my life do they play now? Nothing that I can see. I could care less. Now if you'll excuse me, here is Madame."

"Hello, Imogene!" exclaimed Carlotta as she put her arms around Ernesto. "How nice of you to come to our Ernesto's concert, my dear. Come along, my child. Mrs. Irving, our hostess, has been dying to speak to you before we leave." She turned to Imogene. "We must be kind with such people. You never know how useful they might prove in the future." She grasped Ernesto's hand. In unison, they turned their backs on Imogene, and were gone towards the cackling old dowager.

* * *

Imogene, alone and utterly rejected, watched them wind their way through the crowd. *He had the nerve to call me Imogene in the same tone she uses. He didn't even say goodbye, kiss my ass, or thank you for coming. That bitch called my David, "Our Ernesto!" Took his hand and said, "Come along, my child." Both of them had me here and stepped on my heart. I have never been so hurt and humiliated in my life. But they'll never know it. No one will. It's time for me to go back home to dwell in my own loneliness. He'll be fine. He has his Madame.* No one in that throng was aware of who she was. She ran her hands over Carlotta's hand-me-down cobalt blue sequined gown she had worn especially for him. She studied her refection in a gilt mirror. She raised her hand, touching the glittering sapphires at her neck, ears, hands, as well as wrists. *No one here knows me or that any of these things had ever been hers.* She resisted a sudden impulse to tear the gems off, find Carlotta, and throw them in her face, but no . . . as a southern belle she would not have others see her behave in such a manner. Grief was something a southern lady did not reveal in public. To the curious stares of the passersby, she was just another not-so-young matron among all the others who shone in the light of the ballroom. She smiled bitterly at no one in particular, turned and walked out of the room, her head held high.

Twenty

By mid-September Carlotta started receiving, almost daily, letters and documents from the Venetian theater, *La Fenice.* She thoughtfully put her latest letter into her desk. *I know he is ready for this. I already have an Italian passport for him, as well as the birth certificate that Barbarina sent from Como. Ernesto has his identity now. The entire world will think he was born there and was left at the children's home after his parents' untimely deaths. His father, Enrico Vasselli, was a distant cousin of mine; his mother, Amalia Dolci, an only child, whose entire family died in an air raid in Ancona. There will be no way any of this can be traced. The Colonel and I are identified as guardians from 1947 forward. It's now time to bring Ernesto in on this. He must play his part. Only Barbarina knows the truth and I have bought her silence for all time. And now here is my letter from the desperate Intendant of the Fenice. The time is now.* Resolutely she glanced at the portrait of Madame Blanche and went out into the great hall. She knew Ernesto and The Colonel would be back soon from their boating trip on the nearby Alabama river. They had been gone since early morning. She paced back and forth in the kitchen, unable to relax. *Here I am ready to deal with this and they are still gone.*

She called her travel agent. "Good afternoon, Mr. Blackwell. Yes, this is Carlotta Vasselli. Is everything ready with my reservations? The hotel and ground transportation as well? Good. What's that? An interpreter? Oh, do I need that for understanding the southern dialect you people speak? If you mean when we get to Italy, may I remind you that we are *Italians?* We will have no trouble getting around anywhere in our own country. That's quite all right, Mr. Blackwell. I understand. After all, you have dealt with me many times in the past, and I do pay, do I not? Yes, we have our passports and they are current and in order. Yes, I am aware of all requirements and I don't need any reminders of what I'm responsible for. I am not one of your Selma ladies that you book trips to the Holy Land for. Well then, I expect that the tickets and everything else will be ready when I arrive at your office? For God's sake, Mr. Blackwell, of course I mean today. I will be there in thirty minutes!"

She slammed the receiver down so hard it cracked in two. *If I live to be one hundred years old I will never get used to dealing with idiots. Who the hell do they think they're talking to? This is the last damn time I'll put up with these fools.* She looked at the broken receiver beside the phone. In a fury, she jerked the phone loose from the wall and flung the pieces into the hall. She grabbed her handbag, headed out through the kitchen, slamming the door behind her so hard that she didn't notice the pane of glass that fell, shattering on the steps.

Arriving a few minutes later, The Colonel, noticing Carlotta's car was gone, exclaimed, "Now where can she have gone?" As he and Ernesto approached the back porch he saw the broken glass. "My God, what's going on here?"

"Colonel, look, the door is open too. The door doesn't seem to have been tampered with, but would she have left without locking it? Let's look around and see if anything has been stolen." They went from room to room; everything seemed fine. "Colonel, look here by the door. The phone from the hall is there in pieces!"

The Colonel pushed him aside, looking at the broken receiver. "It's a clean break. But who ripped it out of the wall? This is strange." Walking quickly into the library, he picked up the phone on his desk. "Well this one is working." Walking to the front door he checked the lock. "It's bolted as always. Come on, boy, we'll go back to the kitchen and wait. If she isn't back here in thirty minutes I'm calling the police. She wouldn't have just left like this without leaving a note. Nothing has been started for dinner either. It's just not like her to do this. Make us some coffee and let's try to remain calm. There has to be an explanation, and it had better be a good one."

Ernesto did as he was told. He knew the man loved her, but he had never seen him so close to losing control. He, too, felt panic. It was indeed not like her. He poured them both steaming cups; they sat in silence, waiting.

As he grew calmer, The Colonel looked across the table at the young man. Seeing his downcast eyes and stricken look, his heart softened. The older man reached across the table and brushed back locks of wet, dark hair from Ernesto's face. As Ernesto looked back at him, his eyes glistening with tears, he remembered the way his face looked all those years ago that night when he came to them and fainted in his arms. He took both of the boy's hands in his own. "Ernesto, you must realize that not everything revolves around you. There are three of us living here. She pays more attention to you than to me, but do I ever say anything? No, and it's because I love both of you so much. Love isn't selfish, my child. You and I have both betrayed her, over and over again. Even today when we made love in the cabin cruiser in the old secluded cove I went to when I was a boy, we betrayed her. We have both spoiled you, but you're going to find that others aren't going to do the same always. You can't always have your own way, totally disregarding our feelings. It's not fair to me; it's not fair to her. Does this make sense to you?"

Ernesto jerked his hands away, rising with indignation as he felt the hot blood rise in his face. Flushed with anger he exclaimed, "Betrayal? How do you have the nerve to talk to me of betrayal? Wasn't I still a child the first time you came into my bed and fucked me? Wasn't I a child when you said it was okay because you loved me? I thought Tony loved me, too. I thought his friends all liked me also. That terrible night when they raped me, I thought I had asked for it. He told me it was okay because we were brothers. Do you remember how horrified you were when you saw my face? Yet upstairs in the bathroom that night, you had me standing there naked. You were cleaning me up, yes. The blood washed away, but I remember how your fingers probed my ass that night and how you lifted me, wrapped in a towel, and held me in your arms. Do you remember, as I do, the raging erection you had pushed against me as you held me? I was ten years old, but you wanted me. Don't talk to me of betrayal, you hypocrite! Aren't I still a couple of months away from officially being an adult? Wasn't I still a minor today when you sucked my dick and fucked me repeatedly? Who is the adult here, Colonel?"

The Colonel rose and walked to where Ernesto stood. "Why you ungrateful little asshole, who do you think you're talking to? Don't throw this shit in my face. You know whatever has passed between us was real love. Maybe I have been wrong all these years. I just wanted you to know that love between two men can be something beautiful. You know it's not the same as what Tony and his friends did." He grasped the boy by his shoulders. "You never pushed me away. I never forced you into having sex with me."

Ernesto shook off the man's hands. Hot tears scalded down his cheeks. "I didn't think I had a choice. I wanted you to be happy. I wanted you to know how grateful I was for everything you and Madame had done for me. But I was a child still. You were the adult. You betrayed your wife; I just played along because I was afraid you wouldn't love me anymore, that you wouldn't let her be my mother. Oh don't look so sad now. I'm not going to betray you or expose you. This has been wrong and it has to stop here, today, now. Remember how it felt when you pumped into me today, because it will never happen again."

"What in the name of God is going on here?" Carlotta's appearance stunned both of them. "I could hear you both shouting at each other all the way outside. I'm going to forget some of what I heard because I don't want to know. So don't either of you open your mouths to explain anything. I don't want to hear it."

The Colonel said, "Carlotta, we've both been so worried. What happened here? The broken windowpane, the broken phone in the hallway, the open back door, we didn't know what to think had happened to you."

"Oh, you're so concerned that you didn't even come and look for me instead of standing in here shouting at each other? Shame on both of you. The phone is broken because a fool I was talking to irritated me. I ripped it out of the wall and slung it across the hall because I was furious, okay? I've been out attending to important business which concerns us all. Whatever you were fighting about, forget it. Who cares about a broken window pane, Colonel? Just call the Selma Glass Company and have them send someone over here to fix it."

"Madame, I'm sorry," said Ernesto. "It was nothing. We were just having a difference of opinion." His chin trembled. He put his hand over his mouth and with the other pushed his hair out of his eyes. He didn't dare to raise his eyes to hers. He had no way of knowing just how much she had heard.

She came nearer and looked at him. "Why is your hair so wet? Have you two been swimming in the river again? You know how filthy it is, how horrible to go about with wet hair in the wind? You know better, Ernesto. And you too, Colonel!"

"Darling, we were just having a nice time. Ernesto hasn't recovered completely from the tour. You were going to be busy today with the students so we just decided to have a man's day out to let you have the house to yourself."

"Colonel, I want you to go out and get us something for dinner. I don't care what it is. Hell, even that horrendous barbeque you love." She waved her hands impatiently in the air. "I need to talk seriously to Ernesto anyway, so away with you now." He came close to give her a hug. "No, there will be none of that nonsense for now."

"Oh, all right. I'll be back in thirty minutes. Do you want me to pick up some sweet tea too? I know you won't drink it, but our boy here loves it." She shot him a look full of contempt. He grabbed his keys off the table and headed for the back door. "I'll be back in thirty minutes."

"Darling, make it an hour won't you? And do bring the boy his tea and something like a big salad of some kind if the lettuce is fresh."

"Now my little man, I'm not asking for details, but believe this, I'm not a naive fool. I'm aware of everything that goes on in this house. We European women are a lot more in touch with reality than these southern magnolias that you are used to dealing with. I'm not even going into the deception that the two of you practice on me daily, because I don't care. Nothing matters to me except the future, *your* future. Don't even think of trying to explain anything to me. I have seen and heard it all before. Now come with me to the music room. I have something important to say to you."

Ernesto groaned inwardly as he saw music strewn all about the room, knowing he should have straightened up earlier. He did so now, but she was so deep in thought that she hardly noticed. He knew how she hated disorder and didn't want her to be irritated with him more than she was already.

She threw the papers she was carrying onto the piano and went to her desk. She unlocked the drawer and pulled out several documents which she tossed onto the pile of papers. She turned and faced him, both of them appearing nervous.

Ernesto turned and went to the armoire to pour her a glass of her Madeira. "You look like you are ready for this, Madame," he whispered, as he brought the tray back to where she stood.

"Pour yourself one as well my dear. You're going to need it when you hear what I have to say."

He thankfully ran back to the armoire as he struggled to control his nerves.

She lifted her glass. "Ernesto, how many times have I told you? Don't pour it so full that any of it might drop on our Persian carpets. Now sit down and listen to me." She waved him to the sofa in the center of the room and gathered up all her papers from the piano. She drew her ornate throne chair beside him, waving him back when he tried to help her. "Momentous things are afoot. You and I are leaving for Italy on Saturday. No, don't say anything. I will explain everything. I have been in contact with Carlo Meneghini, intendant of the *La Fenice* Theater in Venice. They are opening their season with a gala new production of *Semiramide.* The stars making their debuts there are to be the sensational Australian Diva, Jane Fremstead, along with the American contralto, Olivia Davis. The conductor? The incomparable *De Sabata.*

" But there is a problem. They have no tenor for the role of the Indian prince, *Idreno.* The singer they had engaged has withdrawn, because he has come to consider the part too small. Signor Meneghini and I both feel that it's because when he finally looked at his two arias that he was afraid of the extremely high and florid writing. There are to be six weeks of rehearsals, beginning the last week of October, with the first performance to go on stage December fourteenth. Carlo is beside himself with worry because Madame Fremstead has cast approval, and without her consent to the quality of the substitute, the entire production is in peril of being cancelled. I of course have convinced him that my kinsman from Como can save the situation. We have to be there for a week to acclimate ourselves to the air in that waterlogged city, and then you are to appear to formally audition before Madame Fremstead, her husband, James

Buffington, and, of course, Carlo. I have assured Carlo that I stake my artistic reputation, still warmly remembered, that the part holds no terrors for you. He had misgivings about your age and lack of experience, but they were put to rest when I sent him a tape of one of your recent concerts. So what do you think, my dearest?"

Ernesto sat, stunned. The *Fenice!* Never in his dreams could he have conceived of such an offer coming from a theater this important. He took a gulp of his Madeira and stammered, "Are you sure, Madame, that I can do this? These are great stars just making their debuts in this opera house. Madame Fremstead's fame has been growing steadily since her Covent Garden performances of *Lucia Di Lammermoor*. I don't think I could open my mouth in front of her. And Olivia Davis, she is singing everywhere these days. Her voice is huge. How can it be possible that Signor Meneghini could consider an unknown like me?" He voice trailed off in silence as he sat transfixed in wonderment.

"Ernesto, you can do this and you must." She patted him on the knee and continued, "All is ready, and you only have to have the confidence to use your gift as you've been taught for nearly ten years. Never fear, my sweet one; I will be with you to be sure your courage will not fail you. Carlo wants to put us up at his villa, but I have other plans. I will stay until after the third performance. Then I must leave you. But before I go, I will have arranged for you to be signed with an agency that I'll choose for you. We will have you set up with a rented, furnished apartment and transportation. Offers will come, of course, if you do your very best. I realize that being an unknown, however great your success may be, that you won't be engaged in leading parts at first, but you have an advantage. You are an Italian from Como in all the world's eyes.

"You will have opportunities that non-Italians would never be eligible for. Even Madame Fremstead, for all her qualifications, will never be engaged as a permanent member on any theater's roster in Italy. Just relax. As always, I have seen to every detail. All will be well. Trust me; your star will shine for the entire world to see." Rising, she took the bewildered young man's hand. "I hear The Colonel coming up the driveway. Let's see what he brought for our supper."

Ernesto was too dumbfounded to speak.

She threw back her head and laughed as she drew him out of the room and back to the kitchen.

The Colonel strode in, arms laden with containers of varying sizes. "I went to that new place, darling. You know, Carollo's. You said their veal *a la marsala* was near the equal of anything we could get in Italy. I mentioned your name and the chef was beside himself. He fixed up the antipastos just as he knows what would please you. Let's eat. I'm starving. Aren't you too, son?"

Throughout dinner, Carlotta observed them closely, watching their body language and trying to make sense of the scene she had witnessed earlier. She talked about the trip to Italy and Ernesto's big chance that had seemingly fallen out of nowhere into his lap.

"Carlotta, why does it have to be now? Surely we can keep the boy here for a few more weeks. I'm counting on him helping me put up the Halloween decorations."

Sipping her coffee, she looked at one and then the other. *Ah, Halloween decorations indeed, you traitor? How well I know what you really want. You plan to fuck him some more.* "Come along, Ernesto, we must pack. The Colonel will bring up the wardrobe trunks from the basement and I'll help you and advise just the things you'll need for Venice at this time of year."

The Colonel started for the cellar. "Hold up a second, Colonel," said Ernesto. "I'll come down to help you bring them upstairs. I know they're heavy and you're tired from all our activities. Madame, maybe he's right, we can wait another week before we leave."

A glance of disapproval from Carlotta silenced him. "What activities? You're both *so* tired? Ha! I can just imagine what the two of you have been doing. But whatever it is, it is finished. Do you hear me? Now come along, Ernesto. Do as you're told. My husband will see to the trunks." When they hesitated, she swept the glasses on the counter to the floor in a furious gesture of contempt. The two men stared at her. Broken shards of glass littered the floor. "Now, darling, after you bring up our trunks you may clean up this mess, too."

Ernesto stood frozen in terror. She seized his arm and drew him away toward the door to the hall. As they were about to go out, she stopped, glared at her speechless husband and exclaimed, "This is my show, and if the two of you know what's good for you, you'll keep your mouths shut and do as you're told. No one is ever going to hurt me again. I swore it to myself before you found me in the opera house that your people had bombed. Carlotta is going to come first in this house." She looked at Ernesto and said passionately, "Yes, and first with *my* husband as well. Don't fuck with me, boys."

Part Two: Ernesto

Twenty-One

"Bella Venezia!" (Beautiful Venice!) exclaimed Carlotta as their gondola headed out on the Grand Canal towards the Hotel Gondolphi. They had arrived at the train station just outside Venice that evening on their connection from Paris. They had first traveled to New York and then across to Paris, also known as the city of light. Carlotta had decided on a leisurely tour of Paris and the Loire valley sights to give Ernesto a view of what life was to be like in Europe. Now they were in Venice at last. "Ernesto, stop gaping at everything. You have to remember not to overreact to the things you see here. After all you are a native Italian now, born just to the north in Como. You can't act like you haven't been accustomed to these surroundings all your life. I have to admit, however, that coming across the lagoon it is so beautiful with the city laid out before us with thousands of beckoning lights."

Ernesto hardly heard her, engrossed as he was in the sights. The gondolier sang as he glided them on the short ride. The gondola was long and narrow, black like the silent water, drawn along by a steering mechanism, expertly in the control of the gondolier. Strange smells told him that the city was very old. The breeze into the lagoon from the Adriatic Sea swept over them, heightening his excitement. The smells were an overpowering amalgamation of mold mixed with the foam of salt water. At length the gondola reached the steps of the hotel, where the staff rushed out to help them disembark. After receiving his tip, the gondolier sped away into the night. He and Ernesto had exchanged smiles on the way and he hoped he would see this handsome Italian again.

"Come along, darling. We must get inside to our suite," Carlotta said as they walked into a magnificent lobby. Everywhere Ernesto looked, he saw luxury in a style so different from anything back home. Expanses of marble floors with towering ceilings stretched out before them as Carlotta led the way to the registration desk. She was in her element now at last. Beautifully dressed in the latest Parisian fashion, she drew stares from staff and guests alike as she swept along, nodding this way and that, carrying herself like the prima donna she was. After signing the register with a flourish, she led the way for the short elevator ride up to their suite. The bellman opened the double doors, handing the key to Ernesto. He quickly waved in two young men carrying the luggage and had them deposit the cases in their respective bedrooms.

"At last, my darling, we have arrived. Isn't this a wonderful suite of rooms?" Her glance fell on beautiful arrangements of flowers on all the tables. The main living room was wide and the furniture arranged tastefully for their comfort. Fruit and wine had been left for them. At the back, double doors led to a balcony overlooking the Grand Canal. Magnificent windows flanked either side with tapestries on the walls. "Ah, yes, this is the only way to travel my dear, first class only. Of course we can afford this since Carlo has taken care of this for us. Well he should, since I am about to save his performances of *Semiramide* for him. Come on, Ernesto, let's go out onto the balcony."

Before them the Grand Canal stretched out with the entrance to the lagoon far in the distance. "Look here, my boy, on the left is Saint Mark's square and the Doge's palace. Aren't they beautiful in the moonlight?"

"Madame, I am overwhelmed. Never in my imagination could I have been prepared for being here in Italy. It's like a dream." He smiled and looked out at the sight before him. Gondolas appeared and departed frequently. *What handsome men. What a wonderful place to be.* He wakened from his reverie as he became aware that she was watching him, smiling.

She gathered her shawl about her shoulders. "Let's go back in. The air is chilly."

He poured wine for both of them. "Well, darling, I can see you are somewhat overwhelmed with everything, but get used to it. As I've cautioned you, you are in your own country now. Our secret must be maintained. This is one reason I declined Carlo's invitation for us to stay at his villa outside the city. It simply would not do to be so soon under the microscope of the curious. I can't stand his wife anyway. She thinks she is so grand, brushing shoulders with the *Fenice* staff and acting as though her origins from a family of peddlers selling sausages in the streets wasn't something that was her life not so many years ago.

"Before the war, when I sang here and also at the *Teatro Malibran*, things were so different than today. People still love their opera, and I sang with so many great singers. Thank God though that at last the *Bel Canto* (beautiful singing) operas are enjoying resurgence and we can hear and see different works than that of the horrible Puccini. I always refused to sing that *verismo* music. It's horrible for the voice, and as I've said for years anyone can get away with it. It requires nothing like the Garcia technique. If you ever have to sing Puccini, confine yourself to *La Boheme.* It's the only one of his works that's worthy of any attention. After Maria Callas sang her unforgettable *Anna Bolena* and *Sonnambula* at *La Scala* the pattern for revivals of our kind of music began in earnest. With your voice, you should figure prominently in what is to come as the old operas are pulled down from the shelves and re-examined and prepared for performances. We have people like Madame Fremstead to thank, Ernesto. All the opera houses are vying for her services, and her interest in *Bel Canto* as well as that of her husband, James Buffington, will be opening opportunities for people like you. It won't come without a good deal of effort, however, as so few people have the proper techniques for these operas."

She sat back in the comfort of the sofa, sipping her wine, when the phone on the table beside her rang. A wide smile burst across her face. "Carlo! How wonderful of you to call. Yes, we have only just arrived and we are settling in here in our suite. Thank you so much for making the arrangements. Yes, the staff has taken care of us very well. I am so delighted to be here again. Ernesto? Oh yes, he is here with me. We plan to have a light supper here in our suite and then get to bed. It was a long train ride across the mountains, but we arrived a little earlier than we had anticipated. How is the production coming along? That's very nice to hear. We will be there Friday morning so Ernesto can sing for you and Madame Fremstead. 10 a.m.? That's fine. He will be ready. You are nervous? No need to be my dear, he will not let any of you down. Thank you also for arranging for a piano to be here for us. We need to unpack and then in the morning I'll take him through his paces. I did receive the score with the recommendations as to ornamentation that the *Maestro* has asked for. Ernesto knows his arias from memory and the opening trio as well. I will need to talk with the *Maestro* about the cadenzas. I have several ideas that I believe will be of interest in making these moments more beautiful for the audience.

"All right then, my dear, we will see you there on Friday. I need to do a bit of shopping and arrange to have some things sent back to the states. We have to get acclimated to this sea air. It is horrible, I know. I had nearly forgotten about the foul air here. It will be as you wish, Signor. Ciao." She hung up and looked across at Ernesto, who had followed her side of the conversation with apprehension.

"Madame, I'm nervous. I know my part is only the two arias and the trio and then brief lines in the two ensembles, but it all seems so surreal to me. I'm so glad you are here to guide me. I don't know what I will do though when you have to leave." *I'm homesick for The Colonel. He seemed so sad when he saw us off at the Atlanta airport when we left for New York. I wonder when I'll ever see him again.*

She waved her hands impatiently and smiled. "What are you daydreaming about, sweetheart? I can hardly wait till tomorrow when I can show you around. It's a bit of a bore to have to depend on gondolas to get around all the time, but we have no choice here. Other places will be a lot easier to get around. I also have to take you by the Sforza Agency to arrange for you to sign with them. Believe me; I'll make sure they don't railroad you on their percentages. You will have to learn to deal with them yourself when I'm gone, but they are the lifeblood of artists here. Unless you are a free lancer like only the biggest names, the agencies are a necessary evil. God, what a shop it can be!"

A soft knock came at the door. "That must be our supper! Do let them in, darling."

The waiters brought everything into the room and set the table for them. Carlotta nodded her approval at the new wine offered for her consideration. After tipping them handsomely, Ernesto closed the door and joined her at the table.

"Ah, they have all my favorite cheeses. God, such things aren't available back in Selma, and never will be," she exclaimed. Lifting the cover of the central silver tray, she smiled in delight at the carefully prepared *pasta a' la pomonardo*. "Have some, my angel."

He poured wine and they filled their plates. He then took a bite, saying, "I didn't realize how hungry I was, Madame. You are right, this is so delicious."

Carlotta frowned. "Ernesto, stop eating like some field hand from the cotton fields. Here people are used to good food and wines, but they are to be savored, not swallowed whole in five minutes. I've talked to you about this so many times. You have to behave here as the natives do. Manners are all important. Courtesy must be observed. It will not do when you are in public at dinners and receptions to behave in such an uncouth manner. Enjoy things, but don't act as if you are starving."

Ernesto pushed his plate away. "I'm sorry, Madame; I just thought that here in private I could eat as I like." He folded his arms across his chest.

"Look, sweetheart, what I say is for your own good. If you eat so fast, you won't realize till you have stuffed yourself silly that you will be sick from the rich food here. Also, it's important that you keep your slender figure. It's so easy to gain weight, and your stage appearance is all important. You won't be eighteen till we are in the midst of the rehearsals and you must look stunningly handsome in the costumes. Remember you need to eat sparingly so that digestion doesn't interfere with singing. That will never do here with these theatrical people. You are so much more than the mere mortals you will come in contact with. Don't ever forget that. You must set the example of one who is disciplined in all things. People notice these things. Are you listening to me?"

"Yes, I am. I'll follow your example, Madame. Please just give me a little time to adjust to life and ways here. I won't let you down. Now, may I sample just a few of the sweets?" He laughed as she nodded her approval.

"Darling, remember that I'm just being severe so that you'll learn quickly how to behave as an Italian. When I'm gone, you'll have to stand on your own. I will arrange for you to meet some people who will make the way easier, but you must never let down your guard. You are an Italian now. Don't forget it for a moment. Now go ahead and enjoy the desserts."

Later, after the waiters had returned and taken everything away, they sat, talking on one of the sofas.

"It's growing late now, dear boy. Let's go to our rooms and get ready for bed. We have to start singing some tomorrow and then do some shopping. After the long train ride I know you are as tired as I am."

In his room, Ernesto put on one of The Colonel's oversized nightshirts, gathering the pajamas that were laid out for him away into one of the elaborate wardrobes. *How my heart aches for him. I'm so glad he let me bring this nightshirt with me. It has his scent on it. Old Spice and thoughts of home they bring back. There will be time enough to think about my new life tomorrow.* He slipped into the luxurious bed with the soft Egyptian cotton sheets and pulled up the quilted coverlet. His thoughts were mixed with a feeling of homesickness and anticipation. He turned off the bedside lamp and lay in the darkness. Outside he could still hear the sounds of the gondolas coming and going and smelled again the sea air as the panels over the curtains stirred with the breezes that fluttered in from the lagoon. *Oh night of beauty, of peace. Here in my new world.* Out of nowhere he suddenly thought of Imogene without understanding why. *No, away with these memories. My future lies here ahead in my country among my people.* He grew quiet as the room filled with filtered moonlight. At last he slept without dreams.

Twenty-Two

Friday, audition day, brought overcast skies. Carlotta and Ernesto were up early, and after a very light breakfast they had warmed his voice up at the piano. Ignoring cries from adjoining suites, they went through the *Marchesi* exercises. Everything had been done at half voice to limber up the instrument. Dressing warmly against the chilly late-October wind, they left the hotel and were soon at the artists' entrance to the theater.

Carlotta rapped loudly on the door. "Where is the attendant?" She fumed in impatience. "Ernesto, stop staring at everything. We've gone over the layout of the theater a thousand times already. It is all familiar to you."

"I know, Madame, its just everything is so beautiful here in spite of the smells. I can hardly believe that Rossini, Bellini, Donizetti, and Verdi once walked through this door. The dust in the rehearsal rooms must be as it was then, only heavier." He laughed and looked around as he caught the eye of a beautiful girl walking by at the corner. "Good morning," he called out as she waved and smiled.

"Oh are you courting street-walking tramps this morning, my dear? You had better get your mind back where it belongs. Now where are these people?" She knocked once more. At last the sound of someone coming down the corridor with clattering keys fell on their ears. The stage door opened. Before them stood an old woman, enveloped in a heavy shawl. She eyed them closely and asked who they were there to see.

"Why, my good woman, we are here to see Signor Meneghini. I am Carlotta Vasselli, and this is Ernesto Vasselli. We are expected. Now move aside, I know where I'm going." She shoved the old woman out of her way, and, taking Ernesto by the hand, proceeded to elbow her way down the hall. Up two flights of stairs they arrived breathless at rehearsal room #1. Flinging open the door, Carlotta swept into the huge space with Ernesto in tow. Before them stood Carlo Meneghini and behind him sat Jane Fremstead and her husband. "Ah, Carlo my dear. At last we are here. No thanks to that old crone who took her time opening the door."

"Oh, my Carlotta, embrace me," cried Carlo as she fell into his arms. "We are so glad you are here. It's been too long since we've seen you. Not since before the war when you sang *La Vestale* for us. Thank you for coming to help us out of this dilemma we have been faced with." They embraced again. Over her shoulder his eyes met the steady gaze of Ernesto, who had steeled himself to contain his emotion at being in the same room with Madame Fremstead. "Is this our tenor? Why have we not seen him here before? I adored the tape that was sent. You have a beautiful voice!"

"Carlo, may I present my kinsman, Ernesto Vasselli, from Como. He is delighted for the opportunity to participate in this production."

Carlo embraced him, kissing him on both cheeks in the Italian manner.

Ernesto drew back in confusion but at a recognized signal from Carlotta, smiled broadly and returned the embrace.

"My boy, you are so young, but Carlotta tells me you are ready and know the role of *Idreno*. We are happy to have you here with us. May I present Madame Fremstead and James Buffington, her husband. They have come down this morning specifically to hear you." He stepped to the side and the red-haired diva came forward with her hand outstretched.

"How nice to meet you at last, Signor Vasselli." she exclaimed. "May I call you Ernesto? This is my husband James, who will play for you."

"Madame Fremstead, I am so glad to meet you," gushed Ernesto. "I have heard only the most wonderful things about you. I've heard so much about your *Lucias* in London and New York, also *Beatrice di Tenda* at *La Scala*. This is so wonderful, seeing you in person."

"Let's not forget her *Gli Ugonoti* too," beamed Carlotta. "May I congratulate you as well, Madame Fremstead? I am Carlotta Vasselli."

"Madame Vasselli! Why yes, I have heard so many things about you from Carlo here about your performances before the war when you sang *Norma* with Gina Cigna. Please, both of you, call me Jane. We are informal with fellow artists. Now, may we hear Ernesto sing?"

"Of course," said Carlotta, heading for the piano with her score of the opera.

"Oh no, Signora," murmured Jane, patting the chair beside her. "Come sit here with me. James will play for him. James, are you ready? Good. Now if we may begin please?"

Ernesto threw off his overcoat and scarf and stood before them. James began the introduction to the aria, *Ma Dov'e, dov'e il cimento*. He sang cautiously, knowing what was at stake. In less than four measures came the first high C, flooding the room with shimmering cascades of sound. At last the allegro portion began with dazzling runs capped by the cadenza, which rose to a high D natural. There was silence as Jane and Signor Carlo exchanged glances. James turned to the second aria, *La Speranza Piu Soave.*

Carlotta stirred uneasily in her seat. *I was supposed to have played for him. This is a surprise. No comments from the diva. He is used to me, but James plays it better than I do and he is an expert.*

Ernesto sang the aria as he had been taught. The high tessitura held no terrors for him. Notes in the extended upper register rang out like a cascade of diamonds, perfectly in place as James followed and encouraged, the dynamics were rising and falling in harmony. Again an even more brilliant cadenza shimmering with thirty-second notes capped with a high C sharp ended the piece. Once more there was complete silence. Carlotta held her breath. Ernesto stood motionless, displaying no visible emotion.

"Bravo!" exclaimed the diva. Nodding to her smiling husband, she advanced and embraced the singer. "Ernesto, the part is yours. It will be delightful to sing with you, though I am so sorry we don't have any duets together. Perhaps in the future, who knows?" She turned to the speechless Signor Meneghini saying, "We shall be ready then, Signore, to begin the rehearsals on Monday. I'll get word to Olivia. She has been waiting on her American pins and needles as to how things were to be. Signora Vasselli, thank you for this gift. He is all I could wish for as I prepare for my first *Semiramide*. Is this all then? Come, James, we must go." Laughing, they left the room.

Carlotta stood, clapped her hands, rushed forward and grabbed Ernesto. "Darling, isn't it like a dream?" she whispered, "Madame Fremstead was astounded, but then of course I always knew she would be. Didn't I tell you that there was nothing to be afraid of? She is of the greatest of singers, but then you are also. You will shine in this part and all the critics will be here to cover the event. It can't help but bode well for you also. Carlo, I must say I was a bit surprised by Mr. Buffington's tempos, but then who am I to question? After all he has discovered Madame Fremstead's *bel canto* voice and all the opera houses are clamoring for her services. It is well, as I knew it would be."

"Carlotta, *mille grazie*," (many thanks) exclaimed Carlo, appearing stupefied by the scene that had just passed. "Now at last we can get down to work. We would have been ruined if she had canceled after all the money and time we've expended. The president of Italy himself is coming. It would have been a fiasco. How can I thank you?" He embraced her warmly.

"Why Carlo, my dear, it is nothing, just an artist doing what he was trained for. Just take care of my child here when I have to leave Venice and make a place for him if anything comes up that he can help you with. That's all the thanks I could hope for."

Ernesto smiled warmly at both of them. "I am so happy, signore, to be of service to you. Thank you for this opportunity to make my debut in this beautiful theater." He laughed, and taking Carlotta by the hand said, "Mother, let us go, I need a glass of wine to stop my knees from shaking." They embraced again and bid the smiling Carlo farewell, oblivious to the cold wind and rain drops that fell softly on their shoulders outside.

Twenty-Three

At ten sharp the following Monday morning the first piano rehearsals began in the same large room where Ernesto had auditioned. Madame

Fremstead, with her mane of bright auburn hair, greeted everyone as she arrived with Olivia Davis, the American mezzo soprano. Ernesto, with Carlotta close beside him, sat, waiting to be called. The first numbers to be rehearsed were *Bel Raggio* and *Ah, quel giorno, ognor rammento.* The conductor, De Sabata, signaled, and Madame Fremstead advanced to begin her aria. Ernesto had been warned not to expect her to sing as though in an actual performance. The extreme high notes were only etched in very lightly. Her voice, in person, was a revelation. Carlotta shivered in spite of herself, trying to contain her excitement.

"Darling, isn't she wonderful? I have only heard that one record of hers that was released recently, but she sings correctly, albeit with that thick tone to her Italian that Australians always have. The public will adore her to be sure, though they do like to understand the words. *Mio Dio*, what a tall woman she is. I can't wait to see how she'll look in her costumes. I've heard they are magnificent, everything having been made in London." She grumbled under her breath, "I can't understand what's wrong with our Italian costumers that this would be allowed, but then she *is* a star, and with a voice like that, such little petty annoyances can be ignored." She smiled brightly as Madame Fremstead returned to her seat.

Olivia Davis was next to sing her opening aria. In contrast to the diva, she was short and chubby, nothing like a typical opera singer. Her voice, however, belied her appearance. The dynamics she used and above all the phenomenal breath control she displayed left those present sitting in stunned silence as she finished. Ernesto had to restrain himself from applause and shouting out *bravas* as he shook with excitement. Carlotta had told him that he must understand the rules of rehearsal: be quiet, listen with attention, and leave all comments to the conductor and his assistants. The pianist asked Olivia about the pacing in a few places to be sure they were in agreement. The conductor nodded his approval and she returned to her seat beside Madame Fremstead.

"Madame, how is in that he makes so few comments? I would have thought he would have been picking things apart, making them start here, stop there, go over the arias again and again. This boggles my mind."

"Hush, child! For God's sake keep your voice down. Don't you realize these women are consummate professionals? You noticed, didn't you, that neither was using music? When you arrive for rehearsals, even with these first ones with the piano only, you are expected to have your part to memory. Don't even dream about taking your score up with you when you are called. It is not allowed."

He was silent, watching everything with keen interest. *How handsome he is! How wonderful he is going to look in the costumes. Thank God my old dresser Giuletta is in charge of the fittings. I must keep him focused. This is the chance of a lifetime.*

"Signor Vasselli, if you please," intoned an assistant, "the *Maestro* would like now to hear the trio of *Idreno, Oroe*, and *Assur*." Ernesto advanced with the bass and baritone, and the trio *Ah quel detti, quel aspecto fremer seno il cor nel petto* began. He was dismayed when they were constantly interrupted due to the imbalance between the voices. He sang his lines as Carlotta had taught him a thousand times in the past, but never having sung with these other singers, he felt unnerved by the process of blending. After several false starts and admonishments from the conductor, they finally were able to sing through the trio without interruption.

"That will do for now, gentlemen," said the conductor, frowning. "Get together separately on your own time and work this out. The complete blend must be obtained." The three singers started back to their seats, looking downcast. "Not you, Signor Vasselli. We will now hear your first aria."

Ernesto shot Carlotta a glance of panic. He had no idea he was to be asked for one of the arias at this initial rehearsal.

Carlotta mouthed the word "courage" as he returned to the piano.

He began the aria, *Ah dov'e, dov'e il cimento,* half expecting to be stopped a dozen times. To his amazement, he was allowed to sing it without interruption. Everyone sat in silence as he finished. Madames Fremstead and Davis smiled in approval as the conductor looked over at them for their reactions. Completely forgetting protocol, Ernesto had sung the aria in full voice.

The conductor cleared his throat and said, "Thank you, signore. I must say you know the part well, at least as far as I can ascertain at this first hearing. You may return to your seat."

Carlotta dabbed at his forehead as he sat beside her. He was sweating even though the room was ice cold. "Bravo, my love. I watched them all closely, they adored it. What a handsome Indian prince you will make. I know it's just a small part, but you have your moments to shine. De Sabata has seen and worked with the greatest singers of the century, even before *my* time. For him to allow you to proceed without stopping you is amazing. But then, it's as I have always said, perfection is simply that. To do what we adore and to do it with no visible signs of any inner struggle, that is the sign of an accomplished artist, and believe me, all of them recognized it."

The conductor, followed by Signor Meneghini, abruptly left the room.

The morning rehearsal was finished.

Madames Fremstead and Davis approached Carlotta and Ernesto. “Ernesto, we both want to tell you how much we enjoyed hearing you this morning,” said Madame Fremstead. "Olivia is astonished that she has never heard your name before. Exactly how old are you if I may ask?”

“I will be eighteen on November twenty-third, Madame” he murmured, feeling at ease with these two huge stars.

“Eighteen! My God, this is incredible,” exclaimed Olivia. “How can it be that you have mastered this technique at such a young age?”

“Ten years study with me!” spoke up Carlotta. “He began as an eight-year-old with me and I have instilled the Garcia technique, with the results you have heard demonstrated today.”

“Madame Vasselli,” said Madame Fremstead, “Please call us Jane and Olivia, and you too, Ernesto. We like informality among fellow singers. We are so pleased to have met you both at last. We had heard wonderful things about you, Carlotta, of your *Norma* and *La Vestale* here and in Milan before the war. Believe me, you are warmly recalled whenever I speak to these Italians here in Venice, but most especially in Milan. It’s so wonderful that you have been able to impart your knowledge to our young man here.”

The three women continued to talk, while Ernesto, distracted by the sound of a Chopin Mazurka coming from the piano, met the steady gaze of James Buffington, who beckoned for him to approach. Never missing a beat in the music, he patted the stool beside him. “Ernesto? May I call you that? Jane and I have been talking about you. We have many projects we are considering, and depending on how the performances go here, we may have need of you in the future.”

His smoldering, direct gaze left Ernesto disturbed, his heart pounding with excitement. The room and the chattering women seemed to dissolve as he looked into James’ dark eyes. He trembled as he gazed at the full sensual mouth of this very handsome man.

“Mr. Buffington, I am only a beginner here in the opera world. I can’t imagine that you and your wife could ever use me for anything.”

“It’s James, Ernesto, and who knows what the future may hold? Perhaps you and I can work some together, just the two of us, on some variations I have been thinking of for you. In time, I will conduct Jane myself as my stock with these impresarios rises. All sorts of things could be possible in the future.” Seeing the women approach, he said, “I’ll call you at your hotel and we’ll arrange everything.”

He grasped Ernesto’s hand warmly, and they rose to greet the women.

"Are you ready to leave, Jane? Olivia, come along and let's get some lunch. I know a perfect place where we can go unrecognized." The three of them left, arm-in-arm.

"What was all that about?" Carlotta asked. "What was he saying to you? I'm surprised he called you over like that. He is thought to be a snob and rarely mixes with his wife's fellow artists."

"Madame, he was just saying that perhaps in the future that he and Jane might be interested in having me sing with them again. That is all; I am just surprised that people of that caliber would be interested in an unknown like me." He returned her gaze with a new assurance.

"Well, my child, exert yourself to your utmost in these performances and who knows what might happen? The fact that someone like James would speak to you in that manner is very flattering. He isn't, from what I've heard, very free with compliments. Consider yourself lucky if you have sparked his interest."

Ernesto hesitated for a moment and then said, "He offered to coach me in some new variations and cadenzas for my arias. Can you imagine that he would want to work privately with me, that he would give me that special instruction?"

Carlotta stiffened, and her smile faded. "So I'm just to be forgotten and cast aside? I know your voice better than anyone, what can be in his mind to think he could usurp my place? I'll have to talk with Carlo about this. I don't approve at all of your being alone with some of the men in this place. I've tried to tell you and you're so naive. People will try to possess you so that you will belong to them, body and soul. I can't watch-dog you forever. I'll have to leave in a few weeks and you'll be alone here." She looked anxiously away, emotion rising. "Well then let's go and get a strong coffee. I am feeling suddenly chilled."

The weeks passed quickly as the opera came together, and the rehearsals with orchestra proceeded to the dress rehearsal. An invited audience arrived in the ornate theater. The huge semi-circular stage projected outward into the theater, with row upon row of seats packed tightly together. Above, a horseshoe of boxes encircled the theater, culminating in the center with the royal box, where only the most important invited dignitaries sat. Lamps gleamed in the boxes, shining light on the gold accents of the very old theater which had been redecorated for this gala opening series of performances. At last the houselights lowered as the stage behind the curtain glowed with light. *Maestro De Sabata* made his entrance and stood at the podium, nodding to warm applause. He turned, and the orchestra began the stirring overture to *Semiramide.*

Behind the curtain, everything was in place. The Rossini crescendos came in quick succession as the overture ended. The curtains opened to reveal ancient Babylon and the kingdom of the Assyrians. The chorus, dressed in glittering costumes of black and gold, stood looking out into the auditorium. The high priest, *Oroe*, intoned the opening solo phrase, *Si, gran Nume, intendo.*

Ernesto was dressed in robes of gold and green, a shining crown on his head. He sang out his first line, *La nel gange, a te primero!* A hush fell on the audience. Tenors were highly prized in Italy and the newcomer drew interest .The baritone in the role of *Assur,* prince of the blood Royal, came forward with his opening lines, and almost immediately the men launched into their trio. As they finished, a few scattered bravos rang out. The audience was too concerned with anticipation of Madame Fremstead in the role of the Queen of Babylon to pay much attention at this point.

A chorus of applause welcomed her to the stage. Dressed in robes of rich gold with a magnificent diadem in her bright red hair, she sang in full voice, *Fra tante Reggi e popoli, Ah perche tremi, palpiti, misero cor cosi?* Her melody was taken up by the other principals as her solo became a quartet, each voice intertwining with the others as each character expressed conflicting emotions. The audience grew restless. Many did not know the opera. It had not been done here since the early 1930's. They expected elaborate arias immediately, but there were none in this opening scene. After the quartet finished, another ensemble began as the ghost of the dead King Nino appeared and interrupted the naming of his replacement on the throne. Semiramide, though queen, was only a temporary regent till she named a male heir. The scene ended in confusion as everyone, in fright, fled the stage in terror.

In her box at stage left, Carlotta stirred uneasily. There had been no applause at all as principals and chorus left the stage. *Let's see how they react now as the long prelude ensues before Olivia comes on stage as Arsace.* Back to the spectacle she turned her eyes as the audience caught sight of Olivia as she entered upstage right. She had her back turned to the spectators as she intoned the opening words of the scene, *Eccomi alfine in Babilonia!* From her shoulders fell a long cloak of red velvet trimmed in gold. On her head she wore a golden helmet from which cascaded bright red ostrich plumes. She turned and, facing the audience, advanced toward the footlights. The audience sat in silence, anticipating a big moment. Olivia began her heroic aria, *Ah quel giorno, ognor rammento.* Her matchless breath control and dynamics filled the theater as she sang. When she launched into the cabaletta, *Ah com'e da quel di tutto, tutto per me cangio,* electricity ran through the listeners. The voice rang out, bouncing off the walls, up and down in trills, shakes, roulades, and huge leaps from high to deep chest low notes. As she finished, the audience was in frenzy. A hurricane of cheers burst forth. The Venetians were swept away by the genius of the singer, who stood stock still waiting for the ovation to subside.

Next came a beautiful duet with the baritone Andrea Ganzarolli in the role of *Assur.* Olivia's and Andrea's singing in the *stretta* of the duet *Va superbo* grew ever more brilliant through the coloratura agility of the baritone. Venetian audiences, used to hearing women sing florid music, were unprepared for such writing for baritone. They left the stage to the acclamation of the public.

The scene changed to the hanging gardens of Babylon, revealing Jane on stage as Semiramide, reclining on a gold-covered litter, dressed in a costume of white with gold bracelets, rings, and a necklace of heavy gold chains. In her red hair rested a glittering tiara of semiprecious stones that radiated light when she moved. Her female attendants were garbed in simple white tunics, gathered at the waist with golden belts, and each wore a band of gold which encircled their foreheads. Jane stood, and advancing to mid stage, turned and began the aria *Bel Raggio.* As she began the final florid section, *Dolce piensiero*, cries of amazement rang out at the dazzling prima donna before them. A magnificent high E rang out as the aria came to its conclusion. A frenetic demonstration, not seen or heard in many years, filled the opera house. The audience rose to their feet in a standing ovation. Flowers rained down on the stage from the galleries.

The ovation went on for some time before the conductor signaled for Olivia to come onstage for the duet, *Serbarmi Ognor,* with Jane. At her entrance, the throng grew quiet, as if wondering how anything could match what they had just witnessed.

In her box, Carlotta realized that she had shredded her gloves in the delirium of excitement at the triumph of the two ladies. She was not used to seeing opera at this level, not since years ago on this very stage. She smiled at Signor Carlo beside her and redirected her attention to the performance.

The duet seemed almost anti-climactic after the great aria that preceded it, but waves of rapture enveloped the crowd as they shouted, jumped to their feet in delight, and were loath to let them leave.

In the wings, Ernesto waited with James. James looked approvingly at his Indian costume and stood with his arm around the young man's shoulders. "Don't fear, my boy; your first moment has come. I'm so glad we've had our moments together, working out the ornaments. Carlotta has done such a wonderful job with you, though her ways are somewhat old fashioned by today's standards. I hope she doesn't resent too greatly my taking you over to refine the arias. Think of the passion of *Idreno* now."

Ernesto swept onto the stage to join the assembled chorus members. His entrance was greeted with dead silence. He knew he was on trial before one of the most sophisticated audiences in the world. He glanced nervously at the box in which Carlotta sat, almost beside herself with anticipation. He fixed his eyes on the conductor and began the aria, *Ah Dov'e, Dov'e il Cimento.* The first high C, grabbed out of mid air, came quickly. Some members of the public began exchanging glances, their memories perhaps taking them back to Cesare Valletti and Luigi Alva, both experts in Rossini characters, though no one but those with the longest memories could remember having heard anything quite like this before. The allegro portion with its dazzling upwards runs poured forth in youthful abandon. Ernesto, with nerves of steel, flung out the final cadenza, culminating with a flourish of thirty-second notes capped by a sustained, enormous, high D.

A moment of silence and then an avalanche of applause broke out. He had come on stage unknown to them and emerged with their enthusiastic approval.

Carlotta dissolved into tears of joy and relief. Her ambition had been accomplished and her prodigy stood center stage at the *Fenice* Theater with thunderous bravos and flowers raining down on him. *Oh God, if I should die in this moment, then so be it. He has faced the Venetians and has emerged a finished artist. What a champion!*

Onstage, Ernesto gestured towards her box. The audience catching sight of her, directed cries of *Brava Diva* to her until she retired to the back of the box. Ernesto turned and left the stage, followed quickly by the chorus.

The opera proceeded after a long intermission. Each aria and duet had been received with mounting excitement. Ernesto's final aria, *La Speranza piu soave,* was received in the most enthusiastic manner, people obviously astonished by this handsome youth and his fearless execution, especially in the highest register. His strength seemed unending. His part in the opera finished, he retired to his dressing room, leaving the leading ladies and the baritone to the final scenes. He started to take off his costume when a soft knock came on his door.

It was James, and Ernesto rushed to embrace him. James gently pushed him back, laughing. "My boy, don't be so passionate now. The makeup will get all over my evening clothes. I want to tell you how proud we all are of you. To think that the production was almost canceled because we didn't think your role could be recast. You've proved all of them wrong. Jane and I both knew when we heard you that you would have a great success. You do need to learn to move with more authority and not be so in awe of sharing the stage with Jane and Olivia. They have paid their dues to be at the top of their professions, and you'll have to also. My God, how you're sweating, even though it's ice cold backstage." He came forward and dabbed at Ernesto's dark hair, wet with sweat. "We've got about another thirty minutes till the opera is over and you'll need to return to the stage to take bows with everyone. Why don't you take a quick shower and I'll help you reapply the makeup. This way the costume can air out a little."

Ernesto began to undress, laying aside the gold ornaments and robes. Finally he stood naked, and blushing at James' admiring smile, he stepped into the warmth of the shower. Reaching for the shampoo, he lathered his hair and washed the makeup from his neck and face. Suddenly he felt hands on his back and turned to face James, who had slipped into the shower with him. He smiled and laughed nervously. "James, we can't do this, not here, not now, there isn't time!" His protests were silenced in the wordless kiss that came onto his mouth. James washed all the parts of his body till be was squeaky clean.

With the water running over them and the room rapidly filling with steam, James sank to his knees taking Ernesto's now rigid penis into his mouth. It seemed only a moment passed till Ernesto, moaning with pleasure, filled that mouth with thick sperm. He leaned back heavily on the wall. James rose with a smoldering smile, turned him around and entered his warm body, plunged deeply two or three times, groaning in rapture as he filled Ernesto to overflowing. Laughing and kissing deeply, they rinsed off and stepped out onto the thick bath rugs. Ernesto dressed back into the robes of an Indian prince and James into his evening clothes. James assisted him with the makeup. He hastily put the gold crown back on his head and James helped him again in putting on his costume's ornaments.

"There now . . . all freshly fucked, you look wonderful. Get ready now, you have to return to the stage, the final scene is drawing to a close and people are going to be wondering where we are." He smiled at Ernesto. "Look, we can have fun like this whenever possible. People are aware, but they could care less, as long as nothing interferes with professionalism. Even Jane is aware of my weakness for handsome young men. She knows I'm dedicated completely to her success. Don't take it seriously. This is going to happen all the time to you now, but you have to take it for what it is, a moment of pleasure, making ourselves and someone else feel happy. Don't let love get in your way. I hope it will always be wonderful for you, though I warn you there are people who are unattractive who will want your body. My advice is to use them as they use you. Don't give in unless there is something in it for you. Now come on, let's go."

Feeling somewhat crest- fallen, Ernesto followed James back to the wings. The performance had ended in screams of delight and thundering ovations. Jane and Olivia came from the stage and greeted them both with happy smiles.

Jane grabbed Ernesto's arm. "Come now, my little love, let's line up for our bows." She drew him onto the stage and they lined up as the curtain rose. The roar of the public was beyond description. Ernesto with the other principals advanced to the footlights and bowed repeatedly with them. The solo bows followed, with each principal coming and going. As Ernesto's turn came, he stepped out before the public to a gigantic roar of applause. Flowers rained down till there was hardly room to walk.

He blew kisses and with a superb gesture, flung a wreath of white roses into Carlotta's box at stage left. Her eyes overflowed with tears as she gestured with both arms towards him.

He returned behind the curtain feeling numb; Signor Ganzarolli, then Olivia, and finally Jane went on to their solo bows. The ensemble bows, with *Maestro De Sabata*, followed. Ernesto and other male cast members picked up the floral tributes and gave them to the ladies to the delight of the audience. At long last they were allowed to leave and retire to their dressing rooms. Ernesto, casting aside the ornaments of gold, felt limp with fatigue. A knock came at the door. Upon opening it, Carlotta fell into his arms.

"Madame, please, your gown! Don't ruin it. My makeup is running." He tried to disengage but she held him fast.

"Oh, to hell with the gown. I could care less. I just want to hold you to my heart now. My dream has come true. You were superb. What scales, the runs like shimmering diamonds. I know you were nervous, but the ordeal is over now." She burst into tears. "Ernesto, Ernesto! Thank you from my heart for the joy you have given to me this evening."

He fought to control his own emotions, thinking of his time before the public . . . and of the kisses of rapture he had shared in the shower. He too, felt hot tears scald his cheeks as he sank to his knees and embraced her. Laying his head in her lap as in days of old when she comforted him when he was frightened. "My mother, to you is the glory. Without you, this night would never have come. Please stay here always with me. I don't think I can go on without you." He raised his face to hers, his eyes brimming with tears.

"Dearest child, I must leave soon. The Colonel is waiting and my place is with him. Your success has brought me a joy I thought I would never feel again in my life. There is no more I can teach you. You are my equal now and your glory is all I desire. I will hold this memory in my heart all the rest of my life. Ernesto, my darling Ernesto!" She kissed him again and again on the cheeks and then drew herself away from his embrace. "I'll wait for you outside, my dearest. Hurry now, shower and get dressed in your street clothes. I know you're hungry, and God knows we both need several glasses of wine. Don't worry about your costumes, the dressers will be in for them and they will be cleaned and ready for you in time for the gala performance in three days. I don't see how it could equal tonight, but Signor Gronci, the President of all the Italians, will be present to sit in the royal box with me as his guest. Okay, be quick now, we need to leave here, the gondola is waiting." She patted his cheek and left him

He mechanically disrobed and went into the shower, looking at the towels he and James had so recently used to wipe up the evidence of their encounter. As the water ran over his body, the memory of so long ago hit him, when he used towels to wipe up the evidence of sex that night back in Selma. *Why now? Why tonight these memories? God, can I ever get used to trying to separate love from sex? That wasn't love, not what Tony and his friends did. But The Colonel? He said he loved me, and I gave my body to him, and now James, who helped himself to my charms and then dismissed my feelings with his advice. Where is love? Where can it be for me? Will I ever know the warm* hello *that's meant only for me with nothing expected in return? Ah, fatal destiny, I go forth to embrace you.* He dressed quietly in silence and joined Carlotta outside his dressing room.

As they passed Jane's star dressing room, filled with dignitaries and fans, he paused as James flashed him a wide smile. They continued through the stage door into the night as the stars shown brightly overhead. Locked in each other's arms, Mother and Son sat in their gondola and sped off across the deep and silent lagoon to the restaurant she had chosen.

Twenty-Four

The next two weeks of performances passed quickly. The newspapers were filled with enthusiastic reviews for all the principal singers. Carlotta clipped and pasted them into a scrapbook she had purchased. True to her word, she left Venice after the third performance. Before leaving, she took Ernesto to the Sforza agency and signed him on to their management. The terms were severe as to percentages. He had to agree to pay them twenty-five percent of his earnings for a period of five years. On their part, they agreed to promote his career and to arrange all negotiations with other opera houses for his services.

Carlotta had carefully read everything and insisted on his right of refusal of any part that he felt was unsuited to his voice, to which the agency reluctantly agreed. She was determined that he not be pushed into parts where the orchestration would be too heavy. As always, protecting the voice was her primary aim. Finally when she had pronounced herself satisfied, she had him sign the contract and they left the offices.

"Darling I know you were reluctant to tie yourself to them for five years, but it's a normal rite of passage for young, inexperienced artists to do so. You are having a great success right now, but the public, especially here in Italy, is fickle. You are only as important to them as your last performance. Take care that they not be allowed to devour you in the process."

The two had made a final sightseeing excursion around the city. She gave him maps of the principal cities and arranged for lodging with an elderly couple. Now they walked across St. Mark's square arm-in-arm. The ever-present flocks of birds flew over them in the overcast skies. In a small café Ernesto ordered them strong coffee, and both sipped in silence, lost in thought, occasionally glancing at each other. The idea of having to say farewell, after ten years, weighed heavily. Ernesto reached across the table, grasped and kissed her hands as he fought back tears. She gazed back at him lovingly and ran her hands through his hair and cupped his face as she had done a thousand times. She stood and looked across the lagoon. Ernesto, his eyes brimming with tears, looked up at her searchingly.

"Madame, when will we see each other again? I love it here and the excitement of working with people at the theater has been wonderful. I thought I would have had stage fright, but as you always have said, as long as one is prepared, nothing is to be feared."

She brushed away a lock of his hair that blew in the cool breeze and earnestly looked into his face. "Let me look deep into your heart as I did that day long ago when you first came to study with me. I want the memory to linger to brighten the loneliness we will both feel when I leave this place to return home. Home, what is that anyway? This country was my home for many years before the war and The Colonel came. Home is really where your heart is. I want only your happiness, you know this. At the conclusion of the opera seasons, unless you are engaged for a summer festival, you can always return to visit us in the summers. For now, just think about establishing yourself here. The Sforzas are a good agency. They will find you work. Just go where you are called to and learn the parts you are assigned without inner murmurings. You won't always be cast in large roles, but the opportunities will come. You've always had an uncanny memory and thus learning new parts will not be difficult. Just always present yourself prepared. There is no room in our profession for amateurs. Conduct yourself with discretion. Above all else, be true to yourself and all will be well. Trust your mother. I have never said anything that was not true."

When she left, Ernesto saw her off with the elderly couple with whom he would be staying. As the gondolier took her luggage, she drew Ernesto to the side and embraced him warmly. An icy wind caused her to shiver and to draw her traveling cloak closer. She laid her head on his shoulder for a moment. She brushed away the tears that burned warm in her eyes and steeled herself to say farewell. "Don't look so sad, child. We will write and keep in touch. Let me know what the agency does for you. Alas, who knows when we will meet again? The time will pass though. It always does. Be kind to these two old people. They won't be any bother to you. You can come and go as you wish. I have known them for many years and they never interfere. You have the piano and can work in your rooms. Study hard and keep out of trouble. Never forget you are Italian now. No chatting in English with the tourists unless they are important. Carlo told me that Prince Ranier and Princess Grace will be coming to the last performance. You'll be invited of course to the reception for them. Just remember what you've been taught and let the royal couple lead any conversation. Ah, the gondola is ready. I must go now."

"Oh my mother, God bless you till we meet again. I promise I will be good. I won't let you down." He helped her into the gondola and they kissed each other. A final hug and she was gone, not hiding her emotion. He stood watching silently beside the water as the gondola turned to the opening of the lagoon. The elderly couple handed him the flowers they had brought, and in the Italian fashion of farewell in Venice, he cast them into the water, one by one. He looked out as she sailed away, each blowing kisses and waving till she was lost in a speck on the horizon. With a great sigh, he turned back to his hosts and they silently followed him back to their palazzo. He was alone now in his country, yet he was happy.

* * *

Carlotta arrived at the train station for the journey to Paris. She looked back across the water and allowed her grief to pour forth in all its bitterness. Her fragile shoulders shook as convulsive sobs burst forth unchecked. *Oh, dearest child, may God guard you. This time has been magic, seeing all my old friends after so many years. Being in the performance process again and seeing his career launched in such a splendid way. I always knew this day would come, but never dreamed of the agony this goodbye would cost me. To return to Selma after this brush again with glory is almost too much to conceive of.* Glancing around at the curious stares of fellow travelers, she wrapped herself tightly in her fur-lined cloak. Its expansive hood hid her tear-streaked face as she was helped into the passenger car and conducted to her private compartment. *Let no one but God ever say they have seen Carlotta Vasselli weep!* As the train pulled out of the station, despair seized her once more, and again she wept. Through the window, she could see clouds near the approaching mountains casting their shadows across the rails. She felt numb as Venice receded rapidly behind her. She caught sight of her reflection in the window and a shudder came relentlessly as she gazed at herself. *Oh God, all my youth is gone, my time is past, my cup has run, but Ernesto's is dawning. It's his time to live and to experience the glory that I have known. Oh God, help me to bear this loneliness. Italy, who knows when we may meet again?* Drawing down the shades over the window, she sought to pull herself together. The Colonel would be there to welcome her back to their house on the hill with the skeletal branches of the great oaks to shelter them. She pulled a blanket over her shoulders and trembled with the cold as she lay down and sought forgetfulness in dreamless sleep.

Twenty-Five

The night before the final performance Ernesto decided to have a night out with a couple of the dancers he had met during rehearsals, Mario and Giuseppe. Both young men were physically breathtaking and very close to his age. After a light meal at Mario's apartment, Ernesto came up with an idea. "Why don't we go back to the opera house and raid the costume department and go out in disguise?" He looked at them, waiting for their response.

The other young men looked at each other questioningly. Mario laughed and came over to Ernesto and gave him a hug. "Well, we actually had something else in mind to do with you, but it can wait till later. I guess it will be okay. We have the performance tomorrow, so let's do this if we can and get through so we can get back here before it gets too late." Mario blushed as he thought of the three of them crawling into bed and making love. He had been with Ernesto several times. His mouth watered at the thought of deep kisses and hard and pulsing penises against his own body. But it would have to wait. Now it was another adventure they were to take in the dim streets near the opera house.

They furtively made their way to the *Fenice,* where a performance of *Tosca* had just gotten underway. Slipping in quietly via an entrance used for scenery removal, they made their way to the room where the costumes for *Semiramide* hung waiting for the following night's performance.

Ernesto rushed towards Jane's costume for her opening sequence. "Tonight my friends, I will be the Queen of Babylon, and the two of you will be my attendants." Quickly undressing to their underwear, Mario and Giuseppe helped him into the ornate costume. He grabbed the huge red wig and put it on his head, laughing out loud. "Okay, boys, dress yourselves in those skimpy soldiers' uniforms and let's go. We'll have these things back in no time and no one will be the wiser. I can hardly wait to see how people will react." The other young men dressed quickly and the three of them made their way stealthily back down the stairs.

They dashed into the cold night and soon found themselves in St. Mark's square. Delightedly they accosted the tourists who were scattered about in the cafés around the square. Laughing and imitating Jane's majesty in her costume, Ernesto danced about with his young friends, people gaping at them in surprise. They grabbed glasses of wine from the waiters who laughed at them. They told the manager at one café to just bill everything back to the *La Fenice.* This madness went on for at least an hour as the three young men laughed and deeply bowed to each other. Suddenly a shrill whistle rang out in the cold air as three policemen appeared in their path.

"Where do the three of you think you're going dressed in this ridiculous manner?" demanded one of the officers.

Giuseppe laughingly shouted back, "Make way for *Ernesta*, Queen of Babylon, and her servants, you imbeciles. Don't you know how to act in the presence of royalty?" Grabbing Ernesto's hands they tried to flee but were stopped dead in their tracks as the policemen advanced on them menacingly.

"Queen of Babylon indeed! We think you three are drunks who have stolen costumes from the opera house. You are coming with us to the police station."

Ernesto, shocked back to reality, haughtily drew himself to full height and addressed them imperiously. "Out of my way, you dogs. We are artists of the theater. Signor Meneghini, the impresario, can vouch for us.

Now I insist you allow us to pass on our way."

With dismay they found themselves seized and roughly conducted to the police station, where they were flung into a cell. They retreated to the center of the large room where they stood in fright.

"Careful, Your Majesty, not to step in the hole," laughed Mario. "That's where Your Highness will have to pee."

Ernesto looked in horror at the hole in the floor that served as a toilet. No furniture, not even a table or pitcher of water. "Damn it to hell. What are we going to do now? I do have to pee. You two stand in front of me now." Turning around, he pulled up the costume and let a stream loose as he emptied his aching bladder. "There now, you two. Be bold and don't let these people intimidate you."

Back and forth they paced. Hours passed. Finally, at one a.m., one of the policemen reappeared. Unlocking their cell, he beckoned them to follow him down the hall to the main receiving room. Standing before them were three officials from the opera house. The assistant manager, Signor Mattei, advanced and addressed Ernesto severely. "Signor Vasselli, what is the meaning of this? Who gave you men permission to take these costumes and parade around the streets like common ruffians? Your behavior is unworthy of artists of the *Fenice,* and has shocked Signor Meneghini. We have taken steps to insure this matter will be kept quiet and out of the newspapers if possible. You three are to come with us back to the opera house and return these costumes. Don't put on airs with us. You are just another tenor to us and after tomorrow night's performance you'll be lucky if you are ever invited back to perform. Now come along and put these cloaks over those costumes and let's go."

They silently followed the officials back to the theater, where they quickly changed back into their own clothes. They were conducted to the stage door and found the door slammed loudly in their faces.

"Fuck them," cried Giuseppe. "Don't let those old queens intimidate you, Ernesto. You have the voice of an angel. No one sings like you do, and if they are going to do more Rossini anytime soon, they'll remember you."

Ernesto, feeling ashamed, said goodnight and returned to his host's palazzo. His rooms were lighted and his bed turned down. No one said anything to him as he made his way inside. He was depressed, concerned about what would be said to him the next evening at the theater. He went to bed thinking of what he would say if this escapade reached Carlotta's ears.

Upon entering the theater the next night, he encountered James on his way to his dressing room. "Well, my boy, I trust your voice wasn't affected by the cold winds in St. Mark's square last night? Jane and I heard about it this morning. She was laughing her head off till she suddenly thought about what state her entrance costume was in, but it all worked out okay. I know you must be worried about what Carlo is going to say. I want you to know that Jane and I have both talked to him, and he's well aware that we may have something in mind for you in one of our future projects. We are leaving tomorrow for London for a few weeks. He isn't going to say anything about last night to you, so don't give it another thought. And as far as Carlotta, she's not going to be told of it either."

Ernesto looked down at him in relieved surprise. "James, for whatever influence you have over these people, thank you for keeping this thing quiet. Mario and Giuseppe had quite a different thought in mind for what they wanted to do with me last night." *And I would have loved that threesome, especially since I haven't yet sampled Giuseppe's body.* "I'm not sure what the agency is going to come up with for me after tonight, but I don't want to stay here in Venice that long. Madame told me that I need a home base. Como is too far to the north, but perhaps Naples or Milan. I want to be on my own, in my own space without chaperones. Now, if you'll excuse me, we need to get this show on for the last time. I'm looking forward to seeing you and Jane in the future, if I can be of use to you."

James smiled, "The future? Yes, who knows? We'll have to see. I won't forget you. I've been too deep in your talents these last few weeks for that ever to happen. I'll talk to you later. My prima donna waits." A quick hug and he was gone.

Ernesto watched him walk away. *Too deep? I know what you meant. My eyes are open now. I have to learn to use others as I've been used.* He turned and went to his dressing room.

At the end of the performance, as he took bows with the cast, he discerned Signor Carlo in the wings. As the curtain calls ended and the cast dispersed to their dressing rooms, Carlo came up to him. "Signor Vasselli, I would like to thank you for your part in saving our production. We hope to be able to use you again sometime in the future. Jane has told us she might consider a return engagement in *L' Assedio Di Corinto* of Rossini in the spring. There is a nice supporting role in that opera for tenor, though not nearly as long as your part has been here. There's only a trio that really shines, but you would be singing with great singers. We will contact your agent about it when the time comes and hopefully you will be available. I'll let you go now, so you can get ready for the wrap party. I just want you to know that you have made a definite impression and we hope to see and hear more of you here before long. We'll be in touch."

Alone in his dressing room, Ernesto reflected over the last few weeks while removing the costume and make up. In the shower, he felt suddenly loneliness as real as if it were a living entity. *No knock at my door tonight. No real invitation to the wrap party. Signor Carlo must have seen to that, even though he politely said something to me about it. His manner was cold, especially now that Madame has left and I'm on my own and no further use to him. Well, I'm going anyway. No one is going to prevent me from meeting Princess Grace.* Dressing carefully into his evening clothes, he stood before the full-length mirror and studied his reflection.

Not bad for an old Alabama boy from Selma. Well, I'm alone now, but I'm going to survive no matter what happens in the future. I may only be eighteen, but I'm going to get what's mine. If it means having to play hardball with the big boys, I don't give a damn. As he left the opera house, he had no way of knowing how prophetic those thoughts would be.

At the Doge's palace, he strode into a magnificent room, realizing he was both weary and very hungry. Jane caught sight of him and approached in a jovial mood.

"Well, my handsome Prince *Idreno*, come along with me. Let's have some wine and gorge ourselves on this food while we may. Then we'll have to gather ourselves up in the receiving line like the paid entertainers we are and receive royalty with due homage. I'm so disgusted with it all, you know. So what if we have talent? Things never change. They want us as long as we make money for them. You have to learn the hard facts, Ernesto. It can overwhelm you if you don't. Now let's smile and nod back and forth to all these people with their titles that their ancestors picked up from their pools of blood and pretend not to be bored out of our minds." Laughing, she linked her arm in his and they moved to one of the food tables. He noticed that she immediately began to gorge herself.

"Jane, are we supposed to just eat as we like? Madame has hammered it into me that I'm to eat sparingly whenever I'm in public." Glancing around, he saw people were staring at them. "Damn, do they think we're some kind of freaks?"

"Get used to it, dearie. They do that because they know we are on a different plane than they are. They do it because somehow they think that talent can rub off, or that they can shine by reflected glory." Grabbing another glass of wine from a passing waiter, she turned her back on an ancient crone hesitantly approaching. "Come on, baby, there's James and Olivia. Let's get over there to them before this old Duchess inflicts her garlic drool on me." They moved away from the tottering old lady and joined James and Olivia at their table.

"Ernesto!" James gave him a big hug and pulled him down into a chair beside him. "Take a load off, my boy." He studied his wife, well on her way to enebriation, as he sat joking with Ernesto. "We're off to London in the morning. Decca wants us to talk about some recording projects, but first we have to get through this reception."

Ernesto gazed about the room, seeing luxury everywhere. The marble floors, centuries old, gleamed in the light of the Venetian chandeliers. The walls and even the ceiling were filled with portraits of famous Venetians who had died centuries ago. Waiters moved silently among the guests with trays of drinks and food. Women and men clustered around in groups watching who came through the floor-to-ceiling massive doors of polished bronze. Lost in thought, he realized Olivia was talking to him.

"Earth to Ernesto. What are you thinking of?" She smiled warmly at him. "Poor thing, you look tired! It'll be over soon. I must have lost ten pounds during this run of performances. Are you staying on in Venice? We were wondering what your plans were."

"I think I will be here for a while, Olivia. I have to see what the agency is going to do for me. I don't really like Venice that much. After a couple of months of all this activity it gets old you know."

"It sure as hell does, sweetie. I can't wait to get out of here tomorrow and get back to the states where we have modern surroundings. Everything here is so old that after weeks of it, I feel like I'm lost in a museum. Enough is enough. I'm from Pennsylvania and I can never get used to the way they cook here. You know, Ernesto, you sure speak good English for an Italian. I can't quite place your accent. Did I hear you were from Como?"

Ernesto stirred uneasily. *If I blow this I'm going to be in trouble. If a single y'all should come out of my mouth it's all over.* "Yes, I am from Como. I grew up at the Villa Pasta on the lake. I studied English from an early age, so I don't have any problem when I have to speak it, and of course Madame Vasselli frequently had me over to the states to work with her in Alabama."

Olivia studied him closely, as if not at all satisfied. A stir of voices near the entrance put an end to all conversation however, as an official from the *Fenice* came over to advise of the royal couple's arrival.

Jane rose to her feet and said "Well, come along, my loves, and let's take our places in the receiving line. James, hold me up and get me over there." They moved over to a spot just inside the entrance doors and took their places beside the conductor and Signor Carlo, as the Prince and

Princess entered the room.

Princess Grace was radiant, glittering with diamonds, her blond hair pulled back in a French twist. People gasped at her beauty; so intense was the reaction to the princess that it hardly mattered to the throng that the handsome prince stood beside her. With a set smile on her face, she turned and greeted each member of the cast in turn, murmuring a few words of congratulations to each of them and holding out her hand to all of them. As she approached Ernesto, near the end of the line, he felt his knees grow weak. He had never seen such a beautiful woman in his life. She smiled broadly at him as he bowed stiffly.

"Signor Vasselli, may I congratulate you on your performance? My husband and I both enjoyed your arias this evening. We hope to hear more of you in the future."

"Your Royal Highness, thank you for coming this evening. I am delighted if you enjoyed it." Before the words died on his lips, she was gone like a vision of loveliness as she continued with her husband down the line. *God, she actually held my hand for a moment!* He was brought back to his senses as Jane elbowed him in the side.

"Well, dearie, we've done our duty. It's time for us to get out of here. These shoes are killing my feet. It's two a.m. and if I don't get back to the hotel I'm not going to be any good tomorrow." She, Olivia, and James hugged him warmly and quickly slipped outside.

Ernesto stood alone, watching the royals as they made their way through all the fawning officials. *I'll never forget her beautiful blue eyes and that she actually spoke to me. It makes all this play acting worth it.* Overcome with weariness, he decided to call it a night. After a short gondola ride he was deposited at his host's Palazzo. The smell of mold assailed the air. The butler let him in and he went up the staircase to his rooms. Crossing over to his bedroom, he carefully undressed and put his evening clothes on a sofa to be taken to the cleaners in the morning.

A tray of cheeses and fresh baked bread had been left for him. He realized he was still hungry, and the cheese and bread were soon devoured. Slipping into his pajamas, he went to the bathroom. Seeing The Colonel's old nightshirt lying on the bedside table as he emerged from the bathroom, he picked it up and got into bed, feeling lonely. He closed his eyes, clutching the nightshirt close against his face. Breathing in deeply, he tried in vain to catch the scent of The Colonel's body. It was gone, though the memories lingered as he fell into a wordless, dreamless sleep.

Twenty-six

During the following five years, Ernesto found that the Sforza agency stayed busy on his behalf. The *Bel Canto* revival was in full flower and the word got around quickly that the tenor who had made a splash in Venice was available. Ernesto learned his assignments quickly, never making waves. His performances were more than competent, though not of the star quality thought to be required by such houses as *La Scala* in Milan. Still, he worked a great deal, giving sometimes as many as seventy to ninety performances a season. The productions in which he was engaged, however, seemed to be confined to small theaters in Pavia, Macerata, Ancona, Trieste, Ferrara, Genoa and other small circuits. He fulfilled his professional engagements without complaints. He steered away from backstage intrigues and respected the prima donnas, being careful never to upstage them. His roles ran from *Nemorino* in *L'Elisir D'amore*, to many other Donizetti works such as *Belisario, Lucia Di Lammermoor, Lucrezia Borgia, Imelda di Lambertazzi, Anna Bolena, Sancia Di Castiglia, Maria Stuarda, Roberto Devereux,* and *Rosmunda D'Inghiltera.* He discovered that people took notice when long-forgotten operas came down from their shelves in dusty old archives. His tenor parts, though often lead roles, were generally inferior to those of the prima donnas with whom he worked. And what dogs some of these singers were.

The productions were often mediocre. Scenery and costumes from other operas were often used that had no correlation to the epoch in which the action was set. All of these slights he tolerated, thinking at any time he could be called to Milan, Rome, or Naples to sing in international houses. He had long ago left Venice after his initial engagement. Milan was the logical choice for a permanent base. He also wanted to get away from whatever spies Carlotta might have had to keep up with his movements. He settled into a little hamlet near Milan called Locate. He rented three large rooms in a sixteenth-century palace that once belonged to the famous nineteenth-century Princess *Cristina Trivulzio- Belgiojoso.*

In spite of many renovations over the centuries, the palace retained much of its former glory. The first thing that Ernesto noticed was the grand central staircase that curled up to the right and left to the floor above. Long corridors stretched down each side on both floors. The once great rooms had been broken up into apartments of various sizes. His rooms on the second floor were spacious, but not as clean as he would have liked. The general impression, however, was of faded glory and the windows and marble floors had a yellow cast to them.

He turned to the kindly old landlady as she stood in the doorway from the hall and asked, "What changes will I be able to make?" Without waiting for an answer, he continued; "You know from my letter that I am an opera singer, and I must arrange for a piano and furniture, and these drapes will have to be replaced, at my expense of course. I see I have a small private bathroom, sitting room, and bedroom. This place seems remote, though it is less than eight kilometers from Milan, so I believe it will suit me if I am able to practice in peace."

"Oh, Signore, there is no problem with your singing. We have had many singers here in the past, though none right now. Mainly we have elderly couples and widows; no children are allowed. You may make any changes you wish. We only require that you keep somewhat the same colors for the walls and that the curtains be dark. You may have a small refrigerator and hot plate if you wish. No one will bother you. My quarters are on the lower floor. The rent is due the first of each month and you may slip payment under my door or in my mail box. We are delighted to have a singer here with us again who is young as you are." As she was talking, she kept her eyes downcast, a simple woman who probably had no idea of the latest fashions. She smiled nervously, all the while keeping her hand to her lips to hide her missing teeth. She need not have worried, as he whirled around and addressed her arrogantly.

"Signora, it will take me about a week to arrange for furniture and draperies to be delivered and installed to my specifications. In the meantime, I need the windows washed of their yellow grime and these floors to be thoroughly scrubbed. I can not abide dirt, nor can I practice my music in unhealthy surroundings. Whoever can do these things I leave to you. Here is some money to cover the expense. I also include a year's rental in advance, as I do not have the time or inclination to think about each month slipping payment under your door. Do we understand each other?" Feeling less confident than the arrogant facade he presented, he crossed his arms and stood, looking at her.

"Signor Vasselli, it will be as you ask. I will get some people in at once to get everything clean and orderly." Clutching the large envelope of money he had disdainfully put into her hands, she bowed slightly, handed him his key, and then turned to leave the apartment.

"Signora, if in the next few days you should need to get in touch with me, I will be at the *Hotel Di Milano*. You have the number I believe?"

"Ah yes, Signor, the hotel were *Maestro* Verdi lived. We know it well. Everything here will be as you have asked. The men will see me to let them in when the furniture arrives and of course whoever is to put up your window hangings. Thank you, Signor." She turned and silently closed the door behind her.

As her steps echoed down the hall, Ernesto looked at his rooms anew. *What is this? Outlets in the floorboards and electrical cables connected to them? Is this some joke?* He carefully followed them with his eyes to where they disappeared near the windows. Looking out one the windows, he noticed the cables for the electricity as well as plumbing ran down the exterior walls of the building. Looking around, he saw no light switches. *Incredible! It's so very primitive. Strip away these cables and it's as it must have been centuries ago, nothing whatsoever modern. But this is Italy, with many buildings so old with thick walls; they couldn't possibly modernize a place like this. Well, good or bad, this will be my home. I'll make it comfortable for my needs when I am here. Transportation is easy. Major railways connect here. It will do, all will be well.* Smiling at that often-used phrase of Carlotta's, he stepped into the wide hall and descended to the foyer, then into the courtyard. He had not seen a living soul other than his landlady. He walked out through the gates, unaware that from many windows he was watched.

In a week's time the apartment was ready and he returned to inspect everything. The walls had been freshly painted in the off-white colors he had chosen. The windows and floors gleamed. He quickly went to the piano and played several scales. *Well, the tuner has been here. This old instrument that I found in the shop in Milan will do, though God knows, I would die for one of Madame's Steinways.* The piano, of indeterminate origin, had a brilliant tone. He laid down an armload of music and looked about the rooms. Dark green velvet curtains hung from each of the six tall windows. The furniture he had purchased in nearby Bergamo had arrived safely. He was pleased that it had been placed tastefully in the rooms. He had found furnishings in an old warehouse which specialized in refurbished pieces from the past. His bedroom had the simple double bed he had selected, and several free-standing cabinets held his clothes which he had sent ahead. He lay down on the bed and found the firm mattress to his liking.

His landlady had hung his thick white towels in the small bathroom and the bed had been made with the linens he had found in Milan. Cheese, salami, bread, and wine had been left for him on a small table just inside the door to the sitting room. *Well, it's not much I guess. Not after Madame's house. Most important though to me is having my own things in my own apartment. After nearly five years of living out of suitcases in crumbling old hotels, it's time. I have been sick to death of sleeping on beds that God knows who was there before me. Get away to the provincial towns where the third-rank opera houses are and I'm back in the nineteenth century. After the grandeur of the Fenice, the work really began.* He crossed over to a window overlooking the courtyard below. The summer heat was not stifling as it was in south Alabama. The high ceilings and thick walls of the old palace made its interiors comfortable. He looked beyond the gates, seeing all sorts of people, ordinary working folk coming and going in the street. Even though Milan itself was close by, none of these people would go there often. Their lives revolved around a narrow compass of factory and domestic work.

Returning to the piano, he sat and looked at the scores of the operas the Sforza agency had sent him to learn for the upcoming season. After all the Donizetti works he had been performing, he looked with pleasure at the three Bellini scores. *Il Pirata, I Puritani, and I Capuleti ed I Montecchi.* His folder containing the indispensable Marchesi exercises sat on the music stand. He thought about the meeting scheduled for the next day with the Sforza agency's Milan branch. Then on the bottom of the pile he saw the score of Verdi's *I Lombardi a la Prima Crociata.* He opened it and saw a note that he was to study the role of *Arvino*. He didn't know this opera, except for the aria *La mia letizia infondere.* But that aria belonged to the lead character of *Oronte*. He quickly leafed through some of the pages. He had one aria, a duet with the soprano, a trio, some ensemble work, a small role, though important to the plot. *Why do they want me to learn this? Who knows where I'll be singing it again? The music is beautiful, but in five years of being in Italy I haven't once heard of it being performed anywhere. Well, I'll know soon enough at the meeting tomorrow. God, what a shop it all is. I shouldn't complain. I've been making money and saving some too, but where is it all heading? The public in these small towns seem to like my voice, but I would have thought by now I'd at least have been singing with better people.*

He crossed the wide courtyard through the gates to a café a block away. He sat at one of the outside tables and ordered a coffee and biscotti. His handsome face and figure drew admiring glances from both men and women. Lost in thought, he was oblivious to them. He had come to understand very quickly the sensual nature of these people in his new country. The men especially, whether married or not, enjoyed affairs with both sexes. No one thought anything about it, though discretion was paramount. There were always the little out-of-the-way hotels where no one asked questions, and physical lust was satisfied with no strings attached. Ernesto had met many men in this manner. Sometimes names weren't even exchanged. It was only momentary pleasure, nothing more.

In the late afternoon sunshine, fortified with too much espresso, he grew aware of his surroundings and moved to another table in the shade to avoid the direct sunlight. He ate sparingly, always aware of Carlotta's demands that he stay slim and muscular. A waiter nearby watched him intently. He had black hair and the slightly darker complexion of a southern Italian. By contrast, Ernesto was pale, but with dark eyes and hair and a full sensual mouth so typical of those from the northern part of the country. He boldly returned the young man's gaze, looking at him from head to toe. They both smiled. The evening waited. He would not be alone tonight.

Twenty-Seven

The next morning, after a light breakfast, he dressed carefully for his meeting with Sforza's Milan representatives. Riding his rented moped, he made his way into Milan. He frowned at the factories he passed on the outskirts of the city. From their chimneys dark, arid, smoke rose, fouling what would have been a bright and pleasant ride. His spirits lifted as he approached the center of Milan with its ancient buildings. *Not so ancient, though. Most appear to be of nineteenth-century origin, and in spite of the allied bombings they have been restored exactly as they were.* He passed by the splendid *La Scala* opera house and made a sharp right turn onto a narrow street behind the smaller theater *La Piccola Scala* where more intimate operas were performed. He found the offices in a small gray building with an ugly entrance. He parked the moped, locking it to a rack where several others were parked.

He walked into the building. At the end of the hall he saw a steel door with *Sforza* painted on it. Without knocking, he walked in to a small office with several doors leading off of it.

A secretary sat behind a hideous World War II issue desk. Glancing up, without smiling, she said, "Signor Vasselli? You may go in by the door to your right. They are waiting for you in there." She looked back down without further comment to her work.

Who in hell does this arrogant bitch think she's talking to? I have half a mind to throw a fit and let her know this is no way to greet an artist who has made a great deal of money for this fucking agency. But no, that would be giving her attention that she is unworthy of. Glancing back at the hunched figure with contempt, he opened the door to the right and walked into a large office. Before him at a long steel table sat the three middle-aged agents. They looked up and wordlessly waved him to a chair in front of them. He sat stiffly and with difficulty tried to appear calm and composed.

"Signor Vasselli, I am Gaetano Fraschini. This is Alberto Barbieri-Nini and Ettore Belladonna. We are to brief you on your engagements for the coming season. We trust you received the scores that were sent to you?" All three gentlemen nodded at him. They wore business suits of dark gray with identical black ties. They had an air about them that bespoke an attitude of businesslike disdain of artists that Ernesto had grown to despise. The original speaker shoved forward a thick sheaf of papers.

Ernesto faced them coldly. "Yes, gentlemen, I have received the music and have been studying it carefully. So this is the list of the cities where I am to perform? If you will give me a moment please to peruse these papers I would appreciate it." The first item dealt with five performances of *I Lombardi to* be presented at the *Teatro Della Pergola* in Florence in November. The document outlined when he was to arrive, the arrangements for his lodging and transportation and the schedule of rehearsals and performance dates. "May I ask who the other artists are to be and who is the *Maestro*?"

The three men looked quickly at each other and then Signor Barbieri-Nini led off. "The *Oronte* is to be sung by Franceso Savarotti, the *Giselda* by Leonora Di Amichis, and the hermit by Signor Ganzarolli. The *Maestro* is Gavazenni. You will take the part of *Arvino*, as indicated in the score you were sent. The terms are the same as usual. We take twenty-five percent of your fees, which will be paid to you, as always, in cash, before each of the performances. All of your expenses are to be paid by the agency, as in our previous agreements. If this is acceptable to you, please sign at the bottom of the page."

Ernesto was staggered at the names of some of the greatest singers in the world. He was inwardly thrilled, but merely stared back at them. "These terms are acceptable to me." He signed the document, carefully putting his copy to the side. "What next?"

Signor Belladonna cleared his throat. "You will be singing *I Puritani* at the *Teatro Massimo Bellini di Palermo* and the *Teatro Bellini* in Catania. At the *San Carlo* in Naples, you are to sing *Il Pirata.* These are for the second run of each opera in the three cities, and you will be covering in each city for the tenors who will be performing in the first runs. These three documents contain the dates you must present yourself for the rehearsals and performances. They also specify your fees, our percentages, and your travel, hotel, as well as food expenses as usual. In the case of the performances you are to cover, you must be in that city available and ready until three hours before the performances. You will of course be paid for the performances you cover with your usual fees, even if you don't have to sing at any of them. The last document concerns the production of *I Capuleti ed I Montecchi* to be presented by the *Teatro Argentina* in Rome with the usual arrangements. If you accept, please sign each of these documents and you will be bound by their terms."

Ernesto looked at each page carefully. The terms for each showed higher fees than he had been earning. He was excited, as each production was to be held in an upper-echelon house which would give him exposure to international press coverage. He signed each page with pleasure, carefully concealing his joy. He was determined not to let these agency men see just how happy these terms made him.

Signor Fraschini leaned over the table. "Signor Vasselli, of course you are free to accept engagements with any other theaters during the season, knowing of course you must keep us informed of your movements and seeing that any other theaters sends to us the usual fees. Your expenses, of course, are their affair and I would suggest you engage counsel to be sure any independent contracts you are offered are in good form. If you have no further questions, you may leave now."

Ernesto left the room without a backward glance. He was furious at their attitude towards him, both as a man and an artist, but he was tied to them for now, though the five-year original contract would expire at the end of the coming season. *When the next contract comes up these dogs are going to find that when they come to me that I'm going to be expensive and they are going to have to accept a smaller percentage. I've toiled too long now with their inferior engagements and I'm not about to accept the same terms that I did in Venice.* He passed the secretary, who didn't look up, and smiled at the soprano who waited her turn with the officials. He left the building and went to a nearby café, where he ordered a strong espresso and biscotti. He was seething with indignation, but carefully concealed it on his chalk-white face. No use scaring off potential bed partners by seeming unapproachable.

Twenty-eight

In late October, Ernesto journeyed to Florence for rehearsals of *I Lombardi a la Prima Crociata* at the *Teatro Della Pergola*. Arriving only the day before, he had no time to look about the city or to take in its many famous museums and galleries. This, unfortunately, had become a pattern in the business. The demands of time in learning and coaching roles, as well as giving many performances up and down the country, prevented him from having any more than a cursory examination of anything he might have wanted to see. He was content with these restraints, however; he loved to perform and was dedicated to being a part of a collective effort in bringing neglected operas to the stage. He was also extremely excited about the prospect of appearing on stage in a neglected Verdi opera with Savarotti, the rising tenor star.

Upon leaving the train station, he went at once to his hotel and settled into his suite. After his luggage had been deposited in his bedroom, he tipped the porters, poured a glass of wine, and tried out the piano, which by contract was to be in his suite wherever he was to perform.

He played the Chopin mazurka he knew from memory. Its scope covered almost the entire keyboard and instantly allowed him to recognize the piano's tune. *This isn't bad. At least they've fulfilled their promise to have something of quality waiting my arrival. The action is a little tight, but the sound is brilliant.* He had arrived with his role committed to memory, as was his rule, a discipline instilled in childhood. Nevertheless, he put the score of the opera before him. All cuts and adjustments had been carefully worked out in advance by the conductor. He played through his aria, the duet of *Arvino* and *Giselda,* and the ensembles in which he was to appear. He hated the fact that he had no duets or solo scenes with Savarotti, but relished the thought of hearing this extraordinary singer in person.

As the afternoon advanced, he called for a cold supper to be served in his suite. He looked around in pleasure at the well-appointed sitting room. His requests, always reasonable in his opinion, had been taken care of by the agency. His favorite wines, cheeses, and bottled water stood on the sideboard. He went to his bedroom and lay down for a brief nap, rising when his supper arrived. A handsome young man delivered a cart laden with what he had ordered. Ernesto looked at him with interest as he sat at his table and waited to be served. The waiter, efficient, smiled broadly at him as he poured the wine and arranged the dishes.

While Ernesto realized that the man was certainly available, his interest in sex, for once, took a back seat to the following day's rehearsal, which weighed heavily on his mind. The role of *Arvino* was not the usual high-flying *Bel Canto* part in which he specialized. Aside from his one aria, which only once rose to a single high C, the part was more of an inflexible father whose sole aim was to dissuade his daughter from involvement with a Moslem prince. He had worked often with Gavazenni, the conductor, and respected his judgment totally, but he had misgivings for the first time regarding his ability to carry off this role as enthusiastically as usual since the part held little interest for him. He dismissed the young man, who hovered nearby expectantly as he ate his meal, and went to bed. Without hesitation, he reached for the telephone and called Carlotta in Alabama.

His mood immediately brightened at her familiar voice. "Madame? Yes, it is me, Ernesto. How are you and The Colonel? I know it's been a long time, but you understand I've been preparing for the opening of the season here in Florence. Yes, the rehearsals begin tomorrow. I am calling because I'm concerned about this small part that I'll be singing. I'm afraid this might be taking a step backwards since I've been singing leading roles the last few years."

* * *

Carlotta nervously twisted the cord with her fingers. Sitting at her French desk in the music room, she was growing impatient with the whining tone of his voice. "Now, Ernesto, let me tell you something. I didn't spend ten years perfecting your technique only to have you feeling sorry for yourself because you've accepted a small role. Of course it isn't one of my favorite operas, but I've looked at the score you sent, and frankly it's a far less-difficult part than most of what you've been doing. What you have to realize is that it's a great compliment that the *maestro* has asked for you. Savarotti and Di Amichis are singing the leads. So what? I'll tell you what. These are singers who are infinitely superior to the dogs you've been singing with in the provinces. The event will attract international attention. And if you do what I know you're capable of, it can't help but enhance your reputation when you next go to Palermo, Catania, and Naples. Also, think of the opportunity of singing the lead roles in the Bellini operas. My God, child! Use your mind a bit. Now I have to go, a student is coming. Yes, well it isn't night here. You know I'm eight hours behind you." The doorbell sounded through the hall. "Mamie!" she yelled. "Answer the door. Where the hell is that woman when she's needed? You see, darling, what I still have to put up with in this hell hole?" The shrill bell once more sounded. "I've got to go let them in myself, so let me go. No, but call on a Sunday my dear in the future if you don't mind. I don't teach then. Don't worry you'll be fine. *Ciao,* my angel!" She abruptly broke the connection and hurried to the front door.

* * *

Ernesto felt better as he hung up the phone. Her voice always steadied him. *She is changeless, ageless, my Madame. Great singers! It's about time.*

He closed his eyes, thinking back to the time when he was a little boy, picking blackberries in Albertville for Aunt Barbara to make her wonderful cobblers. He smiled as he recalled her care-worn face. Sleep overtook him and the thoughts of long ago evaporated in the darkness.

At eight o'clock sharp Ernesto walked through the doors of the main rehearsal room at the *Teatro Della Pergola.* The room was large and cold. As usual in Italian theaters, there was no heat or air conditioning. Singers could not abide either. Officials from the theater directed him to an area where steel folding chairs had been set up for the chorus members. He knew no one but could tell right away that no insult was directed at him personally. This was business. After a few more minutes, *Maestro* Gavazinni and the leading singers made their entrance. The *maestro*, spying Ernesto sitting with the chorus members, shot him a bright smile and waved, but did not call him up to the raised platform where Savarotti and Di Amichis stood. After a few opening remarks concerning the opera by the stage director, the piano rehearsal began. The chorus left for a separate room with the chorus master among much grumbling from members who weren't used to being herded like cattle this early in the morning.

Ernesto found himself sitting alone. In the front of the room the conductor and principal singers were in deep conversation. Near him sat several singers who would be filling small parts, mostly older chorus members who would occasionally be thrown a bone of a few lines. *Damn, when is some singing going to start? I can't believe the short rehearsal time that has been given to this production, less than a month for an opera unknown to most of these people. Madame would be in horror if she were here. The median age for this chorus has to be at least forty, but we'll see how they sound.* An assistant signaled for silence. The soprano began her first aria in typical rehearsal style, high notes only lightly etched into place. Ernesto, while used to this sort of thing, always sang in full voice, only pulling back on volume in the uppermost reaches of his voice. He didn't like the practice, but had learned long ago not to make waves.

He sat back and listened admiringly. She had already been singing major roles for at least fifteen years, with large theaters in Italy and abroad vying for her services. A little, squat older woman followed her everywhere with a large notebook in which she constantly scribbled notes. He was used to seeing such people, though he had never known or wanted the services of a personal assistant. Then the soprano finished her aria after many stops and starts, returning to her seat as Savarotti stood up.

What a handsome man, tall and running to fat, but a wonderful presence with his gleaming black hair, his eyes, bright blue. Very self-assured, but I like that. The tenor now nodded towards the pianist and began the aria *La Mia Letizia en fondere.* The great voice rang out and filled the room. Ernesto listened in rapt attention. This was a major voice and it thrilled him to hear such accomplished technique. No stops, no false intonation. As he finished the aria, Savarotti looked over at the beaming conductor who silently mouthed *Bravo!*

Ernesto was called and the duet between father and daughter began. He hid a feeling of indignation at having been kept waiting for nearly an hour. The blend between his voice and the soprano would have to be worked on, but the basic sound was there. Di Amichis smiled brightly at him and patted the seat beside her as they sat down. She was very animated and chatted with him about his experience. She too had obviously trained in the Garcia method. She spoke of her beginning with a *Traviata* at Flori. He knew her reputation. She had not so long ago recorded *Medea* at *La Scala*. She specialized in *Bel Canto* operas, and since the age of twenty had been singing everywhere. The older woman sat directly behind her, constantly whispering and recording information in her notebook. Only later did Ernesto come to know that this huge notebook was the soprano's date book, divided into engagements as much as five years in advance. This staggered him, as his was only from season to season.

The piano rehearsals went on for two weeks, followed by another week with orchestra. The opera came together. This was Verdi's music, and although unknown to many, it attracted a great deal of interest. The chorus had mastered the difficult music with seeming ease, and at the performances they were warmly greeted by the public with marked approval. Ernesto was pleased with the details given to costumes and sets. Everything was new. The medieval setting of the opera was true to the composer's intentions and directions. The five performances were spread over a twelve-day period. Newspapers raved over Di Amichis and Savarotti. The time passed quickly and the principals left for other engagements.

Ernesto loved the Italian ways. Operas were given in spurts of five to ten presentations in a short while and then put away and a new opera mounted. This was not true in the United States, where after several performances in the fall, they would be brought back in the spring again, often with new casts. He left Florence the day after the last performance on a train for Naples. From there, after a day's rest, it was time to sail across the bay of Naples to Sicily.

Sicily seemed a strange and wild place to him, with mountains and rocky seaports. Ernesto was interested in being in the place that gave birth to his divine Bellini, but he soon tired of these dark people. In Palermo, it was like stepping back in time at least a hundred years. There were few modern buildings. Everywhere old stone buildings swept up from the harbor into the far off hills. People went quietly about their daily tasks, much as had their ancestors for hundreds of years. The fishermen constantly mended their nets and then would set off for their fishing in the bay. Street vendors hawked their wares to the tourists who came and went among the market places. Even in Palermo, the *Teatro Massimo* seemed on a much smaller scale than theaters on the mainland. He delighted in singing *I Puritani.* The part of *Arturo* suited his voice perfectly. The performances were presented before appreciative audiences in a very unspectacular manner.

After moving on to Bellini's birth city in Catania, Ernesto was pleased to visit the house where the illustrious composer had been born in 1801. He visited the church where he was entombed under a magnificent monument. He wondered at how the blond-haired, blue-eyed Bellini could have sprung from this wild place with narrow streets and old gray buildings.

The artists with whom he appeared were predominately drawn from minor houses in Italy. No major stars ever sang here. They were far too expensive and uniformly uninterested in performing off the international circuit. He was ready to leave when, after three weeks, his engagement ended. The undercurrent feeling of fear which seemed to permeate the island unnerved him. He had been warned not to venture into the mountains where the beautiful villas of the ruling classes stood shining in the afternoon sunshine. It was warm here, even in February, though it grew cold in the evenings. The people were frightened of the Mafia. They went about their tasks furtively and quietly. Ernesto was happy when he embarked on his boat, crowded with departing tourists, and sailed from Catania across the bay to Naples.

Naples, he soon discovered, was not like northern Italian cities. Its chief claim to fame came from the fact that many famous operas had been produced over the last hundred and fifty years in its theaters. The San Carlo Theater itself was magnificent, though outside the squalor of crowded streets spoke loudly of the utter poverty of many of its inhabitants. At the rehearsals of *Il Pirata,* Ernesto was impressed with how smoothly music was made here. Everyone seemed to like him a great deal. He had learned most of the part of *Gualtiero* with Carlotta, incorporating the ornaments of its original creator, Giovanni Battista Rubini. He was delighted that Di Amichis was singing the role of Imogene. The eight performances were given great acclaim, and because of the presence of the soprano, they attracted audiences from all over Italy. This opera had been the first great success of the young Bellini in 1826. The orchestra brought it to life in a stirring performance of the overture which set the tone of the action that followed.

Ernesto's opening aria, *Nel furor de le tempeste,* drew a huge ovation. Every aria, duet, and trio held the spectators in rapt attention, rewarded with applause and bravas.

Di Amichis, in her final aria and cabaletta, *Col Sorriso d'innocenza, O Sole ti vela,* brought down the house with great waves of *bravas* as applause descended on her. From all sides of the large auditorium flowers rained down from the galleries. Ernesto had not heard anything like this since the days when Jane and Olivia had sung their arias and duets in Venice five years earlier. The curtain calls never seemed to end as they were called out repeatedly by the enraptured audience.

After so much activity concentrated over several months, Ernesto was glad to have two weeks at home in his apartment in the old palace near Milan. There was much on his mind about future projects. Even here in Milan word of his triumphs was the talk of the city. People thought surely the great theater of *La Scala* would send for him. His old landlady, Signora Eleonora, greeted him on his arrival, throwing off her reserve and embracing him warmly.

He gratefully retreated to his rooms, a welcome refuge. He was tired, but after having settled back in he hurried to call Carlotta. "Madame, how wonderful to hear your voice again. Yes, the performances all went well. I feel rich with the fees I have brought home. In Naples they couldn't seem to get enough of me."

"Darling, didn't I tell you it would all go well?" gushed Carlotta. "The Colonel and I have been waiting for your news, and we are happy for you. Go on like this and the world will be at your feet. It's been so long since we've seen you. Are you thinking of coming back in the summer to spend a few weeks with us? Nothing ever changes here. Just the lessons I give all the time. Ernesto, it's time you began to think of sending some of your earnings out of the country. Italians are so idiotic about allowing major sums to leave their shores, so please start making these arrangements. As long as it's done in small transfers, no alarms should come up against you." He envisioned her in her throne chair, drinking strong coffee and glancing at the portrait of Madame Blanche above the fireplace. "No dear, we are fine, we just miss you so much. Please let us know how the *Capuleti* performances go in Rome."

"Yes, Madame, I will. The part of *Tebaldo* does have that beautiful aria, though it's the women singing Romeo and Giuletta who are the stars.

I'm looking forward to being in Rome. It will be my first time there. The new contract with the Sforza's? I haven't been sent a copy of it yet, but I'm to talk with them while I'm there. I'm reluctant to sign again for another five years. I know they've brought me a lot of work, but with the attention I've been receiving, I'm wondering if I shouldn't become a free lancer like Madame Di Amichis. You would love her. She was so kind to me in Florence and also lately in Naples."

"Well Ernesto, I think you should stay with the agency. After all, they have kept you working constantly. You are still only twenty-three. I stay in touch with them all the time, you know. I just want to be sure you don't accept any roles that aren't well suited for you. I know with your technique that you never force the voice, but heavier orchestrations can make it difficult for an agile voice like yours. Stay with the *Bel Canto* operas is my advice. Okay, I know you need to go. Stay in touch. We send our love, darling. You know that will never change. Goodbye then for now."

He poured a glass of wine, walked to the windows facing on the courtyard, pulled the shutters open and peered at the street. *Nothing ever changes here. People come and go on the street as before. It all has a sense of permanence about it. I'll have to go out later for a coffee at the café. I wonder if Gasparo will be there. I loved the time I spent with him last summer when I first came here. It's time for some fun and letting out some of this pent-up energy.* He laughed and went to his bedroom for a nap. He didn't realize how tired he was till he lay down. He pulled up the coverlet over his shoulders and fell asleep almost instantly.

Twenty-nine

Two weeks at home rapidly evaporated. The important engagement in Rome called him to that ancient city. On his arrival the day before rehearsals were to begin, he briefly took a short self-guided tour of the central city. The Roman Forum, The Castel Sant'Angelo and, of course, the Vatican were places he wanted to see. The Vatican was too immense to be taken in as he would have liked. He simply did not have the time. Reluctantly, he returned to his hotel near the opera house in the late afternoon. He was glad to be in a city where the Italian spoken was nearer the Milanese dialect. He had been appalled at the Neopolitan and Sicilian dialects, so different that he had learned from Carlotta. It had been almost like another language, and at times he found it difficult to converse with people. Happily, he wouldn't have that problem here.

Springtime was showing itself earlier here than in Milan and Venice. Trees were budding; their flowers would soon be a delight to residents and tourists alike. After checking in at the hotel he made his way to a restaurant he had seen earlier, four blocks away.

As the sun was setting, the tables outside were deserted and new arrivals were conducted inside. Walls of dark cypress paneling gleamed in the candlelight. Waiters moved with ease from the seating areas to the kitchens in the rear. Ernesto asked for a single table near the front. He ordered calamari and his favorite red wine along with a dish of baked ziti pasta and a large mixed salad. A flurry of voices at the entrance diverted his attention. A rush of welcoming voices greeted the arrival of the celebrity.

It was the heroic tenor star, Mario Del Aroldo and his wife. This was quite a surprise for Ernesto, who expected just a quiet evening among the tourists. Signor Aroldo swept into the main dining room and was escorted to his table by the beaming owner. *My God, what a man. I have only heard his recordings of Andrea Chenier, Trovatore, and Ernani, but how handsome he is in person. The wife too, is beautiful. I have heard that he has begun to curtail his performances and now seldom sings outside Italy. He is a specialist in verismo operas and has been singing all over the world for more than thirty years.* He was like a gushing fan now as he stared brazenly at the great tenor. He quickly diverted his gaze when he saw that Mario was looking back at him. He blushed and looked down at his food. His appetite was gone. His heart pounded with excitement.

His waiter saw the untouched food. "Signore? Is anything wrong with the supper? We would be glad to replace anything not to your satisfaction. I wasn't meaning to neglect you, but we were all thrilled when Signor Del Aroldo came in. We haven't seen him for a while, and it is always a joy when he honors us this way." The waiter smiled, then looked over to where the couple sat.

"No, I'm fine. I just find I'm not quite as hungry as I thought. Just some more wine please." He smiled back at the waiter. "I had heard that Signor Aroldo had been on tour. Perhaps he is here just for a visit. This must be a favorite place of his here in Rome."

The waiter, whose name was Gaetano, poured another glass of wine and whispered, "Actually he lives here in Rome with his wife near the Farnese palace. They come in here often as he loves the special off-the-menu dishes that our owner always prepares especially for him. His wife Signora Giovanna is a very noble lady, having descended from a very ancient Roman family, the D'Estes."

"I thought that family was from Ferrara," exclaimed Ernesto. "That's far to the north, but who knows? I have sung at the Communale Theater myself there several times." He touched the waiter's back

Gaetano smiled warmly at him. "So you too are a singer? We are all looking forward to hearing the *I Capuleti* of Bellini in a few weeks at the Argentina. Are you with the company here?"

"Actually no, I am only a guest artist, but I will be singing *Tebaldo* in the *Capuleti* there. Will you be going to hear us perhaps?" He looked intently at the young man.

"Oh, I'm not sure, Signore. I love the opera, of course, but much will depend on the availability of tickets. I probably will now though . . . to hear you."

"I'm only singing a supporting role. The stars are the women who will sing *Romeo* and *Giuletta*, but I have a nice aria in the first act." He took out his card case and rapidly wrote a sentence on the back of his personal card. "Take this to the ticket office at the theater. I will see that a ticket is left for you for the first performance." He handed the card to the surprised young man. "You have been so kind to me this evening. I will be delighted to have you as my guest."

The waiter trembled. "Ernesto Vasselli, *Tenore, Milano*. Oh, signore, I am just a simple man, I go to the Santa Cecilia School in the day time and work here in the evenings, but when I show this to the owner I'm sure he'll excuse me to see the opera. What an honor to have you with us. I believe I saw your name in the newspaper review of a performance in Naples. I can hardly wait to tell my wife about this. She will be so excited for me. Thank you so much."

Frowning, Ernesto looked away and dropped his hand from Gaetano's back. "Well that was *Pirata* that I sang there with Signora Di Amichis. It was a much larger part than I'll have here. I need to go. I'm staying at the Hotel D'Annunzio and need to get back to rest. Our rehearsals begin in the morning. Is that my bill that you are clutching there? Just leave it here on the table." He waved the young man off and turned his attention back to his table. He realized he was hungry after all and began to eat the nearly cold food. *Well I can't expect that every man I meet will be obtainable. I hate having wasted my time, but he did give me information about Del Aroldo.* Looking up, he met Del Aroldo's gaze from across the room. He had an amused look on his face. He smiled broadly and laughed out loud. Ernesto blushed crimson and rapidly threw some money on the table for his meal and started to the men's room to wash his hands. As he came out, he ran right into Del Aroldo.

The older man looked him up and down saying, "We hear you are here to sing in *Capuleti* next month. Welcome to Rome, Signor Vasselli. Forgive me, but your friend, the waiter, told me just now while you were in the bathroom who you are. I hope you aren't offended."

"Why of course not, Signor Del Aroldo. The waiter is not a friend, however. I only met him tonight, but I'm delighted to meet you. It's my first time singing here in Rome. The ways of people here are different than in Milan. I apologize for his having bothered you about me." He could feel sweat breaking out on his face. His knees were shaking. Del Aroldo was several inches shorter, but powerfully built with blue back hair and a very sensual mouth.

"Not at all, my boy. I know the management at the *Argentina* very well, having sung there many times in the past. I haven't sung there in some time though, as they keep putting on these *Bel Canto* operas. Not that I don't like them, but my voice is too large for that kind of music." He reached out, putting both hands on Ernesto's shoulders. "What's this? You are trembling? No need for that, I'm just a man like you." He put his palm flat against the younger man's cheek and laughed. "We Romans are warm people. Stay here long enough among us and perhaps you'll never want to leave again. Well excuse me now, Ernesto, I know you are leaving and I have to let some of this wine out." He looked down at his own crotch. "You understand what that's like, I'm sure."

"Yes, sir. Thank you, I'm so glad to have met you." He reached out his hand, which Mario grasped warmly and then the great man abruptly kissed him on both cheeks.

"Good night then. My wife and I will look forward to seeing you perform soon." Ernesto almost ran out of the restaurant.

Outside, he took several deep breaths, still trembling with excitement at actually talking with this huge star. Wiping his face with a handkerchief, he turned to walk back to the hotel. He looked back in the window to where Signora Giovanna sat and caught the steady gaze of Gaetano, who waved at him. He hurried away into the night.

In his suite, sleep evaded him. The events at the restaurant combined with the anticipation of rehearsals in the morning set his nerves on edge. He drew a chair to one of the windows and looked out into the night. *I have to start planning on doing something that can bring my career up a notch. The isolated brushes with greatness that I've known are nothing to compare with the squalor of having constantly to sing in inferior productions in insignificant theaters. I have too much time and effort invested now to put up with that sort of crap much longer. Perhaps I should not have put all my eggs in one basket here in Italy. People love the novelty of the revivals of the forgotten operas, but most of them are for the glory of the prima donnas. Still, it's what I've trained for, and it does bring in money. Del Aroldo nearly swept me off my feet tonight. He must think I'm just a young fool making a small splash in a large ocean. I need to ally myself with powerful people like him. His reputation only could open doors where I could become a permanent member of a company instead of just being a guest artist. Come on, Ernesto, what are you thinking? He's probably already forgotten you. What are any of us really but paid entertainers? Even Mario for all his greatness is nothing more. Yet he is rich as well as famous. He's not the sort of man I'm usually attracted to. He can't be more than five-foot-eight, while I'm over six feet tall. Short then, with a large chest, but he is handsome. Away dreams! I need to rest now. It's so late. Two o'clock. The rehearsal begins promptly at eight.*

He willed himself to sleep.

The morning dawned dark and gray as dim light filtered through the curtains. His sleep had been fitful at best. He was slightly hung over from too much wine and called for strong coffee to be sent from the kitchen. When it arrived, he sat on the sofa in pajamas and savored the hot, dark liquid while his head cleared. He nibbled at the fruit and biscotti and began to hum to warm up the voice. *Good! It's responding. Not a trace of throat constriction. Oh shit, it's nearly seven. Need to get my ass in high gear.* He took a long hot shower, and after shaving, admired himself in the mirror. *Damn, I'm still looking good. No fat creeping on like the pigs I see all the time, my abs still tight and my dick in good working order. Why can't I take all Rome by storm?* Laughing at his foolishness, he dressed quickly in loose-fitting clothing and walked three blocks to the opera house. Tourist buses, filled with old ladies, passed in both directions as he trekked.

The rehearsal got off to a slow start due to the pianist's tardiness, for which he was severely reprimanded when he finally arrived. He was a non-threatening balding man in his forties, running to fat, but played beautifully. The prima donnas who were singing *Romeo* and *Giuletta* began their long first duet, followed by individual arias.

Ernesto was at last called up and sang his aria, *E Serbato, E Serbato questo acciaro.* He knew this was all the part except for some brief interjections with the chorus in the two acts. While he was singing, he noticed the prima donnas stopped their gossiping long enough to listen. The part lay rather low for him. No very high notes, just very beautiful melodies at a point in the story that partly set in motion the tragedy that ended in the deaths of the two major protagonists. The conductor complimented him on his singing. As always, his pitch was perfect.

He sat for most of the three-hour rehearsal, watching the conductor closely to see if he would prove a severe taskmaster. The days ran together after that, with almost daily sessions and at last costume fittings and stage directions. The opera house would be a comfortable place in which to sing for all of them with lively acoustics and shallow orchestra seating. Only perhaps thirty yards from the stage to the rear of the auditorium, and then the typical horseshoe galleries rising in eight tiers towards an ornate painted ceiling. Most Italian theaters were similar, utilizing limited space and designed for bringing the audience as close to the stage as possible.

At the first performance, every seat was taken. Elegantly dressed ladies, glittering with diamonds, called out to friends while their bored husbands sat in silence. As the orchestra tuned up and the lights came down, the audience grew silent in anticipation. The conductor appeared and after a brief prelude, the curtain rose to reveal fourteenth-century Verona. A chorus of Capulet retainers was joined by the character of *Capellio*, father of *Giuletta*, and Ernesto, in the role of *Tebaldo*. The beautiful prelude to the aria *E Serbato* began as Ernesto stepped toward the footlights, singing of the love he felt for *Giuletta* and thanking her father for promising her hand in marriage to him. Many were curious to hear him, as newspapers with reviews of his *I Puritani* and *Il Pirata* in Palermo and Naples had preceded him.

His stage appearance startled many. He was young and tall. Slim, with piercing dark eyes, and above all, a powerful voice and clear diction. The aria was warmly received with applause from the adoring women. As *Tebaldo* is then told by *Capellio* that *Giuletta* will be his even if she is forced to the altar, he stunned the audience as he began the cabaletta, *L'amo, L'amo e me se cara.* His acting and emotional bearing as he sang – the song stating that if his ardor caused her one moment of pain that he would be content to live a life of sadness — caused a sympathetic stir in the audience. *Bravos* rang out in appreciation.

He left the stage as Romeo and his followers entered quietly. The prima donna singing the role of *Romeo* launched into a beautiful aria about love for *Giuletta*, interrupted by the threatening return of the Capulets and *Tebaldo*. Romeo's cabaletta to the aria, *Se Romeo,* was hurled out in furious indignation, beginning with the words *La tremenda ultrice spada.* The action was stopped by a tremendous ovation for the mezzo soprano. Flowers rained down from the galleries almost as though people were seized with delirium. At last they were permitted to continue as the two groups facing each other with angry gestures withdrew to opposite sides of the stage into the wings. Each scene that followed was an undisputed success.

Backstage after the finale of the first act, a furious argument broke out between the two prima donnas, each accusing the other of upstaging her. Ernesto had seen this sort of thing many times when operas had two female singers who were constantly fighting to outshine each other, but as always, he never took sides and merely watched in amused silence until the women left for their dressing rooms.

The second and last act followed after a long intermission, and drew tears with the music of the divine Bellini as the principal singers fell dead on stage before the horrified onlookers. The curtain calls began, to ever-mounting acclaim. Huge floral tributes were thrown onstage.

When at last they were allowed to depart, Ernesto went to his dressing room, greeted by several arrangements of flowers. He looked at the cards. One was from Carlotta and The Colonel: *Best wishes darling for a wonderful success in your Roman debut!* He smiled at their memory. The next card, in gold ink, read, *Our congratulations, Signor Vasselli, on your first performances here in Rome, Mario and Giovanna Del Aroldo.*

I can hardly believe they have remembered me!

The third was in an arrangement of pure white gardenias, which nearly suffocated the room with their pungent aroma. The card read *Good luck tonight from your admirer, La Speranza.* He stared at the obvious female handwriting and thought, *Who can this be? A woman who signed herself, she who hopes? Curious. Hopefully the people managing this theater will know who sent them to me.*

A soft knock sent him to the door, and he saw the Del Aroldo couple before him. "Signor, Signora Del Aroldo, what a surprise. Please come in. What an honor that you've come back to see me." He smiled broadly.

"Please, signor, call us Mario and Giovanna," said Mario as they embraced him. "And we will call you Ernesto if that is okay with you? We are after all friends in this city. We enjoyed so much your beautiful singing this evening. We are always delighted with fresh, young voices."

Giovanna stepped forward and embraced him again. "Ernesto, we've heard so much from the reviews we've read of your *Il Pirata* and *I Puritani*, but why, we ask, in Palermo and Naples, but not here in Rome? We were surprised when *Capuleti* was announced here. We don't hear enough of *bel canto* operas these days, though they are being put on everywhere else it seems."

"I'm sure, Signora, that it has more to do with the availability of singers and having a conductor willing to take them on. I would rather it had been *Il Pirata*, where I have a longer and more interesting role. Please, would you both sit down? I'll call for some wine and cheese for us."

"No, Ernesto," said Mario. "We need to let you change, and we have a late dinner that we need to get to." Handing him his card, he continued "Here's our address and phone number. We would like you to come to our home tomorrow for lunch. We can talk shop some more. Would one o'clock be all right? That is if you are available?"

"Yes, Mario, I would be happy to get to know the two of you better." He looked at the card. "Your apartment seems to be near the Farnese palace. At least the street name is the same. I have been asked to give a song recital there between the fourth and fifth performances of *Capuleti* and would like very much, if your schedules permit, for you to come as my guests."

"We would be delighted," said Giovanna. "We can talk more about it tomorrow and you can give us the date. Well, my dear, we should go and let Ernesto rest."

"Yes, we'll go now, my boy. Thanks again for your performance. We were enchanted. We will look forward then to seeing you tomorrow."

"Thank you both so much for your kind words." Pulling flowers from the arrangement they had sent, he continued, "And from the lovely flowers you sent me, please take these as a souvenir of this evening." Each of them embraced and kissed him once more as they left.

Well, I seem to be in the family now. My God, for them to ask me to their home is more than I could have hoped for. And I have to finally see the Sforza agents in the morning to see what terms they are offering in the new contract. They are not going to run roughshod over me as they have in the past. I want fresh, beautiful working conditions like here in Rome. No more of just third rate provincial towns. I'll just have to see. They can't ignore the successes I've had this season. Turning to the clothes rack, he hung up his costume and took a quick shower, dressed into street clothes and made his way to the stage door.

A cluster of fans were waiting to see the artists as they came out. Gaetano from the restaurant rushed up asking for an autograph.

Ernesto smiled as he signed the programs. "So, Gaetano, you enjoyed the music tonight? I'm happy to see you. Is the restaurant open late for dinner? I'm famished!"

"Oh yes, *Signore*. May I come along with you? It will be wonderful to be waited on for a change and to hear how people have reacted to the opera."

"That will be fine. I'm not used to having fans waiting here like this. In Naples they always scoot us out side doors so the public will give us some room to breathe. Come along then, let's get out of here."

Waving to the applauding fans, he took Gaetano's arm, and the two young men walked into the night, ignoring the light rain that had begun to fall. Ernesto was riding high and smiled at the adoring young man. He thought briefly about the young man's wife, and then shook his head, as he knew he would sleep in Gaetano's arms tonight.

Thirty

The next morning, after a light breakfast, he dressed carefully and left for the meeting. Sforza's Rome offices were located on a narrow old street in a part of the city not frequented by tourists. *I can see why. These buildings must date from the seventeenth century. Certainly not anything a tourist would be interested in.* He arrived at the address and was relieved that the offices appeared clean and spacious in contrast to the tightly packed hovels that surrounded them. He rang the bell; almost immediately a young woman ushered him in.

"Signor Vasselli, if you will wait here, someone will be with you shortly. I was told that you are always prompt with your appointments and I've taken the liberty of having some coffee ready for the meeting, unless you would like some now perhaps?" She smiled warmly at him. She was tall and slim. She was also polite, in contrast to the woman in Milan.

"Thank you, *Signorina*, but I think I'll wait till the meeting begins." He sat in a large leather chair to which she had directed him and waited.

The girl, who said her name was *Antonietta,* sat at her desk some distance away.

Thirty minutes passed. *And to think I knocked myself out to get here on time. Reminds me of some doctor's office back in Selma where appointments times meant nothing, they just saw you when they were ready. Why should things be different in another country? After all, they could care less about me as an artist. I bet Mario is never kept waiting this way. They probably come to him, and then they wait till he is ready to see them. How I'd love to be in that position. Where the hell are these people?*

Disgusted, he decided to leave and addressed the young woman. "Tell your masters that when they are ready to promptly deal with artists at a time they have designated that they can reach me at my hotel. I have better things to do than to keep sitting here."

"Signore, please don't go. There must be a reason the agent is tardy. Here, let me go ahead and bring your coffee and I'll call to see what the problem is." He reluctantly reseated himself, growing angrier by the minute.

"Antonietta, I don't mean to sound rude. It's just that I performed last night and didn't get in bed till two o'clock and then had to be here at nine. I could have been getting some well-deserved rest right now. Unless I have a rehearsal, I never get up before ten. At least leave your work and sit here with me. I'll wait just a little while longer."

"Signore, I need to make the call first. I'm not sure it would be proper for me to be sitting talking with you when the agent arrives. They are very strict about our not being over familiar with artists." Footsteps echoed near the outer door. "Here the agent is, finally."

A middle-aged woman entered. "I am Eleonora Barjaba. I'm so sorry I was running late. An unfortunate accident with one of the tourist buses ahead of me tied up traffic. I trust Antonietta has made you feel comfortable?" She extended her hand, which he ignored as he stood, facing her down in furious tones.

"Are you just a secretary for whoever I'm to talk to? If that is the case, I'm leaving. I have no more time to waste waiting on anyone else. I wouldn't have stayed this long but for the kindness of this young woman here." He reached for his coat.

Obviously stung by his words, her smile vanished. "I am not a secretary to anyone. I am the manager and chief agent for this office. I apologize again that you were kept waiting, but as I explained, it couldn't be avoided. Now if you'll please come with me to my office, we can discuss the contract." She gestured towards the door on the left.

The office was a far cry from that of the one in Milan. Lace curtains hung from the tall windows. A beautiful desk of gleaming polished mahogany stood between the two windows on the wall that faced the street. Two comfortable armchairs stood in front of it with a small table between them. A leather sofa was against the wall to the left, and over all the walls hung lighted, framed publicity photographs of some very famous singers of the recent past. In spite of himself, he was impressed with the imperious nature of this woman, who surrounded herself in a comfortable setting.

She waved him to one of the armchairs and sat at her desk. "Signor Vasselli, we are impressed with the reports we have been receiving concerning your performances this season. Several of the theaters you have sung in this year have contacted us regarding productions they are planning, and have asked that we provide your services once again if you approve their choice of operas. We also have been approached by the management of *La Scala* in Milan, where I know you are living, about providing cover artists for their upcoming seasons. Tenors are always in short supply, especially for the *bel canto* operas that have become once again so popular these last ten years. I'm not sure this would be something you would be interested in, but if you do agree to this arrangement, you would be paid a fee for each performance you cover, and would be required to attend all rehearsals. If you should be called on to replace a principal tenor, you would have to understand that the public, having paid to see a certain singer, would naturally be displeased with a substitute being offered. However, we would expect that you not allow this to intimidate you and that you would step in without complaining, and sing at the highest standards that you are capable of. What would you think of this idea?"

La Scala? The thought brightened his mood. "Well this might be something I would consider, although I have not thought before of such an arrangement. You would need to give me a list of the parts I would need to prepare, the dates and number of performances and so forth. I could then give you an answer. Since I live there, it would be nice to be home more and it wouldn't be as tiring as in the past. You must give me time to think on it."

"Of course, that won't be a problem, but we would need an answer several months before the season opens. We have a new five-year contract that we'd like you to consider after your engagement at the *Argentina* is finished and then kindly forward back to us with your acceptance of the terms. You will note that in light of your many appearances this season that we have lowered our percentage demand to twenty percent of your earnings. We have also allowed you more time to accept foreign offers if they come your way, though whatever theaters that would want you will have to pay for your transportation and lodging. That would be an arrangement you would have to deal with yourself, as we only do that for Italy alone. If you commit to appearances through us in Italy you would not be allowed to accept offers that could cause a conflict. Thèaters here depend on us to deliver, so keep that in mind as well. Now, do you have any more questions or concerns?" She studied him carefully, trying to access the impact of her words.

Ernesto sipped his coffee. "Signora, you have given me a lot to think on. I know our original contract expires with the performances here in Rome, but if you will forward the proposal to my address in Milan, I will consider what you have discussed. I have wanted to sing more Rossini operas, so hopefully some of the theaters will be planning for them. I know the Teatro Reggio Di Parma has spoken in the press about possible productions of *Ermione, Armida, L'Italiana in Algeri,* and *La Donna Del Lago.* If you could make inquiries on my behalf, I would be pleased. I don't want to just become a cover artist alone, though I welcome the opportunity to sing with better theaters that have higher artistic standards. Now if you will excuse me, I have a luncheon engagement and I need to get back to my hotel." He rose, as did she.

"Signor, I'm sure we can come to an understanding when we hammer out the details of the contract. I will be happy to handle the matter myself." She made a beautiful gesture toward the photos on the walls, naming off each of the singers they had managed in the recent past. "Some of these are still with us, now singing everywhere. It is a mutual pact of respect between us and our artists. We work behind the scenes and they have the serenity of knowing they can just sing and leave the worrisome details to us. I hope to add your photograph to my walls very soon. Goodbye then, Signor. Our proposals in contract form will be sent on to Milan in a few weeks."

"Good day, Signora," he said. Antonietta smiled warmly from her desk as he crossed the reception area.

"Ciao, sweet girl. Perhaps next season I'll sing at *La Scala*. Would you come to hear me if I do?" Laughing, he kissed her on both cheeks as she blushed deeply.

She looked away and then returned his joyful smile. "I'm so happy for you, Signor. I must confess however, that I don't like opera that much. Not even Johann Strauss. The operetta I hate most is called *Die Fledermaus*." She laughed and walked out with him into the bright sunshine.

"Who knows, dear girl, maybe I'll convert you to opera one day. It's wonderful to hear the words of the opera all around us. Try to think about it. You are missing a great deal if you leave the theater out of your life." He gave her a hug and walked quickly away.

At one o'clock sharp he presented himself at the apartment of the Del Aroldos. A servant ushered him in and he was joined by his hosts, who, after welcoming him warmly, led him into their music room. Drapes of watered silk moiré in deep purple were tied back with golden cords. A beautiful chandelier dominated the ceiling, casting forth bright lighting even though bright sunlight flooded the room from the bank of six windows which dominated the wall to the rear of the room. Above a marble fireplace loomed a life-sized portrait of Mario as *Otello* in the opera by Verdi. In a glass cabinet beside the fireplace stood dozens of awards and commendations he had received during his long career. Statues and busts from the Napoleonic era stood in the four corners, with green plants and flowers scattered around on tables. A brocaded high-backed sofa stood in the center of the room with a low table of polished marble before it and four matching chairs of an indeterminate period. Ernesto had rarely seen such a room in a private residence and stared in undisguised admiration.

At the opposite side of the room, a grand piano dominated the wall space below an even more magnificent portrait of Mario in *Francesca Da Rimini.* On the piano itself, as in Carlotta's home, at least two dozen autographed pictures of colleagues stood in ornate gold frames, while on the floor beneath it, to Ernesto's amazement, heaps of golden laurel crowns and wreaths were scattered about in complete disorder, all souvenirs of performances and gifts of fans from countless engagements all over the world. Stunned, he stood in amazed silence while his hosts watched in amusement.

"Ernesto? Ernesto, would you please sit down and enjoy some wine while we wait for the luncheon to be served?" Giovanna smiled and gestured to an arm chair while her husband poured the glasses of Venetian crystal with the rich wine *D'Serucusa*. "We are so glad that you accepted our invitation, even after singing last night." They sat facing each other. "We trust that you slept well, after the storm that passed during the night?"

"Yes, Giovanna, thank you so much. I slept like a stone, though my small role wasn't in the least tiring. Bellini's music is such balm for the voice and I found the acoustics in the theater to be very good. What a beautiful room you have here. Why, I can't take my eyes off it. Everything is in such perfect harmony. My kinswoman, Carlotta Vasselli, back in the states, has a beautiful music room too, though nothing quite on this scale."

Mario exclaimed, "Carlotta Vasselli? You are from that family? I met her in my youth when she sang in *La Vestale, Beatrice di Tenda,* and *Norma* in Milan and Venice. I was always amazed at the scope of that voice which enabled her to sing both soprano and mezzo roles. A very great, a marvelous singer, but we lost track of her after the war. Did you study with her? Your technique recalls hers in many ways.

"Yes, Mario. She instilled in me the Garcia method when I was still a child. I came from Como, where I grew up in the Villa Pasta on the lake. After the early deaths of my parents, she and her husband became my guardians and arranged for my education. I spent a great deal of time with them at their home in the United States, so music was always of primary importance to me growing up. Madame Vasselli was a stern mistress when it came to developing my voice, the results of which you and Giovanna may judge for yourselves." He paused; Mario was watching him with intense interest. He willed himself to stop shaking. He felt uneasy talking about his manufactured past.

The opening to turn the conversation to the present came from Mario. "I have begun to curtail my own performances. After my last appearances at the Metropolitan in New York, I have decided I don't want to tour or be a permanent member of any company. I've been in the position for years now of being my own agent and I prefer it. These agencies can have their advantages, but they will try to arrange matters in such a way that they dominate your entire life. I promised Giovanna, who hates to travel anyway, that I would confine myself to only selected appearances. Our children are grown now and we are at a point in our lives where we want more stability."

Giovanna seemed content to let her husband lead the conversation, but Ernesto could see clearly that she adored him. Presently their servants served the meal in the adjoining small dining room.

Giovanna raised her glass in a toast. "To Ernesto! May your career continue always upwards to even greater successes. We are both pleased to have you as our friend. Anytime you are in Rome in the future, we would love to have you stay with us. We know how it is to live out of suitcases and to endure hotels and separations. Mario has been taking in a few students of promise lately, which relieves any boredom that might creep in. Our apartment as you can see is quite large. Ten rooms; I keep busy just keeping everything in order."

Mario smiled with what appeared to be an air of condescension and redirected his attention to Ernesto, who sat silently playing with his food. "Ernesto, if I may be so bold, I understand you will be singing at the Farnese Palace in a couple of weeks. I'm sure one of the rehearsal pianists from the *Argentina* will be working with you, but may I ask what you are planning to sing?"

The younger man struggled to control his rising emotion. He was used to men looking him up and down, but he felt strange to have it happen in front of Giovanna, who sat serenely and oblivious. Or so he thought.

"I am planning on singing Rossini, Bellini, Donizetti, and of course Verdi; some beautiful songs. Vittorio Canzonolli from the *Argentina* is going to play for me. I need to pin him down about the arrangement of the program. I also need to check out the hall where it's to be held. I can't stand dead rooms, and with only about a hundred people, I would like it to be relaxed and intimate."

"Intimate? An interesting word, don't you think so, Giovanna?" Husband and wife exchanged a knowing glance. Ernesto blushed deeply.

"I mean by that of course a relaxed atmosphere where the singer is not far removed from the hearers. These songs need to be presented in a way where they will go straight to the hearts and minds of people. If I can do that, then I will feel satisfied."

Giovanna said, "We will have to see if we can come. Would you please let us know the date? Mario isn't singing anywhere for awhile, so we should be able to attend." She got up suddenly. "Excuse me please, Ernesto, but I must go. I promised my daughter Mariella that I would go shopping with her and I need to get moving. We always meet at the church of San'Andrea della Valle, and she starts pouting very soon if she's kept waiting. Please stay as long as you like and talk with Mario." Both men stood, and she embraced and kissed each of them.

Ernesto began to feel uncomfortable, unaccustomed to being alone with a man as imposing as his host. "Mario, this has been wonderful, but I feel it's time for me to go back to the hotel and not impose further on your time. I love talking music with you and Giovanna, but I need to practice my scales before it gets too late." His voice trailed off as he perceived Mario was laughing.

"I would like you to stay awhile if you will. Let's go back to the music room and talk like we've known each other for years. We like you, my boy, and would like to spend more time with you." He impulsively reached out and led Ernesto back into the music room, where he insisted he sit on the sofa. Ernesto began feeling a sense of panic as Mario closed the doors and sat beside him.

"Now, Ernesto, let's talk more about you. You spoke of being from Como, which is strange as your accent doesn't sound like a northern one, but no matter. I would think at your age that love is something that must be high in your priorities. Do you have anyone special in your life?"

"Mario, I don't think about such things often. I stay very busy with learning new operas and there's not room in my life for anything but fleeting moments with people. I try to control emotions by directing them to the roles I portray. Better that than getting too close to people when I have to travel so much. After these *Capuleti* performances, I will need to get home to Milan to study the proposals of my new contract with the Sforza agency. I have no plans for the summer except for perhaps a concert at the *Teatro Comunale Aighieri* in Ravenna, and even that is only in the preliminary stage of discussion."

"When I was your age, music was important. I know what ambition is, how totally encompassing it can be to put music first in your life. Giovanna and I married when we were both very young, some thirty years ago. She traveled with me a great deal until the babies started to come. Things began to change over the years. I was gone so much and when I began to have extended engagements in other countries we wouldn't see each other for months on end. You'll find, if you ever marry, that intimacy is something to be nourished and reinvented if you tie yourself to one person only. We love each other deeply, but she has the problems that many women in middle age develop. She is no longer interested in sex."

"Mario, stop! You must not say such things to me. They are too personal, especially speaking to me of intimate sexual matters. I will be leaving in a few weeks and who knows when I'll be returning here. I need the summer months for study and reflection."

Late afternoon shadows began to fill the room. With the wine making their thoughts grow fuzzy, Mario drew closer. He boldly put his hand on Ernesto's thigh and rubbed it gently. "You are so handsome, sweet boy. Your face, in the glow of the afternoon sun, so white and fair." He slipped his arm around Ernesto's waist and held him tightly. "Your mouth, so beautiful, come, bend your head down to mine in forgetfulness."

Ernesto thrilled inside as he let his hand slip down over Mario's dark hair. "Are you sure this is what you want? I am nothing. What do I have that I can give to someone like you?"

Mario kissed him. "What do you have to give? Your youth, your sweetness, your wonderful body." His hand reached onto Ernesto's lap, grasping his now rock-hard penis through his thin linen trousers. "I want to make love to you here and now, to know the nearness of you close against my body. Come, give yourself to me."

Hands fumbled with clothing, and they at last lay naked on the sofa. Mario's lips tweaked the younger man's nipples as their mouths hungrily dissolved together in passionate kisses. Their hands entwined their bodies and sought out secret places, rushing to a shattering climax of lovemaking. At last, passions satisfied, they lay against each other. Twilight engulfed the room. They reluctantly drew apart and dressed.

"Mario, this has been wonderful. I never dreamed this could happen. Giovanna must be coming back soon though. She mustn't find me still here with you."

"Don't worry about her. She doesn't care what I do. She knows I have needs and she doesn't ask questions about my comings and goings. She is content with things as they are. What has passed between you and I this afternoon was fated. From the night in the restaurant where I first saw you, I wanted you. I don't give myself to people who don't deserve the gift. This is only the beginning for us. I want to see you again . . . as much as possible given our schedules. I can help you in so many ways, share so much with you, and further enhance your voice with new music. I will come to you in Milan and look over your contract. The Sforzas are a great agency, but I'd like to acquaint myself with their proposals. Trust me,

Ernesto, I am a powerful man."

"It is enough for me, Mario, that you would want me, want to help me. I don't expect anything more than you can give. I know how busy you must stay. Think of what has passed between us this afternoon. I am content if I've brought you some happiness today, but time and distance have a way of changing people. You will soon forget me."

"No, you are wrong. Time will prove that to you." He kissed him again, and they made their way back to the entrance hall. Ernesto slipped out reluctantly.

What can he do for me? We will see. His name and fame may open doors that I thought would be closed. I know he knows powerful people too. La Scala! If he can help me appear there, perhaps my career will truly take off. It's worth letting him fuck me if these things can happen. But love? What he feels now is for the passion we shared. I can never let myself be destroyed by love. It must not take over my goal. I want to be as great as he is, to take my place with the stars. Nothing else matters. No matter what it takes, this must happen while I'm still young, before time takes away these dreams.

He made his way back to the hotel without realizing how he got there. He realized that he was very hungry. Another performance lay ahead the next night, but for now he dismissed that from his mind as he left for his favorite restaurant and his Gaetano. *What is this that I'm doing with these married men? Gaetano is so sweet, Mario so handsome. His body I loved. His huge dick was like thick steel as he came into my body, but away with these thoughts. Emotion must be contained. I can not lose control. Madame would be furious with me if I let anything detract me from the goal we have set in motion.*

He walked to the restaurant, greeted by the staff as an old friend. In the dim light of the flickering candles scattered across the tables, he smiled, as Gaetano approached.

Thirty-one

Ten days later, after more performances of *Capuleti*, Ernesto found himself deeply involved in planning for the recital at the Farnese Palace. He and Vittorio practiced as their schedules allowed, at the rehearsal room at the Farnese when available. The piano, a Bosendorfer, was acceptable, though Ernesto still longed for a Steinway and the sharp, brilliant sound. Vittorio did not understand this. Steinways were foreign to him, uncommon except in households of the very rich in Italy. European instruments were good enough for him as long as they were kept in tune.

The program came together, as well as several encores. As he had promised, he had sent a note to the Del Aroldos, giving them the date and time. Like Carlotta, he fussed over every detail, insisting that the hundred chairs were all alike and comfortable. A photograph on the front of the program depicted him in the role of *Edgardo* in *Lucia Di Lammermoor. Teatro Argentina*, the evening's sponsor, paid all expenses, including his fee of $2,500 in United States currency, to be paid in cash before the recital commenced. When questioned as to why he asked for American money, he merely replied that he was planning a trip there and wanted to save the exchange fees, especially important since the dollar was strong against the Italian lira.

He received the program a few days before the recital and was satisfied. It read:

The Teatro Argentina presents in recital:
Ernesto Vasselli, Tenore Lyrico.
Vittorio Canzonolli, Piano

Rossini: 1792-1868
La Regata Veneziana: Tre Canzones
I Gondolieri
Crudel, perche finora
Bellini: 1801-1835
Vaga luna che inargenti
Melinconia, ninfa gentile
Vanne, O rosa fortunata
Bella Nice che d'amore
Quando incise si quel marmo   Scena ed Aria
Donizetti 1797-1848
A Mezzanotte
Ah, che miro o sventurato   Aria
Eterno amore
Come volgeste rapidi, giorni de'miei primi anni
Mentre del caro lido
Verdi: 1813-1901
In solitaria stanza
Nell'orror di notte oscura
Stornello
Non t'accostare all'urna
Lo Spazzacamino

Alone in his dressing room after the fourth performance of the Bellini opera, Ernesto again scanned the program. *Madame will be so pleased when I send her a copy. These Romans are going to hear some of these songs for the first time. Madame spent a great deal of time running down unpublished songs by our beloved composers, even those held in private hands. I have sung them for our own pleasure for years. I hope Mario and Giovanna will be pleased.*

The anticipated evening finally arrived. Ernesto and Vittorio, along with a piano tuner, appeared at the Farnese an hour before the program was to begin. Once they were satisfied with the piano, the two men played through several of the songs. Ernesto could see that Vittorio seemed deeply moved. He was aware that the older man was infatuated with him, but he wasn't interested. He allowed the older man to perform oral sex on him. It meant nothing to him, but he knew it made Vittorio happy.

"What's this, Vittorio? Am I singing so badly that it's left you in tears? What foolishness. I wouldn't have expected you to be so emotionally connected to these songs." He smiled in a patronizing manner and laughed.

"And you are not emotionally involved? Impossible, for you sing like a god. The colors and feelings you bring to these pieces amaze me. You make your hearers feel the impact of the words. It seems so different hearing you like this without the trappings of the stage. Here you communicate with one's very heart. I'm so glad you asked that I accompany you this evening. I'll be sorry to see you go next week. It's so seldom we have young artists like you to realistically portray their roles this way."

"Nonsense, Vittorio, you are just an old pushover. I do nothing that has not been carefully worked out in advance. What you see on stage is not reality, though as a child I was taught to combine words and music in such a way that it seems that I become the person I'm portraying. I feel their pain or joy. It's no special gift. I look to the words and music for what I do. I listen to what the stage director says, yet if in performance it works better that I move this arm this way or that, then it's what I do. To be true to the composer's intentions is our goal as artists. We owe this to their genius, to sing their music as close as possible to their original intentions. If I can wring tears from people by using certain colors, certain gestures and facial expressions, then I have done my duty. Look, they are bringing in the flowers now.

"Let's go back and have a glass of wine. If you play well tonight, then I promise you'll have my dick to nurse on." He laughed; the older man licked his lips. "God only knows who has been invited, and they can do as they like. Who knows when I'll be back here? People talk in vague ways about upcoming or projected operas, but I never believe any such promises unless a contract is placed in my hands. When I have that commitment, then, and only then, does the work begin for me. This is my pattern, my friend. An ironclad agreement with every particular ironed out is first, and foremost, the only way for me." He turned and walked away. Vittorio followed him like a love-sick child.

The hall began to fill with the invited audience, who sat in assigned chairs. Shimmering chandeliers glowed, casting reflections on the polished black and white marble floor. The palace was from the early nineteenth century and the salon itself was spacious. The artists were to be on eye level with the audience which lent an intimate atmosphere to the program to come.

* * *

In the second row, Mario and Giovanna sat with officials from the *Argentina*. The appearance of the heroic tenor caused a stir of excitement among the stuffy ladies of Roman society. Mario's aloofness towards all but a few of the guests affronted many, who gossiped among themselves at his arrogance. Mario had long ago dismissed the chatter of mindless people whose only recommendation was their money. That he had taken gladly, but to allow such boring people into his inner circle was anathema. His privacy he guarded passionately. Many knew that he kept mistresses. They knew there were illegitimate children, but they would have been surprised to know that he also had a hidden secret when it came to handsome young men. His wife, descended from the *D'Este* family, presented a picture of domestic harmony. Mario had not seen Ernesto since the afternoon of their encounter in his music room. Still, the young man was much on his mind and he was determined to play a role in his life and career.

* * *

Ernesto and Vittorio came on to polite applause and the program commenced with Rossini. A stir came over the audience as the *Regata Veneziana* ended. This singer — young, slim and tall with dark eyes and hair — was so unlike the short, fat tenors they were used to seeing. The voice rang out without visible effort. As he launched into the Bellini and Donizetti songs, the impression was further enhanced. Singing of love and longing, the burst of colors and facial expressions he employed moved many to tears, as they had Vittorio. Here was a singer who merely with the voice, not outlandish grimaces and exaggerated gestures, conveyed deep emotions. The Verdi songs were familiar to most of them, and as he finished *Lo Spazzacamino* with its ending cadenza rising to a high D in alt, waves of bravos rang out. Ladies seemed to be beside themselves and smiled back and forth among their neighbors. Even their husbands were caught up in the enthusiasm. The audience stood as one in a standing ovation. He left and after many cries for an encore, came back and addressed them.

"Ladies and gentlemen, I would like to dedicate this encore to Signor and Signora Del Aroldo, who honor me with their presence this evening. I will sing *Tirana alla spagnola* of Rossini." A scattering of applause greeted his words, as many in the audience knew the song. He produced a set of castanets and launched into the exciting song with its variations growing more florid with each repeat of the melody. He played the castanets as he sang. Faster the words and music went till a climatic high C was grabbed out of mid air. Great cheers broke out as the audience jumped to their feet once more.

Mario seemed beside himself with joy and came forward to embrace Ernesto to an even greater burst of bravos. Aristocratic old ladies threw off their stuffy reserve and moved with more excitement than their creaking carcasses had demonstrated in years. After several deep bows and gestures of appreciation, he again withdrew. Still the people had not had enough and after several more calls, he consented to another encore. "I would like to thank the management of the *Argentina* for their faith in me. I have enjoyed my time in Rome, and rest assured I will take the memory of this evening with me when I go home. I am now going to depart from what was basically a song recital and sing an operatic aria which I would like to dedicate to my teacher and kinswoman, Madame Carlotta Vasselli. This final selection will be *Fra poco a me ricovero* and *Tu che a Dio spiegasti l'ali* from *Lucia Di Lammermoor* of Maestro Donizetti." The emotionally drenched aria of initial agitation followed by heartbreaking pathos and despair left the audience stunned, with many wiping away tears. Indeed he was the tenor of the beautiful death.

If this doesn't go to their very souls then they are made of stone, thought Mario, as he and Giovanna both came forward to embrace and congratulate him.

Near the piano, Vittorio had given way to floods of tears. Ernesto laughed and called him up to bow with him. At last they were permitted to leave and the audience dispersed. The evening had been a triumph. Surely now the operatic establishment would open the doors of *La Scala* at last.

Ernesto returned to his suite in a reflective mood. He was exhausted emotionally, but he felt happy. He had given Vittorio what he had promised, then sent him on his way. The invited audience of the highest denizens of Roman society had been met and conquered. Mario and his wife had publicly acknowledged him. From the faces of the old men in charge of the *Argentina,* his reception had not been lost on them. He would be called on to return. Still, behind his euphoria, nagging self doubt spoke to him.

Carlotta's words rang our emphatically, *Never take anything for granted. Success can be a fickle mistress. Until you see a contract with terms in writing, do not commit either your heart or mind to something that, like sand, can slip through your fingers.* The memory of her words was sobering.

As he undressed, he threw the envelope containing the $2,500 on the bedside table. He showered and stood naked before the cheval mirror in the bedroom. He breathed deeply as he admired himself. Bitterly, he reflected on times when fat old impresarios had exacted their pleasures from this body. He knew, as much as he would have liked to deny it, that talent wasn't enough. If you played with the big boys, there was often a price to pay. For such a price, one could get bumped up a notch or two on the ladder of success. Still he despised the times these men had used him. It took away a bit of self worth to think that sex with the right people was more important than the voice he had worked for years to draw ever closer to perfection. Always there was a sense of shame, of violation, reminding him of the horrible night when he had been raped.

Shaking his head to clear away the horror, he looked into his white face. A wide forehead stood out in contrast to the dark eyebrows, and the eyes, framed by a double row of eyelashes, shone like dark, bottomless pools. The secret in his mind was an unending longing to be loved for himself. His hair fell on his shoulders, thick and gleaming from the ever present gel with its slight scent of The Colonel's Old Spice. His mouth had full sensual soft lips that curled easily into a smile revealing the milk white teeth, all straight and perfectly even. He had turned many heads yet love eluded him. He had sex when he wanted it, but fleetingly, and seldom ever twice with the same person. Nothing was allowed to gain such a hold on him that he would relinquish the goal of stepping to higher success. He looked even closer. Not a hint of the decay he saw in others. He was God's and Carlotta's creation. But was the price he paid worth what he had endured? Carlotta would have said so, as would Mario.

He turned away, and walking into the sitting room, the scent of gardenias assailed him. A small white card read, *La Speranza. She who hopes? This again? Tonight they must have been delivered while I was at the recital. Who can this woman be, if indeed it is a woman? Maybe it's just an infatuated admirer? Why gardenias? What significance can this choice hold?* He crossed to the small table beside the sofa and poured a glass of wine, carrying it with him as he climbed naked into bed. The Roman adventure was drawing to a close. He fluffed the pillows and drew the soft linen sheet to his chest. Loneliness settled over him. In spite of ovations, applause and adulation, he always came back alone. He was always alone. Outside, only the muffled noises of cars and mopeds came up to his high floor.

Sometime in the early morning hours before dawn he awoke suddenly.

Mario! He wore a gardenia last night. Could he be the one who hopes? But for what? Oh no, it's not possible. What am I but a quick fuck to a man like that? Could he be falling in love with me? After tomorrow's performance I go back to Milan. He won't remember me for long.

Thirty-two

After the final *Capuleti*, he left for Milan on the early morning train. Everything was as he had left it weeks earlier. His landlady had left a fresh supply of his favorite wine and cheeses. His penchant for cleanliness in his personal surroundings had become an obsession, something he inwardly knew was from Carlotta. He leafed absently through a great quantity of mail. There was a large parcel from the Sforza agency, which contained the projected contract for the following season. Also cards from admirers, and several letters from Carlotta. *I'll deal with all this later after I've had some rest. It's good to be home with nothing planned for the oncoming summer.*

Suddenly he heard the soft words and melody of a very old song, *Amarilli, mia bella.* He rushed to one of the windows overlooking the courtyard, but could not see anyone. The street seemed unusually quiet. But when he turned around a huge voice burst forth from his bedroom with the opening word from Verdi's opera *Otello. "Rejoice!"* Before him, completely naked, stood Mario with outstretched arms.

"Surprise, my boy! Did you think your old Mario had so soon forgotten you? Come give me a hug."

Ernesto flung himself into the older man's arms, laughing, thrilled and astonished all at the same time. "Mario! How could you have beaten me here? I didn't know you even knew where I lived. It must have been very late when you got here, how did you get in?"

"I drove down two days ago, as I had some business here in Milan. I thought how nice it would be to be here to welcome you home." His wide smile thrilled Ernesto who gazed back in wonder. "Come on now, take off those traveling clothes and let's go to bed."

Ernesto rapidly took off his clothes, pausing as he did to fold them and put them on a chair as he had been taught as a child. Mario took him in his arms and kissed him deeply, drawing him onto the bed.

As they lay with bodies pressed closely together, Ernesto grew aware of the heavy scent of flowers. Arrangements of pure white gardenias were scattered about the room. Filtered sunlight came through the curtains, casting a golden haze over the room. He pulled back for a moment, grasping Mario's face in his hands, and exclaimed," So you are *La Speranza?* I could never have dreamed after that afternoon in your music room that I would ever be with you like this again. That I would find you here and feel again your body close against mine." He broke off, looking up at the ceiling, joyously lost for words.

Mario held him tightly, drawing his head against his chest. There were no more words now, only passion that seized both men as their hands sought out the places to give each other pleasure. Mario slid his hand down the younger man's chest and grasped the rock-hard penis. Ernesto thrilled at his touch as Mario lowered his head and hungrily opened his mouth, taking everything in. He trembled as a gasp came and died in his throat.

"No, not yet, sweet boy, don't get off, I want us to take our time, to be with each other where there is no hurry as before. No one can disturb us now. Come kiss me again . . . and again." Hands fumbled under the sheets, reached out to the bedside table drawer for a lubricant. Mario turned him on his side, cupping his body tightly, and with his free hand liberally spread the lubricant. With a thrust, their bodies blended together. He pulled tightly against Ernesto's hips and tried to hold back, but passion denied restraint. Hips pulsing forward, a final push and he filled Ernesto with a shattering climax. How long they lay still, closely entwined, neither of them knew or cared. Then Mario lowered his head, taking the throbbing penis in his mouth.

The younger man grasped his head. Moaning, he thrust deeply and emptied sperm into the hungry, soft mouth. Pulling him up, he laughed. "Never has it been like this before for me, Mario, to be with such a man. I have shared myself this way so many times in the past, but it was always hurried, over as quickly as it had begun and I would be alone again." His mind whirled, long-repressed emotions sweeping over him. He curled his hands through Mario's dark hair and kissed him again deeply. "Thank you for this happiness. It's been so long for me." He thought suddenly of The

Colonel and the times they had shared, but it didn't touch what he felt now. It was like remembering some lost dream of long ago. This was reality.

"We have much to talk about, my handsome young stud, but first let's clean ourselves up and take a shower."

After showering, they donned soft robes and walked hand in hand back to the sitting room. Ernesto poured them both big glasses of wine. "Are you hungry, Mario? I only have some salami and cheese and crackers here. No kitchen, I'm afraid, just a tiny refrigerator and hot plate. No way to make a proper meal. I'm sorry for that."

"No need to apologize, you've filled my tummy very well for a while. Later we'll find some place and have a proper supper, but now, to business. I want to see the proposals and contract the Sforzas have made to you. Forgive me, but I couldn't help being curious when I saw all the mail on the sideboard and recognized their name on that one large parcel. Do you mind if we look at it together?"

Ernesto crossed to where the mail lay and brought back the parcel. "I'm surprised you would bother with this, Mario. They just present things in such a cut-and-dried way. I know you have better things to do than look over my contract." He took out the thick document.

Mario frowned. "What's this? They want you to commit to another five years at twenty percent? That might not be so good. Considering what you have been doing this season for them, twenty percent seems high to me. I see they are offering you cover assignments at *La Scala*, the *San Carlo*, and again Palermo and Genoa. Do you realize the time you will be required to be in these cities, having to be on call at a moment's notice? Incredible. Still maybe twenty percent would be okay, but they need to make major concessions for you to agree to that again."

"But, Mario, I have longed to sing at *La Scala*, and if this will just give me a chance to get my foot in the door, who knows what might come of it for me? The agency has lowered the percentage by five percent which is good."

"What can come of it could be nothing, all your study, the anxiety of having to be ready and not knowing if the call may come or not. I know that you would be prepared. I've seen you in action, but ask yourself something. The fees they are offering are nothing special. Even if you do get to sing, it would be at a far lower rate that these big names you would be covering for. Also you would be locked into having to be in one place during the run of the performances where you couldn't accept outside engagements. This means you would have to have their permission for everything, and you could lose opportunities that might not come again. Always read the fine print. So much is hidden in there. Remember you are just a piece of meat to them, passing on you and several dozen other artists together with maybe one huge star." He frowned, looking at each page closely.

Ernesto studied him carefully. "Mario, I'm not known outside Italy. I can't imagine that theaters in France, England, or Germany would have heard of me or even if they would have occasion to consider me. My French is good as far as it goes, but it doesn't go far enough. I've never sung in a French opera, just duets or arias in concerts. German is completely foreign to me. Theirs is not *bel canto* music. English I can handle, though I wouldn't want to sing often in that language. It's puzzlement for me. Madame has always told me to direct my efforts only to Italy where beautiful music is performed."

"You poor man," said Mario. He looked earnestly into confused eyes. "Only beautiful music? You are dreaming. There is so much mediocrity thrown on stage here that it's hardly worth mentioning. They still have you singing in the provinces and I well know what dogs those people can be. I think you should not be singing so much in places where no one important sees you. This contract has you having to be available for as many as eighty or more performances, and where? Piacenza, Torino, Macerata, Livorno, and Ancona. This is not much more than a beginner's contract that dozens of other artists could do. You've been singing now for what, seven years, and have not been asked to be a regular member of any theater?" He disgustedly looked again at the contract, glancing up and down at Ernesto, trying to gauge the impact of what he was telling him. "Are you really this hard up for money?"

Drawing back in hurt pride, Ernesto said, "Well, yes. I have to have money to live in the manner I'm used to. Of course I despise some of the things I've had to endure, poorly prepared performances in shabby falling-down places. Horrible colleagues and indifferent stage directors and conductors, but I'm only twenty-five. I think I have to put up with some of this, if only to have a shot at the big time." *It's so easy for him to dismiss all that I'm doing. He is a gigantic star and can dictate his own terms to any opera house in the world. He is a freelancer and can sing what he wants, where he wants. He can't remember or has forgotten what it is to struggle. God, am I always to have someone telling me to do this or do that, like I'm some mindless puppet to be used and then thrown back in a corner till they need me again?* He looked at the floor, trying to keep resentment from rising to a point he would be unable to control.

"Look, Ernesto, I wouldn't say these things, I wouldn't bother at all, except you mean something to me. I wouldn't be here if I didn't care about your future. Let yourself be at least advised by someone who has seen it all. Do you think it was always easy for me? You have no idea what it was like after the Great War. Careers had gone up in smoke. Theaters had been closed and very few performances were available to anyone. Those who had associated themselves with Mussolini or the Nazis found their names disgraced. Carlotta could tell you these things if she hasn't before. We had to tread our way cautiously through a narrow compass, always looking over our shoulders, suspecting everyone. It wasn't easy. I had to sing with dogs too, but slowly the situation with the occupation of the major cities cooled down and some of the larger theaters began to open again. Success came to me slowly. I had to work hard and keep my eyes, and above all, my mind open.

"My wife's immense inheritance was tied up for years until the banking fiascos were cleared. We had the babies to deal with too. They came like clockwork. Believe it or not, she and I were sometimes hungry and we had to change and wash diapers just like common people. I swore to her we wouldn't have to live like that ever again. After much perseverance my time came, and I quickly became a sought-after star. I shook off the yoke of having to have an agent and throwing money made by my efforts into the laps of others. Giovanna and I worked hard together. You've seen how we live now. Things are easy now in comparison, but for you, you have to tread the mine fields with caution if you are to go anywhere."

"Mario, I am flattered that you take an interest in me. I have heard from Madame for years about how difficult it was in those years after the war, but her career ended too soon and she married and left Italy for the United States with her husband. Now she lives on memories. I don't want my life to go in that direction. I feel I'm only just finding my mark and I too long for success as well as the material things that come from it. Let's put the contract aside for now. I don't have to give them an answer for a while. I have the whole summer ahead without engagements, but if I go with what they are proposing then I have much music to prepare myself for."

They dressed and went out for supper. Mario knew a place in the city, and they were soon seated in a café near the opera house. Mario ordered for both of them and they sat, drinking wine and watching people pass by. A buzz of excitement went through the staff; Mario Del Aroldo was actually in their establishment. Ernesto was stunned as he watched people falling over themselves to attend them. Occasionally a timid young fan would approach, asking for an autograph or just wanting to stare at the great man. Mario took it all in with practiced calm, speaking kind words to the young people and smiling broadly at the flattering compliments directed to him.

The food was marvelous, though Ernesto ate sparingly. He had to keep himself slim for the stage. The trend in the theaters had become to actually be able to look the parts as opposed to being huge and fat and giving concerts in costume.

"Tomorrow I want you to come with me to the *Cimeterio Monumentale*, Ernesto. Many famous musicians are interred there, and the statuary and monuments are a marvel to behold. We will go in the morning, though, before the tourists get there. I don't mind being recognized, and people by and large will leave me alone. You have to be firm but kind with fans and keep them at bay, but always keep in mind that they buy records. That is important, even for me. I love the royalty checks coming in." He laughed and studied the young man closely. *Giovanna wouldn't care. Not really. She is content with things as they are these days. I can be gone for days and she never questions me. Not many people have a relationship like ours. How handsome he is with his blooming youth and beauty. I can help him. I want to be a part of his life and guide him if I can get him to understand how things are in our profession. He has had some success, but perhaps I can shield him from some of the ugliness that greedy people might inflict on him.*

"Mario, let's leave now and go back to my rooms. I want to be alone with you and make love again and again before you leave, to feel your mouth on mine, your hands on my body."

"Yes, sweet boy, look, the stars are coming out now. We need to be alone again together. Let's shut the world outside and only think about ourselves. I want to feel the soft inside of your body, to feel the warmth there and the nearness of you."

They left and were soon in bed again, making love, lost in themselves till at last they slept with bodies close in happy forgetfulness.

Thirty-three

They did not go to the cemetery the next day. Or the next. They lay in bed all day, not being able to get enough of each other. The only thing that roused them from lovemaking was hunger, which they satisfied with fruit, wine, cheese and biscotti.

On the third morning, Mario said he had some business in the city and was gone for several hours. Upon his return, he insisted they try many other restaurants that he knew, far away from the curious stares of the tourists and opera fans . . . safe places where the staff were discreet and kept their distance unless summoned. In these candle-lit places they could admire each other without fear or intimidation.

A new understanding beyond sex was apparent in both of them. Mario was in no hurry to leave. He was determined that Ernesto would be his, body and soul. His mission was to dominate and enhance the younger man's career as well as winning his heart. It had become an obsession.

Early one morning, a few days later, Mario again broached the subject of the contract. Rising from bed, he retrieved it from the sideboard. Gently he began, "Look, Ernesto, I have re-thought my position on some of the things in here we had discussed earlier. The idea of being a cover artist at *La Scala* I believe you should accept with some stipulations. I would like to suggest that you call the Sforzas here in Milan, arrange a meeting for this afternoon if possible, and I will go with you to prevent you from being intimidated. No, don't protest. You know how I feel about you. I'm not about to allow them to run over you is all. Let me do the talking. All they can say is no, but I don't think they will. Your ability to learn new roles and to be ready at a moment's notice is a valuable asset for them. Your penchant for the *bel canto* operas and the shortage of tenors willing or able to fill those roles is important. No matter that you are often asked to sing them in places off the international circuit. The prima donnas who want to do these operas want at least adequate singers to perform with, and you are more than adequate. The roles you sing were once portrayed by some of the greatest singers who ever lived. If they are to gain a foothold again as standard repertory pieces, then they have to be done with more than just adequate artists. Even the prima donnas would have to agree, as much as they might want to deny it. They can't carry performances by themselves alone. No one can."

"Mario, I had my misgivings as to your interest in me. To be honest, I figured all I was to you was a piece of ass, and after our Roman encounter, I never thought you'd have given me another thought again. Yet these last few days you've shown me a softer side. I don't just mean the great sex we've been having, but a genuine interest in me as an artist and human being. I know now that your being here speaks of something deeper than a casual affair which either of us could have. Not a just fuck them and forget them one night stand. I do trust you, and I will call the Sforzas right now."

Reaching across Mario's chest, he paused for a kiss, then brought the phone between them. "This is Ernesto Vasselli. I want to come in today to discuss the contract proposal I received a few weeks ago from your office in Rome. Yes, of course I mean today. Two o'clock? I'll be there." He hung up and smiled coyly. "Well, show time, as we say in the trade. I hope you know what you're doing. This is going to be interesting. Now, if you've nothing better to do, let's fuck again and then clear out of here for something to eat before throwing me to the wolves."

His laughter was silenced with Mario's mouth which descended on his. Chest against chest, they made love, slowly at first, then with white-hot intensity. At last they slept in each other's arms for several hours.

Precisely at two o'clock Ernesto and Mario walked into the offices of the Sforzas near *La Scala*. Mario carried the large parcel containing the proposed contract. The old woman with whom Ernesto had dealt sat at her desk, seemingly as rude and sour faced as he remembered. She glanced up at the two men and said, "Signor Vasselli? You may go in. They are waiting for you."

She looked up again suddenly, and a smile that Ernesto would never have dreamed could light up that vinegary countenance, broke across her wrinkled face. "Signor Del Aroldo? Is it really you, *maestro*?" She moved faster than she probably had in many years as she jumped up and ran around her desk to curtsey and kiss his hand. "Oh, God, that you should come in here! I saved for a week to get tickets when you last sang *Francesa Da Rimini.* Oh, Signore, how may I be of service?"

"I require nothing, my dear, thank you. I'm so glad that you would remember me and I'm happy indeed that you enjoyed my modest efforts. I am here on business with Signor Vasselli, so if you'll excuse us, we'll just go on in now."

He smiled at her in such a way that her poor old heart melted as she dropped another curtsey and flashed Ernesto a warm look. She kissed both men's hands. As they walked down the hall laughing, she could hardly contain her excitement as she lunged for the telephone to alert everyone she knew about who had just walked in her office.

Mario strode majestically into the room with the attitude of a great star. Ernesto followed him in quickly, still laughing over the woman's about-face. Advancing to the gray steel conference table, he threw down the parcel with a tremendous thud. In the bright light that beamed from the overhead fixtures, it appeared to all as if a god had swept into the room. The two men, thin and pale, with their identical gray suits, jumped to their feet in surprise, absolutely astonished at the presence of Mario Del Aroldo.

"Well, gentlemen, shall we begin? I am here in the role of mentor to Signor Vasselli to talk about this ridiculous contract that you have sent to him." The two men on the other side of the table looked at each other in ill-disguised terror.

"Signor Del Aroldo, we are honored to see you here in our establishment," said the older of the two. "Everyone in the city has noticed that you have been here for quite a while. It's the talk everywhere, but we could never have been prepared to see you here this afternoon. Welcome, welcome indeed, Signor. Ah, Signor Vasselli, how nice to see you once more. Please be seated. I am Alberto Barbieri-Nini and this is Gaetano Fraschini in case you don't remember?"

"Of course he remembers! He has told me of the last meeting he had with the two of you before the beginning of this past season, and the impudent manner in which he was treated. So be assured, we know who you both are and your names are of no consequence to us. You may dispense with your compliments and any offers of refreshments. We are here on business matters. We are interested in you solely in your capacity to act and commit on behalf of the Sforzas. Do we understand each other?" His words shot out in furious contempt as he fixed an imperial stare at the two shaking men. He refused to shake their hands, held limply out in mid air, and put his hand on Ernesto's arm to prevent him from doing so. Spilling the papers from the parcel in front of him, he said. "We see you each have your own copies. We will discuss each item, one by one, as to your proposal and what Signor Vasselli is prepared to accept."

Ernesto sat stunned. *My God, what is this, to address my employers in this manner? What can be in his mind? If he offends these people I may never sing anywhere in Italy again when the word gets out.* Under the table, he wrung his hands in worry, but a glance from Mario told him not to let any of this register on his face. *Damn, he actually looks like he's having fun, and at my possible peril.*

"Now, gentlemen, as to this first item, you propose that Signor Vasselli is to be a cover artist at *La Scala* and the *San Carlo*. This is acceptable to us under the following conditions. He will have the absolute right with immunity to refuse any assignment he considers detrimental to his voice. He is not going to be forced to sing anything that is not in accord with his inclinations. He is also not going to cover anything other than leading roles. No walk-on, one line servant or comprimario parts. Are you both making notes? I do not intend to repeat myself. He is also to have the right with a week's notice to accept offers from other theaters, here or abroad, and the agency is to pay his first-class travel expenses both for transportation and hotels. His meals are to be charged to your account and not to be deducted from his fees. You will deliver to him within one month the scores of all the operas he is to cover for both theaters and the dates he will be required to be in each city to attend rehearsals.

"He is to be paid $1,000 for each performance he covers and $3,000 for each performance where he appears on the stage, all fees to be paid in cash before each presentation. He is to be notified no less than twelve hours in advance if he is to sing, and his cover fee to be delivered to him two hours before the performance is to begin if his services are not required that evening. He will also not sing more than three times a week and never on consecutive evenings. Now we see that you have lowered your demand on his earnings to twenty percent. This is acceptable. However, your demand that he sign a five-year exclusive agreement is not. We propose that this is to be no more than a three-year agreement, with the terms we have stated to remain in effect and for there to be a yearly meeting here in Milan at his convenience, to discuss whatever plans you have in mind for him for each upcoming season. He is to also be free during the months of June, July, and August from any arrangements from you so that he may freely accept engagements abroad. You will of course pay, as I've outlined, his travel and accommodation expenses and you will be responsible to recover your outlay from whatever theaters he will be singing in. Let this be understood without discussion, gentlemen." He paused to drink from a flask, handed it to Ernesto, who sat spellbound.

Signor Barbieri-Nini stirred uneasily in his seat as Mario poured out these demands and looked cautiously at Signor Fraschini, who nervously lit a cigarette and inhaled deeply.

Before either of them could think of responding, Mario was on his feet. Bending across the table, he slapped the cigarette from the trembling man's lips, furiously exclaiming, "How dare you smoke in our presence! We are opera singers and will not tolerate tobacco of any kind within fifty feet of us. If you repeat this behavior I will take Signor Vasselli out of here and treat with a more courteous agency. Do you hear me, you imbecile?" His lips curling back in furious contempt, he looked across as the two men shrunk into their chairs. "I know how to deal with the likes of both of you. I didn't get to this point in my career without learning how to do that, so be silent while I finish with this final section."

Ernesto listened to Mario's rambling on about dates and loopholes with astonishment. He couldn't understand how easily he handled these normally aloof people. He watched in wonder as they nodded to each demand without protest. *I'd have never gotten away with such behavior. One cross word and they'd have thrown my ass out into the street. But this is Mario Del Aroldo talking to them. So this is the way a truly great artist behaves, letting no one run over him? I hope to God one day I have the clout to be able to do this.*

At long last the meeting ended with the agents and Mario laughing and smiling. A revised contract, incorporating Mario's demands, would be delivered to Ernesto's residence the next morning. Mario kissed the surprised secretary on their way out.

They stopped at a hole-in-the-wall café for strong coffee. As they sat at a small table, Ernesto felt something stirring inside, something that made him a little afraid.

"Well, my man, how do you think the meeting went? Did you see how easily they gave in and agreed to everything? This is the way to deal with these people. If you don't work, they don't get paid. Bottom line, you are more valuable to them than they to you. From now on they will treat you with respect, that's for sure. I don't want you to worry about agencies anymore. I'll go to all your yearly meetings with them from now on. All you have to do is study and sing, always just sing, and you'll become rich."

He broke off as he noticed Ernesto had suddenly buried his face in his hands. He put his arm around the young man's shaking shoulders. "What's this? Tears? Come on now, stop it or you'll have me crying too." He anxiously looked around. No one could ever be allowed to see the great Del Aroldo weep in public. Ernesto looked up, eyes brimming with tears. He hurled himself into Mario's arms, and slowly, gaining control of his emotions, he quietly began to speak. "Mario, my debt to you is immeasurable. It seems like such a dream that in these last weeks in Rome, and now here in Milan, that you have taken such an interest in a young artist without much clout. I have had success, yes, it is true, but for someone of your experience and celebrity to take up my cause is beyond my comprehension. No, don't wave me off. Let me finish. I am happy to share whatever I have with you, to make wonderful love with you. It's the least I can do for one who has brought me such happiness. Your warmth and regard for me are a gift I don't take lightly. I know you have to get back to Rome and Giovanna soon. I want you to know that even if I were never to see you again that I will never forget all you have given to me, both as an artist and as a man. You make me feel unafraid and ready to accept whatever challenges that fate might throw in my path." He broke off; Mario's face had blushed red..

"Stop this nonsense at once, my boy. I have done nothing except to recognize your genius. I want to be sure that others do also and treat you with the respect you deserve. Yes, I have to leave soon for Rome. I have some performances of my own to prepare for, but don't think I will forget you. I intend on being a part of your life from now on. What a look on your face! You seem so fragile and vulnerable that I could crush you to dust with one hand. Who though could do such a thing to someone they love? Your success will be my reward, and having you as near as possible in the future is all I want. Just let yourself be guided by me, now and in the future, and you'll come to know how powerful an ally I can be." Rising, he pulled the younger man up and said, "Now let's get out of here and go somewhere and have some proper wine and supper, and then we'll go back to your rooms and fuck ourselves into oblivion." Laughing, they walked arm and arm into the gathering darkness as it fell softly from the early summer sky.

Later in the night, they lay together naked in Ernesto's bed. He gave himself, his body, everything in his heart into their passionate lovemaking, but this time a sense of something deeper and more meaningful lingered in the quiet room. After the fluids and sweat had been washed away with a warm shower, they lay entwined, gazing into each other's eyes and talking. He laid his head on Mario's chest as the older man carelessly ran his fingers through the thick, dark curls. Hesitantly he spoke, without looking up as his lips tweaked the dark nipples.

"Mario, do you love me? No, don't answer yet. Even if you love me just a little it will be enough for me. I know now that I don't want to be with another man. I love you. It fills all my heart and soul, but I promise I'll never cause you a moment's worry. I know you are married, that you have a reputation to preserve. I will never betray your trust." He finally found the courage to look up into his eyes, his heart full of wonder and joy.

"Of course I love you, you silly boy. It's not just your wonderful body and beautiful smile. I want you to be mine. We'll see each other often and have moments like this. When I am away, never doubt for a moment that I won't have my vigilant eyes on all you do. It doesn't matter if you have sex with others. I know what it's like to be young and need passion satisfied; just hold your love only for me as I will for you." He smiled and Ernesto's heart melted again as he trembled in the throes of love. "Now let's get some sleep so we can make love again before dawn. We could search the world over for a perfect lover and end the quest with ourselves. Never doubt me, my dearest. I love you." He reached down and put his mouth on the young man's once more, but Ernesto heard and felt nothing. He was asleep and lost in dreams of love eternal.

* * *

What Ernesto did not know was that the scene at the Sforza agency was contrived for his benefit. Mario had called on them several days earlier and had made the arrangements that all correspondence in regard to

Ernesto was to first pass through his hands. He would dictate the terms, and then they would be passed on to the unsuspecting young man. In return for their silence, Mario had agreed to let them manage his own career for the next few years. He also reminded them of the fact that he had powerful friends in Sicily.

Mario thus had set out and succeeded in the future domination of every aspect of Ernesto's professional career. The ramifications of this deception would one day be brought home to the young man, although at the moment he was completely in the dark about Mario's intentions. The force of destiny was set in motion against him. Mario thus became his Svengali. Like the despicable magician, he would become the one who would pull the strings behind the scenes for an indefinite future. Like a lamb to the slaughter, Ernesto had put his fate and his love into the hands of a man who could destroy him with a single stroke.

Thirty-four

Weeks passed. Mario returned to Rome. Ernesto received the scores of the operas he was to cover at *La Scala* and the *San Carlo*. They were to be *Lucrezia Borgia, Anna Bolena, La Sonnambula, Norma, La Favorita, and Lucia Di Lammermoor.* Only *Norma* and *La Sonnambula* were operas he didn't know well. He set about learning the roles and reacquainting himself with the others. As September neared and the rehearsal period for the opening of the theaters would begin, he felt at peace. His love for Mario was never far from his thoughts. He rejoiced that he had found such a champion. He spoke frequently with Carlotta back in Alabama about his plans.

She wholeheartedly approved, though she wondered out loud why someone like Mario would interest himself in her young protégé. Had she acted on her suspicions, perhaps the future would have turned out differently, but she kept her misgivings to herself and hoped for the best.

One day, out of the blue, Ernesto was called to the offices of the Sforzas on urgent business. A call had come from a London impresario. Three concert performances of Halevey's opera *La Juive* were being given at the Royal Albert Hall. The tenor engaged for the part of *Leopold* was not going to be able to appear for the first performance. No one could be found who knew the part. It was a second lead, but because of the fiendishly high tessitura, hardly anyone was available who would or could perform it. It was a part which couldn't be cut since the action hinged greatly on this character. Agencies all over the world had been contacted without success until the Sforzas heard of it and proposed Ernesto for this one performance. As he sat in their offices and heard the proposal, he was astounded.

"Signor Vasselli," said Signor Fraschini, "this is a great compliment to you. Of all our artists, you are the only one we could trust with such an assignment. Are you familiar with the opera?"

"All I know of it is the duet in the prison scene between the two women. I sang it in a concert with my teacher years ago before my voice changed. I have never seen a score of the entire opera, and it being in French, which I don't specialize in, I've never even thought about it." He felt both a thrill and trepidation at the same time. The agent pushed a copy of the vocal score across the table to him. He opened it and scanned the first few pages.

"We have marked the pages of the music you would be required to learn. Scores will be used by the artists at the performance, so memorization would not be required. What we would like to know is: do you think you could learn the part in a week?"

"A week, are you insane? I've always been a quick study, but wait while I look through the part." *Vocally there is no problem here, though this music is not the bel canto I am used to. An opening aria, two duets, a magnificent trio? Yes, I can do this.* Clearing his throat, he began by saying, "The part is difficult, but relatively short. The range is easier than most of the roles I've been singing. Strange intervals and leaps from low to high, but yes, I could do it. I want to know though about the financial arrangements." He looked at the agent, fancying that he could adopt Mario's imperial manner.

The agent looked at the contract, then returned Ernesto's look. "The terms are that for this one performance, which will be a Royal Gala., you will be paid the sum of $5,000. You will report to London in eight days time with your part perfected. You will have one run through with the other artists and the conductor. Two days afterward the performance will take place in the presence of the royal family. Do you accept the terms?"

"My only misgiving is ignorance of the orchestration. I will not force my voice beyond its natural compass. If the orchestra plays too loudly, then they will just have to cover me. With this understanding, I will accept and learn the part within the next week. I trust this will not interfere with my cover assignments?"

"No, Signor, it will not. You will only be away for that one performance, and you will be back here in ample time to attend rehearsals for the opening of *La Favorita.* Your tickets will be delivered to your residence and a car will be sent for you. Of course transportation and hotel will be first class as per your contract that you kindly signed in June when Signor Del Aroldo was here. If you have no further questions, you may take the score with you. The services of a pianist from *La Scala* are at your disposal to coach you in preparing the role. May we wish you every success?"

Something in the agent's manner disturbed him, but he dismissed it as he left with the score in his hands and rode back on his moped. Eight days later he caught a flight to London. As he saw the lights of the city approaching, he sipped champagne and looked again at the score he had been given. Large sections of the opera had been cut, as evidenced by pages having been stapled together. He knew his part, though the French pronunciation had been more difficult to master that he had remembered from his student days. It wasn't a very good libretto, but there very highly effective scenes, and if performed well he felt there would be good results.

He was met at the airport by a driver who spoke very bad Italian. The poor man was visibly relieved to learn Ernesto spoke perfect English and soon reverted to his native cockney accent which amused Ernesto. Arriving at the hotel in the heart of the city, he was conducted by a bellman to his suite overlooking the Thames in the distance. After settling in, he scanned the several messages that had preceded his arrival from the impresario who had arranged the performances.

His impression of London was not good. He found a pretentiousness about the British offensive. He had seen it many times in the past in Italy at performances and the receptions that invariably followed. The brushes with British society in Italy, however, were nothing compared to finding himself in their midst. The messages informed him of the general run through set for the next morning and that a car would be sent for him. He frowned at the curt, cold tone of the typed messages. Wasn't he stepping in to save their performance since the Spanish tenor would not be available for the gala?

That tenor was the heralded, Diego De Los Angeles from Barcelona. His agent had stupidly double booked him and the tangled web had been unable to be unraveled. The other theater had refused to release him for the first *La Juive* and had threatened legal action if he didn't appear that evening in Paris.

Ernesto mused on the circumstances. *A beautiful voice, or so I've heard. Only twenty-seven, he specializes in my type of operas. Too bad for him if I get my foot in the door first. The Royal Gala is being attended by all the critics as well as Her Majesty, the Queen. Well, bring them on. I'm ready.*

A soft knock on the door startled him back to reality. It was Jane and James. He excitedly greeted them with huge hugs and kisses and escorted them into the living room.

"Ernesto! How wonderful to see you again and here in London!" exclaimed Jane as she seated herself on the sofa and kicked off her shoes. "We have been hearing good things of you via our connections. You naughty boy, you should have let us know you were coming. You could have stayed at our house near Windsor instead of this drab old mausoleum."

"Yes indeed!" chimed in James, who embraced him in a huge bear hug. "Sit and tell us how this came about. We had heard about the performances, but only learned this morning that you were filling in at the first for the tenor. We are coming, of course. Jane has been singing at Covent Garden recently, so it's good luck for us that we're here."

"Thank you both for coming to see me. I hardly know where to begin. I have been so busy these last few years singing all over Italy. Mostly in rat holes, but occasionally in the better houses. I had no idea how to get in touch with you, and of course this all came about very suddenly only a couple of weeks ago." He sat back in his chair, delighted to see them again.

"Well, dearie," intoned Jane, "I'm sure you've heard I've been dragged everywhere. Took us years to get this far, but no fee seems to be too high to demand these days for me. Everyone seems to want me in whatever I wish to sing. Best of all, James is now my only conductor, so we travel always together these days. He knows my voice best, though as you well know, I'm the one who has to go out there and make it happen." She threw back her mane of red hair and roared the laughter that had thrilled him so long ago in Venice.

"I know you've only just arrived, Ernesto, and I hope you don't think us impertinent," said James. "As we were coming in, I took the liberty of having ordered a cold supper sent up. We will pay for it, of course. Poor Jane was recording most of the day and is simply famished. We have our wunderkind with us for the recording. You've heard of Savarotti, I know. He's one of the few tenors tall enough to look right on stage with Jane, and he is so anxious to sing everywhere now with her. They will be doing *La Fille du Regiment* in New York in the spring, but now we have to finish up this *Sonnambula* so the recording will come out before the performances at *La Scala*."

His gushing words were interrupted by waiters. Cold slices of rare beef, a large chef's salad, oysters, various cheeses, and assorted breads were quickly laid out, along with several bottles of Italian wines and champagne.

Ernesto, studying his guests, thought, *I guess I should have this billed to the room, but what the hell. James is even more of a pompous asshole than he was in Venice, so let him pay. To see Jane again is worth putting up with him, though I have to admit, he did help me back then, though God knows they never called on me about future projects. Savarotti is now a huge star, due in part to his association with Jane, but it should have been me.*

"Ernesto, have you wandered off to another planet?" said Jane impatiently. "Just like in Venice, always dreaming unless you're on stage. Quick, James, pour me some champagne. My throat is so dry that I could drink a bottle by myself. I'm glad we ordered Italian wine too, I can't abide the French. Do you know, of all the places I've been that I hate France the most. I mustn't say that out loud though as they are always buying my records and coming over to hear me when I'm in London or Milan. Now to you, dearie, what are your plans for the fall and winter season? Still singing in places like Trieste, Turin, Bergamo, et al?" She giggled like a school girl as she sloshed down her drink in one gulp and then held it out to James for a refill.

Ernesto ignored the unsubtle reference to his singing in third-rate opera houses. He chose his words carefully as he said in a stifled voice, "As a matter of fact, Jane, I've signed on as a cover artist for six operas at *La Scala* and the *San Carlo* for the upcoming season, so I doubt I'll have much time to be crooning away in Bergamo, Trieste, or Turin. In fact one of the operas I'll be covering will be your *Sonnambulas.* So I'll definitely see you since I have to attend all the rehearsals."

"That will be so nice," said James. "Of course Savarotti almost never cancels, so the chances of your singing with Jane are slim, but nevertheless it will be a joy to see you there. Jane is going to have some costumes made while we're there, so while she's involved with that maybe you and I could do some running around together. I would so much like to renew our friendship that was so dear to me when we were all in Venice when you made your debut." He fixed a look on the younger man as he spoke that left no doubt as to what he meant. Jane just shrugged and smiled.

"Actually, James, I doubt very much that I'll have much time for flitting about with you. Things have changed greatly with me the last several years. I was a naive beginner in Venice, but I now know my worth. The rehearsals for the other operas will overlap Jane's, but we can see. Perhaps Mario could come down and we could have three men together driving about the countryside. I don't get much time for sightseeing as you can imagine, but he knows all the right places to see." He laughed in spite of himself at their consternation at the mention of Mario, and nibbled on a celery stalk.

James poured himself a stiff drink from the flask he carried with him. "Do you mean Del Aroldo? When did you meet him? Jane has never sung with him since they are specialists in different types of operas, but I'm surprised that you'd have run into him."

"Actually, James," said Ernesto, refilling his glass, "I met him and his lovely wife last spring when I was singing in *Capuleti* in Rome. Both of them were very kind and did me a great honor in inviting me to their home for lunch and came to the recital I gave at the Farnese palace. He was even kind enough to look me up when he came to Milan on business in June. I owe a lot to him. He even bothered to advise me and to help negotiate with the Sforzas on the new contract I signed with them this summer. To have an artist of that stature take an interest in my career has been a great blessing as you can imagine." He walked back to the table. Peeling a grape, he smiled brightly at them.

Husband and wife exchanged a look. Jane staggered to her feet and said, "My goodness! Look at the time. James, we must go. We've bothered this poor boy quite long enough. He needs to get some rest and get accustomed to our London air. We too, have to be up early for the recording session." She smiled and embraced him warmly. Taking her husband's arm, she headed for the door. "It was simply divine seeing you again, Ernesto. We hate it that your time here is to be so short, but good luck. We'll look forward to seeing you in Milan."

"Yes, my boy" said James, "break a leg, into the wolf's mouth, and all that nonsense you Italians carry on. Take care of yourself. We'll be sitting in the fourth row at the Gala. Wave at us if you get a chance." A quick hug and they were gone.

"Ciao," said Ernesto as he closed the door behind them. Rage erupted as he furiously threw his glass against the wall. *How arrogant they are. Especially James, thinking he could even suggest our getting together in Milan. They are both so full of themselves. They are on top of the world and she makes references to my singing in the provinces? God willing and with luck, maybe I'll get to actually sing one of the performances at La Scala, and show them I can rub shoulders with great singers as well. The looks they gave each other as I mentioned Mario's name were priceless. I thought James would choke when he heard Mario had seen me in Milan.* He laughed bitterly as he sat back at the table looking at his untouched plate. *To hell with him! Probably thought he could get me off somewhere for a quick fuck. Well, I hope he still has memories of fucking me and blowing me in the shower at the Fenice, because hell will freeze over before he ever gets a piece of this ass again.*

Shaking off his disgust, he reached for the phone and called room service to remove the dishes. They came shortly and filled up a cart with the leftovers. "No, leave the wine and cheese. I'm not through with them yet." The two waiters stood hesitating at the door. "Are you two waiting for a tip? I suggest you add it to Maestro Buffington's bill since it was he who ordered the meal. Now get out, both of you, and leave me alone. Tell the chef, if he cares, that the food was atrocious." He slammed the door behind them, and grabbing the open bottle of wine, he walked into his bedroom. Undressing quickly, he showered and then got into bed naked. He was tired. He carelessly drank down the wine and propped himself up against the pillows. He must rest, it was late. As he closed his eyes, he wished with all his heart that Mario was with him. He yawned, and smiled, knowing that soon he would be back in Italy where he belonged. His last thought, before sleep overtook him, was of the morning run through at the Royal Albert Hall. He would be ready.

The next morning, precisely at 11 a.m., Ernesto walked into the backstage rehearsal room to meet the other artists in *La Juive.* The star of the opera was veteran American tenor Richard Peerce, who was the first to greet him with personal thanks for stepping in on short notice in the role of *Prince Leopold.* It was to be a piano rehearsal only, consisting of the scenes in which the character appears. The other artists, all French singers, grumbled at having to do this run-through with a singer none of them knew. They quieted down, however, when the conductor admonished them.

Ernesto was called immediately for his solo aria with chorus in the opening scene. The aria was very high with repeated high B's and C's, and ended with a top D. A stir went through the chorus and principal singers as he finished. They no longer considered him an unknown, but an unmined talent which had been thrust into their path. The conductor congratulated him with compliments and saw no reason to make adjustments.

Next they went over the duet with the character of *Rachel*, the heroic trio with the star tenor and Natalie Levaseur, the *Eudoxie*. The effect of the trio which blended the voices as each entered singing the principal melody was electric. Ernesto instinctively made dynamic adjustments to create balance between his voice and that of the other two singers. Even the cold soprano was caught up in the moment, and, abandoning her arrogance, sang out in full voice as the trio ended with her sustained high F. The chorus members burst into applause.

The conductor silenced them with a gesture, and then went on to the concerted numbers with finales for the first two acts. Again the grumbling began as the singers wanted to get away for a late lunch. The conductor apologized to Ernesto for not staging a full orchestral rehearsal, explaining the costs that would have ensued.

He did get to finally look at the orchestral score and tried to gauge the impact of the instruments on his voice. He was somewhat relieved when he realized that in his solo passages the orchestral writing was such that his voice would carry easily over it. Only the concerted ensembles concerned him; he perceived places where he knew he would be swamped by the sheer volume. Even with the cuts, there would be at least two hours of music, not counting one brief intermission. As they dispersed, he was grateful for the smiles of approval he received, even from the French artists. Singing French opera was very different than the Italian way.

Later that afternoon he met with several of the chorus members who had offered to show him around the city. He visited the ancient Tower of London and saw the places where so many famous (and infamous) people had met their ends. At the Chapel of St. Peter of Viscula, he saw the places where rested the remains of Anne Boleyn, Catherine Howard and others buried beneath the floor. He saw the houses of Parliament, and was taken on a boat ride on the Thames pass the Tudor Palace of Richmond, now a museum. He was generally unimpressed and was happy to return to his suite to rest.

The evening of the performance found him homesick for Milan and for Mario. As the large audience assembled and the singers gathered backstage, anticipation levels were high. The royal family would be in attendance. Dressed in evening clothes, the artists took their places with scores on music stands, the orchestra members began to file in and, behind them, the two-hundred-voice chorus on risers. At a signal from the conductor, the artists and orchestra, as well as the audience rose as one when the royals filed into the central royal box, unchanged since the days of Queen Victoria. The British national anthem began, followed by a scattering of applause as the royals took their seats. The audience followed suit.

Each aria and duet was greeted warmly, the rest of the audience taking cues from the royals, who consistently expressed pleasure. At the performance's conclusion, cheers broke out, especially for Richard Peerce, the undisputed star of the evening in the heroic role of *Eleazar.* The opera itself was gaining performances in several cities across the world due to his prestige and was scheduled to be performed in New York's Metropolitan Opera in tribute to Peerce's thirty years with the company.

Ernesto was glad it was over. There had been two instances of unprofessional conduct during the duets with each of the two French sopranos. Both of them, against the rules of professional conduct, had held final high notes as he broke his off. His signals to each of them to let go of the high notes at the end of the duets had been ignored. Even the conductor sent the women glances of fury. Ernesto made mental notes to never sing with either of them again.

Backstage, Richard Peerce warmly embraced him as they took their places in line to meet the royal family. At the end of the line, Ernesto stood nervously as Queen Elizabeth, the Queen Mother, appeared in a white gown. She was ablaze in diamonds. A glittering tiara in her still dark hair recalled the time of Queen Victoria and Queen Mary. Behind her Queen Elizabeth and Prince Charles walked in, followed by Princess Margaret, the Princess Royal. The Queen, also dressed in white, wore beautiful diamonds, which shone in the backstage light. Prince Charles was dressed in a dark military uniform with decorations he had received. Behind him came Princess Margaret, who unlike her mother and sister, had chosen a cherry-red gown. She too wore a tiara of diamonds and pearls in her dark hair and appeared to be even more beautiful than Ernesto could have imagined. She also appeared to be aloof and terribly bored with the whole affair. The royals proceeded down the line of the artists, greeting each with well chosen words of congratulations and thanks.

At the end of the line, Ernesto was thrilled. He and the others had been warned not to touch the royals unless they first held out a gloved hand. The Queen Mother, Elizabeth, turned her beautiful smile on him as she approached, extending her hand to him. Overcome with the moment, he sank to his knees before her, tears raining down his cheeks as he took her hand.

She smiled warmly and said, "Ah, no, we must not have this. It is we who are honored by your presence, Signor Vasselli. Please rise." Turning to her daughter, she said, "Isn't it so, my dear?"

"Indeed." answered the Queen. "Please rise." He did so with shaking knees as Prince Charles grasped his hands and raised him to his feet.

"Your Majesties, your Royal Highness, thank you for this honor. I am so pleased that you enjoyed the opera."

The Queen Mother, apparently delighted with him, suddenly embraced him, kissing him on both cheeks. He felt like he had died and gone to heaven at her touch, unheard of in his experience. His knees were still shaking as each of them held out their hands to him, though none was quite as effusive as the Dowager Queen.

Princess Margaret gave him an amused smile and nod as she brought up the rear. All the artists followed them with their eyes as they made their way out to their waiting cars. The conductor, too, seemed amazed at the signal honor afforded Ernesto by the Queen Mother.

As Princess Margaret went through the door, her driver stood smoking a cigarette. To the utter consternation of all present, she reached out a gloved hand, slapping the cigarette from his lips and exclaimed, "How dare you smoke in my presence without my permission!"

Everyone fell silent. As she passed the offending driver, she glanced back at Ernesto with a beaming smile and nod.

Ernesto smiled. *What an incredible Princess! I would never have dared to do such a thing.* He watched the royal party disperse into the dark night. He was still in the afterglow of the moment as he left for his hotel, declining to join the others for a post-performance dinner.

He asked that a tray be sent up to his suite. After it arrived, he poured a large glass of wine and sat on the sofa. He felt an enormous sense of relief that he had met and passed this challenge. Singing was the only thing that could take over his emotions, losing himself in his roles. Concert performances, shed of the trappings of costumes and sets, were quite a different matter. The rudeness of the two sopranos had highly offended him. He never felt envy for other singers. He felt that working together to present a total victory was the only professional goal they should have. *Those French bitches were insufferable, just little people whose arrogance outstrips their talents. It's so disturbing to be subjected to such pettiness from people who profess to be professionals. Why is it that a success has to leave such a taste of bitterness about it? Madame warned me about such things. It's like a victory won through a hard fight, instead of the accomplishment of the moment. Why must it always be so?*

He would be glad to be gone out of this arena for Italy. Only there would he ever truly feel at home. He slept deeply, with dreams of a reunion with Mario foremost in his thoughts.

Thirty-five

Back in Milan, he was soon fully engaged with his duties as a cover artist for both *La Scala* and the *San Carlo*. Several operas were being rehearsed at once, so almost every day he was at the theater from morning to late afternoon. He met the greatest conductors, stage directors, and superbly gifted singers. Everything he absorbed like a sponge. He had never before seen such attention to detail . . . from the costumes of the stars down to the most insignificant members of the chorus, everything was first class. All was not perfection, though. Furious arguments over tempos, dynamics, and even the smallest details rang out in the great rehearsal rooms. Jealousy reared its ugly head often. Leading artists often disagreed with the stage director, grumbled about the fit of a costume, the weight of a wig, even the makeup and lighting they insisted set them off to greatest advantage. Often the singers would look at their cover artists with contempt, declaring openly that they were insignificant to themselves, that they would never cancel a performance. Ernesto knew better. He had seen it all. He would be ready. He would sit in silence and listen and watch, gauging how the conductor worked. Eventually he became bored as the prima donnas and tenors would insist on going over and over the same ground, no doubt thinking that they were the only contributions to creating a triumph. At last the first of the operas, *La Favorita*, was to be performed before one of the most sophisticated audiences in the world. The great chandeliers gleamed over the orchestra-level seats. Seven tiers of boxes arranged in the typical horseshoe pattern went upward to the ceiling level. The acoustics were first class. There was no need to force the voice here. Even the smallest nuances could be heard without effort.

The Milanese gathered on opening night, setting the theater abuzz with conversations from leading ladies of society. Dazzling jewels blazed from the ample, though severely wrinkled, bosoms of the ancient dowagers. Now and then a soprano, singing in another production, would sweep down the aisle to her seat, smiling radiantly at her fans in the galleries as they caught sight of her. Ernesto hated these displays, which were planned to draw attention away from the evening's opera to themselves. But he carefully observed the prima donnas; he would be working with many of them if his chance ever came.

He was the cover for Diego De Los Angeles in this production. He had listened attentively to the Spanish tenor during the rehearsals. Diego was making his debut at *La Scala* in this opera, and from the conversations leaked to the press (and thus to the homes of the matrons of Milan) great anticipation was centered on this production. Everything was new, as were many of the operas being offered that fall. Italian theaters enjoyed great government subsidies. With so much support, *La Scala* could offer huge fees to the stars.

Great interest was also in the air as the magnificent mezzo-soprano, Fiorenza Pirazzini, a favorite in Milan, was to make her first appearance in several seasons in the role of *Leonora Di Guzman.*

Ernesto had entered with Mario and Giovanna Del Aroldo, who had come from Rome. Mario, a great favorite in Milan, had not appeared there in several years. He was immediately noticed and a great burst of applause greeted him as he led Giovanna and Ernesto to their seats in a box on the first tier. He beamed brightly at his fans, nodding to the right and left. Many in that sold-out theater wondered who the handsome young man with him could be. They ignored the stares of the curious and settled into comfortable seats. Ernesto was relieved that he would be able to enjoy being with his friends. He and Mario exchanged smoldering looks as Giovanna looked on with amusement, her radiant smile concealing whatever her private thoughts might have been.

A hush fell and conversations quieted as the chandeliers and box lights dimmed and the footlights came up on the great curtains. The orchestra members were tuned up by the concert master, who then sat down waiting the appearance of the conductor. He did not appear.

The audience began to stir uneasily when a spotlight came up on the curtains and the impresario of the theater appeared. Gesturing for silence, he said, "Up until five minutes ago Signor Diego De Los Angeles was prepared to sing the role of Fernando in tonight's performance. He now finds that he can not sing this evening! Is Ernesto Vasselli in the audience?" He peered out into the darkness as the house lights came up.

Ernesto was stunned. He looked anxiously at Mario, who gestured for him to stand. An usher appeared and tapped him on the shoulder. The manager caught sight of him as the audience broke out into murmurs of displeasure.

"Signor Vasselli, please come backstage. Ladies and gentlemen, the role of *Fernando* will be sung tonight by Ernesto Vasselli. If you will please indulge us, the performance will begin shortly after he is in costume." With that he retired behind the curtain as a noisy stir came over the spectators.

Ernesto, in a daze, followed the usher from audience to the stage. He encountered the anxious *La Scala* officials backstage who thanked him for being there in spite of his contract which specified he was to receive twelve hours' notice.

A furious argument had broken out backstage between Diego and Signora Pirazzini. Word had reached him that a demonstration by her fans was to mar the opening scene in which he has to immediately sing a highly exposed aria. He had demanded that she send word to her supporters not to choose that moment to ruin his initial appearance. She had refused, stating that she didn't know what he was talking about and that it was beneath her dignity as a prima donna to dictate the behavior of anyone. He denounced her, screaming out that she was a whore who was trying to hog the spotlight, yelled that she was old enough to be his mother and shouted out for her to call off her dogs. The management attempted to calm him, saying that the rumor was unfounded. He ground in his heels, saying if they could not order her to comply that he would not sing. As the hapless officials approached her, she said they could replace her as well if they demanded anything of her. She was an established star in this theater and they could not dare to announce to the gala audience that their favorite would not appear in the title role. Diego retreated to his dressing room, calling down curses on all of them. Into this highly charged scene Ernesto appeared.

Madame Pirazzini walked directly up to him and, smiling sweetly, said, "Just so you know, Signore, I am the star of this opera. Don't get in my way and we won't have a problem. Just so you know where things stand." She looked around at the other cast members and shouted, "I'm going out there and I'm going to get mine. I don't give a damn what the rest of you do. I give and take no quarter in this business." She turned and left for her dressing room. "Call me when it's my time."

Ernesto was dragged to a dressing room, where a swarm of people assisted with his makeup and costume. He went through some scales with a house pianist, and was then hurried to the stage to take his place on the set with the bass who was singing the role of the Father Superior of the monastery. On the other side of the curtain he could hear the stamping of feet and loud cries of impatience from the audience. Suddenly they grew quiet as the conductor made his entrance and the performance, delayed by thirty minutes, was finally to begin. The prelude started and the stage lighted behind the curtains. His moment had come. All the work of years was to be rewarded.

As the curtain went up, he stood onstage in his white costume emblazoned with a large red cross. Absolute silence greeted the two singers as they exchanged their opening phrases. As *Fernando*, he began the opening aria, *Una Vergine, un angel di Dio.* A hush came over the audience as he sang the final phrase of the aria which rose to a high C sharp. A split second of silence was followed by a tremendous roar, as cries of delight rang out all over the theater. Standing stock still in character, he absorbed it all with no visible sign of emotion. He lowered his gaze to the floor, then lifted his head gazing toward heaven. He briefly touched his hand to his heart acknowledging the ovation, then broke out into the heroic cabaletta, *Cara luce, soave conforto.* With a cry of despair over the denunciation of the Father Superior, he rushed from the stage as the scene ended to tumultuous applause.

The rest of the opera's four acts unfolded in unbroken glory for all the principals. He was careful not to offend the prima donna in any way and she rewarded him with beautiful smiles of appreciation as he would step back from her at the climax of their duets, allowing her to take the principal ovations. The final act of the opera opened on the same scene as the first in the monastery. He quietly entered with the bass. Left alone on stage, he began his final aria, *Spirto Gentil, Ne'Sogni Miei.* His voice rang out in all its youthful beauty as he wrung the hearts of the hearers with the subtle despair of the character.

Madame Pirazzini made her entrance dressed in the simple robes of the religious order. Absolute silence hung in the air as they began the final duet that ended with her dying in his arms. His final cry of despair as he realizes she is dead, *E Spenta!* was hurled out in agony as he fell to the floor, cradling her in his arms as the curtain fell rapidly. Backstage the prima donna, radiant with joy, embraced and kissed him.

The curtain calls began to great acclaim, as each principal artist came forward again and again. When they were finally allowed to leave, Ernesto walked back to his dressing room, graciously receiving the thanks of the management for literally stepping in at the last moment.

He sat before the mirrors and drew from his costume the small portrait of Carlotta in the role of *Violetta* in *La Traviata* which he carried during all his appearances. Burying his face in his hands, through tears of joy, he whispered, "Madame, this night is for you, my own diva and mother. To you is the glory."

Suddenly Mario rushed into the room. "Darling boy, bravo! You were magnificent, superb. I love you so much. Oh, my own dearest, Giovanna and I are so proud of your achievement. She is waiting outside for us. Hurry and dress and let's go out to celebrate at the restaurant." He kissed him over and over again.

Ernesto approached and threw himself into Mario's arms, laughing with relief. Slipping to his knees, he grasped him around the waist and held him tightly in a wordless embrace.

"Hurry now, my angel. Take your shower and dress and let's get the hell out of here. We'll be waiting for you at the stage door." He swept out of the room. Ernesto took off his costume and makeup and took a warm shower.

At the stage door he and the Del Aroldos were greeted by a crush of fans as they made their way to a waiting car. Young men and women looked at him adoringly and showered him with flowers.

At the restaurant they were greeted by the staff and were conducted to a private dining room where a wonderful dinner had been prepared for them. Ernesto looked at the couple and embraced both in contentment. They were famished and dove into their food like starving refugees. Many toasts to his success followed. Other cast members and officials of *La Scala* came and went, all offering thanks for his part in saving the performance. Ernesto thought himself an overnight star as he gloried in his reception by all these people. The night grew late and cold as they made their way back to their car.

The Del Aroldos were deposited at the Hotel Milano. Mario whispered he would come to see him in the morning. At last the car drew up to his palace apartment. Going up the grand staircase and down the corridor, he was alone, still in wonder of what had transpired. He got into bed and was asleep almost immediately.

He knew well that the recognition of his achievement in *La Favorita* would recede and that he could never rest on his laurels, especially from the fickle audiences in Milan and Naples. That same season he was called on to replace leading tenors in *Anna Bolena, Norma, and Lucrezia Borgia* at both Milan and Naples. In spite of the momentary glories, he found himself called again and again to provincial towns to sing in third-rate performances, hastily thrown onstage with inferior singers and indifferent conductors.

He, as always, avoided the usual antics of erratic singers. He did his work and moved on to other cities, constantly moving up and down Italy in an endless succession till it seemed like an unending nightmare of work. He was called on many times to appear with the great Turkish soprano, Elvira Dencer, principally in *Lucrezia Borgia,* an opera that he eventually sang more than ninety times. He joined her too for performances of *Belisario*, *La Vestale, Maria Stuarda,* and *La Gioconda.*

The *La Gioconda* was for the *La Fenice* Theater in Venice and marked his return there for the first time since his Italian debut nearly ten years before. This time he did not engage in the foolishness of his first appearances. Gone was any inclination to run about incognito in the costumes of the prima donna.

On a break of a few weeks, he met Mario many times, always seeking moments where their passion could be given free rein. He continued to be completely dominated by him. Nights of lovemaking followed and also intense discussions on the direction, or rather lack thereof, that his career was taking.

Mario had through the Sforzas arranged for him to sing in Brussels at the *Theatre Royal De La Monnaie,* the *Palais Garnier* in Paris, and the

Theatre Grasin in Nantes.

Ernesto reluctantly learned roles in *Faust, Romeo et Juliette, Robert Le Diable, and Les Huguenots.* He found the French and Belgians cold, and the French works totally foreign to his training. As a result, he made little impression, and gratefully returned to Italy as soon as possible. He continued to wonder why it was that in spite of swipes at glory in major houses that he seemed to have only the drudgery of appearing in the provincial towns. Mario had told him it was his job to perform without complaint. Still, he was uncomfortable.

A constant stream of letters from Carlotta came regularly, full of advice and concern that he seemed to be allowing himself to be pushed into uncongenial roles, expressing worry that his top notes and incredible ease in Rossini works was being compromised. He read her letters and replied evasively. Mario was now his sole guide.

Mario's own career was drawing to a close. He sang his last performances in the title role of Verdi's *Stiffelio* in Rome, then retired. No one saw it coming, though he had often confided to Ernesto that he was weary. The constant traveling all over the world had worn him down, and the once heroic voice had begun to falter. He said it should come as no surprise after having sung for more than thirty-five years. He was extremely rich and was still a powerful man in promoting his *protégés*. Ernesto was only one of many.

Several years passed. Mario remained, unknown to Ernesto, dominant in all decisions made concerning his career. The contracts he received had first passed through Mario's hands, even eliminating many of his previous cover assignments. Still he worked almost constantly, singing hundreds of performances.

A South American tour, mainly centered on the *Teatro Colon* in Buenos Aires, kept him away from Italy for more than six months. There he met the sensational Argentine soprano, Leonora D'Negri, who befriended him and appeared with him in more than ten operas, even taking him with her to Mexico, Brazil and Ecuador.

In this last country he appeared with her in the first revival in one hundred years of the opera, *Jone,* by the now completely forgotten Errico Petrella, which is set in Roman antiquity in Pompeii, ending with the spectacular eruption of Vesuvius. It was a triumph and for a time the talk of South America. Though beautiful, it quickly returned to silence after D'Negri lost interest.

He loved the audiences and the Italian-style theaters. Here there seemed to be none of the back biting and jealousies he had known in Italy. Colleagues were, for the most part, concerned that everyone had their moments to shine. The Argentines loved their prima donna and anything in which she wished to appear was eagerly anticipated. The operas here were his *bel canto* favorites. Donizetti, Rossini, Bellini, and early Verdi were the composers.

As the triumphant tour drew to a close, he received an urgent letter from Carlotta asking that he return to Selma for a visit. He had been away for thirteen years, and having nothing more planned that summer, he agreed to come home. Her letter had been vague but insistent. It was June of 1976, and his Italian commitments would not call him back till late September. He flew from Buenos Aires to New York and then to Atlanta. From there he rented a car and drove to Selma.

Thirty-six

As he approached the outskirts of Selma, memories flooded his mind in a cascading torrent. In the humid June morning, he saw the towering Edmund Pettis Memorial Bridge over the Alabama River. He felt strangely detached from this place where he had grown up. As he reached the other side of the bridge, he noticed how the river turned off sharply toward the Old Live Oak Cemetery near the downtown area. Many of the adults that had touched his life now rested there, and he made a mental note to visit this island of reflection. Little had changed in the downtown area. The old post office and the courthouse of Dallas County still stood like silent sentinels, untouched by the passage of time. He saw the old Methodist church and the schools he had attended as a child. He remembered the heat that would inexorably follow as the sun rose higher in the sky. This would be only a passing visit, a swipe at the life he had once led. Three miles outside the downtown area, he turned down the broad avenue leading to The Colonel's mansion. As he reached the driveway a sign proclaimed, *Vasselli School of Singing.*

He remembered as if in a dream, when he had first seen that sign, then fresh and pristine in its white and black lettering. Now it looked faded and weather-beaten. He rounded the slight bend in the driveway and before him the house stood at the end of the double row of great oaks. The house glistened white in the morning sunlight. Behind it stood the grove of pecan trees, now towering more than seventy feet above ground, planted by The Colonel's ancestors. He pulled into the parking area, which contained two unfamiliar cars: a Jeep he knew must be The Colonel's and a cherry-red Mercedes. He smiled; that one had to be Carlotta's. As he got out of his car, he saw the back door open, and Carlotta appeared.

With a cry, she rushed down the steps and fell into his arms. “Ernesto! Oh, my child, is it really you? After all these years you are finally home again?” She cradled his face in her hands, searchingly gazing into the dark eyes that she remembered so well. He smiled and kissed her on both cheeks as always he had done in the past.

“Madame, I have looked forward to this reunion all these many years. It has been so long, too long.” They stood in sunshine at the bottom of the stairs, holding each other in a wordless embrace.

“Well, come along inside now. It will soon be so hot that we won’t be able to stand to venture outside again. I have made some of the lemonade you loved as a child, a sure remedy for all that could ail us in this heat. No, don’t bother with your luggage. I’ll send old John out for it in a little while and he can carry it up to your room.”

Inside, much had changed. Gone were the 1930's kitchen appliances, replaced by a modern stainless steel stove and refrigerator. The great white pine table, however, was still in the center of the room. He gazed around the room and exclaimed, “Why, Madame, so many new things. I’m glad to see you’ve updated things for your comfort.”

“Why of course, my little love. Do you think I could have endured living indefinitely with those old things? We have even installed air conditioning now. Come, sit down and let’s have some of the fresh lemonade I’ve just made.” She filled two glasses and put them on the table, drawing her chair over to sit close beside him. “You have changed so, my dear. You left us a young man in the full bloom of youth, and now here you are, handsome and mature now as a fully grown man. Let me look at you! You have the same sweet smile that always warmed my heart and memories. I know you can’t stay that long, but let’s just enjoy our time together like the old days. There are so many things we need to talk about. You must tell me everything. I am so happy that you appeared at last at *La Scala*. That was always the pinnacle we worked so hard for when you studied here with me and prepared yourself to experience the opera world.” She looked away, her eyes conveying nostalgic remembrances from the days of her youth.

He, too, looked away, lost in the memories of what had passed here with these people he loved. “Mother, I hardly know where to begin to tell you all the things that have happened these last thirteen years. So much you already know, but I’ll be here for a couple of weeks and we can catch up. Where is The Colonel? Is he not here?”

Her smile faded, and she reached across the table and took his hands in hers. “Ernesto, all is not well here. You know, I’m sure, that he is seventy-six now. In the winter he had a light stroke. That’s why we have old John now. I found him through a health agency and he is here now almost every day to look after The Colonel. You may go up to see him in a while, but I want to prepare you in advance. He is still able to get around with a little assistance and John takes him for rides to the places he's loved so much all his life. There's the cemetery, of course. He likes to go there and we've made some repairs to the old family mausoleum, had it pressure washed till it looks new again. He had two benches put outside and he sits there and thinks of the past. He had the four Tiffany windows refitted. We've been told they should stay intact now for many years. His thoughts now seem to bend ever towards death, which has been a bitter pill for me to swallow. You remember him as he was when you left . . . still going strong with an optimistic outlook and engaging always in his golf, fishing, and gardening. Alas, my darling, you will find him so changed, but you mustn't let your concern show when you see him. It would distress him so much."

Ernesto said, "I had no idea. You haven't hinted at this in any of your letters at all. I have just thought of you both here always the same, unchangeable."

She smiled bitterly. "Nothing lasts forever. At thirty you are still too young to know what it is like to grow old, to feel regrets, to have to face aliments, and the shortening of years, but you will some day. We only pray that your inner strength will carry you through when we are gone. As for me, I refuse to give in to it. I still have my pupils, though most are those silly girls who don't really want to work and aspire to have careers. At least with you I have had the satisfaction of passing on the Garcia method to a new generation. You must promise to do so also one day when your singing days are over. Now let's not be so somber. Let's go to the music room and talk about you. Come along now, and bring the pitcher and our glasses with you."

He gathered up the tray and followed her, hesitating as they passed the staircase and the familiar old portraits of the Garcia sisters. In the music room the large portrait of Blanche Marchesi now stood over the French writing desk. In its original place over the fireplace now hung a magnificent full-length portrait of Carlotta in the role of *Norma*. The artist had captured her beautifully. On her head was the entwined mistletoe crown of the Druid priestess and her left hand held the sickle used to cut the mistletoe for the Druid rites. He put down the tray and gazed at the portrait in silence. The pose was from the opening scene with Norma's eyes lifted to heaven as she begins the aria, *Casta Diva, che inargenti.*

Carlotta watched him in amusement. "So what to you think of the new painting? The Colonel had it done ten years ago by an Italian artist from old photographs. The expression has been captured well, don't you think?" He said nothing, continuing to stare. "Come on now. It can't be that beautiful." She sat in her usual throne chair beside the piano, trying to conceal her laughter.

"I am mesmerized, Madame. I have never seen the photograph this was painted from. It's magnificent, spectacular. Why have you never shown me your photos before?" He sat beside her on the lower chair.

"Well, you've never asked to see my old scrapbooks, but it doesn't matter. It's so long ago now, but the photographs capture moments frozen in time from long ago." She held his hand as he continued to look from the portrait to her.

She too had changed. She seemed smaller to him now. Her once lustrous blond hair was now streaked with silver, though her blue eyes retained the luster of old. She still dressed in the latest fashions, though now with a more severe cast than before.

After a few moments, she stood. "Well, my sweet, it's time you went up to see The Colonel. John! Come down here, I need you."

From the floor above came the sound of approaching footsteps. John was a black man, middle-aged but straight as an arrow in a dark black suit and tie. He approached her almost in reverence with downcast eyes. "Yes, Madame? How may I be of assistance?" He looked from her to Ernesto and back again.

"John, this is Ernesto Vasselli. He is here for a visit. Please go out and get his luggage and bring it upstairs to the bedroom on the right at the end of the hall. Ernesto will be going up to see The Colonel. You may then come back down and wait in the kitchen for Mattie to come and start dinner. I will call you if I need you further." With a slight bow, he silently turned away to attend to her wishes.

Carlotta said, "We were lucky to get him. He helps a great deal and takes the burden off me so I may go about the business of running this old house as I always have. Now go on up, child. Yes, alone. Just remember not to let surprise register. You must be calm. Just sit and talk with him. If he's asleep, just wait for him to awaken. Keep the curtains closed. Oh, and close the bedroom door when you go in so that you won't be disturbed. I'll be in the music room if you need me." She gave him a hug and kisses and turned to walk away. "I can't tell you how wonderful it is to have you home, even for a short time." She left him standing at the bottom of the stairs.

For a few moments he gathered his thoughts as to what he would say to this man he had loved so long. At the top of the stairs, he trembled as he approached The Colonel's bedroom. He silently closed the door behind him. The room was in deep shadow. He walked to the bed. Heavy white curtains from the canopy had been drawn back. He heard quiet breathing as The Colonel slept deeply. He pulled up a chair and sat looking at him, propped up on thick pillows. White sheets were in stark contrast to the sleeping man's dark blue pajamas. He peered deeply into familiar features; oh, how he had changed. His once-dark hair was now completely silver, his features pale against the pillows. Ernesto involuntarily reached out and quietly took one of his hands. The skin was nearly transparent and he could see the dark blue veins that crisscrossed beneath it. The Colonel's eyelids were heavy and his face heavily lined. How long Ernesto sat there he didn't know. Time seemed to stand still as memories came flooding back. He felt tears gathering in his eyes, but he brushed them away as he sat there waiting.

The Colonel coughed and opened his light blue eyes. "Ernesto, is that you, my boy? Carlotta told me you were coming. It's so dark in here. Draw the curtains open so I can see you better."

Ernesto opened the drapes across the three floor-to-ceiling windows. The room was filled with sunlight. He ran back quickly to the bed and sat again in the nearby chair.

"How sweet it is of you to come to visit us, my child. You look so well, no longer the boy who left so long ago. You have grown into a handsome man." He reached out his hands. "Come closer, no, not so far away. Come and sit on the bed. You have made me so happy to have come to see us. Here, help me to sit up. Give me a hug."

Ernesto took him into his arms in a silent embrace. He held him a long while against his chest, his hands stroking the silver hair. Both their eyes filled with tears. "Oh, my Colonel, how is it with you? I have missed you so much. My life is so full now with music making, but I have never forgotten how you saved me so long ago and gave me the means to pursue my career. How can I thank you?"

The Colonel smiled. "By loving me as you have for so long, so well. I'm afraid I've turned into a gray old thing now, but love is eternal. When passion ends, what remains is love, it's the only thing that lasts, you know. What we have shared over the years is evergreen in my thoughts. Inside I still feel young, though you would never know from looking at me now. Where is John?"

"Madame had him go for my luggage. She told him to wait in the kitchen for Mattie to come to fix us something to eat. Does she make the charlotte like Viola used to?"

"Oh yes, but Carlotta taught her. Carlotta hasn't changed as I'm sure you noticed. She always supervises everything. It's a wonder I'm still thin since I don't get around as much as I once did." Looking over Ernesto's shoulders, he continued, "Looks like another hot day coming. We'll have to go down to the river to our old haunts near the cemetery. I guess Carlotta told you I had some work done on the mausoleum. It's quite waterproofed now, though the seals on the crypts were still intact when I had the cleaning done. My place beside my sister is waiting. It will be needed soon. I've had my own as well as Carlotta's engraved with our names and birth dates. It's all arranged, you know, and when we are gone, the final dates will be chiseled in. My lawyer will make sure you have the key to the outer doors. Don't mention this to Carlotta; she gets so distressed about it all."

Wiping away his tears, Ernesto looked tenderly at him. "I wish you wouldn't talk about death, Colonel. I want you to live long enough for me to retire so I can come back to look after both of you."

"Well, dear one, I'm afraid we can't wait that long. Don't look so sad. I don't mind really. In fact, I think I'll almost be glad. I'm so useless now since I can't do all the things we used to do. But you're still young. You will yet live long and our memory will fall into its proper place when we are gone." He reached out and put his hand against Ernesto's chest. "I'm afraid passion is spent in this old body now, but I still remember the way your young body felt when I held you so long ago. It was wonderful being with you that way and not having you turn away from a man old enough to be your father." He drew Ernesto close and kissed him on both cheeks. "See, I do it in the Italian way. Carlotta has trained me well after more than thirty years. Now, come help me to the bathroom. This old right side is numb all the time. I'll lean against you."

Ernesto felt his heart in his throat as he helped the man to the bathroom. The Colonel sat on the commode while Ernesto ran his bath, then helped him to undress and lowered him into the warm water. With a large sponge he helped him bathe. The familiar scent of Old Spice filled the room. He shaved him and toweled dried and brushed his silver hair. The Colonel smiled gratefully. They returned to the bedroom and he helped him dress in the clothes Carlotta had laid out for him. A walker stood in a corner of the room.

"Okay, my boy, let's go downstairs now." The Colonel moved slowly, but with minimal assistance, to the landing with Ernesto close beside him. "No, not the stairs. I can't manage them anymore. Carlotta has installed an elevator for me." Ernesto had not noticed the gleaming brass doors as he came upstairs. A moment later they were in the hall outside the kitchen.

John hurried out to the old man. “Colonel Kelly? Mattie has your coffee waiting and the biscuits are hot the way you like them. Come, I’ll help you.”

“Never mind, John, I’m not dead yet. I can still walk; just you stand close till I sit down.”

They sat at the great pine table. A smiling Mattie poured the two men steaming cups of hot coffee. The table was already set and she brought a tray of biscuits from the oven. Fresh churned butter and maple syrup were close at hand alongside the blackberry preserves that The Colonel loved.

“Did you fix the thick bacon too, Mattie? This is our son, Ernesto. He has to be hungry after his drive from Atlanta.”

She curtsied and brought the bacon to the table, then she and John withdrew to the back porch.

“Come on, boy, let’s eat, nothing wrong with my digestion. We’re lucky to have John and Mattie. They are here from morning to night. After supper he helps me get ready for bed and then leaves us alone. I wish Carlotta would allow Mattie to help her, but you know she is not going to let anyone mess with her things. She could have all the help she needs, but wants to do it herself. The young people still come for their lessons and I sit out on the porch and listen.”

Ernesto dove into the fresh biscuits with gusto.

Carlotta entered, hands on hips, and frowned at both of them. “Damn, I turn my back and then here are my two men eating like field hands. What am I to do with you two? Ernesto, stop eating like a pig and pour me a coffee.” She sat, looking at The Colonel. “No, dear, no biscuits for me, too fattening. Bring me my lemon wafers there. They will be quite enough. Ah, this coffee is good. Took me long enough to teach Mattie to fix it the way we like it.” She frowned, looking about the room. Ernesto and The Colonel knew that look and were careful not to say anything while she inspected the room.

Rising, she walked about the room. Not a speck of dust in sight. She shrugged. “All right, Ernesto, let’s talk shop. I try to stay informed as to what is going on with your career, but the details seem to elude me. Are the Sforzas treating you with respect?” Without waiting for a reply, she rushed on. “After thirteen years, I would have hoped you would not have to deal with them so much. Its time you were permanently on the rosters of the greatest houses instead of being buried out in the provinces where performances are always off the international circuit.”

“Well, Madame, I do sing in the great theaters from time to time when I cover performances. I sing often at the *San Carlo*. And over the last five years I've sung five times at *La Scala*. Signor Del Aroldo comes with me always when I visit the Sforza's offices to get my assignments for each upcoming season. They arranged for the South American tour and the concerts I have done at Rio and Buenos Aires. Mario is indispensable these days. I wish I had been able to make some recordings. I know there have been discussions from time to time, but he feels there's time enough for all that. I'm still only thirty and I perform all the time. In fact when I leave here I'm going to have ten performances in Philadelphia of *La Favorita* and *Lucia* before I return to Italy."

Carlotta's eyes narrowed. "And what about *my* advice? Do *I* have no influence on you any more? You know your career would never have been launched without me, yet you keep me in the dark and listen only to Del Aroldo? I know him well since before the war, but I question why he looks after all your contracts. Why should a man like that who has been a star since the late thirties have such control over what you sing and where? Stay with him and he'll soon push you into *Verismo* operas, and then it's goodbye voice. I know you've been doing a lot of Donizetti and early Verdi operas, which is good, but what has happened with Rossini? Festivals are always in full swing in Pesaro and Florence. His old operas are being done everywhere, but you aren't doing them, why is that?"

Stung, he fought to control his composure. "Madame, I still sing those operas when I receive offers. It's just that they seem to just want me for Donizetti and Verdi now. I haven't forgotten or lost my facility in Rossini. I practice the Marchesi exercises every day. Please don't think I would ever forget the *bel canto* training you've given to me." He looked at her defensively.

"Well, do as you wish. It's no longer in my hands what you do since you listen only to Del Aroldo. Just remember, I was a *Prima Donna Assoluta,* while he was crooning those hideous Puccini and Mascagni operas. Why people adore all that screaming I will never understand. No, don't say anything else. Let's just drop it and enjoy your visit. You will one day regret you didn't listen to your old teacher when I'm gone."

She looked at her husband. "Darling, sorry to bore you with all this music talk, but you know how it is with me." He smiled at her, but said nothing. She brushed some crumbs from his shirt, then called for John and Mattie. "All right, you two! I've got to go into town for the steaks I've ordered for tonight. You both know your duties, so see to them. Ernesto, why don't you take The Colonel for a ride? I'll be back later and we can get ready for our supper." A moment later the Mercedes thundered down the driveway and turned toward town.

The Colonel waved off Mattie and John. He looked at Ernesto with a sad smile. "Forgive her, Ernesto. She is unchangeable. Remember that she gave up her career and her country to come to live with me. All that she became here was a sacrifice to dedicate her life to being my wife. Is it any wonder that she clings to her old way of life? No, rather let us rejoice that she is a blessing to me and to you. How sorry and empty my life would have been had I not found her at the war's end. We can't regret what might have been. Without her we would have been the poorer. Her love sustains me in my faltering steps, ever leaning towards the tomb. She has given me the courage to face whatever comes next as life slowly ebbs. Without her what kind of life would you have had? Now, let's go for a ride past our old places the way we used to."

Nodding, Ernesto helped him to his feet and to the Jeep. The heat of summer gathered about them as he helped the Colonel into his seat. They drove out onto the avenue toward the river.

At the end of the first week of his stay, Ernesto drove into town alone to the bank to be sure his accounts were in order and that the money he was sending out of Italy had been received and properly credited. He had begun to do these transfers regularly, but in small increments to avoid being questioned by the Italian authorities. He left the bank after half an hour, assuring himself that the total of close to $500,000 was safe. In this unassuming town, such accounts were treasured by the banking community. His holdings didn't rival those of Carlotta and The Colonel, but they were substantial and would provide handsomely to his expenses when his singing days were over.

As he walked down the sidewalk to his car, he ran into Imogene. They both stood, looking at each other for a moment.

"David? Is it really you? Here in Selma after all this time? How changed you are from the last time we met before you left for Italy. I almost didn't recognize you. When did you arrive? How long are you going to be here?" Her colorless lips trembled with emotion.

"I came a week ago at Madame's invitation. She wanted to see me and have me spend time with them. The Colonel is not well as you may know. I'll only be here for a few more days and then I will have to get back to Italy after some performances that I'll give in Philadelphia." He felt keenly the awkwardness of the moment and then suggested, "If you have a moment, let's go into the drug store out of this horrible heat and have some iced tea."

She nodded in agreement, and they walked the few steps into the old Craig drug store which had been there since the 1930's. As they settled into a booth, he ordered two large glasses of sweet tea. She did not take her eyes off his face. "David, I mean Ernesto, how have you been? I never have news of you. I see Madame from time to time in town, but avoid talking with her. What would be the use? She and The Colonel live in their world and I in mine." She looked around, nodding or waving occasionally at ladies she knew who stared at her sitting with the handsome man. Gossip, she well knew, would soon be afoot behind closed doors about the stranger in their midst. "Are you not interested in knowing what has been going on with me, with your brothers?" She broke off as she saw his face blanch at the mention of his family.

"Actually, Mother, I have little time for dwelling on the comings and goings of people who have no effect on my life. I trust you are all well, but I have little interest in discussing the past. What purpose would it serve at this point?" He paused, taking a drink of his tea as she fell silent. "Madame sends me news of you now and then in passing. She assures me that you are in good health, still working at the air force base. If anything were amiss she would have told me."

She smiled bitterly. "Well, I suppose that if we hadn't accidentally run into each other that you would have come and gone without contacting me? I shouldn't be surprised, I guess. Your life turned away from Selma long ago. I never could understand the hold on you that music became, but I know it was instilled in you long ago by her, so there's no need to go back over old ground. I am still your mother, even if they took you away from me. If you are at peace with yourself then I suppose we have nothing else to say to each other."

The bitter, self-pitying tone of her voice registered on him as he felt impatience rise. He wasn't about to engage in a battle of wits with her. "They have given me everything. Both of them gave me the opportunity to aspire to a life more meaningful and full of purpose. They made the road easier, so don't even attempt to say anything against either of them to me. I am well aware of your own motives and how you profited in the matter, so keep any negative thoughts to yourself. You haven't done too badly in the bargain. You look fine and content, so let's leave it like that." He rose, leaving money on the table for their drinks. "I have to go now. It was nice to have seen you. I have no idea when I'll be back here, so I wish you the best."

Imogene opened her mouth to protest but the words died in her throat. She looked at the table.

"Mother, stay and enjoy your drink. I must get back for dinner."

She stood and addressed him indignantly. "So this is the way it ends then. Ernesto? Without a kiss or a hug you abandon me again?" She shoved the money on the table toward him and threw down a couple of dollars. "I think I can afford my own glass of tea." She glared at him, her face pale. They stood for a moment staring at each other, each lost in their own thoughts. She reached out her hand to touch his arm. He flinched. She then quickly walked outside and rapidly went back to her car. They were strangers now.

He watched her make her way down the street. *Nothing ever changes with this woman. Serpent! Let her go. It's of no consequence either way now. Let the door be closed forever. Your time is coming, Mother, of that there is no doubt.*

On the morning of the last day of his visit, at The Colonel's request, the two of them drove over to the Old Live Oak cemetery. They parked and slowly approached the family mausoleum, sheltered in the shade of the towering cypress trees. They sat on one of the two marble benches outside its doors.

"Well, my boy, it's time for you to leave this afternoon. I can't tell you how much it has meant to me that you've come back to see us after all these years, but we know you need to return to your career. I wanted you to come with me on this last morning to this place. It occurred to me that you've never seen the inside of the mausoleum. Help me to my feet and let's go inside." He drew a large key from his trousers and turned it in the lock. "Here are my grandparents and great grandparents on the top tier. Below them my parents and little sister, Georgiana, rest in their crypts." The stained-glass Tiffany windows cast a warm glow against the walls. The marble floor gleamed in the morning light. "I want to show you the inscription here on the marble bench at the back I've had it inscribed with the words my grandfather wrote for his wife before his death."

Ernesto was moved as he read the words:

While drooping winds among the branches sigh,
And sluggish waters heavily roll by.
Here to my fatal sorrows let me give
The short remaining hours I have to live.

The Colonel sighed deeply. "Here are the crypts on the other side for Carlotta and me. You will need to have our death dates added when we are gone, or at least hers. She will see to mine, I'm sure." Gazing toward the tombs he said, "Soon I must join them. Don't look so sad. My time has come, my glass has run, here I will lay down for my last rest. Try to be here for Carlotta if you can. She will have more than enough to live on for the rest of her days. All I ask is that you take care of seeing that she is placed here with me when her time comes. Will you promise me, my dearest child?" Tears welled in his eyes as he looked beseechingly at Ernesto.

"It will be as you ask. I promise you. I wish we had the time to be together as in the old days, but you have both taught me that love is all that matters. No one who has loved as we have is ever truly gone as long as they are remembered." He wept as he held the old man in his arms and kissed his silver hair.

The Colonel whispered," Below, here in the floor, is the final vacant tomb. It is for you if you wish one day to lie here with us in silence. First though, we wish for you to live long, to grow old easily, and to at last die in peace. It's all any of us can wish for, Ernesto. Oh, there's one final thing I wish to give you before we leave, it's what I want you to have inscribed on Carlotta's crypt when she is gone. I have written it for her, though she doesn't know about it." He drew a paper from his jacket.

Unfolding it, Ernesto read the words written there, The Colonel's last for her.

The beautiful is vanished, and returns not.
'Twas but as yesterday, a mighty throng,
Whose hearts, as one man's heart, thy power could bow,
Amid loud shoutings hailed thee queen of song,
And twined sweet summer flowers around thy brow;
And those loud shouts have scarcely died away
And those young flowers but half forgot thy bloom,
When thy fair crown is changed to one of clay —
Thy boundless empire for a narrow tomb!
Sweet minstrel of the heart, we listen in vain
For music now; THY melody is o'er;
Norma hath ceased o'er hearts to reign,
Sonnambula hath slept to wake no more!
Farewell! Thy sun of life too soon hath set,
But memory shall reflect its brightness yet.

"Again I promise you, Colonel, it will be done. Comfort yourself and let's return to the world of the living. There will be time enough for tears when you are gone. My heart is so full. I know we will probably not meet again in this life, but keep in mind the love we have had all these years for each other. Love never dies."

There were no more words, just an unspoken understanding. Ernesto helped him to his feet and they walked outside, locking the melancholy doors of the mausoleum behind them.

After lunch, The Colonel and Carlotta walked with him through the great front door to the porch and bid him God speed. They both embraced and kissed him. At last, disengaging from his arms, Carlotta said, "Who knows when we will meet again? Please try to remember all I have taught you, my darling, and don't allow yourself to take up roles that will be detrimental to your voice."

The Colonel turned and went back inside.

Carlotta regarded him searchingly. "You have such a great gift, Ernesto. The Garcia method will serve you well as long as you keep it always in mind. I will be here, loving you always. Remember us now as you leave this place."

"I will, Mother. I'll stay in touch. I won't do anything without consulting you." A final kiss and he descended the steps with a heavy heart to his car. Looking back, he saw her framed in the doorway waving goodbye. He blew her a kiss and drove slowly away and turned at the end of the driveway towards the road that would lead him to Montgomery, then Atlanta, and his flight to New York for the return to the world of music, first in Philadelphia, then again to Italy. Though he didn't want to admit it, in his heart he knew he probably would never see the old couple again.

Thirty-seven

The performances in Philadelphia of *La Favorita* and *Lucia di Lammermoor* unfolded with a warm reception for him in his first staged performances in the United States. He forwarded his fees of $30,000 to his bank in Selma and spent his last few days in New York by auditioning at both The Metropolitan Opera and the New York City Opera. At the Metropolitan he was thanked and told that they would keep him in mind. He had sung well but knew their roster was filled with tenor stars. He also knew that The Met seldom, if ever, mounted the kind of operas in which he specialized. Besides, he had seen their auditorium with its hundreds of seats and knew he wouldn't like to perform in such a barn with its horrible acoustics.

The audition at the New York City Opera went better. He sang for their general manager, Wolfgang Budel, and the resident prima donna, Olympia Duplessis. Maestro Budel complimented him and said, "I understand the scope of the career you have led in Italy, but, Signor

Vasselli, you are unknown to our public here. You have made no studio recordings that they could buy, and here in the States, attendance at performances are fueled by record sales. The most I could offer you at this point would be *Madama Butterfly* and *Tosca*. We would also consider you as a cover for several *bel canto* operas we have in planning for Madame Duplessis. Would this be of any interest to you? Of course if you had a bigger reputation there wouldn't be a problem."

Ernesto curtly replied. "Maestro, what you are offering is essentially a beginner's contract. I have already been thirteen years on the lyric stage, singing in London, Paris, Brussels, and Buenos Aires, not to mention Milan, Venice, Naples, and Palermo. If you would bother to check with my agents, the Sforzas in Milan, they would be happy to supply you with reviews of my performances as well as references from opera houses. I am no beginner, but a specialist in *bel canto* operas. I have over sixty roles that I have performed on stage with some of the greatest singers in the world, and you offer me Puccini? I do not sing his operas, except for a few isolated performances of *La Boheme.* Any fool could get away with it. I am used to fresh new performances and productions like those at *La Scala* and the *San Carlo*, where I have sung to great acclaim in such operas as *Anna Bolena."*

Budel smiled and looked at him patronizingly. "*Anna Bolena?* Oh, that's just an old bore of an opera. It wouldn't attract the public here. In that case, I recommend that you make some commercial recordings and increase your visibility in front-rank theaters. Then come back to me and I'll sign you up." He reached across the desk to shake Ernesto's hand.

"Thank you Maestro, but if I increase my European reputation to the point where the American public hears of me, then I won't need you. I do not sing operas that are not suited for my voice, nor do I sing routine operas like those presented here. My mentor, Mario Del Aroldo, has never sung in your theater either, but I'm sure you will agree that he hasn't done too badly. Thank you for your time, I wish the best for you and Madame Duplessis for your upcoming season." He turned and left the office. *What an idiot. They know nothing of presenting fresh performances of bel canto operas, even those they have done with Duplessis are merely puppets surrounding this one big star.*

A few days later, he was back in Milan. He had been away for months but was pleased that his landlady had seen to opening up the rooms and having everything thoroughly cleaned. His sideboard was loaded with mail that he needed to sort. While in South America he had received a renewal contract from the Sforzas. This time they had only asked for ten percent of his earnings, which pleased him greatly, but he was not pleased with the fact that the dozens of engagements they had arranged did not include the *La Fenice, La Scala* or the *San Carlo*. He was, however, encouraged by the new operas they had proposed. Over the next five years he was to sing in *Ernani, I Masnadieri, Luisa Miller, La Battaglia Di Legnano, Rigoletto, I Due Foscari, I Vespri Siciliani,* all by Verdi. Also, *L'Italiana in Algeri* and *La Cenerentola* by Rossini. Rounding out the proposals were ten Donizetti operas, and four by Bellini, all of which he had sung before. Ample time for outside engagements was also included, as well as concerts with various artists.

He called Mario to discuss the details. "Mario, have you had a chance to hear about what they have offered me? I told them that I wanted you to be included in any discussions before I commit myself to a five-year contract."

"Yes, Ernesto. I took the liberty of talking with them while you were away, and I heartily approve of what they're offering. I encourage you to sign immediately to avoid any delay in the fall, winter, and spring seasons. I also want to let you know that Giovanna and I are closing up our apartment in Rome and we are moving to Milan, so I'll be able to be with you nearly every day. Would that please you, my darling?"

Ernesto beamed, "That would be fantastic, but where am I going to find the time to learn all these new operas with you wanting to fuck me morning, noon, and night?"

"Oh there will be plenty of time for our lovemaking and your study. I will coach you in learning all the new parts. I know several pianists in Milan we can call on for that. My new apartment there will be on the top floor of the old hotel near *La Scala*. You know the building, I believe. They've turned it into apartments and ours is ready . . . ten rooms, including a wonderful room that we'll turn into our music room. You remember my wonderful concert grand piano. It will do very nicely. Giovanna, as usual, will be visiting our children and old friends of hers for weeks at a time, so there will be many days when we'll divide our time between the bedroom and the music room. In fact, I think we should christen all the rooms, except for Giovanna's bedroom, of course. The poor old dear needs one room to be hers alone."

Ernesto laughingly agreed. "There is so much to be done, so much new music to learn. I'm excited that the first new part is to be *Ernani.* I know it was one of your favorite parts. I'm a little concerned though that it seems to lie lower in my range than I'm accustomed to. My chest voice is something I was always taught to use sparingly. Too much of it results in the loss of the highest notes." He walked to the windows. A young man from the bakery was entering the gates of the palace. "Well, Mario, I need to go, I see someone coming with the baked goods I've ordered."

"Okay then, enjoy your sweets, but remember not to eat everything those young men have to offer. We don't want you to be known as the tenor whore of Milan." They hung up as a knock came at his door.

Ernesto had entered the most intense period of his career. Up and down the Italian boot he traveled, to Pesaro, Turin, Genoa, Ferrara, Reggio Calabria, Ancona, Bresscia, Macerata, Pavia, Livorno, Cremona, and Parma. Although he worked constantly, the big theaters eluded him. No recording companies approached him, though he was well known in some circles for his facility in learning new roles. Occasionally a call would come from a major opera house to step in for an ailing tenor, but he received few cover assignments. The emergency calls brought his highest fees. He kept careful registers of his performances and the money they brought in and continued to send large sums back to the bank in Selma where his assets grew larger.

A call came in mid-March of 1977 from Carlotta to report the death of The Colonel at the age of seventy-seven. His health had continued to grow more fragile, and finally pneumonia had set in. Ernesto listened in sadness as he looked out the windows of his ancient hotel suite.

"Oh, my dearest boy. His last thoughts included you. We were both so happy that you were able to visit us that last summer. After you left, we sat together so often and he spoke of you with pride and love for your accomplishments. Ernesto, that last night was so terrible. His breathing became more and more labored. The doctor had come to spend the night and warned me that in a few hours it would all be over."

Ernesto felt more alone than ever in his life. His tears fell unheeded down his face as he paced the room. "Oh, Madame, was he in much pain? I feel so helpless that I can't be there with you, but I have been performing non-stop now for weeks. I don't think I could break away to come now."

"Don't worry yourself, sweetheart. Your commitments are sacred. You must never cancel performances, and though you sing through tears, you must give the public what they are paying for." She broke off for a moment, but pulling herself together with her customary discipline, she continued, "No, darling, at the end he wasn't in pain. I sat beside the bed, holding his hand through the night with the doctor hovering near. My nerves were so bad that I nearly screamed at him and he, sensing my agitation, retreated to sit in the corner. The poor man called for light, and I lit the candles, which calmed him. He looked at me so sadly and whispered that of all the things in life that he was about to leave, that he regretted nothing, except being parted from me, from you. I told him to be comforted, that we would be fine. He asked me to give you his love and to remember the promises you made to him that last morning at the mausoleum. He seemed to fall asleep, and I, too, dozed in my chair. The morning light had begun to rise as I came to myself again, and looked at his face, so pale against the pillows where he lay propped up to help his breathing, I sensed the time had come. His hand, still in mine, had grown cold. I called the doctor over. He felt for a pulse and then shook his head. He reached over to close his eyes and I seized his arm saying it was my duty to do that. I got up and did so. I looked long in to that noble face for the last time. The doctor called the funeral directors and they came and took him from the house. Only as the hearse drove away and I was alone did I give into my grief. Tears release pent-up emotions held too long in check and I fully indulged myself."

Ernesto tried to talk through the spasms of sorrow. "Madame, know that my heart and my love are with you always. He was a father to me and saved me so long ago. That last morning in the cemetery, I realized that there was nothing left unspoken between he and I. As we sat on the bench in the mausoleum together the moment was so full of understanding and poignancy that I could hardly bear to see it come to an end. What's that, Mother? No, I'll be fine. I will dry up my tears for now. I've had rapidly to learn *Il Trovatore* for Trieste. The first performance is this evening. Mario himself has coached me in the part. I know it's a stretch from Rossini, but it's still *bel canto* and I don't think it should cause any adverse effects on the voice."

Carlotta listened in silence over the crackling connection and finally said, "I'll say goodbye for now, my dear. There are simply a thousand details to see to regarding the entombment. I must get to it. Keep in touch, my angel."

Ernesto gave full vent to extreme sorrow; his cries rang out in agony as he collapsed into a chair. There was no one there to hear him. The Colonel's voice was stilled for all time. The memories flooded back of nights drenched with love, but now he was alone in another country. Mario was in Milan. The performance was looming closer. He wiped away his tears, washed his face, dressed, and left for the *Teatro Lirico de Giuseppe Verdi*. Sadness must be pushed to a distant corner. His muses, Carlotta, as well as Mario would see him through the ordeal.

Thirty-eight

Weeks and months turned into years. From his base in Milan, he traveled ceaselessly. Occasionally he would be summoned to far-off places with traveling companies that offered large fees. A bad experience was his appearance in *Eugene Onegin* at the Marinsky Theater in St. Petersburg where he sang the role of *Lenski* five times. He had learned the role in a week at the urging of Mario and the Sforzas. The Russian language was completely foreign to him, but he sang it phonetically, and was thus successful in a completely different kind of opera than his training had prepared him to perform. He found the Russians cold and unresponsive and his colleagues uncongenial. Only the briefest time was given to rehearsals. He was appalled that the star baritone refused to rehearse. Such things would never be tolerated in Italy. Even the splendor of the Romanoff palaces didn't impress him. He was miserable and lonely for Mario. The weather was bitterly cold with snow falling heavily during his entire stay and with ice forming on the inside of the windows in his Spartan rooms in a hotel that seemed to date to the 1920's. As soon as possible he returned to Milan and took up the interminable traveling that was his lot.

Though he was making money, which he immediately sent out of the country, he was becoming more and more discouraged that his career didn't seem to advance toward the stardom he felt was always just beyond his grasp. Mario constantly reassured him that it would come. They were together almost constantly now and the older man would often travel with him. Even off the international circuit, all Italy knew Mario, and his coming with his protégé to their provincial opera houses lent glamour to the events. Ernesto noted often that there seemed to be more excitement in the audience than on the stage when Mario would choose a moment to sweep down to his seat and the public would have eyes only for their now-retired star. Jealousy was never a part of Ernesto's thinking. He would shrug and just go about his professional duties like he always had, always superbly prepared and emotionally involved with the characters he portrayed. He fell completely in love with Mario in spite of the fact that he was always in his shadows, believing that at any moment recording contracts would come his way as well as beautifully prepared performances at the large international houses.

Each summer he would leave for two or three months in South America with his friend from Argentina, soprano Leonora D'Negri. These were always independent of the agency's control and the fees he received were among the best he had ever earned.

Mario never came with him when he joined Madame D'Negri. Mario disliked Spanish-speaking countries, even though he had garnered a fortune in earnings years ago in these same theaters. Like most Italians, especially now that he had retired, he thought anything that happened beyond the borders of Italy to be an enormous waste of time. Ernesto, on the other hand, looked forward to going there each summer and he was greeted with great acclaim by an appreciative audience.

Leonora, like him, was a specialist in *bel canto* operas and an acclaimed actress as well. She had appeared all over the world. Even the Metropolitan Opera of New York had come to her when their own resident prima donna had faltered in the demanding role of *Norma*. She received an open contract to save the performances. She demanded and received $10,000 per performance and insisted on three more seasons, where she appeared in *Ernani, Lucia di Lammermoor, Macbeth,* and *Il Trovatore.* Her fees were greater than any artist who had appeared there since Adelina Patti.

As the calendar rolled into the 1981-1982 fall and winter seasons in Italy. Ernesto's contract with the Sforzas would be up in May of 1982. He sat alone in his apartment, looking over a new three-year contract that had been forwarded to him. The terms were almost identical to the last. Even with Mario's constant urging to accept, he had summoned enough backbone to resist signing too quickly. He would be thirty-six in November; nothing of any significance was happening with his career. He questioned soberly if he could go on like this, always being just a step away from the fame that Mario still enjoyed. People told him that he was singing like a god. Although his voice had begun to falter in the highest register, overall his maturity had given it a sheen and warmth which were talked about in newspapers in all the small cities he visited. The middle and lower registers remained intact, but from overuse his high D's were gone. Rossini and much of Bellini had become problematic.

But no one in Milan looked at small-town newspapers, and *La Scala* and the *San Carlo*, as well as the *Fenice* in Venice seemed permanently closed to him. *Why after eighteen seasons on the lyric stage is it this way? In the early years I appeared in those places and everyone loved me. I sang with great singers even if I was a substitute and now I can't even get a foot in the door? Where have I gone wrong? I've paid my dues. I can't abide another three years of working in the provinces. I have seventy roles now that I have sung here, and it's like no one cares. I'm not signing this contract. I need to try to figure out what is going on.*

The fall season had begun in Genoa where he was to perform in Donizetti's *Poliuto*, a role that troubled him because it called for a more declamatory style of singing. Comparisons with the great tenor of the recent past, Franco Borelli, were inevitable. Borelli had sung the part in the December 1960 performances at *La Scala* and had created a sensation with his trumpet-like high C's. After more than twenty years, Genoa was the first city to take on a revival. Mario had urged him to take on this role, and against his better judgment he had agreed.

In the first performance, in the second act during *Poliuto's* great aria, disaster struck. He had to abandon the concluding high C to cries of displeasure and hisses; for the first time in his career his voice had failed him. After the second performance, the management of the theater cancelled the remaining performances, putting on instead routine representations of *Tosca*. Ernesto left the city in a fury, threatening legal action if he wasn't paid for the performances he was contracted to sing. Another theater's doors closed silently on him.

In the months that followed, the golden voice gave him more problems than successes. A distinct wobble crept into notes above the staff, and he was forced to lightly etch in his high B's. This sort of cautious singing was not tolerated, even in the provincial cities. His performances began to dwindle as theater after theater grew disinterested. Still he went on, hoping for the best and attempting to rest his voice, hoping its former glory would be regained. Carlotta's warnings had been ignored as Mario and the agency forced him into accepting heavier roles. He went like a lamb to the slaughter. He loved Mario, and still believed his mentor knew what was best for him, but a dear price had been paid.

After several more months, he found himself back in Milan. He had refused to commit himself to the agency for the three-year contract. He was also disheartened; Mario began to distance himself from him. The Sforzas nagged him constantly. His performances in Parma in April of *Simon Boccanegra* had been undistinguished and resulted in angry exchanges between his fans and the fanatical Parma public which booed him without mercy. He began to cancel appearances and felt totally alone and adrift.

Late one afternoon, he encountered James Buffington at the famous *Biffi Scala* restaurant. Mario and Giovanna had been out of town for several weeks and he sat alone at his usual table in deep depression over his career that had come to a complete standstill. James saw him from across the room and came over to join him at his table. The two old friends embraced warmly and James led off the conversation with inquiries as to how he was feeling, and what he was doing.

"Jane and I have been concerned with the things we've been hearing of you lately. What has happened with your voice?"

Frowning, Ernesto answered bitterly, "I really have no explanation other than I've been wearing myself out singing non-stop the last several years. I have taken the advice of people that I realize now were not interested in what was best for me, but rather lining their own pockets at my expense." He was close to tears as he spoke. "James, things could not be worse."

James glanced cautiously at the hovering waiters, waving them off so that he could speak frankly. "I don't mean to bring you down, but I want you to know that Jane and I have been concerned. We have not forgotten you and I have personally spoken several times with your agents here in Milan and also in Rome. We had inquired through them as to your availability several times when we've found ourselves needing a tenor. There was a *Fille du Regiment* that we were trying to cast for Venice, and also a recording we were thinking of doing of *Beatrice di Tenda.* Savarotti had indicated he might not be available for the recording sessions, and we immediately thought of you. He did, however, clear himself in time and the recording was a great success. Jane, you know, is not far from retirement herself. She is just sick of all the globe trotting we've been doing for the last twenty-five years. By 1986 she will no longer be actively performing anywhere. I will go on conducting because I'm in demand for our *bel canto* operas with a new group of singers. It's just a shame that you were either unavailable or not interested when I made offers through your agents. Were you really so disillusioned with us that you could never give us a personal reply?" He broke off as he perceived a look of astonishment sweeping over Ernesto's face.

The younger man looked at him as though struck by lightening. His wine glass fell from his hand, shattering on the floor. Waiters rushed to attend; James angrily told them to back off. "Ernesto? Are you okay? You've gone completely white. What's going on?"

Ernesto felt a creeping sense of horror sweeping over him. His words poured forth between gasps of disbelief. "James, what you're saying is incredible. I have known nothing of any offers you have made through my agents. *Nothing!* I would have dropped anything I was doing to work with you and Jane again. With the world at your feet, I would have been insane to pass up anything like what you have mentioned. My God, to sing with Jane would have been to turn the world's eyes on my contribution. In this last five-year contract which will end in a few weeks, they eliminated any cover assignments at *La Scala*, the *San Carlo*, and the *Fenice*. They told me that these theaters had not made any offers. I have been singing like a dog in the most horrible places on the face of the earth, sometimes as much as eighty times a year. Mario had urged me to do as the agency asked, saying international stardom would come. Now you tell me this news?" He buried his face in his hands as sobs racked his body. From all sides of the room people stared at him.

James dragged him to his feet and pulled him into a private dining room. Ernesto sat at the table with his face on his arms.

"My God, Ernesto, this is monstrous!" He stood behind the singer's back and held him, trying vainly to assuage his grief. Great wails of agony burst unchecked into the silent room. Ernesto rushed about the room with tears and heart-rending cries coming in waves. James called for wine, which he grabbed from a waiter, closing the doors behind him.

"Ah, James, I am done for at last. They have finished me for all time. I have trusted these people and they have served me up my heart on a platter. I have lost my highest notes from all this constant work, singing sometimes on consecutive nights in different cities. Oh God, what am I to do now?" He flung himself into a chair, downing in a single gulp the wine James offered him. At long last Ernesto raised his head and looked at James with an expression of sorrow.

"The first thing you have to do is to get a lawyer and confront the Sforzas in their own lair here in Milan. I know someone to send you to. You must do this, and quickly, before word gets out and they are forewarned. I will give him a letter outlining the dates I have contacted them about using you on our projects and the names of their representatives who told me you weren't interested in our proposals. He will demand an accounting of them regarding their conduct. Believe me, their house of cards will fall when he gets the facts. They will rush to settle with you. On that you can depend." James paced, growing more agitated. "Come now, my friend. This is not the time for tears. You must be calm and play your part in this drama to its bitter end. Let revenge guide you. The lawyer will arrange a handsome settlement. You'll never have to worry about money again."

"Oh, James, it isn't the money. It's the abject betrayal of me, both as an artist and a man. I have worked like a galley slave for these people, made them rich, and this is how I am rewarded? Yes you are right, they are going to pay dearly for this. But what about Mario? I thought he loved me and had only my best interests at heart. Could he have been deceived by these people too? I can't believe he could have known about these deceptions, but he always told me to go along, to bide my time. I have taken on heavier roles because he has urged me to do so and now my voice is paying the price for this folly. What an utter fool I have been." Calm now, but horribly sad, he took a napkin and wiped his face. "James, thank you for telling me these things. I have imposed on you far too long, ruined your dinner with my childish tears. Jane has to be waiting for you. I'll just go home. I need to think and then tomorrow talk to the lawyer about how to proceed against the agency."

James embraced him. "No, I don't think you need to be alone tonight. Jane isn't with me. She's in London. Come with me, back to my hotel. I'll order dinner and wines sent up. I can be with you through the night."

"Yes, lead me where you will. The night ahead will be less lonely and barren with a true friend nearby." They walked out of the room, ignoring the curious looks of the staff and diners and were soon at the Hotel Verdi. As they walked into the marble-lined foyer, a clap of thunder burst over the city, followed by torrents of rain which poured down in waves from black skies as a starless night fell on the city.

In James' suite, the two friends sat at an ebony table as dinner was laid out for them. Ernesto could eat nothing. He sat on the sofa, staring off into space. James hovered near him, unable to console him. Finally he sat beside him on the sofa and held him. James briefly excused himself to make a couple of business phone calls.

Ernesto sat in silence. *Why have I been treated this way? I can't understand how or why, but if it's the last thing I do I'm going to get to the bottom of it if only I can get through this night. Traitors! They will pay for this.*

James returned, approaching him cautiously so as not to disturb his reverie. He poured them both more wine. "Ernesto? I was just speaking with Jane. She, like me, is in shock that you were never told that we had tried to offer you the performances and the recording. We both remember the promise that you showed so long ago when we first met you in Venice. You were just a baby, but so full of enthusiasm and your talent was so immense. We just knew you would have the world at your feet."

From somewhere deep inside the recesses of his heart, something stirred within the younger man's soul. His mind cleared as he looked back at James, and he spoke with deep sadness. "James, you and Jane were so kind to me all those years ago. I thought then that the future would stretch out before me in a series of unbroken triumphs. It seemed that way as those early years came and I sang in the big theaters, even if, like in Naples, it was just as a second cast singer, or because I learned my music so easily and the public was eager to see operas revived to live again. I served the composers as I had always been taught. I can't even tell now where it all began to go wrong. Madame had always hammered it into me since I was a child never to overtax my voice or it would rebel. I have been arrogant and full of pride because I believed people had my best interests and that of art at heart. Now I sit here with you, looking at my career in ruins and my voice perhaps unrecoverable, too much singing and in such miserable places where no one who mattered could hear me. It's been such a waste. I thought with my heart and not with the clear head I should have. Now it is finished." He went over to a window, still holding his wine glass. He looked out at the dark streets as the lights of the city began to grow faint. The rain had stopped.

Coming up behind him, James put his arms around him, kissing him gently on his shoulders. "Why don't we take a shower? It will do us both good. In the morning we can call the lawyer I know and get some sort of resolution to this tragedy." His hands slipped down the younger man's chest and rested against his waist. "We could pretend we were back in Venice the way we were eighteen years ago. You have hardly changed at all. You are still so lovable and handsome, your body firm beneath my hands as it was then when your dreams were fresh and new."

Disengaging himself, Ernesto looked at him thoughtfully. "James, who does not dream in their souls? I was still a boy then. Now I am a man. Nothing remains the same forever. I realize that now that it's too late. We can never go back again. You have been so kind to give up your night for me so I won't have to be alone. I should go; you and Jane are at the zenith of your careers. You don't need to think of me, I will be fine, I'm sure, when this whole sorted story is played out. If you want me to stay, I will sleep with you tonight, but I can't promise you anything. I hope you understand."

"Come then, Ernesto. It grows late. Let's take our shower and go to bed. I expect nothing beyond trying to comfort you." They showered, the warm water relaxing them. At length, they slipped under the sheets. James drew him close; Ernesto lay on his back looking at the ceiling. James' hand rested on his chest and stomach, slipping lower to give him pleasure. The time ticked away. At last James' breathing grew quieter as he drifted off in sleep.

Ernesto, as though in a dream, looked at the sleeping man. He only saw Mario in his mind. *Mario will know what to do if I can ever get him to return my calls. I have no idea when he will be back. I need his reassurance so much. Until then, come my most steadfast companion and dwell in my heart as you always have in the well of my soul, you my sweet well, my loneliness...* He fell back on his pillows, pulling the sheet over his chest and turning his face to the wall, never realizing when moonlight, flooding the room in a warm glow, cast shadows over their two naked sleeping bodies.

Thirty-nine

After seeing the lawyer James recommended, Ernesto was ready to face the agency in a final confrontation. Armed with James' letter outlining the times he had contacted the agency and the replies he had been given, the two men arranged to go together. The lawyer had cautioned him to remain calm and to listen while he talked to the agents. The lawyer picked him up and drove in silence through the quiet streets. They passed *La Scala*, seemingly deserted now that the season was ending, and were soon at the low gray building which housed the offices of the Sforzas. They had called ahead, though the agent had been given no warning regarding the reason for the meeting. They entered the reception area and were served strong coffee and *biscotti* as they waited. Presently the secretary led them to the familiar office that Ernesto knew so well.

Gaetano Fraschini stood and reached across the table to shake their hands. The unsigned contract lay on the table before them.

The lawyer said, "Signor Fraschini, I am Franceso Fiesco. I think you know Signor Vasselli well already. I am here to represent him in this matter."

"Yes, gentlemen. Please sit down and let's get to business. We are quite anxious for Signor Vasselli to sign the contract. We have been concerned about the number of performances he has been cancelling the last couple of months and have been receiving reports that he is in some sort of vocal trouble? We hope these rumors are unfounded and that we can soon be expecting everything to be normal again."

Ernesto started to open his mouth, but was silenced by a stern glance from the lawyer.

"First of all, Signor Fraschini, the state of Signor Vasselli's voice is not of concern to you at the moment. We are here to discuss your agency's handling of his career over the last few years. If you will ask your secretary to bring in the files you have on him we can get started."

"What files are you speaking of, Signor? Do you only want to look at last season?" The agent's face conveyed a growing sense of alarm. "Aren't we here to discuss the new contract?"

"Just do as I've asked and we can get on with it," answered the lawyer coldly.

The files were placed on the table before them in two large folders.

From his briefcase, the lawyer produced an official document from the chief court of Milan and handed it to the speechless agent. "As you can see, Signor Fraschini, this gives me authority to take possession of the files you have maintained on Signor Vasselli. I trust they are in order and that nothing is missing?"

"Of course they are in order. I resent you saying otherwise. Every scrap we have is contained in these files, all our dealings with Signor Vasselli, his contracts, our communications from the theaters and other managements concerning him over the last eighteen years. I would like to know why you want them." A defensive tone had crept into the agent's voice as he looked back and forth at each man.

The lawyer scooped up the files and put them in the large briefcase he had brought in with him. Palatable tension hung in the air. Ernesto gazed across the table at the stunned agent with undisguised hatred.

The agent cleared his throat, trying in vain to hide utter surprise. "Well, Signor Fiesco, these papers do give you the authority to take our files, though I must protest how you have gone about it. Do you also want to take the new contract and examine it also?"

"That won't be necessary, Signor Fraschini. Signor Vasselli will never sign it or any other with your agency ever again. His current contract is at an end. You are dismissed from any further concern with his career." He drew out his letter from James and gave a copy of it he had prepared to the agent, who quickly scanned it with shaking hands. "Frankly, as you can see, offers were made to you from Mr. Buffington and Madame Fremstead for Signor Vasselli's participation in projected performances and a recording. I represent to you that your agency never presented these offers to Signor Vasselli. He was only made aware of this a few nights ago by Mr. Buffington, who has correspondence from your agency, stating that Signor Vasselli was either not available or uninterested in performing with them. Mr. Buffington and Madame Fremstead are prepared to appear in open court to confirm these charges if necessary. We intend to bring a suit against you in the central court of Milan where you will be required to answer these charges."

The thunderstruck agent looked at the court papers and James' letter. He finally spoke, his voice shaking, "Signor, we don't believe we have acted in bad faith. The records will show that everything we have done for the last few years was done with the approval of Signor Del Aroldo, the personal representative of Signor Vasselli. Every offer, every contract, has first gone through his hands. We have acted through him and after consultations, passed on his recommendations directly to Signor Vasselli."

"No indeed," thundered the lawyer." It was your responsibility to communicate directly with your client and not through some third party without his knowledge and written consent. I hope you have something in writing from Signor Del Aroldo authorizing his handling affairs for Signor

Vasselli. I believe that you don't, and I'm sure Signor Del Aroldo would deny it in open court. I suggest that you consider with your colleagues your agency's position in this matter. We are open to a settlement offer to keep these matters from becoming public knowledge. Your agency stands to lose every important client you represent if your conduct in this sorry business is revealed for all the world to see. We will give you time to consider. In the meantime, we are going to go through these documents with a fine-toothed comb to reveal your complicity with any other individuals. You may contact me directly at my offices in the Via Sacarando here in Milan. We expect an answer from you in a short time or we will go forward with this lawsuit for gross mismanagement of an artist. You have gleaned thousands of dollars from his work over the years and you are going to give him satisfaction for it. You are forbidden to contact Signor Vasselli about this matter. All dealings are to be done through me. I trust you understand and will comply. Your handling of his career is at an end."

He stood, signaling Ernesto to follow him. "We will await your reply. Let it be swift if you know what's good for you. Come, Signor Vasselli, you are through with these dogs."

The agent jumped to his feet, his voice dripping with contempt. "We, too, are pleased that the association is at an end. I don't appreciate being threatened, but I will talk to our managers and lawyers and you will have an answer soon. Now if you will both please leave."

During this last exchange, Ernesto walked over to his framed photo on the wall of the office. He threw it to the floor in a furious gesture, and stood face-to-face with the hapless agent, his voice shaking with fury. "I am done with you and your inept agency. You have ruined my career, blocked my advancement at every turn. I will have satisfaction on the lot of you. On that you can be assured, Signor Fraschini!" His lips curled back from his mouth in ill-disguised fury. His eyes blazed with anger. He began to shake visibly.

His lawyer seized his arm. "Don't descend to their level, Signor Vasselli. "Our business here is at an end." They walked out onto the street and turned to go to the lawyer's offices.

Forty

Alone in his office, the agent fell back into his chair, reeling from the implications of the meeting. He reached for the phone, ordering the secretary, "Call everyone for an emergency meeting, and contact Mario

Del Aroldo. I don't give a damn where he is. We have to talk to him at once. Track him down with dogs if you have to and have him call me here immediately. Do it *now!*" *My God, if this gets out we will be ruined. It must be contained. We can't afford public disclosure.*

Forty-one

Three days later the lawyer summoned Ernesto to his offices in Milan.

"Good morning, Signor Vasselli. Please be seated. We have much to discuss today."

Ernesto, unusually nervous and apprehensive, tried his best to appear positive. He knew part of the story, but now he was prepared to learn the worst of it.

"Since the Sforzas began to handle your career there was initially only the best of attentions given to your interests. You had these early successes with appearances in some major opera houses. Your cover contracts gave you access to the potential you early enjoyed in your first years with them. Everything is here and above board. The cover assignments at *La Scala* and the *San Carlo* of Naples brought a few appearances in those theaters. However, about nine years ago a subtle change began to occur. Your cover contracts began to evaporate, and more and more you were sent to third-rate venues with little fanfare. As you know, Mr. Buffington contacted the agency on several occasions to try to engage you with offers to appear with Madame Fremstead. It's all here, Signore, the letters and cables that were exchanged where the agency replied that you were either unavailable or uninterested. We know that you personally were never made aware of this and many other offers that came in for emergency situations where you could have had major exposure with the greatest theaters and artists. I hate to tell you this, but your mentor, Signor Del Aroldo, when he first became involved with your career nine years ago, had his own arrangement with the Sforzas. I know you've told me that he often would go with you when contract offers were presented for your approval. What you were unaware of is the fact that all offers and contract proposals were first sent to him. He called the shots and pulled the strings.

"While we have nothing here in writing from him personally, we have many instances where agency employees have written in the margins of documents, *approved - Del Aroldo, or do not share - Del Aroldo*. The most surprising thing in regard to his insidious dealing behind the scenes is the fact that there are copies of drafts paid to him for the last nine years in which he and the agency shared the percentages, fifty-fifty, of the fees paid to you for your services. This in itself is something that happens more often than not in musical circles. It's like a finder's fee that someone is paid to ease dealings with difficult artists intent on furthering their careers under the most favorable circumstances. I tell you frankly, Signor Vasselli, that a systematic effort was made here to contain the scope of your career to a very narrow compass. They have had you mainly confined to Italy, where your hundreds of performances have taken place in little towns off the international circuit. We have here offers of new cover assignments at *La Scala*, the *La Fenice* of Venice, the *San Carlo* of Naples, even Covent Garden in London and the *Palais Garnier* in Paris, that were repeatedly turned down, with margin notes indicating, artist uninterested. Thus these major houses thought of you as impossible to deal with, and eventually offers from them dried up. Had it not been for your chance meeting with Mr. Buffington, none of this might have come to light."

Ernesto stared at the lawyer, stunned. He walked around the room, trying vainly to contain his outrage. At last he said, "What is to be done here, Signor Fiesco? I want all of them to feel the full fury of my vengeance fall on them. What are your suggestions in regard to how we should proceed?"

The lawyer looked thoughtfully at him. "I can assure you that they will settle rather than to have this revealed in open court. I have prepared a copy of the suit that will be sent to them. I am asking for compensation for you in the amount of $500,000. They will doubtless make a counter offer, but I believe they have no room to negotiate any reduction. You can always sign later with another agency if you wish, but it appears that at this stage of your career that you would have little chance of recouping a shattered reputation in opera houses here who believe you have blown them off. That and the vocal difficulties you have mentioned you are having, would to me seem to have resulted in a loss of credibility that you'd have an uphill battle to regain. If you are to sign with another management, it is my opinion that it should be one outside of Italy."

Ernesto sighed heavily. "This is not how I would have hoped matters would go. I have been betrayed by so many people that I hardly know which way to turn. I accept your advice, Signor Fiesco. Please proceed on my behalf. I know your fees for this will be high, but at this point it doesn't concern me. I just want it over with and then I'll see what, if any, career options will be open to me." He stared out a window to the street.

"Signor Vasselli, we usually ask thirty-five percent of any settlements we obtain, but in view of my personal dealings in Italy for Mr. Buffington and Madame Fremstead, we are prepared to do it for twenty-five percent. I have a contract here for you to sign accepting those terms if you'll be so kind as to return to your chair and examine the papers."

Ernesto gave the document only a cursory glance before signing it. "Signor Fiesco, I leave this matter in your hands for the moment. I would like to ask if you know how much of my earnings were sent to Signor Del Aroldo, if you know?"

"Approximately, over the years, $125,000 was paid to him by the agency. He may have had arrangements with them not covered in these records, but I believe from your earnings, he has received at least that much." Ernesto was silent. The lawyer rose and shook his hand and led him to the door. "Try not to worry, Signor Vasselli. They will move to settle, I'm sure, in a very short time. I've only given them a week to respond before the suit will be made public."

"Thank you, Signor Fiesco. I hope to hear then from you very soon. I want the matter settled quickly and quietly. You know how to get in touch with me." He walked out of the office onto the street and walked the several blocks past La Scala. He thought of the great theater and its reputation for excellence. He could at least tell himself that he had appeared there, however briefly. No one could take that from him.

At his apartment, he slowly climbed the grand staircase and walked down the corridor. An envelope had been stuck under his door. He recognized Mario's handwriting and tore it open. Its language was cold and to the point. It was a request for a meeting the next day at Mario's apartment to discuss an issue of importance to both of them. The familiar use of the word *tu,* for you, had been replaced by the chillingly formal *voi*. He slowly read the words again of his hero, his mentor, his lover, and guide. He realized it had all been a sham, a dream born in passion and imagined love. It was finished now. He quickly wrote out a return note and called for one of the street boys to hand-deliver it. After paying the young man, he was alone. The greatest sadness he had ever known fell on him, smothering him as surely as if he were dying. He went to his bedroom, closing the heavy drapes to shut out the bright sunshine. He lay on the bed and wept like his heart would break until at last he fell asleep.

The next day, at exactly ten in the morning he arrived at Mario's top-floor apartment. To his surprise, Mario himself opened the door. He was alone in the apartment, his wife and the servants gone. No smiles were exchanged as Mario led him into the music room, only glances of restrained fury. The room contained the familiar paintings of Mario in his most famous opera roles. Everywhere the opulence of celebrity was evident. The drapes at the windows were of the richest fabrics, the central chandelier of the most beautiful and costly Venetian crystal shed bright light above them. Ernesto noticed a copy of his lawsuit against the agency lying on top of the piano.

He said nothing as he watched Mario advance to the large fireplace at the center of the room where he suddenly turned to face him head on.

"Have you lost your fucking mind?" He advanced and screamed out, "What is the meaning of this crap that your lawyer has come up with?" Reaching out suddenly, he pushed him back roughly with clenched fists. "Do you have any real idea of who I am, who you are fucking with?"

Ernesto was not surprised by the cold tone of his voice and returned his gaze without flinching. "I see before me a vile collaborator in the ruin of my career. I see an aging, famous opera star who I thought loved me, a villain who has betrayed me at every turn and trampled on my feelings as both an artist and human being." He paused, his voice cracking. "You have walked on the love and faith I have had for you and thrown it back in my face. I think that here in the morning light that I am seeing clearly what you are for the first time. How could you have done these things to me when I have allowed you to guide me without question only to learn you have enriched yourself at my expense while containing the advancement of my career?"

The two men, in a contest of wills, stood staring at each other, remembering the moments of love they had shared. A shared sense of loss hovered over both of them. In an earlier time, they would have been sharing kisses. Ernesto's heart ached with desire, even now, as he realized the intimacy they once had was in ashes.

"Why you arrogant little fool!" His shout stuck in his throat. "What consequence do you think you are to me? I am one of the greatest singers who have ever lived and I apologize for nothing." For a moment he fell silent, as if trying to gather words. Finally, he spoke, after a long pause, somewhat more quietly, but with anger simmering beneath the surface. "You would have been nothing more than a flash in the pan if I hadn't taken an interest in you. Don't fuck with me or I'll crush you out of existence. Do you really think that you could drag me into court with your insipid little lawyer? Hell will freeze over first. This suit is going to be settled by the Sforzas. They will pay whatever damages you are demanding, but my name is to stay out of it, and you are never to speak a word of it to anyone that would result in my reputation being damaged. Do you hear me you miserable little shit?" Hot tears filled his eyes. He turned away to brush them away and continued, "With what I have on you, you would be lucky not to be dragged into court yourself for misrepresenting who and what you really are." He poured himself a large glass of wine. His face was white with pain.

Ernesto drew in his breath, not even able to grasp the implications of what Mario had said. But he finally looked back at him coldly and said in a suffocated tone, "Now what are you talking about? What do you think you have to threaten me with? You're just grasping at straws trying to make me feel afraid." He did feel afraid, very afraid.

"Trying? Trying? Oh I'm not trying. Remember years ago when we first met in Rome and you said you were from Como? I remarked then that your accent seemed strange, that it was odd that you could have just sprung from nowhere. Well, I made it my business to find out the truth. I hired an investigator, who with little difficulty found out the truth behind your facade. Have you ever heard your beloved Carlotta speak of a woman named *Barbarina* in Como? I know that she paid that woman to secure a false birth certificate saying you were born there. We both know perfectly well what lies were created. Money opens mouths and my investigator paid her for the truth. She didn't care. She was paid twice, once by your precious Carlotta and then again by me. This false birth certificate enabled you to obtain an Italian passport and to make everyone think you were an Italian." He searched vainly for some shred of meaning to hold onto as the ache in his heart gnawed at his soul. "You know it and I know it was all based on lies and forged papers. No one knows about this except me. I have the file on you in a safe place, Mr. David Atkins. You and Carlotta might have deceived a lot of people, but I know who you are and don't believe I won't use it against you if you force my hand. So who here is the deceiver? Who here has been living a lie for nearly twenty years? You don't have to answer, nor should you. There is nothing you can say to redeem yourself. Poor Giovanna. She doesn't even know. She thinks of you as another child. Do you think she or anyone would ever trust you again if they knew what I know?"

Ernesto felt the hair rise on his neck. He felt fear for the first time since he stepped into the room. Without asking permission, he poured a glass of wine, cleared his throat and said quietly, "So you know the truth about me? If you've known all this time, why haven't you confronted me before now? I had to assume an Italian identity to work here as I have. I'm not ashamed of it. The tax advantages alone would have been impossible to ignore, and I'd never have had the freedom to send money out of the country as I have. But still, why have you never mentioned this to me before? Why did you keep it to yourself?

"Why? Because I cared about you. You could never have gone so far without my handling things for you. You don't and never have had the savvy to deal with either the agency or the management of opera houses. I could have just let you shipwreck yourself, but I wanted to keep you near me. I would never have left my wife for you. I was always up front from the start with you about that. You were young, and your body and soul I have made it my business to possess. You should be on your knees now before me, begging to suck my cock as you have for years now. My head was never in the clouds when it came to you, and in spite of what you think, I have protected you, even loved you in the only way I could."

"No!" Ernesto shouted. "It wasn't love that made you want to protect me, Mario. It was contempt. I could have had many other men. That was never a problem. If you couldn't love me, you should have let someone else try. I don't know that another lover would have mistreated me or starved me for affection. Besides dominating my career and keeping me on a leash like a dog, you have ultimately enriched yourself at my expense. Yes, I know about the arrangements you made with the agency. How could you have done that? Didn't you have enough money of your own without stealing mine?" He turned away as hot tears fell down his face. He gazed across the gulf between them. Immense pain struck into his heart. He cursed himself for still loving this man. For even now wanting to make love with him one last time. His voice broke as he sobbed, "You have finished with me at last. Mario, my torment! My career and my heart are in ruins, and you can stand there and say you did it all for love of me?"

Mario picked up an envelope from the mantel and advanced close to him. He shoved it toward him. "Here is $125,000 in U.S. currency. This is what you say I've made off of you. I don't want it. Take it and get out of here. I never want to hear from you or ever see your face again. I suggest you go back to your own country. I am powerful. I have friends from Sicily here in Milan and they can, at my command, silence your mouth for all time. Remember what happened to Mario Lanza? I know it was before your time, but you must have heard of it. It was said he had a heart attack, dead at the age of thirty-eight. Not so. He was silenced because he didn't play ball with the big boys. He forgot the people who made him into a movie star. Don't make the same mistake, Ernesto, or should I say David? Leave now, while you have a shred of remembered dignity and glory to look back on. You've had a good ride, but now it's over." He poured another glass of wine. A motion behind him caused him to whirl back.

* * *

Ernesto was gone, leaving a single white gardenia on the piano. Mario grimly saw that he had taken the envelope of money with him. Returning to the fireplace with the flower, he hung his head and broke into tears.

Looking up at his reflection in the mirror, he looked silently at himself, saying sadly out loud, "It had to end this way. Maybe not today, but I always knew one day he would walk out of my life. Oh God, all my youth is gone! What is left for me without his love? I only did the things I did because I wanted him always near me, to warm my bed, to banish my loneliness. Now, now I'm alone. I'm old, so old. With him I felt young and strong again. Farewell, my greatness. You were but a dream of paradise, now lost. Now I will go down into eternal night with only his memory, only his name on my lips." Clutching the gardenia, he turned his face to the wall.

* * *

The next day, Signor Fiesco called to announce that the agency had settled the lawsuit out of court. The damages asked had been paid without protest or even a counteroffer. It was as he had predicted. The agency couldn't afford to let such dirty linen be aired in public. He told Ernesto that he would be receiving a bank draft shortly by messenger, less the agreed twenty-five percent.

Thanking him profusely, Ernesto hung up and sat on the sofa in his living room. Speaking out loud to no one except the silent walls, he said, "Finally it is finished, the living nightmare over at last. Eighteen years! Where has the time gone, so much work, and for what? People who are fans and wannabes never realize that to be a singer, to stand on a stage, is a thing more glorious for them who see it than to those who bear it. They desperately try to be close, to bask in the reflected glory of an opera star. Alas, and when you cease to be a money-making machine for them, they turn their backs and walk away. Fuck it! I don't give a damn. I will go without shame. I have played a part here and now it's over, time to go home and make a new life if I can. Farewell, vain glory. Sleep and rest in peace. The singers come, they sing, and then are forgotten, but *La Scala* remains."

Reaching for the telephone, he called his landlady and asked that she come up to his apartment. She came quickly.

"Come in, Signora, and let's sit and talk awhile." After guiding her to the sofa, he sat in the armchair facing her. "Signora, I am closing up my apartment. I want to thank you for protecting my privacy over all these years. My voice has rung out in these rooms for years. Here I learned almost all my new roles as they came to me. I know it can't have been easy with other lodgers constantly complaining of the noise at every hour of the day and night. I just want you to know that I have enjoyed many good moments here and their memories and that of your many unspoken kindnesses have warmed many often lonely times that have come. Now it is time for me to leave." He poured her a glass of wine, smiling as he did so.

"Oh, Signore, I am sorry then to see you go. I know you had mentioned the possibility before, but I always prayed to the Virgin that it would never come about. We will miss you terribly. Even though I could never afford tickets to the opera, I sat so often in the courtyard with my old friends and listened as your voice poured forth from your windows. It comforted me many times. I always have tried to keep my place, as it is my custom not to inject myself into the lives of the lodgers here in the palace. I am happy if ever I have been of service to you, Signore." She burst into tears and fell silent.

Deeply moved, he embraced her. He looked at her careworn face and simple clothes and realized he was looking at her for the first time as a fellow human being. He had cast off the aura of an opera star, and now in leaving, he finally saw her true worth. She was just a simple old widow woman, yet her appreciation of him and her heartfelt tears mattered now more than any empty applause that came from the public he had courted and lost. He said softly, "I will miss you too, and the life I have known here, but my time here is finished, nothing more to say except goodbye. I will be sending a few things out of here to my new home across the sea. I've paid, as you know, for the rest of the year. I can't take the furniture with me, so, when I'm gone, please take anything you wish and dispose of anything that you and your friends can't use. Do this in memory of me and I will be forever grateful to you. Now if you will excuse me, I have several letters to write and have to arrange for my few souvenirs of yesterday to be packed up and sent overseas." He took her hand and led her to the door. He smiled and kissed her warmly on both cheeks. She smiled bravely at him as she closed the door behind her, and he quietly listened in silence as her retreating steps grew fainter. His life in Italy was at an end.

Forty-two

He was in Buenos Aires for three months. He made his way quickly to the home of his friend, Leonora D'Negri. She had her servants take his luggage to one of the quest bedrooms, and then arm-in-arm, guided him into her drawing room. Everything there was Spanish in nature, but of an old-world quality that spoke of the opulent lifestyle of a Prima Donna Assoluta. They spoke in Italian since he had not mastered conversational Spanish. She called for refreshments and asked him to sit on a comfortable divan with her. They looked thoughtfully at each other and she said, "So, old friend, I hear that you are through with Italy? I must know all the details, but we'll save that for later. What are your immediate plans? Have you formulated anything concerning your future?" She smiled warmly through her quizzical expression.

"Leonora, beyond the season here with you, I have not thought ahead. I believe I'll be going back to the United States to stay with my old teacher, Carlotta Vasselli. I do want to discuss with you the problems that I'm having with my voice. If you want to replace me, I will completely understand, it's just that I have to be honest with you. I have lost the high C and my top D seems to be gone forever too. Everything else is problematic. I can barely trust a high B now. The facility remains, though the seamlessness between registers is wearing badly. The operas we have agreed to perform seem beyond my powers now without major repositioning of the vocal lines. I'm aware of the public's love of extreme high notes and I'm afraid of facing them or doing anything that will distract from your own success or cause you embarrassment of any kind."

He looked down at his coffee and fell silent.

She looked at him thoughtfully, then drew nearer and took his hands. "Is this all, my little angel? Trust me — I know how to deal with vocal difficulties. There are remedies, known only to me, for preserving the voice. How do you think I have managed to retain all my notes all these years? My age of course is a secret known to very few, but I have not maintained my voice for thirty-five years for nothing. We are both trained in the old Garcia method, but beyond that, I have learned how to keep the voice from shortening. My range of over three octaves remains intact, the same now as when I made my debut in *Lucia Di Lammermoor* when I was sixteen. An old woman from Bolivia, whose mother lived at the time of the last tour of the divine Adelina Patti here in South America, gleaned the secret from the diva herself. It requires discipline and the use of certain herbs taken at all times of the day with hot teas. I undertake that you take the remedy at once. I promise your voice will return in all its former glory. We have ten days before rehearsals of our first opera, *Anna Bolena.* You will stay here with me and take the cure. You will talk little beyond a whisper and sing only in a quiet manner, saving your strength for the stage. We will have a triumph as always." She laughed as she saw his doubtful looks. "I'll make you a believer, Ernesto. You'll be able to sing the Rubini roles with his ornaments like you always have. The public will go mad over both of us."

"I don't know what to say, Signora, but if you can promise me a cure like that from taking herbs and resting the voice then I would be a fool to refuse." He laughed for the first time since his arrival, and embraced and kissed her.

"My sweet, all will be well. We'll make a lot of money and make people happy in the process. Now come on. Let's get the hell out of here and do some shopping and let you reacquaint yourself with the city. Be sure to wear the sweater you brought in with you. Its June, but here in the Southern Hemisphere we are in winter and must protect ourselves from drafts." They walked out into bright sunshine where her driver waited to whisk them away down the steep drive to the city spread out below.

After a week or taking Leonora's cure, Ernesto felt his voice began to loosen up. With her there was no stress. Everything was provided for his comfort. Staying in her villa was relaxing in a way no hotel suite could match. He sat each day in her music room with its Goya and Picasso paintings dominating the walls, listening as her pupils came for lessons all day long. Like Carlotta, she was a stern mistress, but the kindness she presented with it gave results. The students were able to make debuts singing with her and gaining experience for international careers. She had forsaken the *Teatro Colon* long ago and now held court at the *Teatro Alvenida* where she was treated with the adoration due a Diva of her stature. The rehearsals began and to his complete surprise, his high C, C sharp and top D had returned, which was fortunate because he was to appear in nine other operas with the diva for the next three months.

The season began with the wildly successful *Anna Bolena,* followed by *I Puritani, La Sonnambula, Il Pirata, La Straniera, Lucrezia Borgia, Tancredi, La Traviata, Norma,* and finally *Semiramide*. After performances in Buenos Aires, the tour began, taking them to Rio followed by Bogata, Lima, Cordoba, and several other cities. Everywhere the public received them with an adoration bordering on delirium. Ovations and showers of flowers greeted all their appearances. The great D'Negri and the handsome tenor were acclaimed and feted with banquets in magnificent palatial mansions.

Happiness and contentment so filled Ernesto that he almost could forget the bitterness of leaving Italy behind. His final performances in *Semiramide* created a sensation. The irony of singing again the role of his Italian debut was not lost on him. He still felt, however, that even though D'Negri's herbal brew had restored temporarily the golden top notes that in the freshness of youth had gushed forward with no apparent effort, it was indeed only a short-term fix. He was weary and longed to go home.

After the tour ended, they returned to Buenos Aires, where he spent another unforgettable week with his diva. At last the time for his departure came and after many hugs and kisses from his beloved friend, he was taken by her driver to the airport for his flight back to the United States. His career as a performing artist was now at an end, but such an end. He had sung like a God with all the strength of his youth. He now left it all behind to go into retirement. He did so without regret or a backward glance. He flew into New York and then to Atlanta, where after a few days rest, he returned to Selma and Carlotta.

Part Three: The Return

Forty-three

Autumn, with its usual palette of bright colors in red and gold, was coming on slowly as he drove over the familiar Edmond Pettus Bridge. The leaves seemed reluctant in the cool air to reveal their magical glory. He could see the muddy waters of the Alabama River below as they turned inexorably towards the bend that carried them past the Old Live Oak Cemetery and beyond to the Gulf of Mexico. It was a Saturday morning, and on the other side of the bridge people went to and fro as they had for as long as he could remember. He had written to Carlotta of his impending arrival so that she wouldn't be surprised when packages containing his personal effects were delivered to her mansion. He dreaded having to explain everything to her and hoped she wouldn't question him in her usual forthright manner the moment he stepped across the threshold. He came to the fork in the road; the left path led to the old Evans road house where Imogene still lived. He turned resolutely to the right and continued till he arrived at The Colonel's old estate. Above him the twenty towering oaks reached high above to form the familiar canopy where their branches joined. The leaves were beginning to turn gold. At the end of this oak alley the house came into view. Nothing had changed, as if time had stood still. The same hedges of mountain laurel formed on each side of the house, and the ancient pecan trees in the back of the house stood like silent guardians. As he pulled to the parking area in back, he noticed one thing new to him. A four-car garage, modeled after the main house, now stood where before there had only been an asphalt parking area. He pulled into the empty space to the right. Carlotta's cherry red Mercedes was there, along with The Colonel's old Jeep. He saw a new Mercury Marquis in the third spot. A refurbished brick pathway led up to the rear entrance of the house. As he approached the steps, the back door was suddenly thrown open.

Carlotta stood in the doorway. Her mouth was open with joy as she cried out to him. "Ernesto! Beloved child, welcome home!"

He rushed up the steps and she literally threw herself into his arms. They stood there for a moment in the bright sunshine as she held him closely and showered kisses all over his face.

"Come in, my darling. I have strong coffee waiting." In the old kitchen, everything was unchanged by the passage of the years. Two maids, dressed in black with white aprons and caps, curtsied as she led him to the great white pine table at the center of the room. At a signal from their mistress, they sprang into action. The old silver coffee service was laid out on the table with two massive silver trays laden with sweet cakes and fruit. One of the maids stepped forward to pour the coffee when suddenly she stopped dead in her tracks at a severe look from Carlotta. "Away with you, Mattie! I will serve as I always have. Now be gone, both of you. I will ring if we need anything further."

The two black women curtsied and left in haste. Carlotta poured coffee into the fine cups and motioned for him to draw his chair up beside hers. She had changed little since he had last seen her five years before. Her once-blond hair had turned pure silver. She was as slim as ever. She had dressed in her usual European fashion in a stunning sky-blue silk sheath. Her makeup, as always, had been carefully applied. From her neck hung ropes of Mikimoto pearls, and on her left hand she wore the wedding set of rings The Colonel had given her long ago. The central stone was a five-carat diamond set in platinum in a raised setting, and her band was of smaller, but no less beautiful, stones.

She saw him gazing at her from head to toe and suddenly laughed. "My darling, are you taking inventory of my attire and jewels? They are just the same old things you've seen for years. Now let's enjoy our coffee. I'll send the butler out for your luggage after while." They drank, never taking their eyes off each other. "Why you have hardly changed, my boy. Thank God you've kept yourself slim and youthful." She reached out a hand and passed her fingers through his still-thick hair. "What's this? Silver beginning to come into your auburn curls? Ah well, it's only natural After all, time stands still for none of us. Even I have started having a few aches and pains since I'm now seventy-eight."

He smiled warmly at her. "Seventy-eight? Why it's not possible, Madame. You look at least twenty years younger than that!"

"Only twenty? Why you sly young man. I would have hoped you'd have said thirty. Alas, my dear, I am not so young anymore, though I employ dozens of beauty aids to keep my looks intact, with the results that you can clearly see." She laughed again.

His heart was warmed by her relaxed manner. That had not changed. Her posture was as erect as ever and he was amused to see, in the exchange with the maid, that her imperious manner had remained intact.

She cleared her throat and looked at him thoughtfully. "So you have abandoned your career to return to me? You know I will want to know full details, but not now. Not for the moment anyway. I just want to look at you and make sure I'm not dreaming." She poured another cup for each of them and insisted that he sample the sweet pound cake. She nibbled on some seedless dark grapes.

"Madame, I am so glad to be here with you once more. I will never leave here . . . leave you . . . again."

Her smile faded. "Not to bring you down, my sweet, but I have news of your other mother. You know Imogene and I have always maintained an uneasy truce when it comes to you. She has just retired from that horrible old air force base where she worked for forty years. She had her house enlarged a few years ago and installed a big new master suite and bath, though I'm at a loss to know why she bothered. Seems that house was big enough for one person the way it was, but it's no matter to me. I just have my ways of finding out how things are with her. You may not know that she has four grandchildren now. She has remained somewhat attractive in the way of so many faded southern women. She still accepts with thanks the clothes and accessories I still send on to her. You know how I am with clothes; I just get so bored with them after a short time. She must be the second-best dressed woman in all of Selma after me. Her health is good and she keeps herself busy at that old Methodist church and with her bridge parties. I read sometimes in the society pages of the newspaper about her being on this or that committee. Don't laugh, Ernesto, but somehow she has gotten herself appointed chairwoman of *The Ladies of Selma, Society for the Preservation and Beautification of the Graves of our Sainted Confederate Dead* at Old Live Oak Cemetery. I even drove over there on one occasion to be sure fresh flowers were placed at The Colonel's family mausoleum when suddenly I noticed she and a bunch of old crones were gaily decorating the soldier's graves with the Confederate stars and bars, hundreds of little flags. Can you imagine? It didn't dawn on me till later that Memorial Day was fast approaching. You know well I never keep up with old ways here, though my husband always did, but then he was of these same people, just nicer.

"Anyway, that's enough of my long speeches. Let's take ourselves upstairs for a nap. I've ordered a light lunch to be served about one o'clock and then we can talk in the music room about you and your career."

Together they walked to the hall leading to the grand staircase. "No dear, not the stairs. Let's take the elevator. I still make my sweeping descents in the evenings for dinner, but it's a bore to climb up them now." They stepped into the elevator and she pushed the button to take them to the second floor.

He noticed she seemed to shiver a bit as she wrapped her heavy shawl closer around her shoulders. They arrived at the landing; he gave her another hug and kiss and started down the hall to his old room.

She called after him, "No, dear. You are now to occupy The Colonel's suite which adjoins mine. It was his wish that you do so after his death. All of his things are as he left them, but you are welcome to make any changes you wish. After all, you are now the man of the house." She smiled and walked into her suite, leaving him alone outside the door to The Colonel's rooms.

He looked down the staircase at the three life-sized paintings that hung below. They were as they had always been. The Garcia sisters, dressed in the roles of *Desdemona* in Rossini's *Otello*, and as *Saffo* in the opera by Pacini. In the center stood the relatively new portrait of Carlotta in the role of *Norma*. He smiled and walked into The Colonel's suite, smelling again for a moment the scent of Old Spice in the bedroom. "I'm home. I'm home, Colonel. Here, where there is love. How I miss you kissing me good night." Taking off his traveling clothes, he went to the bathroom and splashed water on his face, drying off with the familiar thick white towels which hung from gold rings. He lay on The Colonel's great king-sized bed and was soon asleep. Unseen by him, the ghost of The Colonel materialized and lingered near the window seat in the quiet room, silently watching him.

Two months passed as Ernesto became quickly reacquainted with the slow pace of life in Selma. The dreaded explanation of what had taken place those last months in Italy was never demanded of him. Carlotta had let the matter drop. He had noticed an uncharacteristic quietness about her. She still left no doubt as to who was mistress of her house, and the servants would flee in terror whenever she reacted with displeasure at little mistakes they made. Ernesto sensed that all was not well with her though. With him, her imperial haughtiness would drop, and she would spend hours just staying close to him when he played for her in the music room. She would rally when she perceived mistakes, but the flashes of temperament grew less frequent.

One morning, just after his thirty-seventh birthday, they were talking over their light breakfast when the butler delivered a silver tray to her. The tray contained a letter from Milan. She picked the letter up and with her usual dramatic manner slashed it open with her silver letter opener. She scanned the contents quickly and looked at Ernesto.

He looked up from his newspaper as he sipped his coffee. "What news, Madame, from Italy? Is anything exciting going on with your old friends?" Not receiving a reply, he began to read once more.

Watching him closely, she turned the letter in her hands. She reached out and touched his arm. "Darling, you must prepare yourself for a terrible shock. My friend Caterina writes to me that Mario Del Aroldo died two weeks ago, curious that he had cancer and no one seemed to have been aware of it. You know as well as I what a stupendous voice he had. Too bad it was so wasted on some of the horrible operas he specialized in, but then that instrument was always like a loud trumpet. Why, my dear, your face has gone quite pale. Were you not aware that he had been ill? I know you saw him shortly before you left."

A long pause followed. "Ernesto, what are you thinking, my dear?"

He looked at the wine decanter on the counter and wished with all his heart he could justify getting up to drink it all down in a single gulp.

"By the way, she has enclosed a note from him for you. She said his wife knew she would know how to contact you. Apparently it was found in his papers after his death. Strange, I would have steamed it open myself. The seal with his coat of arms is still intact." She handed it to him. "You can read it when you're alone, dear. I'm surprised you hadn't heard the news, but then considering how recent it was, I guess you wouldn't have known yet."

"I had no idea. My last meeting with him did not go well, but I didn't see any sign of illness. He just looked old with that silver white hair. I'll have to write my condolences to Giovanna." He was ashamed that inside his heart he felt relief mixed with shock. Mario's thinly masked threat now evaporated. He started to go into The Colonel's old study to write the letter.

Carlotta seized his arm. "Don't bother, dear. I'll write her for both of us. I've known them both slightly from the early forties when our paths would cross on occasion. I'm ashamed to admit that in those days I found him extremely attractive, but his little wife was such a dear, I couldn't do that. In those days, believe it or not, people were a bit more discreet than now. These days it's just flung in people's faces with a total disregard of decorum, or good breeding." She left for the music room and her French writing desk

Alone in the kitchen, Ernesto found he was unable to react at all except to feel relief. At least now he would never have to worry about being murdered by a hit man from Sicily. There were no tears, just a feeling of sorrow for the great man's loss to his family. They had all adored him so deeply. He opened the note. In it Mario said that during their last meeting he was already aware that he didn't have long to live. He was writing now to assure him that anything he had done was done from love because he couldn't bear to become an afterthought had Ernesto become a sought-after international star. He said that he realized too late that he had been wrong, and prayed that Ernesto would forgive him and think in the future of only the loving moments that had passed between them. He folded the note and put it in his shirt pocket.

As he stood by the windows, he began to shake violently as grief bubbled up from deep inside. *Oh God, Mario, I loved you with all the longing that anyone could have dreamed. Perhaps you did love me. If only we could go back to those nights when we lay together satiated and drenched with love. A single smile, one tear to fall on my lips as they did that first time in Rome would stop this horrible ache inside. If only we could have always been honest without fear or deceit, perhaps the story would have ended for us in peace.* Tears fell as he stared out into the morning sunshine. There was no room in his heart for anger, only memories of a love that had known no equal. Brushing away his tears, he walked to the back door. Fall had come in full force. Brisk winds blew leaves from the pecan trees all over the new garage.

Suddenly, a shrill bell rang from the music room. Carlotta had little bells on her desk for each of her servants. Their tone let them know who was being summoned.

A new bell had been added and he recognized that it was he she wanted. He quickly picked up a tray, filled it with cake and coffee and rushed into the room where she sat at her desk. A fire burned brightly in the fireplace, casting warmth into the room. Carlotta disdained the new central heating and kept the house very cold.

She looked up crossly. "Quickly boy, pour me a coffee and one for you as well. We need to talk about some boring business. Pull that chair up here. That's it." The desk was littered with various documents. "Thank you, my dear, now let's talk. I know you've never seen the inside of my desk. It holds all my personal papers. I want you to see what is here. Here is my will and our lawyer's name and phone number. When the day comes that I croak, you will need to know the key to the desk is hidden in a compartment here. All you have to do is press the rosette on the right side here and the drawer will open. Now . . . pay attention. My service is to be conducted by the Rabbi who lives near the center of town beside the Union bank. The clothes I am to wear are at the funeral director's. Everything has been taken care of. You just simply have to make the call to the lawyer and he'll take it from there." She broke off, staring off into space, then looked about the room. "Souvenirs of a lifetime, what are they my darling except vanity, something for someone else to have to clear away when we're gone? For me the important thing is the memories we create. Those will never die. If helping you to the career you have enjoyed counts for anything then I feel I have accomplished something in this life."

He put his arm around her shoulders, drawing her close and kissed her forehead. "Be comforted, Mother. I am here now and I want to make things easier for you. I know you've closed the school and aren't dealing with pupils any more. Why don't we reopen the studio and take on teaching responsibilities together? I want it to continue, to bloom again the way it used to, and to pass on the Garcia method to a new generation. Isn't that something that would bring you back some joy?" He looked at her searchingly, trying to bring some measure of comfort to the sadness he could see in her face.

"Yes, I think that's a good idea, but you'll need to be the one who does the most work on it. I'm just so tired, Ernesto. I also think we should talk again about Imogene. She is a good deal younger than me, though you'd never know it since I am a thousand times more beautiful, but she'll be around a long time after I'm gone. Perhaps there's a way for you to bridge the gap of years with her and have her in your life again. I know The Colonel and I took over the role that she had when you were a child, and believe me, I have no guilt about that. It took you far from this place. You are still young, only thirty-seven. So much more of life will come for you. I don't want to think of you alone and unloved in this house with only memories to sustain you. You must be practical. Reach out to her. Perhaps there's a way you could be friends again."

She rang the butler's bell and on his appearance handed him the condolence note she had written to be mailed to Giovanna in Milan. She then settled in her throne chair and waved Ernesto to the piano.

"Now, my dear, play me some Chopin or Schubert. Either will do. I want you to look at the waltzes and learn some of them. Oh yes, and the nocturnes of John Field that came the other day, they are so hauntingly beautiful."

Sitting at the piano, he looked through the music. He began to play, first Chopin and then Schubert. Stillness settled on the room as only the notes sounded in the air. As he played, he glanced at her. She dozed off. He silently got up, took the soft lap blanket she adored and gathered it around her lap. The fire crackled warmly in the chill of the late November day. He walked to the window. Leaves fell heavily from the great oaks in the brisk fall winds. Soon, he knew, the winter must come. The sense of loss was keener at this time of year over The Colonel's absence. He knew that she grieved inwardly over the loss, but he knew no way to comfort her except to simply love her. He started to go to the kitchen to see about having their lunch made ready. Looking back, he could see that she was still asleep. He backed out of the room as he always had, like a courtier before royalty, reluctant to leave her, wanting to be always near her.

December came. The house was festive with light and, always, music. Ernesto had seen to the decorations. Red and gold ornaments from Italy were scattered everywhere. The servants had outdone themselves to make the rooms glitter for their mistress. Carlotta did not like the idea of live trees in the house. She preferred them to be outside where she could watch the colored lights twinkle. Inside, great sprays of rosemary sent forth a wonderful fragrance into the air. Poinsettias of all colors adorned all the principal rooms. Even little arrangements of statues and pictures from The Colonel's youth decorated tables. His old miniature trains were carefully put on their tracks so they could circle the music room, sending forth little toots from the engine. Carlotta grumbled about all the fuss, but she loved it.

She was failing. Ernesto had seen it. A sense of foreboding and dread filled his thoughts. If this was to be her last Christmas, he wanted no expense spared to bring her happiness. Being Jewish, she had never known such things as a child. She was not religious, but she did have a few friends who came to see her from the Temple. The Rabbi was close to her, but knew, as others learned the hard way, to give her space. She couldn't stand to be smothered, but homage was always welcome.

On Christmas Eve many of her former students came to see her. The chandeliers in the front rooms gleamed brightly above as the young people came laden with gifts of sweets which she adored. She sat in her throne chair, surrounded by the girls. Ernesto played and sang Christmas carols with some of the young people, always closely watching his prima donna. The girls begged her to sing for them. She protested at first, but Ernesto approached her and said, "Come now, Madame, to satisfy our guests, you must sing."

Her eyes glittered as she allowed herself to be helped to another armchair next to the piano. She leafed through some music and handed it to Ernesto to play, saying. "Little man, little man. The word *must* is never to be spoken to a prima donna. All of you should remember your places. Now, yet I will sing."

The room grew quiet with anticipation as he began the introduction and the great voice poured forth in the Schubert Ave Maria. The power of the voice was like that of a young girl. He alone could see the effort it had cost her, but she was determined to sing as she always had. To her it was just a simple song but laden with deep meaning. The girls all congratulated her when the last notes died away. At a signal from Ernesto, two of them helped her back to her throne chair. She seemed quite exhausted, and the others respectfully began to leave. Wishing her joy in this season, the last of them left. The servants took away the glasses and great silver and gilt trays, leaving the two of them alone.

She raised her head. “Darling, it grows late. Come help me. Let’s go to bed. Where is Mattie? She needs to help me with my night clothes.” She rang the bell, the maid appeared, and the three of them rode the elevator to the second floor. He went to his own room to put on his pajamas as the maid helped Carlotta into her suite. A few moments later a soft knock came at his door.

“Sir,” said Mattie, as he opened the door. “She is settled into bed with one of her books. She said to tell you to come in. Sir, I knows it ain’t my place, but I think you ought to call her doctor. She ain’t looking too well. Ain’t ever seen her looking so tired. I’ll stay over the night if it’s okay down in the kitchen in case you need me.”

He looked back at her, relieved. “That will be fine, Mattie. I’ll call the doctor. When he arrives, send him upstairs to Madame’s rooms. I’ll wait with her till then. She is just worn out and needs to rest.”

“Yes, sir. You won’t forget then, sir, to call old Mattie if you need her?”

“No, I won’t. Now go, I need to call the doctor and then go to Madame.”

Returning to his room, he called the doctor. “Please come at once. I believe she won’t last out the night. I need you to be here. I know it’s Christmas Eve, but death keeps no schedule, so please come. After all, doctor, as Madame always says, we do pay our bills, don’t we?” He hung up the phone and hurried to be with her. Hoping that his premonition was unfounded, he knocked softly at her door. “Madame? May I enter?”

The reply was faint. “Of course, darling, come in at once.”

He was shocked by her appearance. Lying in her bed clothes, she was so pale as to fade into the white linen around her . . . all except her eyes, which shone blue as cornflowers in summer. “My heavens, what a look you give me. Come here, my child. Pull up that chair beside me and let us talk for a while.”

He did so, never taking his eyes off her face. “You must forgive me, Madame, but I have taken the liberty of calling your doctor. He will be here shortly.” He reached for her hand. It was icy cold.

“Called my doctor? Why, my dear, no need for such a thing, and on Christmas Eve of all nights. I’m sure I will be quite well in the morning. I just seem to feel a little congestion in my lungs. Tonight with the girls and you, I felt something coming on. I’ve had this many times before. You know how we singers catch cold so easily. Well, when he arrives, I’m sure he will have a tonic that will quite knock me out.” She chuckled at the thought of The Colonel’s old family doctor. “What a sour, disagreeable old man he is. We will have to send him on his way shortly. Yet I am tired tonight. I think though that my rendering of that old Schubert song will echo in those silly girl's heads forever. Would you mind child, just sitting here with me till he arrives? No need for small talk among we two, is there?"

"No indeed, Madame. We will just sit here quietly. The house, though, is creaking tonight with the winter winds outside." Seeing her shiver, he pulled up the pale blue coverlet that had been turned back. He touched her cheek and forehead. Both were warm in spite of the chill in the room. She looked back at him adoringly and he saw with alarm that there was blood in her mouth. Taking a tissue, he wiped it away as best he could. Her eyes were alight with fever. He stood and quickly said, "Where in hell can the man be? I told him to come at once." He looked back and said, "Perhaps I should start a fire for you, Madame? It seems bitterly cold tonight." He rang for the butler, but she silenced him with a look.

"That will not be needed. I feel quite comfortable. In fact, I'm feeling warm. No, send the man away. No need for a fire. You know how I love a room to be ice cold. Germs can't live in the cold, you know." She threw back the coverlet and sat up in the bed. "Come and fluff these pillows up behind me. I don't want to sleep right now." A spasm racked her chest and bright blood dripped from the right side of her mouth as she signaled for him to pass her some tissues. She coughed slightly and looked steadily in his eyes that were brimming with tears. At that moment the doctor hurried in the door. Carlotta weakly cried out, "Sir, you are no gentleman to enter a lady's boudoir without knocking first. Oh very well. Come and examine me. You, Ernesto, remain."

The doctor called for water. Mattie, hiding outside the room, complied. He washed out her mouth, catching the darkening liquid with a small steel bowl. He listened to her lungs and looked back at Ernesto. He called the maid back into the room and beckoned for him to step out into the hall.

"It is pneumonia. Her lungs are very congested and probably inflamed as well. It's just like The Colonel was that night, and he was dead by morning. Prepare yourself, she won't last till then."

Ernesto looked back at him. It was what he had feared. He had noticed lately that she seemed weak, but she had waved away his concerns with feigned laughter. "She seemed fine earlier when the girls were here. She sang with strength and was quite herself, I don't understand."

The doctor looked at him in ill-disguised amusement, saying, "It is often this way with this illness. They really seem to be themselves for a few hours, then total collapse."

Ernesto glared at him. "Don't *patronize* me, doctor. I don't tolerate that sort of behavior from anyone, especially when I am paying them for professional answers. Now get back in there and give her something to help quiet her. Do it now."

He dragged the old man back into the room. Mattie curtsied and walked past them to wait outside. The doctor took her pulse as she tried to shake him off. He made her drink a narcotic-based cough medicine, which she immediately spat back out at him.

"You dog!" she snarled. "Come here to choke me to death with that foul tasting crap. I should pour it down your own wrinkled throat and kill you as you are trying to do to me. Now get the hell away from me. Wait outside till my child summons you." The doctor fled. Carlotta reached out her hands to Ernesto, who came running across the room. "Don't let him call an ambulance. If I'm to die, it will be in my own bed and in my own time and not hooked up to needles and tubes in a hospital. Promise me, child."

He had never seen such a look of fright on her face. He stared at her helplessly. He remembered one time nearly thirty years before when he crawled up onto the wide front porch that night and she saw his face and screamed for The Colonel. To see her losing control astonished him. He stuck his head out the door and shouted, "No ambulance! I will call you both if I need you." He walked back into the room and sat beside her and stared, trying to contain his emotion "How about just a little pure water, Madame?" She nodded, and he raised the glass to her lips. "Just a swallow. Another?" She shook her head.

She motioned to the bathroom, and he called Mattie back to help her. With difficulty, they both helped her from the bed to the bathroom. Mattie took her in as he closed the door and waited outside. A few moments later, he heard Mattie scream and he threw open the door.

Carlotta had fallen and Mattie was trying vainly to help her to her feet. "Oh, sweet Jesus, save us all!" she wailed. "Sir, I tried holding her up, but she just keeled over right there to the floor. Lord, have mercy! I tried, sir."

He gathered Carlotta in his arms and carried her back to bed, carefully smoothing her nightdress to try to make her more comfortable. She curled up in bed and threw her head back against the pillows, staring at him like a bird caught in a trap. She was delirious. The doctor returned, gave her a sedative and stood helplessly watching.

She looked up from her pillows and said "Leave us, old man. Don't you see that I am dying with the one person I love in this world near me? Now, be gone!" He left the room, Mattie at his heels. She beckoned to

Ernesto. He sat in the chair beside her and held her hands. "No darling, closer." He reached over to put his arm around her shoulders. "No, here in the bed beside me."

He got into bed and held her frail body against his chest, wrapping her protectively in his arms.

Her head rested against his shoulder and she looked at him lovingly. "Open that drawer there, darling. There's something I want to give you." He reached in and drew out a gold box that had her initials engraved on it. She took it from him and weakly opened it. Inside was a oval miniature portrait of her, painted on ivory in the role of *Amina* in *La Sonnambula.* It was surrounded with a double row of diamonds. "Take this, child, and keep it in memory of the one who loved you so."

Words failed him as he gazed from the portrait to her face and back again. She smiled as sleep seemed to come over her. His eyes filled with tears as he looked at her. "Oh, my mother, I love you so much. Thank you for loving me, for all those who didn't. I will keep it with me always. Be at peace, Mother. I am with you." He sat up in bed, holding her close in his arms as tears fell and grief broke his heart. She tried to answer, opened her mouth to speak. No sound came. She moved her colorless lips to form the word *Ernesto*. The room grew deathly still. Only her soft, shallow breathing filled the air. Hours passed as he held her in his arms; thousands of memories flooded back of their years together. From far off, the sound of a rooster announced the coming morning. Closer still, just outside, a rare December snow began to fall. As the great grandfather's clock in the hall began to strike six, he felt a slight shudder as her hand fell away from his arm and a long-held breath was released. Her heart had stopped. He sobbed, holding her closer, trying in vain to keep her spirit near. Behind him, The Colonel's ghost passed through the wall and drew closer. Her ghost passed from the still form in Ernesto's arms. Husband and wife, clasped in reunion, together rose over him, smiled at him, then passed through the windows as snow engulfed the world outside the house. He silently laid the lifeless form down, and as he closed her eyes, he saw there a look of happiness. A smile lingered on her face as he pulled the coverlet over her and reluctantly left the room to make the necessary calls.

Forty-four

The funeral directors came swiftly and carried the small body to the mortuary. He stood alone on the veranda watching them drive away. The white hearse, emblazoned with the words *Kimbrell-Stern* turned at the end of the long drive, then turned to the right toward town. Many times he had seen the mansion converted into a funeral home. The residents of Selma had always avoided allowing the owners from joining their closed society because they were Jewish, but they were the overwhelming choice of anyone who wanted the dearly beloved conducted to the grave in style. Even at this early hour on Christmas Day, they went about their duties as consummate professionals. Beautifully dressed in matching black suits and ties, they spoke quietly and respectfully as they went about the duties to the dead and took from the living the burden of dealing with the physical reality of death. Ernesto turned away and walked back inside to the wide hall.

The butler and maids stood quietly in their uniforms, helplessly silent. He smiled at Mattie, who was weeping. "There now, Mattie," he said, placing an arm around her shoulders. "Thank you for your service to Madame. Please, all of you go about your duties as usual. Nothing will change for the time being. We must go on maintaining her home as she would have wished. The funeral directors will take care of everything. You are all invited to her internment. It is to be two days from now. Mattie, you and Thelma go upstairs and see to straightening up the bedrooms. I have to make some more calls in the music room and will ring when I need you. John, there may be callers coming by as the news spreads. If you would please see to them I would appreciate it."

The great three chandeliers gleamed with light in the front rooms. In the music room, he admired the new, dominating portrait of Carlotta in the role of *Violetta* in *La Traviata* over the fireplace, the other portrait of her as *Norma* having been transferred to its central position at the landing on the staircase. Grimly, he went to the French writing desk and mashed the rosette on the right. A hidden compartment sprang open. He took the key and unlocked the central drawer. He took out the papers inside and carefully laid them out before him. He poured himself a cup of black coffee from the silver service thoughtfully left for him by Thelma and Mattie.

He saw the will, then found the phone number and name of the lawyer. He reached for the gilt-encrusted phone. "Mr. Stein, this is Ernesto Vasselli. I am calling to inform you of the death this morning of Madame Carlotta Vasselli. Yes, thank you. I know you have a copy of the will as well. No, I have not read it yet. If you could put in motion her wishes and handle the legal affairs it entails I would appreciate it. The funeral will be in two days at the Kelly Mausoleum in Old Live Oak cemetery. Yes, of course Kimbrell-Stern will be handling all the arrangements. If you could let me know when you can arrange for reading the will I would be grateful. A few days' time? That will be fine. Whatever people locally who may be named should be contacted so they may attend the meeting. Rabbi Jacobson? Yes, Madame had mentioned he would conduct the services at the temple. I have already called him. I believe it's to be at one p.m. Thank you for your services both to The Colonel and Madame. I'll be talking to you then later."

He hung up and continued to look through the papers. He saw the great key to the mausoleum doors and made a mental note to get it to the funeral home. He saw the bank books and a few bonds, all carefully annotated in her firm handwriting. He couldn't bring himself to peruse them. He was tired from the long night's vigil and felt emotionally spent. Passing her empty throne chair, he patted its back. He sat at the grand piano and began to play some of her favorite Schubert impromptus. The immortal melodies of the Austrian master rang out in the stillness of the house. From the large windows, light from the gloomy skies crept in, casting shadows on the furniture as he played on for more than two hours.

In the afternoon, visitors began to arrive. Thirty to forty girls, many with their husbands, came to pay their respects. The two maids scurried to and fro, taking coats and depositing them in The Colonel's library. Coffee and refreshments had been laid out in the music room, as one by one they came in and spoke to Ernesto, who sat in Madame's throne chair to receive them. Most of them were former students and each had a special story of Madame to impart to him. Food began to arrive as the matrons received the news and prepared, in the southern tradition, the "funeral food" as it was always designated. Caramel cakes, pecan pies, cold salads and many delicacies including the inevitable fried chicken soon clustered the sideboards. Visitors came and went through the rest of the day. The Rabbi's wife brought a magnificent platter of tomato aspic with garnishes of fresh greens. Biscuits, cornbread and gravy, dressing, green beans and corn puddings came with some of the ladies from the Temple. Mourners feasted while looking about the richly furnished room, waiting their turn to approach the host. He ate nothing, preferring from long habit to drink countless cups of coffee.

As nightfall came, the final visitors departed. The maids took everything away to the kitchen, depositing the cold dishes in the refrigerator and wrapping the cakes, pies, and dozens of cookies in plastic and leaving them on the counters. Left alone, Ernesto walked through the great principal rooms, unable to relax. A stern inner reserve prevented him from breaking down in front of others, his southern upbringing teaching him to keep such displays to time alone. He thought of all the people who had come. Many of The Colonel's old friends had stayed only a few moments. They were old and walked with difficulty from various aliments. All were uniformly quiet and spoke in respectful, hushed voices. The former students, in contrast, were teary-eyed as they spoke of the great prima donna they held in awe. He dismissed all these thoughts as best he could, pausing in the hall before he went upstairs to look out at the piles of leaves, now covered and white with snow. It would not last long. Such winter scenes were rare here in southern Alabama.

He picked up one of Carlotta's shawls from where it lay on a chair in the hall and carried it upstairs with him. Alone, he wept for the woman who had given him everything. The shawl smelled of her perfume which lingered in its heavy folds. For a moment he thought of Imogene. He wondered why she had not come, but perhaps it was just as well. He took another shower and went to bed. The day ahead would be difficult and he needed to rest. Still clutching the shawl, he fell asleep.

The next morning, after a light breakfast of scrambled eggs and donated Virginia ham, he left the house and drove to the funeral home. As he entered, he was ushered into the viewing room above which were emblazoned the words *The Reposed,* where Carlotta's body lay in a magnificent casket. The funeral directors spoke softly and respectfully to him, then quietly withdrew, leaving him alone in the huge room. He approached the casket and was pleased to see how lifelike the remains appeared. Her hairdresser had arranged her hair in a very different manner than it had appeared in life. Instead of the usual severe French twist she favored, he had parted the hair in the middle and entwined two loose and thick braids on the sides of her head in imitation of the style she had adapted when she had once sung the role of *Violetta Valery* in *La Traviata.* Each of the two braids contained rows of faux pearls and made a stunning effect. Ernesto knew she would have been displeased, as never in her life had she worn fake jewelry of any kind. The hairdresser had also done her makeup so expertly that she looked merely asleep. She was dressed in an approximation of the costume she had worn in the opera *Semiramide*. The color was a beautiful mauve, accented at the shoulders with gold medallions. A sheer white veil covered her body, encircling her arms and folded across the bosom, disappearing from the waist down. He admired the Belgian lace handkerchief in her hands, which were covered with soft white gloves. He gazed into the still face. A soft cough sounded behind him and he turned to see the chief director of the funeral home behind him.

"Excuse me, Mr. Vasselli, for intruding on your privacy at this time, but may we talk for a moment?" He motioned to a sofa to the left of the casket. Tall funeral lamps cast soft light on the two men as they sat. "Mr.

Vasselli, let me begin by expressing again my condolences on the loss of this very great lady." Without waiting for a reply, he continued, "Madame had come to us several months ago to deposit her requirements regarding her services. There is no charge to you. She paid for everything at that time and selected the casket and gave us the gown that she is now wearing. She was of the Jewish religion, as you know, and asked that Rabbi Jacobson be in charge of a brief memorial service at the temple, during which time she is to be privately interred at Old Live Oak cemetery in the Kelly Mausoleum that I know you are familiar with. She told us that she would prefer that you accompany her remains to the grave rather than have you attend the service at the temple. She also asked that only you were to be allowed to view her, after which the casket is to be closed. She said that she wished the entombment to be private as well, with only you being allowed to be present in the mausoleum. Here are the papers she signed that day. She had asked that if you were not in Selma at the time of her death that she be placed in a cooling room to be preserved until you could arrive. This, of course, is not now necessary due to your being present in our community. She asked that when the time came we were to speak with you concerning her wishes and to assure you that you have the power to veto anything that you disagree with. We need to call *The Selma Times* so her notice will appear in this afternoon's paper. Oh yes, and she asked that there be no flowers but rather that people make a donation to the charity of their choice. Time is of the essence regarding the newspaper article, so may I ask that you indicate your approval at this time?"

Ernesto seemed overwhelmed, but was silently grateful that she had made all arrangements in advance. "I agree with almost everything that you have said Mr. Solomon, especially so since it was Madame's wish. However, I would like to ask that there be no visitation here this evening. I know this is something she would have wished as she would like people that she knew to remember her as she was in life. The only thing I would ask is that the internment at the cemetery be open to the public. I trust you received the key to the mausoleum that I had sent to you?" The director nodded. "Good. I know that her many students and acquaintances would welcome the opportunity of being present there. Please have the paper indicate that they are to gather there thirty minutes before one tomorrow. I will follow the hearse in a car that I wish you to supply and we should promptly be there at one o'clock. Only your staff and I are to be permitted to enter the mausoleum. There is to be no ceremony there and as soon as the tomb is sealed, the doors are to be locked and the key returned to me. Is that understood?"

The director nodded. “Thank you, sir, I am sure that Madame Vasselli would be pleased with only the slight alteration you have made to her wishes. It will be as you ask, of course. Please stay as long as you like and we will close the casket when you leave. Oh, by the way, I have two messages for you. Madame’s lawyer, Mr. Stein, called. Your staff at the house told him you were on your way here. He said if it’s convenient with you that he would like you to stop by his office after lunch. It is directly beside the Selma Bank and Trust building downtown. The other message was from Madame’s bankers, who would also like to talk to you at your earliest convenience.”

“I have no experience of dealing with such people, Mr. Solomon. Is it customary that matters of this nature be conducted with such haste? My God, Madame isn’t even in her tomb yet and people are calling here looking for me?”

The director looked at him with sympathy. “Please allow me to apologize to you on their behalf if they appear to be in haste over the matters they need to see you about. However, this is Selma. Here people wish for legal matters to be concluded as soon as possible. It’s easier for most people to do so and to put such business behind them as quickly as possible. You may, of course, do as you wish. I am just conveying to you these messages as I was asked to do. As I said, please stay as long as you like. I need to call the newspaper and we will send our car for you at 12:30 tomorrow. Good day, sir.”

Ernesto walked to the casket in the richly decorated room. He gazed at Carlotta’s silent form and said out loud, “Madame, I know your spirit has fled and now is numbered with the dead. No more on earth you have a home, only I am left here, your loss to mourn. I will do so all the rest of my life. You were the bright angel of my childhood. You and The Colonel taught me everything I needed for my career. I am so grateful that we had these last months here together.” Leaning into the casket, he kissed her for the last time. He wept softly and with a final backward look, left the room.

After lunch he made his way to Mr. Stein’s office by the bank building. He was ushered into the lawyer’s private office and sat down in a comfortable leather chair facing the desk. “Mr. Vasselli, let me again express my condolences for your loss. Madame wished me to talk with you as soon as possible after her death, hence my request that you come here today. First of all, here are her safety deposit keys. You will need them when you see her bankers. I also have several copies of the death certificate for you. As for the will, I know she had a copy at the house. Have you had an opportunity to acquaint yourself with its contents?”

Ernesto gazed across the desk incredulously. “No, as a matter of fact,

I have not had time to do so. Even though she had already made a great deal of her arrangements herself, I have had to deal with people coming to the house. I also am extremely tired from the sorrow I am suffering and lack of adequate sleep. I still have tomorrow to get through. I don't mind the responsibility thrust on me with little warning, it's just there is a limit to what any reasonable person should expect from me at a time like this." Frustration showed in his voice.

The lawyer looked at him sympathetically. "Well, I'll take up as little of your time as I can. Madame's will, which was redone after The Colonel's death, is pretty simple. There are several small bequests to old friends in Italy, as well as to her personal maids and butler. Here in Selma, besides her personal servants, she has left the sum of $50,000 to Mrs. Imogene Atkins. Mrs. Atkins was here this morning and I will see that a check is sent to her. She did not wish to be here at the same time as you for reasons she explained were personal in nature. The remainder of the estate is yours, Mr. Vasselli. It includes the house and all furnishings, and the fifty acres surrounding the house; also, all assets in the Selma Bank and Trust, real estate holdings, jewelry, investments and so forth. On your behalf, I have already moved to have everything put in your name. This process should be complete within the next week to ten days. The sum total will be somewhere approaching three and a half million dollars before inheritance taxes. You can minimize your losses financially by immediately having funds transferred to certificates of deposit that are only taxed as money is withdrawn. Madame had advised me that you have dual citizenship both here and in Italy, therefore you will not have the problem of transference of assets that a foreign national would encounter. I suggest that you engage counsel of your own to handle legal affairs and investments that you might want to retain or liquidate at your pleasure. I have served Colonel Kelly, as well as Madame Vasselli, for the past thirty-five years and would be happy to do so for you as well. That, of course, is up to you. I have nothing further at this time and will be in touch with you as matters come to a conclusion. Now, do you have any questions or requests that I can help you with?"

Ernesto could hardly take it all in. He replied in quieter, friendlier tones by saying, "Thank you Mr. Stein, for both your service to Madame as well as myself. I would like, since you are already familiar with the estate holdings, that you continue in that capacity for me as well. I do have a question, however, in regard to Mrs. Atkins. Are you aware, or can you tell me to what extent Madame's financial dealings have been with her in the past?"

"Sir, all I can tell you is that since January 1956, continuing till the fall of 1982, that The Colonel and Madame Vasselli have made yearly allowances to Mrs. Atkins of $10,000. After The Colonel's death, Madame instructed me to make the same payments to her each year, and I have done so. I am unaware of their reasons for doing so, as it is not for me to question the actions or requests of my employers. The payments of course are suspended with Madame's death. Would you like me to continue the payments to Mrs. Atkins at this time?"

Ernesto looked at him in astonishment. "No. Absolutely *not* at this time, but I will get back to you about it later. I am acquainted with the lady and I will be talking to her soon. At that time I will let you know my decision." He reached across the desk and warmly shook the lawyer's hand. "I appreciate all you have said and done. I will be back in touch with you soon, I am sure."

From there, he went into the bank next door and asked the secretary of the bank president to announce him. They went down a long corridor and he was soon in the office of the president.

"Good afternoon, Mr. Vasselli. My name is Hoyt Edge. Please be seated." The two men shook hands and sat facing each other. "I am happy you received our message and could come by this afternoon. We have instructions from the law firm of Mr. Stein to make arrangements for Mrs. Vasselli's accounts to be converted to your name. I have documents here for your signature to do so. We are aware that you have your own account with us that you have been making deposits to for a number of years now. Madame and The Colonel had several accounts with us for many years. I would suggest if this is acceptable with you that the account numbers be kept intact with only the name changed to yours." Ernesto nodded his agreement, and Mr. Edge continued, "I see you have the keys with you for Madame's safety deposit boxes in our vault? My secretary will show you to the vault where the drawers may be taken to a private room where you may examine their contents to familiarize yourself with them. When you are through, just ring when you are ready for our clerk to return."

Ernesto signed the documents and shook hands once more with Mr. Edge.

The secretary showed him to the vault. "Sir," she said, "there are six large boxes. If you will put your keys in each on the left, I will insert ours on the right to unlock them." They both did so and the clerk took each box out, setting them carefully on a two-shelf rolling cart which she pushed into the examining room. She put each box on the large table and left the room, closing the door behind her.

He was stunned at the treasures they contained. One box was filled with bonds. The others contained Madame's personal jewelry collections as well as those handed down through four generations of The Colonel's family. Bracelets, necklaces, tiaras, rings, gold bars, silver bars, pearls, rubies, emeralds, diamonds, and endless chokers and numerous ropes of pearls poured out in a great flood, each more beautiful and glittering than the last.

Ernesto sat, stunned beyond comprehension. It was like a king's ransom, so vast were the contents of the combined boxes. Some he had seen Madame wear over the years, but he had no idea before today that The Colonel and she had anywhere near the wealth displayed in the boxes. He took only a beautiful five carat solitaire ring of diamonds set in platinum with him.

Looking around warily, he got into his car and drove back to the house. He could not take in the extent of his fortune. Never more would he have to want or worry about anything. A feeling of loneliness and detachment settled upon him. He knew practically no one in Selma with the exception of Imogene. He would think about it all later. Right now, he didn't know how to even think about the future. He only knew that his heart ached in sorrow in spite of the incredible wealth that was now his alone.

Forty-five

The next day, at precisely 12:30, a funeral car drove up to the house. Ernesto dressed in beautiful highly formal mourning clothes that he knew would have pleased Carlotta. The maids and John, the butler, followed in a separate car. In contrast to the past two gloomy days, it was bright and sunny, the winds still. Ernesto wore dark sunglasses; his eyes were dark from weeping. They went by the funeral home, where he saw Carlotta's casket already placed in a white Mercedes hearse. His driver pulled in behind it, with the maids and butler following behind him. The short procession wound through the old streets into the downtown area and turned south to the cemetery adjacent to the Alabama River. The cemetery was encircled by thick granite walls. The great nineteenth-century iron gates were open. Tall marble monuments, obelisks, and pedestals topped with towering marble statues stood like watchmen on each side of the main road. They drove to a row of large mausoleums and parked. He was surprised, but pleased, to see approximately two hundred people standing in respectful silence.

The Kelly Mausoleum, of white *Cararra* marble, gleamed in the bright sunlight. Above its double doors was carved the date 1840, the year it had been built. Ernesto donned his top hat. He was dressed in a dark black mourning coat, cut away to reveal gray pinstriped trousers. His formal white shirt had a black ascot at the neck, to which he had attached the small oval portrait Carlotta had given to him that last night of her life. His figure was tall, slim, and handsome. People looked at him admiringly as he lifted his hat and nodded to some of the girls who had been students of the departed. His dark auburn hair, shot now with premature silver streaks, drew approving nods from the older ladies.

He knew few of the people. Fewer still would have remembered that he, as David Atkins, had grown up among them long ago.

As the casket was carried into the mausoleum, men removed their hats and stood with their hands over their hearts. He entered through the doors after the casket passed inside. People drew closer, admiring the Tiffany stained-glass windows, trying to see into the beautiful monument.

Inside, the polished marble walls rose toward the ceiling from which a circular rose window cast light. On both sides from floor to ceiling, tombs of past generations were emblazoned with their names and dates inscribed in bold letters. Each crypt had brass handles fastened to their covers. Ernesto looked at the top tier where The Colonel's grandparents' and great-grandparents' names were written. Alternating from left to right where The Colonel's parents, his little sister, Georgiana, and finally The Colonel's own crypt. The space assigned to Carlotta was open. He nodded to the undertakers, who signaled the pallbearers to slide the casket inside. The cover was attached and sealed. The funeral home's staff left the building. At the door, Ernesto signaled for the two maids and butler to come inside. Mattie wept. He put his arm around her shoulders and the four of them walked outside. The funeral director closed and locked the doors and handed the key to Ernesto. The crowd unexpectedly broke into applause in tribute to the prima donna and then began to disperse.

As he was walking to the car, Ernesto saw Imogene standing in front of the mausoleum. He signaled the driver to wait and then walked up to her. "Well hello, Imogene. It's been a long time. I was wondering when I might see you. I am happy that you came today." He smiled, trying to swallow down the lump rising in his throat.

"I, too, have been wondering when I might hear from you," she said, "considering you have been back here for several months now and haven't taken the time to call me." She spoke through clenched teeth, obviously trying to be civil.

He cleared his throat and replied quietly, "You are quite right there. I should have called you. This is not the time, certainly not the place for us to talk. However, if you don't already have plans would you like to come by this evening, say at seven, for supper? We need to talk about many things, I think."

Something in his voice caused her face to soften, and she answered affirmatively, "Yes, David, I mean Ernesto. I would be happy to come by. Please don't go to a lot of trouble, however, on my account. I am just a simple old woman now. Something informal and small would be fine for me."

He bowed slightly and said, "Well, I'll expect you at seven then. We can dine on some of the dozens of dishes that have been sent over to the house. I need to get it all cleared out and the platters and so forth returned to those who sent them. Very well then, I'll see you this evening." She turned and walked away. He watched her retreating form until she was out of sight. "All right then," he said to the driver, "take me home."

A few moments after seven, a loud knock came at the front door. Ernesto stood back as Imogene came inside. He closed the door behind her. He took her coat and hung it on the hall tree saying, "Thank you for coming. Please come in the dining room. I believe you remember where it is?" He led the way, and pulled out a chair for her. He rang a bell to summon the staff, and then sat down across the table facing her. "I hope you are well this evening. May I pour you a glass of wine?"

She shook her head. "Actually, if you don't mind, I'd like something a little stronger than that. Do you have any liquor in the house?"

He returned her steady gaze without flinching. Mattie and Thelma came into the room and curtsied. "Mattie, please bring Mrs. Atkins a mint julep. In fact, make it two. You may both serve dinner in a few minutes after we have had our drinks." The maid curtsied again and left the room.

High above their heads, the shimmering Venetian crystal chandelier filled the room with bright light. Sitting across from each other, mother and son watched each other with caution.

She was dressed in a dark green suit. A necklace of five rows of fine pearls hung from her neck. Matching pearl drop earrings, accented with diamonds, were on her ears. Her hands shook though she folded them together trying to keep them still. Her dark auburn hair, so like his own, was pulled back severely from her face. He noticed silver streaks running through it as they did in his own. Across from her, he sat in a dark blue jacket with a white shirt to which was attached the miniature portrait of Carlotta.

He led off the conversation. "It was nice to see you at the cemetery. I'm very grateful that you came today. I'm sure Madame would have been pleased that you did so. It was rather chilly, but at least the skies cleared and the sun came out this morning. I have forgotten what this season of the year is like here in Selma, since I have been away for so long, except for the brief visit I made that summer five years ago."

Mattie served the mint juleps in frosted silver cups and withdrew to help Thelma bring in the carts with their supper.

Raising the cup to her lips, Imogene sipped the cold beverage. "I felt I needed to be there at the cemetery. I have seen The Colonel and then Madame infrequently these past years. We didn't run in the same circles, but I would occasionally see and speak with them when we happened to run into each other when we were all in town at the same time. They were both kind to me though in many ways over the years. Both of them helped make my life more comfortable and free of financial worries. They would keep me informed of what was happening with you and your career. Not that it has anything to do with me of course. I'm still active in my church and spend a lot of time with my four grandchildren when I'm able to do so. I retired this fall from the air force base as you may know."

He looked thoughtfully across the table. "Yes, Madame told me that you had. I'm sure it has to be a relief to not have to work anymore and to be able just to do anything you like without that bother."

She stiffened slightly. "Oh, I never minded work. I've always worked, as you well know. I like to be active, to be useful. Nothing was ever handed to me on a silver platter like it was to some people."

He, too, stiffened and returned her steady look. "Oh, really? Nothing? Excuse me for saying so, but I doubt that. You don't seem the worse for wear for the life you've led. You seem quite serene, relaxed and taken care of to me." His smile faded as he looked across at her.

She opened her mouth to speak, but checked herself as the maids entered and began to put the trays on the table. Both of them were hungrier that either would have admitted. When they were finished he said, "Let's move to the music room now for our coffee and charlotte if you please, like we had that time years ago the afternoon you returned from Albertville." He pulled back her chair and she followed him silently. They sat in armchairs, facing each other. A tension crackled in the air as they both looked into the warm red flames in the fireplace.

She looked across at him and said. "Well, I guess you'll be leaving to return to Europe soon? I know it's a life you must miss and that you're anxious to return to?"

He looked thoughtfully at her. "Actually, my plans are quite indefinite now. I'm no longer singing professionally, though I won't bore you with the details as to why. No, for now, I plan to stay here in Selma and reopen the singing school. I believe that would have pleased Madame. I need to look after the house now and maintain it as she and The Colonel would have if they were still living."

The coffee and charlotte arrived and he poured for both of them. "You still take it black? I do too. Never could stand to have anything ruin the flavor. Mattie, you may leave now. I'll take care of things from here."

Imogene smiled slightly. "You always did love your coffee black. You got that from me, you know. Even when you were a little thing, you'd sip it from my saucer. That's one habit you didn't get from her."

At the reference to Carlotta, he began to feel anger rising in his heart. He checked himself, however, and continued drinking his coffee.

After an awkward silence she put her cup down and said. "All right, David, or Ernesto, or whatever you call yourself today, I see now that this house must be yours now. I would like to know why you asked me here tonight. Our words have been stiff and formal and I'm sick of skirting about whatever it is that you want to say to me. " She shot him a defiant, hostile, glance.

Blood rushed high into his face as he exclaimed, "How *dare* you take that tone with me! Who the hell do you think you are, woman? You may call me whatever makes you most comfortable. I'm sure David is what you prefer, though you know that my name was legally changed many years ago. So call me David if that makes you feel better. You are here at my invitation. I think this meeting between us is long overdue. It should have taken place many years ago, Mother." He glared at her. "There are so many things I want to say to you that I hardly know where to begin." He broke off, trying to regain his composure.

She answered with the bitterness born of years of being shunted out to the shadows of his life. "Well, David, why don't you just start at the beginning and get it off your chest. I'm woman enough to hear whatever it is that you wish to say. Thank God Brad and Tony haven't shut me out of their lives as you have. They both married well and have good jobs and families. They haven't looked for the vain glory of an opera star the way you have. They have included me and loved me, given me grandchildren, while you were over there, across the sea, making faces to strangers from your stage of make-believe." She returned his look. "Brad is a rich man now. Tony too, is doing well and has moved his family back here to Selma. They didn't go off to live with some old opera singer and her doting husband. You are my son too, even if you were torn away from me all those years ago by those people. Well, you aren't going to shut any more doors in my face, young man."

His eyes narrowed. "Yes, I am your son. You are the woman who gave birth to me, but it was The Colonel and Madame who raised me and groomed me for the life and career I have known for all these years. Why? It's because you were an unfit mother. You speak to me of Brad and of Tony and tell me how well they have done? Well, this man before you hasn't done too badly either, even if my success seems lost on you. Now you come here. Sit down!! It's my turn to talk and you are going to listen. Maybe you'll learn some things tonight about your two precious sons that you adore so much." He seized her arm and forced her down into Carlotta's throne chair. "Now don't you move, Mother. You are going to listen to me."

He turned away and almost ran to the French writing desk. He opened the central drawer and pulled out an old envelope of pictures. Returning to where she sat in dumbfounded silence, he handed her the envelope. "I think you have seen these before, but I want to jog your memory if you can take off your rose-colored glasses and listen to the truth. Now, look at them, Mother!" He stood over her shaking with fury as she looked at the pictures, now faded, of a beaten and battered little boy. "That was me. Do you remember Madame showing them to you?"

She looked through the pictures, then laid them on the piano. "Yes I have seen them, and I wish to God I never had. The boys and then these two people here told me you had an accident, that you fell down the steps of our house, hurt yourself and then came over here to them, so they could take care of you. Yes, I remember. I know you never spent another night in my house again after this incident. But why do you bring this up now? What difference do these old pictures make to the present? David, tell me. I am your mother, and in spite of everything, I love you. I *never* stopped loving you." She turned away as tears began to gather in her eyes.

He looked at her in contempt and screamed, "Oh God! You Love me? You have no idea what love is." In spite of himself, he felt blood rise in his cheeks. He reached out and steadied himself by putting both hands on a chair. "What difference do they make? Do you understand nothing you hypocrite? You stand there, telling me about how your other sons have succeeded in life, how happy and loved they've made you feel, while you denigrate everything that I have done in my life, everything Madame sacrificed to make it possible for me to stand alone? What those pictures don't tell you is what happened that night. What your precious Tony and his friends did to a ten year old boy. You have believed what you wanted to believe, but tonight you are going to face the truth. Then, I hope God will forgive you and that you can live with it."

"All I know is what I was told," she stammered. "I came home from my mother's and the boys told me you were here and there had been an accident. I walked in this damn house to take you home, and there all three of you sat in that dining room, dressed in all your fancy dinner clothes. You did look like you'd been knocked around a little and I wanted to take you home, but he took you upstairs and then this woman pulled me in here like you have tonight and showed me these pictures. She threatened me with legal action to have all of you boys taken away, to have me declared an unfit mother because I had left you alone for two weeks without adult supervision. Who was I to fight against people like that? I was afraid." She moved toward the windows, trying to control her shaking hands and to make sense of what was happening. "She told me that she'd have me in court and that you'd have to testify, and Brad and Tony, too. She said The Colonel's uncle was the judge of the superior court of Dallas County, and that I would be in big trouble if what had happened came out. I felt I had no choice. She backed me into a corner. What was it David? Tell me now."

He snarled and leaned to her face, saying, "Misguided and miserable wretch that you are, Mother, you didn't fight for me because you thought it better to lose one son than all three. You let money and intimidation get the best of you. Of course these people were rich and powerful, but my life would not have had any meaning had they not intervened. Now prepare yourself to hear the worst. What I am going to tell you is not out of hatred for my brothers, though I despise them both. Tony for what he and his friends did. Brad for knowing the truth and doing nothing. I don't care if I ever see them again. But you are still my mother, even after all this time, and I am your son." He reeled back as tears scalded down his cheeks. He sat in an armchair, weeping as though his heart would break.

She drew nearer. "David? It's all right. I am your mother and I love you. Please tell me. Let it out and let's try to deal with it." She reached across and grasped his hands. He jerked them away. "I'm ready." Her voice had grown calm as she looked at him.

He poured himself a large glass of Madeira from the decanter on the sideboard. He looked at her with all the sadness of his soul. His face was red from his tears which he choked back. With great effort, he calmed himself and brushed aside his tears impatiently and at last spoke, saying, "That night, after Brad left for his date, I was alone in the house. I was coming over here for dinner. I was taking a shower when I heard the front door open. I grabbed a towel and walked around the corner into the living room. Tony and his friends were all sitting there. They were drunk and stank of cigarettes and beer. I tried to go back to my room, but Tony grabbed me by my hair and threw me naked to the floor. He kicked me in the face. All of them, one by one, took off their clothes. They beat me, called me a girl-boy, and each of them raped me. Blood was everywhere. I screamed, but they wouldn't stop. Tony said, as he fucked me, 'It's okay that I do this, because we're brothers.' The others laughed and said how good it felt to fuck a girl-boy, a sissy like me. When they were through, they left. I don't know how long I lay on the floor, but I could see how torn up the room was. Beer cans everywhere, chairs knocked over, and I crawled on my hands and knees to wipe up the blood and filth and to set the room straight again so that you wouldn't be mad when you came home. I got back to the bathroom and ran water over my face till my head cleared. Oh, Mother, they had hurt me so bad. I pulled on my jeans as best I could and a sweatshirt. I gathered up all the towels and took them with me out the front door. I came over here, not even knowing how I walked those five blocks. Madame and The Colonel were here waiting on me. I didn't know what to do. I crawled up the steps of this house to the porch and knocked. She came out as I turned away towards one of the chairs on the porch. She saw me and screamed for The Colonel. He came out and took me into the house in his arms. They told me later that I had fainted.

She had blanched out white as a ghost as she heard the story. Suddenly, she jumped to her feet and screamed. The ghosts of Carlotta and The Colonel passed through the walls, watching the drama intently. "Oh God! Give me light. Oh, my baby, my David. I had no idea. I wish to God I had died before I ever heard this. How you must have suffered. If only I had been home, none of this would have happened, but how could I have known? My mother was ill. I had to go up there. Surely there can be no guilt, my darling. Not now. Thank God they were here for you. I can't even imagine what it must have been like. If this had come out, what would have become of us?" She began to cry but had enough presence of mind to walk over to the armoire where the liquor was kept and poured herself a large glass of straight Kentucky Bourbon. She flopped down in her chair and looked back at him.

He had regained his composure and watched her as she gulped down her drink "You're right at home, aren't you, Mother? Just help yourself to the booze? Well, that's okay. I need one myself." He poured an even larger glass for himself. "Well, Mother, where do we go from here?"

She looked into his face and took another gulp from her glass. "I don't know, David. I just don't know. It's going to take me a while to deal with everything I've learned tonight. I do feel that you've tried to reach out to me, and I appreciate it. Maybe there's nothing we can do about the past, but I tell you this, I am going to have this out with Tony. His behavior was unforgivable. I know that my eyes are wide open now. I have many friends here in Selma, but I know that you don't. If you're going to stay here and maybe reopen the singing school again to the students, it's going to take a while. I don't know anything about that kind of music, but you always sang so sweetly when you were a little boy. I should have been more demonstrative towards you, but I had so much to deal with back in the old days. My parents never hugged, never kissed me. I knew I was loved; it's just that they were always working. We all were. There never seemed time for what they considered nonsense.

"Maybe people should just try to show their love more. I'm sorry for what you had to go through. I wish I could make up for it, but it happened and you went on to a very different kind of life than you could ever have had with me. These people who raised you were rich. Their money opened doors. I guess you haven't done too badly in that sense."

He smiled. "Well old girl, you didn't do too badly yourself in the bargain either did you? Madame's lawyer told me yesterday when I was in his office that she left you $50,000, and that since 1956 they have settled $10,000 a year on you. That's a lot of money. With what you earned working, your life must have been pretty comfortable. It's okay. I don't mind. I'm glad for you if it helped you."

She smiled back at him as she finished her drink. "Yes, they were good to me in that sense. The Colonel paid off my house. He even paid for the addition I had put on, and put in central air and heat. I finally got rid of that old oil furnace that never kept that damn place warm in winter. My friends always wondered but never had the nerve to ask where the money came from. Certainly not from that good-for-nothing father of yours. As soon as he could he stopped my child support as each of you turned eighteen. He still sends me my alimony checks every month . . . one hundred dollars. God, I know it galls him to have to do that. I don't give a damn though, I deserve it." She laughed.

He laughed too and felt a lightness of heart towards her for the first time since she had come in the front door. He reached across and took her hands in his and smiled warmly. "Maybe we haven't accomplished a lot tonight, but we've both got a lot off our chests. It's a first step, Mother. The past is what it is. We can't change it. I'm glad it's all out in the open. Maybe we can go on now and be friends again. Perhaps even mother and son once more if it isn't too late, if it's something you would like to see bloom again?"

She looked earnestly at him. They embraced each other before the fireplace. "I'd like to think we could try, David. I'm willing to try if you are. Perhaps we can both bridge that gap. It's terrible that I didn't know the truth before tonight. And to think that all these years we might have been friends." They walked with their arms around each other out into the hall where he helped her put on her coat.

"Mother, about this business with Tony, just let it go. It's enough that you know the truth. The Colonel always told me that the more you stir shit, the worse it smells. There's no need for you to confront him about it. It was so long ago. I'm fine now and at peace with the past. There isn't any point in your revealing it to him. I'm sure he has thought about it every day of his life. Why don't you bring the grandchildren by to see me sometime when they are with you? Maybe they would like to meet the uncle they've never known. Who knows? All I can say is that I welcome you back into my life for whatever we can be to each other."

"I'll do as you've suggested, David. I won't mention what you've told me to Tony. I feel for the first time that maybe we can all be a family again. I'll call you and we can continue these first steps. Maybe I can even talk you into coming to sing for my Susannah Wesley Sunday school class? Nothing fancy you know. Those old biddies wouldn't know what long hair music is like anyway. Maybe an old hymn like you used to sing? What was it? The one I loved? Oh yes. *Brightly gleams our Father's mercy, from his lighthouse ever more?* Yeah, *Let the Lower Lights Be Burning*? That would do nicely."

He smiled warmly; they stepped onto the porch. He again took her into his arms, warmly embracing and kissing her on both cheeks. From his pocket, he drew out the magnificent five-carat diamond ring he had brought home with him the day before and placed it on her finger. She began to cry. She opened her mouth to speak, but he raised his hand and shook his head. She smiled and walked down the steps to her car. He stood on the front porch and watched her drive slowly away. He sighed and went back inside, closing the heavy door behind him. He looked around the silent hall and turning out the lights, walked up the stairs. Unseen by him, the ghosts of The Colonel and Carlotta, smiled at each other and passed through the front door to return to their cold tombs.

Forty-six

Outside The Colonel's mansion, at the entrance to the driveway, a new sign went up, reading as before: *Vasselli School of Singing*. Ads had been put in various neighboring newspapers, including the venerable *Selma Times*. Applications began to pour in. Though he abhorred the idea of teaching beginners, Ernesto was resigned to the reality, that as in the days of Carlotta before him, accomplished intermediate young singers were not to be found. Advertisements specified that admission to the program was to be on an audition basis only. After one-by-one auditioning the applicants, the new teacher agreed to take on twenty students who he felt had the potential of becoming artists in the future. He had pored over Carlotta's list of contacts, both in Selma, and in out-of-state locations to find venues to present the young singers. The lessons began in mid-April, 1983. Selma society was abuzz with gossip of the presence in their community of the handsome relative of Madame Vasselli. Curiosity regarding the new teacher, as well as the old mansion where he lived, was as discussed by nosy people as it had been before when the former mistress lived there.

Between Ernesto and Imogene, a mutual respect had been established, and she often visited him, sometimes bringing her four grandchildren with her. She continued to call him David, but by agreement, the name was confined to their private conversations. He retained his enigmatic identity. He was legally Ernesto Vasselli, and that was enough for him. Like Carlotta before him, he preferred not to try to enter Selma society. His servants were steadfastly loyal and guarded events at the house from the scrutiny of the curious. Imogene continued to live in her home on the Old Evans road; her various bridge parties and church activities continued unabated.

At the beginning of June, Ernesto received a call from Dr. Wilson, pastor of the First Methodist church of Selma. Sitting alone in the music room, drinking his omnipresent strong black coffee, he picked up the phone. "Yes, I'm Ernesto Vasselli. What is that, Dr. Wilson? You have a young man in your children's choir that you wish me to audition? I'm afraid I already have a full slate of students at this time. Mrs. Atkins gave you my phone number? Well, in that case, I'll listen to him and perhaps he can be admitted as a special case. Twelve years old? I was only eight when I first came to study with Madame Vasselli. No, I can't promise anything more than to say I will be happy to audition him since Mrs. Atkins has asked. Let me see. I could hear him this afternoon at four o'clock if his mother could bring him by. All right, if you'll pass that on to her, I'll expect them at that time." He hung up as his first student of the day, a fourteen-year-old soprano, knocked at the door. The day thus engaged passed by as usual with only a brief break at lunchtime. At four-fifteen the young mother and her son knocked on the heavy oak front door.

He opened the door himself and ushered them inside. "Come in, Mrs. Ward. So this is your son Robert? Well, let us go to the music room then."

The young mother and her son, who held her hand tightly, stumbled into the wide entrance of the house, gaping at the portraits on the walls and the imposing furniture. Ernesto stood at the entrance to the music room, and looking back impatiently, he exclaimed, "Well, come on. I am waiting. I don't have all day you know. You are already fifteen minutes late. I hope, Mrs. Ward, that this is not your usual practice. We practice discipline in this school and expect precise acceptance of such by anyone who seeks to enter. Now, don't waste any more of my time. Come in here at once." Mother and son followed him timidly. As they entered the music room, he impatiently waved them to a sofa in the center of the room and turned to face them. "I am Ernesto Francesco Vasselli, teacher of singing. I teach the method of Manuel Garcia. It is the only correct and sure method of learning the ancient Bel Canto technique. I have agreed to hear your son, Mrs. Ward, at the special request of Mrs. Imogene Atkins and Dr. Wilson of your church. If I accept him as a student, I expect to be addressed as Signore. Is that understood?"

Mrs. Ward nervously took her eyes off the splendor of the room to stammer out, "Oh yes, Signore. I will certainly be sure he will cooperate. Isn't that right, sweetheart?" The little boy nodded his head while fixing his eyes on the floor. The mother was a quiet woman, dressed in a simple yellow street dress and practical shoes. The young boy was also very timid. His blond curls gathered around an oval, pale face accentuated by beautiful light-blue eyes.

Ernesto looked searchingly at the slight child and then turned to the mother once more. "Well, Mrs. Ward, you may go. I will run the boy through some scales at the piano of the famous Marchesi exercises to see how his voice is settled and its compass."

"Signor Vasselli, my son is only a child. I think I should remain with him while you work with him. He isn't used to being alone with other adults, you see." She smiled nervously.

He turned a furious look in her direction. "Mrs. Ward, this is absurd. You bring the child by here for me to see if he has a voice worth cultivating. I have only agreed to hear him as a favor to Dr. Wilson and Mrs. Atkins, and you have the nerve to question my methods? I tolerate no interference, and you will leave him here this instant and leave yourself. If this is not acceptable, then I will bid you both good day."

The young mother looked back at him, stunned. "Oh please, Signore, I am so sorry. I didn't mean to offend you, It's just the boy is so shy and he is used to me being nearby. I'll leave then and return for him in an hour if that's okay?"

He looked at her impatiently and said, "Mrs. Ward, do not bother yourself to return in precisely an hour. I do not teach by the clock, but rather it is I who will summon you back here when I am through with Robert. Now, the sooner you leave, the sooner I can begin to work with him."

She gathered her coat from the sofa, and after admonishing the boy to do as he was told, she left the house.

The boy sat in silence as he watched his mother leaving. He then looked up at Ernesto in awe. Ernesto smiled at the child and said, "Is that the song that you are going to sing for me? Well come over here and stand beside me at the piano and we'll run through it." He sat at the piano and played some scales, then took the battered old album of Marchesi exercises, put it on the music stand and opened it to the first page. He then took the music the child brought and opened it to the beginning. "What is this song? Oh yes, *I walked today where Jesus walked*." He raised his eyes to the ceiling. "Now look, Robert, we need to warm your voice a bit before we begin. I will play a scale and you follow. There are no words, just repeat as I play and sing the vowels, A E, I, O, U. You do know what I'm talking about, don't you?"

They began, and the boy followed him in singing the vowels. The voice was a clear soprano, but already showed the signs of approaching puberty. He vocalized the child from low A to a high C. He noticed immediately that the basic quality was pleasing and that the child sang on pitch. "Now, that is good, Robert. We will begin your song now." He played through the introduction and the boy's voice rang out in the room. Watching him closely, Ernesto perceived that the child had talent. "All right, Robert, you have a pleasant voice. I believe I can make something of you if you are willing to work hard. Is this something you want, or are you just doing this to please your mother?"

"Oh no, Signore. I like to sing. I sing in the children's choir and you know Mrs. Atkins is one of our adult sponsors. I mean she's a swell lady, even if she is old, and she spoke to Dr. Wilson and told him I should come out here and study with you. I want to learn. Mrs. Atkins told me you were a famous opera singer and that the lady who taught you once lived here." The child smiled and seemed completely unafraid.

Ernesto looked back at him and wondered at the similarity of the boy to himself. Directing the boy's eyes to the large portrait over the fireplace, he said, "Robert, that lady was Madame Carlotta Vasselli. She taught me as a child. I lived here in this house with her and her husband. They were very kind and raised me well. Now don't stare at the portrait, just remember that Madame still watches everything that happens here. She insisted, as I do, in absolute adherence to the rules of singing by the method of Manuel Garcia. I know that name doesn't mean anything to you now, but in time it will. There will be so much for you to learn. Do you play at all?" The boy nodded. "Well, I'm not sure I trust the proficiency of piano teachers in this town, but for now we will take a wait-and-see attitude. You need to learn so many things, Robert. Not just the basics of correct singing, but also languages, history, composers and the like. I do not teach church music. I will have none of that here. Your voice is approaching the change that is coming for you sooner than it did for me. When that time comes, we will have to direct it into its mature form, whether that is tenor, baritone, or bass. Trust me, apply yourself diligently to all I say, and possibly I will be able to make something extraordinary of you. It will take time and study. You have an instinct for it and your pitch seems true." He reached over and rang a bell on the piano.

Mattie appeared and curtsied. "Mattie, this is Robert Ward. He will be coming here to study with me. Please take him to the kitchen and give him some of the fresh lemonade you made this morning and some cookies too. I need to call his mother to come and fetch him." He reached out and ran his fingers through the boy's hair and smiled at him. The young boy suddenly threw his arms around his neck, kissing him on the cheek. Startled, he gently disengaged himself and looked thoughtfully at the small boy. "There will be none of that hugging and kissing business in this house. Do you understand? Now be a good boy and run along with Mattie to the kitchen. Your mother will be along soon."

Mattie took the boy's hand and led him out of the room towards the kitchen. In the hall, they passed the grand staircase with the life-sized portraits of the three famous singers.

The boy paused. Looking up at Mattie, he asked, "Who are those ladies? They sure are pretty in their swell dresses."

Mattie smiled warmly saying, "Oh, child, Mattie doesn't know who those two on the left and the right are, but the one in the middle was Madame Vasselli who taught the Signore. She lived here in this house for many years with her husband. They're dead now, but they were such nice folks. You'll like it here and the Signore will teach you all about the folks who once lived here. Child, she was a famous singer. Maybe you will be one day too. Now come along with Mattie to the kitchen. What the Signore says goes, just the same as it did when Madame was alive." They passed on down the hall and disappeared into the kitchen.

Back in the music room, Ernesto sat at the piano, lost in thought about how time had come full circle for him. He was no Colonel, it was true. Nothing would happen between him and this child that was improper. He rose and went to the French writing desk and picked up the phone. "Mrs. Ward? Yes, this is Ernesto Vasselli. You may return for Robert now. Why yes, he behaved and cooperated as he was told. He is in the kitchen with one of my servants having some lemonade and cookies right now. Come along then and we'll talk when you arrive." He hung up and surveyed the room. Everything was the same as when he'd first come here as a child. He glanced up at the portrait of Madame Blanche and then to the one of Carlotta as *Violetta.* The eyes of the portrait seemed to follow him as he went to the armoire and poured himself a glass of Madeira from its crystal decanter.

He walked across the hall toward the library, pausing in the hall as he heard the Robert's joyous laughter coming from the kitchen. Moving aside the large vase of flowers in the library, he drew back the white eyelet lace curtain and saw Mrs. Ward turn into the driveway. He dropped the curtain and walked back out to the front door. Opening it, he made a mental note to have Mattie or Thelma oil the creaking hinges. He stepped out onto the wide veranda. He glanced to his left at the old wicker furniture. He looked at the chaise and thought back to a time so long ago when he lay there in The Colonel's warm embrace and remembered how the older man took his hand and put in on his lap. He shook his head to banish the memory.

The ghosts of Carlotta and The Colonel materialized on the veranda and flanked him on each side as Mrs. Ward came up the steps.

"Signore, did it go okay? I hope Robert behaved as he should. He's a good boy. He does as he's told and is never any trouble. Are you going to take him on? He needs to come out of his little shell and do something useful." She looked at him and he smiled warmly.

Taking her hands, he laughed. "Why of course I accept him, Mrs. Ward. Robert is a delightful child. He shows great promise, but let's not be too strict and drown his spirit. That will never do. Come on in and I'll call him from the kitchen so you can be on your way."

A moment later, Robert came around the corner and ran to his mother, who hugged him.

The two ghosts had come through the closed front door unimpaired and stood behind them.

"Robert, let's go home now. Thank the Signore for the lemonade and cookies."

The boy looked up and said, "Oh yes, Signore. Thank you so much. Mattie is sure a nice person. She told me that you used to eat something here called charlotte. What is that anyway?"

The ghosts looked at each other and smiled.

Kneeling, Ernesto gave the boy a hug. "Robert, it's just an old dessert that a lady who lived here used to make when she came here from Texas as a bride many years ago. Mattie will give you some the next time you come. It's very good; you'll like it I'm sure." He smiled and opened the door for them to leave.

Robert rushed through the door and laughed as he ran down the steps to his mother's car. Mrs. Ward stepped out onto the porch and looked back, saying, "Oh, I forgot to ask you Signore about how much you charge. I hope it's not too much. We haven't been here that long, just a few months. My husband and I are separated, you know. Mrs. Atkins has been so kind to both Robert and me. She helped me get a job over at the air force base. We like Selma and our church." She looked at him earnestly.

"Mrs. Ward, there will be no charge. I accept Robert as a full scholarship student. Just please have him here promptly for his lessons. If you haven't access to a piano, I have one here in the library that he can practice on. I look forward to seeing him again soon."

She smiled and shook his hand and walked down the steps to her car. Robert looked back and waved as they drove away.

Closing the door, Ernesto stepped forward and flipped the light switch, activating the chandeliers that brightly illuminated the hall and front rooms. Night was falling. Mattie hummed in the kitchen as she prepared the evening meal. Ernesto approached the staircase. He would go up and dress for dinner as he always had in the past. Imogene was coming this evening. As he reached the landing he paused before the central portrait of Carlotta as *Norma.* He smiled and said out loud, "It begins then, Madame. I will not fail you. I remember your words from so long ago as I spied on you that first day in the music room." The eyes in the portrait seemed to come alive and gaze at him. "The past is mine, and I remember everything." Reaching for the banister, he made his way up the stairs, not seeing the two ghosts who stood on the landing beneath the three portraits.

The Colonel's ghost, reaching for his wife's transparent hand, said, "It is well then, Carlotta, with our child. Let us leave here now and return to the world of the shades in our tombs."

She smiled back at him. Raising her hand, she looked imperiously into the darkness of the steps where her Ernesto had gone. "Do as you will, Colonel." She reached out and caressed his face with her hand. "Death reveals all secrets, my love, my sweet. I am mistress of this house. I always will be. Death is nothing at all. We have merely stepped into another world which exists alongside that of the living. I am she who must and will be obeyed. My youth and beauty have been restored in our spirit world. Ah no! Here I will remain to watch silently over my child and what happens here. Return if you will to rest in your tomb. That is not for me!"

He smiled at her and said, "No, my dearest. Where you are is where I want to be, beholding you now as when we first met. We will be together, forever, to guard our child."

"Yes, my beloved!"

He took her hand, and together they rose upward into the darkness to guard the well of loneliness.

If you liked this book, perhaps you'll also enjoy these books from the Divacity Press division of ThomasMax Publishing.

A Kept Promise
by Debra Ann Barre

There's more than just power in positive thinking. When combined with the power of prayer and spirituality, that positive attitude turns into a promise of good things in life. This motivational book has earned praise for inspiration and a plan to live life to its fullest, taking nothing for granted. $ 11.95.

The Moulin Huge
by Robert Preston Ward

You can't help but fall into the flow of this story of Evan, Lloyd and Diva. Poor Evan wants to be a performer, even if he has to do it in drag. Oh, wait, he WANTS to do it in drag. Lloyd teaches school by having the kids watch soap operas and drives around with his pants off in pursuit of sexual hijinks. Diva is a Hollywood star with a split in her personality that rivals the Cumberland Gap. She has a Hollywood bigwig wooing her, and her personalities can't agree on the outcome. They all follow the yellow-brick road ... okay, it's probably just regular pavement ... to a trailer park in Niceville, Florida, for Evan to make his performance debut as Lowla. Not for the gay-paranoid but a well-crafted plot spiced with a lot of laughs for everyone else. More than a comedy, though, as the characters all show their darker, unhappier sides too. $ 13.95.

www.ingramcontent.com/pod-product-compliance
Lightning Source LLC
LaVergne TN
LVHW091036080826
845145LV00002B/514

* 9 7 8 0 9 8 2 2 1 8 9 6 9 *